CAVEAT EMPTOR

— The America Incorporated Saga —

MIKAEL CARLSON

WARRINGTON
PUBLISHING

Danbury, Connecticut

Caveat Emptor
Copyright ©2025 by Mikael Carlson

Warrington Publishing
Danbury, CT
www.warringtonpublishing.com

Printed in the United States of America
First Edition
ISBN: 978-1-944972-48-6 (Paperback)
         978-1-944972-49-3 (Hardcover)
         978-1-944972-46-2 (E-Book)

Book cover designed by JD&J
Edited by Mike Waitz at Sticks and Stones Editing

This story is a retelling of the 2015 novel *America Incorporated: Caveat Emptor*. This saga is meant to be read in the order it was written.

Novels by Mikael Carlson:

– The Michael Bennit Series –
The iCandidate
The iCongressman
The iSpeaker
The iAmerican

– Tierra Campos Thrillers –
Justifiable Deceit
Devious Measures
Vital Targets
Revealed Secrets
Decisive Endgame

– Tierra Campos Thrillers Prequels –
Narrow Escape: The Summerville Massacre

– Watchtower Thrillers –
The Eyes of Others
The Eyes of Innocents
The Eyes of Victims
The Eyes of Addicts

– The America, Inc. Saga –
The Black Swan Event
Bounded Rationality
Boiling the Ocean
Caveat Emptor

– The Santa Trilogy –
Banning Santa
Delivering Santa

– The Dancing Trilogy –
The Dancing Life

CAVEAT EMPTOR:

The business principle declares that the buyer alone is responsible for checking the quality and suitability of goods before a purchase is made. The Latin translation is literally "let the buyer beware."

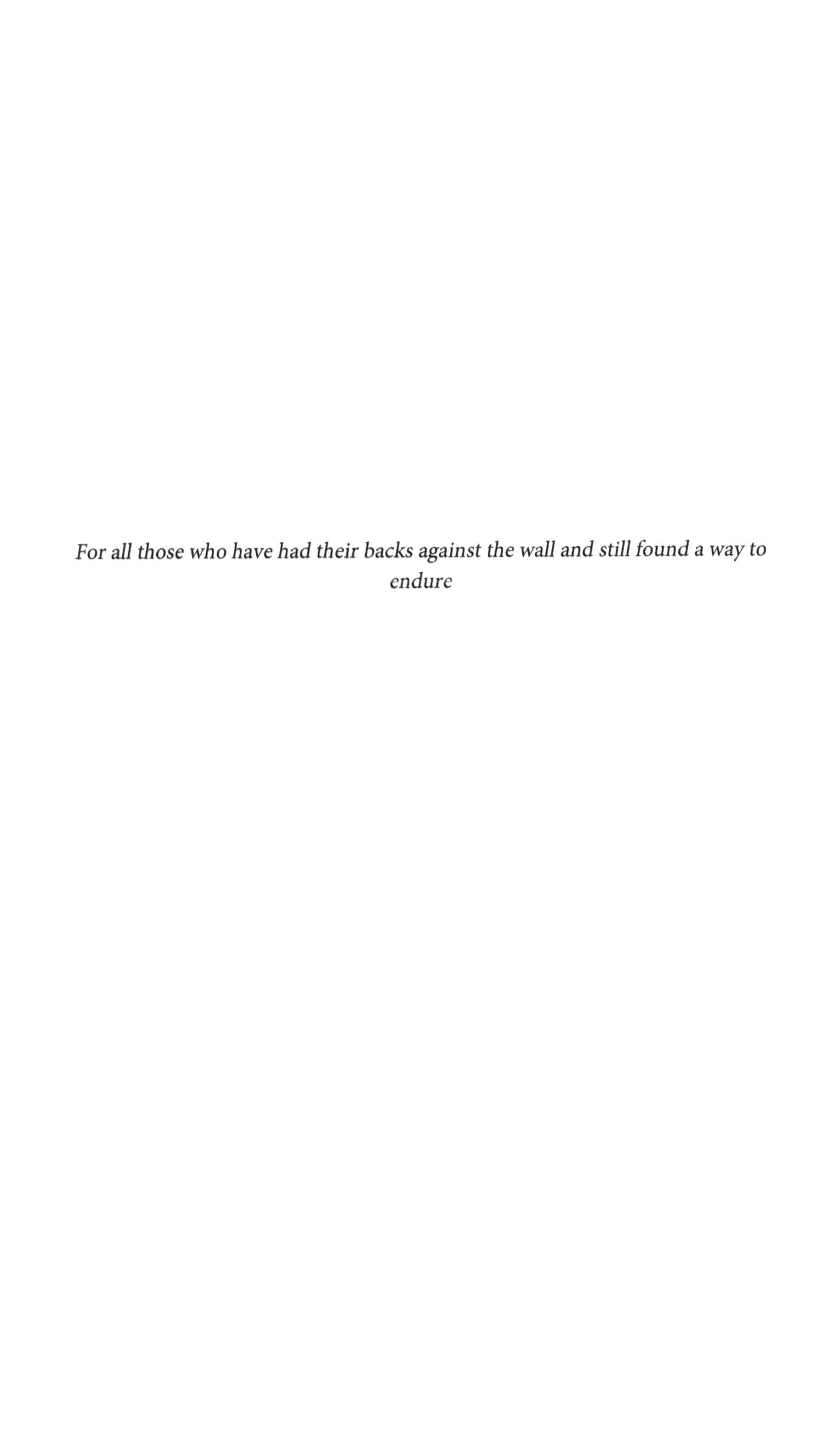

For all those who have had their backs against the wall and still found a way to endure

CHAPTER ONE

RYKOS

Long Island Sound

I close my eyes as the wind fights to beat away the warmth of the sun on my face. It's a strange feeling. The dingy confines of old tunnels, sewers, and building subfloors offer no opportunity for either sensation. I don't know how Michele, or any other urch, survives living that way.

She's not a complete stranger to the above-ground, but she has never spent this much time outside of the relative safety the underground provides. Michele was born an urch, and that made venturing out onto corporate-controlled streets hazardous. New York City is one of the most heavily surveilled places on Earth. It must be a lesson everyone who flees to the underground quickly learns.

I turn to face the rear of the boat. The Manhattan skyline has faded into the distance, but the still smoldering Intercorpex campus serves as a reminder of the chaos the city's been plunged into. Despite our best efforts to stop him, Haven managed to become the greatest mass murderer of the Corporate Age. The myth of Pax Corporacana, or corporate peace, is dead. Even those who perpetrate that lie must admit that now. Haven wanted to create mayhem and kill as many as possible, and he did his job well.

Nobody has spoken since Michele delivered her ultimatum to Zyree. He accepted her offer to tag along with us, much to my surprise and Farron's clear annoyance. The patrician has never been an advocate of deviating from the plan. To him, rescuing Zyree from the public safety guardians and corporate security agents hunting him was an unwanted distraction.

The rush of adrenaline from our harrowing trip out of Manhattan is beginning to subside. In its place, fatigue and weariness are taking hold. I'm not the only one who feels that way. Michele is wearing it on her face.

Archimedes failed, which means that she couldn't fulfill her father's dream. Her whole life was spent building for the moment and longing for the day they would put the plan in motion. She has a grand dream of rescuing humanity from the clutches of the corporations and patricians holding dominion over it. There were going to be challenges, but I don't think she ever anticipated just how much of a nightmare it would become.

I want to say something optimistic. There is a remote chance she can still bring positive change to the world so long as her Valhalla stronghold remains undiscovered. That is a long shot at best. The corporation is looking for it, and it's only a matter of time before it's uncovered.

"We're here," Farron says as the boat captain throttles down the engine on the small craft.

I wouldn't have guessed that the large gray structure looming in the distance is Denali Keating's manor. Maybe I should have. It looks every bit like the massive medieval fortress it's meant to portray. Unlike its neighbors along the coastline, the mansion forgoes the ornate and ostentatious symbols of material wealth like gaudy statues and decorative trim. It projects a very different message: power.

Men swarm through the back yard and take up positions along the beach and quay as the boat swings wide to approach the dock. I would have thought it was a prudent security measure had they not leveled their weapons at us.

"This isn't the welcome I was expecting, Farron," Michele says.

"Yeah, you really know how to roll the red carpet out for your guests," Zyree says from behind us, piling on.

"Red carpets only get laid out for patricians of a higher stature," Farron says, "not that there are many higher than us. But I didn't expect this reception either."

The boat pilot guides the craft alongside the dock. Two men secure the lines while their comrades cover us. Koltayne shifts his gaze down to his weapon and then back at Michele. She shakes her head.

"Everyone, stay calm."

"Easy for you to say," I mumble.

"Kindly keep your hands where we can see them," the leader orders.

We do what we're told. Security personnel force us off the vessel and into a line. They relieve us of our weapons and pat us down for hidden ones. They aren't being gentle with the frisking. The only one who isn't treated like a prisoner is Farron, who is more interested in watching the approaching figure than protesting our treatment.

"Welcome home, Master Farron," a lanky, impeccably dressed man says as he joins us on the dock. "Your father will be pleased you're finally here."

"Thank you, Abbot. Where is he?"

"In the study, of course. These men will accompany you and your…entourage there."

We meander up the path that bisects the manicured grounds and enter the mansion through large doors in the back. I can't stop myself from looking around in awe. I know that patricians lead opulent lives, but this surpasses anything I could imagine.

Denali Keating watches as we file into his study. Farron brushes past us to greet his father with a firm handshake. The family reunion is about as warm as a New York winter.

Farron introduces us to his father, who studies each of us in turn. The exercise is not a technique to remember our names – he's taking measure of us, especially Michele. There's nothing on his face that leads me to believe he's remotely impressed by what he sees.

"The mysterious leader of Liberteum," Denali says, settling on Michele after Farron finishes the introductions. "I'm sure the last place America Incorporated would ever look for you is in my study. From everything I've been told, you are devilishly hard to kill. You've lived up to your reputation."

The alarm klaxons immediately go off in my head. Everything about our arrival has felt wrong. Zyree and Koltayne glance at Michele out of the corners of their eyes. They sense it, too.

"It has been a long day for you, so let's show you to your accommodations. We have a large, spacious home…that you won't see most of."

In an instant, the guards seize us from behind. Zyree and Michele know that resistance is pointless, but Koltayne and I pay the price for trying to break free of their grasp. Koltayne is struck in the back of the head, and I get butt-stroked in the abdomen with a rifle. I stare long and hard at Farron from my knees. He begins to wilt under my heavy gaze and meekly turns to the elder patrician.

"What are you doing, Father?"

"What must be done. You know how this ends, Farron. You've always known."

"Are you going to be a man and kill me yourself, Denali, or just have your henchmen do it like the coward you are?" Michele asks, still defiant under these circumstances.

The provocation earns an amused look. "The world has always been filled with two types of people: winners and those who whine about losing. You lost. Luckily for you, there is a long list of people who want the honor of ending your life. That increases your value as a bargaining chip. Abbot, please show our guests down to the vault."

CHAPTER TWO

AMERICA, INC.

The White House
Corporate Governance District
Washington-Arlington Municipal Corporation

The VidLynk disconnects, and Chief Executive Zeykala closes her eyes and exhales as she moves to the window overlooking the Rose Garden. That was the fifth call she's fielded in the past half hour from a foreign CEO questioning their stability, and more are waiting. This view is one of the only perks of this office that she's been able to enjoy. Not that she's had much time to appreciate it.

The corporation has been gripped in chaos since the moment she assumed leadership. Terrorist attacks have only stepped up. Talya Bettancourt's request to strip the qulis of their independence by making them full employees has set off a chain reaction of protests and riots throughout the sphere of influence. Everything is falling apart, and she's the one getting all the blame.

"Chief Executive Zeykala," her digital assistant announces, "you are being requested in the Situation Room. High priority."

"I'm on my way."

Departing the Oval Office, Zeykala navigates the hectic halls of the West Wing to the elevator leading to one of the sublevels. She could make this journey in her sleep despite it being among the last places she wanted to be this familiar with.

"Keep your seats," she announces as the door swings open. She moves to the front of the long rectangular table. "Somebody had better have some good news."

"We have the traitorous CEO of New York and her chief guardian in custody," Virtari barks from the large display in front of the room.

Zeykala scowls. "I want to hear good news that I wasn't already informed of, Director."

"Then I'm afraid you're going to be disappointed. Liberteum has escaped Manhattan."

The CEO slams her hand down on the table in frustration. "How is that possible? You said you had them in your grasp. You assured me that there was no escape from the trap you laid."

"And that was true given the circumstances. The terrorists drove right into our blocking force. The only avenue of escape was the exit off the autoway into the ambush we set up for them. Then, we were attacked by an unknown force."

The men and women around the table start whispering amongst themselves. Nobody "attacks" the BCS. It's completely unheard of.

"What do you mean '*attacked*'?" Zeykala prods.

"Three attack helicopters engaged our agents to clear the way for the terrorists."

"Did you say helicopters?"

"Not the passenger variants that we ferry executives around in. These were heavily armed combat aircraft. Dozens of my agents were killed or seriously wounded."

For years, corporations have alleged that patricians were increasing the size and capabilities of their security forces to protect their own interests. Speculation ran rampant that some had grown to the size of small armies. They've always been bound by the Zurich Canon, but faith in relying on the exchange to maintain order was clearly misplaced.

"Armed helicopters are operating in our sphere of influence, and we don't know about it? Who was it?" Zeykala asks after Virtari fails to provide the one detail she actually needs.

"We're investigating. I've commandeered public safety's Emergency Operations Center and have a team poring over video footage from the area. We've confirmed that the vehicle they fled in is owned by Farron Keating. We've also confirmed that members of Liberteum, Registrant Rykos, and that rogue ICX chief inspector we were hunting were with him."

"Quite the ensemble," Zeykala mumbles.

"They boarded a small watercraft and headed northeast into Long Island Sound. My guess is that they're heading to the Keating Estate in Greenwich."

The room erupts into another flurry of side conversations, none of which are helping move things forward. It doesn't take a genius to figure out that the Keating Family is the likely culprit behind this.

"I want you to confirm that and whether Denali Keating's people attacked your agents. Most importantly, I want to know why."

"There were reports that Denali Keating and Shalius Covington may have been involved in Liberteum's previous attacks on Intercorpex," the liaison to Intercorpex interjects from the far end of the room. "We dismissed it as ICX propaganda, but given the current situation, we must accept that there might be truth to them. Let's not forget that neither family was at Assembly Hall when it was destroyed."

The analysis gets a spate of nods around the room. "You have your prime suspects, Virtari."

"Yes, ma'am. I'll send word back to the EOC and oversee the inquiry myself when I depart Rikers."

"Do that. Speaking of Rikers, has Ilaria been moved out?"

Virtari scowls. "Yes, against my better judgment. We should have shot them right after we finished with the chief guardian."

Zeykala bristles at having her orders questioned in front of these executives. "Killing them would further inflame the situation with the qulis. I'm not about to make her a martyr."

"Nothing sends a louder message than showing what will happen to those who disobey the corporation. If you want to spare Ilaria's life now to make a spectacle of her death later, fine, but she should have been properly secured at Rikers."

The BCS director is responsible for America Incorporated's security. That role requires a certain foresight into the activities of their global adversaries. Virtari possesses neither the intellectual acumen nor the assessment capability to be successful in his position. He's a blunt object with no understanding of people or politics.

"Your orders remain. Separate Ilaria and her associates. Keep them under house arrest and off the grid. When the time comes to use her to speak to the qulis, I want her near AME News studios. Is that understood?"

"If you insist. What makes you think she'll cooperate?"

"Ilaria's son is a terrorist. When we find and capture him, she'll have no choice but to do whatever we tell her. No mother will willingly watch her son die before her eyes when offered an easy chance to save him."

CHAPTER THREE

THE PATRICIANS

Keating Family of the Gentez-Majorez Estate
Greenwich Geographic District
Southern Connecticut Municipal Corporation

Denali watches with a great deal of satisfaction as Michele and her counterparts get removed from the study. The great leader of Liberteum is now a "guest" in his home. Several months' worth of manhunts by some of the most capable security forces in the world couldn't capture her. He accomplished that feat with minimal effort.

"Father, what are you doing?" Farron asks after they are left alone in the study. "Taking my friends prisoner when we are so close to completing our mission wasn't part of the plan."

This is a conversation that has been a long time coming. Denali simultaneously looked forward to and feared the day it would happen. Farron has worked with Liberteum long enough to make the reaction to what he is about to say somewhat of an enigma.

"Farron, you succeeded in your mission beyond my wildest dreams. My plan never required Liberteum to actually force a halt in trading at Intercorpex. I never expected Raimius would permit the exchange to go offline for even a second."

His son recoils. "What are you talking about, Father?"

"Have a seat," Denali says, gesturing at the leather sofas.

He's rehearsed this conversation in his head a hundred times. Now it's here, and he still feels unprepared. Farron is young and idealistic, and his loyalty extends beyond his family to his friends. He's not going to like this betrayal. Succinctly explaining the reason for it will be the difference between acceptance and resentment.

"Liberteum was meant to be a nuisance that Raimius would struggle to handle, thus expediting his removal as administrator-general and subsequent replacement with someone more…controllable."

"I don't understand."

"Sure you do. The easiest way to balance an equation is to remove a variable. Isn't that the reason you killed Narik?"

Farron's face registers the shock of the question. "What?"

"Are you surprised that I found out? I'm proud of you, son. You did what needed to be done to maintain control of the situation."

"You're proud of me for killing my best friend?"

"You did what was needed in the name of the family. This world is full of people willing to do unspeakable things for control and power. Narik's father was murdered by the BCS for the same reason."

"I didn't kill him for control. He was going to compromise…."

"Compromise what?"

"Nothing," Farron says, popping off the sofa and scurrying to the bar to pour himself a drink.

Denali might not have been the best father, but he knows when his son is holding something back. Farron is a terrible liar. Whatever he was about to say is definitely not "nothing."

"Farron, if there's something you need to tell me, now is the time."

"We thought Narik was feeding information to Haven. We figured he leaked the details about the patrician meeting and were concerned that he might compromise Valhalla's location. When Michele confirmed he was working against us, I was so angry…."

"Go on."

"I didn't hesitate to shoot him right between the eyes. I felt nothing when I did it. I mean, Narik was my friend."

"A friend who betrayed you. The Covingtons were allies, but their agenda cost them their lives. What I do know is Narik didn't help Haven attack Intercorpex."

"How do you know that?"

Denali looks up at his son with determined eyes. "Because I helped him."

Farron returns to the sofa with a dumb look on his face. He can't believe what he just heard. Perhaps he should have broken that news more gently, but they're beyond that now.

"You were working with Haven?"

"Don't be ridiculous. Haven was a psychopath. You can't work with a man like that. I manipulated him into doing what needed to be done."

"How is that diff—? You ordered the murders of all those people?"

Denali checks the length of his fingernails. There isn't a speck of dirt under them, but it's time for a trim.

"Farron, I know you didn't shed a single tear over their deaths."

He meets his father's stare but doesn't offer an objection. "Did you manipulate him into trying to kill Michele, too?"

"That didn't require either manipulation or convincing."

"Why would you want her dead?"

"Her services were no longer needed. Once Liberteum had the login information to the ICX trading platform, we were capable of crashing the market from here if that step was needed."

"So, you ordered Haven to kill her? I almost died that day!"

Denali stares hard at his son. He's struggling to come to terms with these decisions. It's a hard world out there, and Farron is young, naïve, and impressionable. This generation is soft, and he's learning lessons he should have long ago. Denali knows he should have kept a tighter rein on him while he was working with Liberteum.

"I let Haven off his leash. You never should have intervened."

"Liberteum was a pawn," Farron says, shaking his head. "You were using them."

"Son, every piece on a chessboard has two purposes – to vanquish an opponent and protect the king. Some pieces are more valuable than others, but to win the game, you must be willing to sacrifice them all."

"We are one of the most influential families of the gentez-majorez. What more is there for us to win?"

Farron doesn't understand the world they live in. Money, power, and status replaced kindness and generosity long ago. Winning is the whole point of existence. He needs to understand that before he inherits this empire Denali is building.

"There is no America Incorporated without our family. There is no corporatism system without the patricians. We guided the world through the Pirate Wars, were instrumental in the creation of Intercorpex, and pushed for the adoption of Bytecoin as a single currency."

"I'm aware of the history, Father," Farron says with a sneer.

"Good. Do you know what our reward has been? Intercorpex and corporations finding ways to strip us of our influence."

"And this is how you fight that? Humiliate them so they know their place?"

Denali frowns. It's time to tell Farron the whole plan: why he infiltrated Intercorpex, allied himself with Haven, the arrangements made within America Incorporated and other major corporations, the creation of The Trust, and why he needs Liberteum as bargaining chips.

"Corporations have forgotten who created them, and a reminder will only reset the clock before they forget again. The way to ensure our family's place in history is to make our dominance unquestioned. We will no longer be content influencing the world. We're going to run it."

CHAPTER FOUR

AMERICA, INC.

Human Resources Center
Rikers Island Geographic Area
New York City Municipal Corporation

Corporate executives are idiots. The head of the Bureau of Corporate Security came to that conclusion long ago. Zeykala is no different, only more manipulative and power hungry than Valen. Virtari agreed to assist in her little coup out of necessity, but not because she's an upgrade over her predecessor.

Executives don't understand what corporate security does or how it works. They sit behind their big desks and bark orders with little regard for those doing their bidding. Employees lament that their leaders are "echelons above reality." It couldn't be a truer statement.

Virtari wasn't planning on having to jump on a VidLynk and deal with his neurotic CEO until he got to the EOC. Because of her boneheaded decision, he had to send Ilaria and her complement of guardians back to Manhattan. She should have let him put bullets in the heads of the traitors. That's how you show strength.

The thought leads the director to another, even less pleasant one as he exits through the double doors of the Rikers Island administrative building and climbs into the waiting conveyance. They had Liberteum right where they wanted them. The trap was expertly laid. There was no avenue of escape, yet they still managed to.

Of course, it took the private army of a patrician for it to happen. The terrorists deserve credit – they're better connected than previously thought. Nobody had reason to plan for that. Everyone turned a blind eye to the reports that the gentez-majorez were acquiring huge private armies. It was ignorant but understandable. Any notion of Liberteum working with patricians was preposterous until now.

Virtari's tablet chirps just as the conveyance stops at his destination. "Yeah?"

"We confirmed that Liberteum is holed up at the Keating Estate just as you said they would be," an agent in the EOC relays.

"Pull whoever we have in Stamford, Bridgeport, and New Haven and send them to cordon off Denali's mansion in Greenwich. Pull agents from Hartford, too, if you have to."

"What about the uprisings in those cities?"

Virtari scowls. "Let public safety deal with them."

"Yes, sir," the agent says before disconnecting.

He exits the conveyance when it arrives at the training area. Rikers Island was home to a large transitory prison before the collapse. When corporations took control, incarceration was no longer necessary. As a result, Rikers is used for terminations and not much else.

The PSS uses this part of the island as a training area to hone their rudimentary skills. This building is a live fire environment called a "kill house" used to practice raids on urch raves. That may be an appropriate name for it.

"These are the oldest and most influential of all the urches the PSS swept up in the city," an agent whispers in Virtari's ear.

He nods and immediately commands the attention of the urches herded into here. The disheveled, unintelligent, and unambitious men and women in front of him are deplorable. They left a system that provided them with everything, and for what? To live a wasteful existence. It's disgusting.

"The offer I'm about to make you will not be repeated. I don't know what drove you into the underground, nor do I care. Each of you is a freejack who was stupid enough to get caught by the PSS. What's done is done. I'm giving you a chance to atone."

"Atone for what?" one of the men in front challenges.

"Your sins. Right now, I'm your church, priest, and savior. Announce your allegiance to the corporation and cooperate with our investigation. Do that, and we'll pretend all your past transgressions never occurred."

"And if we don't?"

"Look at where you are. Do you have a better alternative?"

"You want us to trade our freedom to become slaves again?" another urch asks.

There's some grumbling among the group. Urches aren't a bright bunch. They don't even recognize the gift Virtari is giving them.

"I almost admire your naiveté," he says when the group quiets. "You actually think you are free. Nothing is further from the truth. You live a life in squalor, without sunshine or the promise of a better future. I'm offering safety, security, and opportunity. Only a fool would decline it."

"Opportunity? Who are ya kidding?"

"Ya pass off only what's in you's best interest as 'opportunity,'" another urch chimes in.

There is universal agreement amongst the group. Living beneath the streets for so long has poisoned their minds. Virtari didn't think they would cooperate, but it was worth a try. He smirks and decides to make one last attempt.

"I'm not going to debate the merits of this offer with you. Accept it or don't."

The angry shouts and disparaging insults telegraph their answer. This is a lost cause. These people are beyond being saved.

"Ya know history?" a man shouts as Virtari turns for the exit. "I've read the old books. Ya ever heard of Patrick Henry? Ya know what he'd say? 'Give me liberty or give me death.'"

The director turns over his shoulder and flashes a smile. "Have it your way."

His men raise their rifles. Shock registers on the urches' faces a split second before tongues of flame belch from the muzzles of their weapons. The first few freejacks die with that look on their face. The rest are gripped in horror as the agents pump rounds into them until the screaming stops. When the shooting is over, the men reload and check for survivors. There is only one.

Virtari climbs over the bullet-ridden bodies and recognizes him immediately. Already dying from his wounds, the man stares at the BCS director in defiance. That is almost worthy of respect. Almost.

"Instead of quoting a man who's as dead as the ideas he spewed forth into the world, perhaps you should have paid more attention to practical idioms. I like the one that says, 'Be careful what you wish for. You might get it.'"

Virtari pulls out his weapon and smiles as he blows a hole into his head. He stands over the man's body for a long moment before holstering his sidearm. Liberty or death. For him, that's an easy request to grant.

"Get the guardians on this island to clean this mess up. If they refuse the order, shoot them. How many urches are we holding at Rikers?"

"Nine hundred and fifty-seven, minus these," the agent in charge of the detail says.

"Bring them here in groups and make them the same offer I just did. Extract information from anyone who agrees and submit them for reeducation. Anyone who doesn't...."

Virtari gestures at the carnage.

"Consider it done."

The men sling their weapons and jump into action. He hopes the crematorium is fired up because there won't be many takers of the offer. Let the feckless executives in Washington dream up political responses to this crisis. Virtari is a man of action who will make the tough choices. By the end of the day, New York's urch problem will be more manageable.

CHAPTER FIVE

NYCMC RESISTANCE

Chief Guardian Teman's Domicile
Upper West Side Geographic District
New York City Municipal Corporation

The two burly BCS agents who escorted Ilaria home look around in amazement as the lights come up. They brusquely shove her out of the elevator into the living space. She listens for the normal Maester greeting, but it never comes. It's either silenced or disarmed.

"Will you get a load of this place?" one of her escorts asks his partner. "Look at that view!"

"It's a shame this place gets wasted on housing a useless guardian."

Everything is just where Ilaria left it before her life took a turn to the surreal. The mess is even still on the counter…a jarring reminder of a difficult, yet somehow still saner time. It's a strange feeling for her. This may be home, but without Teman, it feels anything but.

The trip here was an emotional rollercoaster ride. Anguish, hatred, sadness, and rage about Teman's fate took turns tugging at her soul. She fears her own fate and worries about Dzamko and Deyago. Waves of emotion constantly washed over her and receded, only to be followed by more powerful ones. She's determined to remain strong, but every minute marks a new challenge. Coming home is just the latest.

The agent pushes her hard onto the couch. With her hands still locked in electromag cuffs behind her back, Ilaria has no means to stop her momentum. She bounces off the cushions and lands awkwardly in a heap on the floor.

"Contact the EOC and tell them we arrived," one of the agents orders his counterpart as he laughs and makes a wide loop around the room. "Confirm they disabled the Maester. We don't need it contacting the PSS should our prisoner require a lesson in manners."

"Aw, I'm kinda hoping she needs a good spanking," the agent says, ogling her like a predator.

Ilaria stares at her tormentor impassively. Antagonizing him will only make her treatment worse. He has already telegraphed his intentions. She knows what's likely going to happen to her tonight. There's no point in being openly defiant to make it worse.

"Just make the call," his supervisor impatiently demands.

"Ops, this is Gulag One. Mornym and Ryax are checking in. The prisoner is secure. Confirm that the Maester system has been deactivated."

"Gulag One, this is Ops," the voice replies over his tablet with a hint of attitude. "Confirmed. We're not guardians. Did you think we would forget to disable it or something? Babysit your target, not us. Ops, out."

The agent disconnects the VidLynk. "Asshole."

The other agent is rummaging through the kitchen cabinets and dumping contents on the counter below. "Lighten up, Ryax. You've seen what's going on in this city. Everyone's stressed out."

"Just make yourself at home," Ilaria says, not being able to hold her tongue as she watches him act like a slob.

Ryax's reaction is as swift as it is fierce. In one smooth motion, he smacks her hard across the face with the back of his hand. Her vision explodes into a kaleidoscope of color, and nerves report the pain in her cheek. He grabs a handful of Ilaria's hair, drags her to her feet, and moves his face inches away.

"I'm under orders not to kill you. That doesn't mean I can't *hurt* you." He reaches down and grabs her between the legs. Ilaria reflexively stiffens in shock. "One more snide comment comes out of your mouth, and I'm really gonna make you scream."

"Whoa! What do we have here?" Agent Mornym asks from the kitchen. Ilaria doesn't need to look over, not that she could. There is only one item in there that would get that reaction, and it's a blessing and a curse. "Is this urch shine?"

"You're kidding!" Ryax exclaims, releasing Ilaria's hair. "This is the last place I'd have expected to find a jug of the underground's finest. This might be a good assignment after all."

"It looks like your saintly husband was a closet drinker," the lead agent concludes. "Not very becoming for a PSS chief guardian."

"It's mine."

"Yours?" he asks, finding a pair of drinking glasses. "You do like to party, girl. Lock her in the bedroom, Ryax. She won't give us any trouble in there."

The agent grins and ushers her down the hall. Most BCS agents are physical specimens, and this one is no different. He's rock solid and as strong as any man Ilaria has ever met. There is zero chance of her ever physically overpowering him. If she has any chance to escape his clutches, she will have to outthink him.

"Don't worry," he whispers in Ilaria's ear as they stop in the master bedroom's doorway. He runs his hands up the insides of her thighs and then over her breasts. "I'll be back later to tuck you in."

CHAPTER SIX

AMERICA, INC.

Meade Human Resources Center
Seven Oaks Geographic Area
Baltimore Municipal Corporation

Fiolla's eyes strain to adjust to the light after the black bag is removed from her head. She's woozy from the injection at the quli protest, and the mixture of drugs and bright light is disorienting. The paralytic has begun to wear off but is still sapping her strength and energy.

Not that she could fight if she wanted to. Her arms and legs are secured to the inclined metal bed with the thin mattress. Tears roll down Fiolla's face despite her desperation to stifle them. She doesn't want her captors to see that they're breaking her, even if she feels that she's already been broken.

"Where...where am I?"

"The Meade Human Resources Center," the fuzzy silhouette of a man she assumes is a BCS agent says, his voice completely void of emotion.

"Why?"

"You have been found in violation of corporate law on charges of murder, attempted murder, battery, resisting detention, assault of a corporate security figure, and high treason. By executive decree, you are to be processed for immediate termination."

"Don't I get a hearing?" she mumbles, her voice raspy and uneven from a combination of the drugs and her nerves.

"It's a summary judgment issued by the chief executive," the agent says, handing the tablet to an underling. "Normally, this is where the torture begins. I would love nothing more than to make you suffer in the most horrible way imaginable. You can call it revenge, but it'd be justice. I knew the two men you killed in Washington."

"I was defending myself. They tried...tried to push me in front of a train."

The agent leans close to her face, and she can see him more clearly. "They had orders. You killed them for doing their job."

When Fiolla doesn't respond, he smirks and backs off. The extra distance doesn't put her at ease. If anything, his standing over her is more intimidating.

"A quick death would have been preferable to what I planned. Unfortunately, Director Virtari has something else in store for you. You may wish you were dead if you don't provide the information he wants. You are going to die either way."

A surge of nervous energy races up Fiolla's spine, causing her to shudder. It's not an empty threat. The BCS doesn't need to bluff because they answer to nobody. They can make her life agonizing right before they end it.

Fiolla's mind races as she tries to weigh her options, but it's difficult to fight through the haze of the drugs. She wants to make this painless…she needs to make this painless. She's not prepared to suffer. The best thing to do is give in and tell them whatever they want to hear.

Then Dutch, Boomyr, and Jzahn pop into her mind. She can still see their faces. They gave their lives trying to help a stranger who is an executive and technically their enemy. How can she dishonor their courage by not fighting for herself now?

The door to the gray interrogation room opens, interrupting her thoughts. The BCS agents in the room stand rigid at the entrance of the unexpected visitor. He eyes them as he moves to the middle of the room and clasps his hands behind his back.

"Leave us," the man commands.

The BCS agent gives him a hard look but doesn't protest. Whoever he is, he wields considerable power. Without a word, her interrogator ends his questioning and storms out of the room.

"You'll have to excuse the special agent, Executive Fiolla," he says, walking to the corner and retrieving a metal stool to sit on. "To say my colleagues are militant about their jobs is an exercise in understatement."

"I know you," Fiolla says, recognizing the distinct tones of his voice more than the hazy and vague silhouette.

"Yes, you do," he says, taking a seat. "Our paths have crossed on a couple of occasions. I'm Administrator Lutroq. I run this facility."

She nods in recognition. Prior to her White House assignment, she spent time in Washington Corporate Affairs. Executive terminations are the nasty side of the business, and that responsibility fell on her shoulders. Hating that position motivated her, and the resulting climb up the corporate ladder led her to the White House and ultimately here. How's that for irony?

Lutroq was a reasonable man in their dealings. He's been at Meade forever and is one of the most competent administrators in the entire sphere of influence. He's not by the book, leaving room for the application of common sense while completing his duties. That thought gives Fiolla a faint glimmer of hope.

"Why are you here?"

"To look after your welfare."

"You can start by letting me go."

"I'm sorry, Executive Fiolla, that's not permitted. Your treatment could be far worse. The protocol is to strip you naked for your interrogation."

"Why? So, your agents can get their jollies by staring at me?"

"Being naked makes subjects vulnerable and self-conscious. Everything that happens in this facility is designed to create a heightened state of fear to make our guests more compliant and cooperative. Allowing you to keep your clothing is the only charity you will get from me. We're not friends, Fiolla, and we're no longer business colleagues. You are an enemy of the corporation."

The HR process is a testament to corporate efficiency. America Incorporated has decades of practice perfecting these techniques. She is already vulnerable, self-conscious, and frightened. There's no need to enhance that.

"All because of one person's vendetta," she murmurs.

"Fiolla, every action in this world satisfies one of two needs: power or profit. That was true before corporate rule, and it's true now. People have been used as pawns to achieve those two ends for millennia. Nothing you say will change your fate. You're going to be terminated tomorrow at noon, and nothing will stop that."

Lutroq rises and sets the chair back against the wall where he got it. She feels the strength draining out of her again. As much as she doesn't want to admit it, she knows he's right. It's pointless to fight a system that has become too big to fail.

"You're wrong, Administrator," Fiolla manages to say. "There's much more to life than power and profit."

He stops when he reaches the door. "That belief is what landed you here. Our system may not be perfect, but it'll never change. Employees are too invested in it now. The brilliance of corporations was how they made everyone dependent on the system they created. Those who fight it are fools lost in a hopeless struggle. You chose your side, and that decision is about to cost you your life."

CHAPTER SEVEN

LIBERTEUM

*The White House
Corporate Governance District
Washington-Arlington Municipal Corporation*

Zeykala's head pounds like a freight train is barreling through it. The stress headache that began with the Intercorpex bombing in New York grew in intensity following the Manhattan firefight with Liberteum and quli uprisings throughout the sphere of influence. Now, she returns to the Oval Office from a discouraging briefing in the Situation Room to find another unwelcome sight waiting for her.

"You've made quite a mess of things, Zeykala," Talya Bettancourt says from behind her desk.

"Leave now," the CEO orders the staff who accompanied her to the Oval Office. Not wanting to stick around, they scurry back out the door and close it behind them.

"I see your unsurpassed people skills are still inspiring loyalty."

"Get out of my chair," Zeykala growls.

Talya channels her theatrical side, making a show rising from the high-backed leather executive chair and running her fingers along the top of it. Zeykala is surprised she moved. Patricians don't like taking orders or agreeing to demands. As Prima, the largest shareholder of America Incorporated, Talya Bettancourt is the worst of the lot.

"You might not be saying that for much longer, Zeykala. The list of executives in this corporation who want you replaced is growing by the minute."

"I have bigger concerns than the bleating of the sheep."

"Yes, you do. *Me.* I warned you not four hours ago that you could be replaced if you failed to gain control of the situation. What have you done to effect that end?"

"We're working on several initiatives."

"So, nothing?"

Zeykala fights to control her temper. This woman hasn't ever worked a day in her life. Talya has never led an organization or felt the pressure of making decisions that impact anyone except her house staff. She has no business passing judgment.

"I've declared corporate law. The BCS is planning to eradicate the quli uprisings. Liberteum was chased out of Manhattan, and we're now ascertaining their whereabouts. What more do you think I can do?"

Talya smirks and shakes her head. "Corporations around the world are uncertain of your leadership. Planning and plotting is not the *actual* action everyone needs to see."

The Prima's idea of "actual" action is what got Zeykala into this mess. Listening to Talya's advice regarding the qulis was a mistake that cannot be repeated.

"The CEOs I've spoken to conveyed a much different message. They've all expressed their support."

"I'm sure they have, at least to your face. My sources informed me that foreign corporate leaders think America Incorporated has become weak. They're looking to exploit that. When the exchange comes back online, the corporations who have solidified or enhanced their power will benefit first. Where do you think we fall on that list right now?"

"Do you really think so little of this corporation's health? America Incorporated has been the standard bearer of stability since the collapse."

"And may very well become an example of what happens when you rest on the laurels of those who came before you. Past success is not a predictor of future results."

Using an old financial services disclaimer is a slap in the face. A woman who was once Zeykala's most ardent supporter has become one of her biggest critics. Instead of helping foster a smooth transition following Valen's removal, she's done nothing but undermine the woman she selected to run the corporation.

"This conversation is over," Zeykala decrees, asserting a semblance of authority after recognizing that it's time to begin treating the patrician like the enemy she's become rather than the ally she once was.

"This conversation is over when I say it is."

"No, that's not how this works. You may be Prima, but this crisis is—"

"Why is Ilaria still alive?"

The question throws Zeykala off, and it must show. Talya rolls her eyes.

"Chief Guardian Teman's wife is a traitor who rallied the qulis to defy corporate orders. She attempted to usurp a termination decree at Rikers and attacked BCS personnel in the process. Tell me why you spared her life when she should have been marched in front of her husband's firing squad."

The CEO frowns. Talya Bettancourt is nothing if not well-informed. Wait until she finds the person in the BCS leaking information to her. Only a handful of people know the details of what happened on that island.

Talya cannot think more than an hour ahead of the time on the clock. Great executives fix present problems while looking toward the future. There is no point in explaining that to a woman who believes her birthright entitles her to know all the answers.

"Keeping her alive gives us more options. Ilaria will help us pacify the qulis. If she refuses, we'll terminate her. The BCS is amassing outside of Manhattan to take the city back by force if needed. That's a message the qulis in other cities will understand. Once the uprisings are quelled, I will do whatever it takes to ensure the success of this corporation. Now, if you'll excuse me, I have meetings."

"That's going to be hard to do when the world's corporations are feasting on our dead carcass."

There's no convincing this woman. They stare at each other for a long moment before the masculine voice of the automated assistant fills the room.

"Chief Executive Zeykala, you have a priority VidLynk from the Office of the Chairman of the Board. Shall I connect you?"

"All glory is fleeting, Zeykala," Talya says with a knowing smirk before starting for the door. "Perhaps more fleeting for you than others. I think you're going to want to take that VidLynk."

CHAPTER EIGHT

LIBERTEUM

Keating Family of the Gentez-Majorez Estate
Greenwich Geographic District
Southern Connecticut Municipal Corporation

Denali's guards lead the group down to a vault and herd them through a large, thick door. The strong room is windowless but brightly lit and void of any décor on the steel gray walls. A pair of bunks with pillows and wool blankets stacked on them lines the back wall. A metal table and four matching chairs occupy the middle of the space. It's one of the most uncomfortable places Zyree has ever been in.

"This is a rather sad turn of events," he mumbles, lying down on the bottom bunk and folding his hands on his abdomen. Since he can't catch a break these days, he might as well rest.

"So, what happens next?" Koltayne asks. It's the first time Michele's young henchman has spoken since Zyree was picked up outside of Central Park.

"I don't plan on sticking around to find out," Michele says, studying the walls as she moves around the room.

"You know we're probably being watched," Rykos says.

Zyree smirks. The kid is growing increasingly paranoid. You'd think he was used to being held against his will by now. He's had enough practice.

"We're not," Zyree reassures his rescuers. "The point of this room is to keep anyone confined to it entirely off the grid. There aren't any cameras or microphones. It's designed so no sound or electronic signals can get in or out."

"Nothing is foolproof," Michele argues.

She's an optimist. Strong rooms are constructed with steel-reinforced concrete covered with titanium panels. The only way to exit this room involves going through that vault door.

"This is. Denali built it, and he doesn't do anything halfway."

"That's reassuring," Rykos grumbles, easing himself down into one of the chairs.

"You know the Keatings?" Michele asks, getting a nod. "Then maybe you can explain why they turned on us because I don't understand it. Farron and his father supported our efforts every step of the way. It makes no sense."

"It makes perfect sense, actually," Zyree says, straining to swing his legs off the bed and move into a seated position on the bunk. "I know Denali far better than Farron, and he likely never intended to help you achieve your objective. He used you to accomplish his."

"Which is?"

Michele is the converse of her depiction as a ruthless, egotistical, maniacal personality. Instead, she's intelligent, analytical, and curious. Assumptions that she ruled the terrorist group with an iron fist and wielded fear as a weapon within her own ranks were dead wrong.

"Ultimate control of everything."

The three of them react as expected. They don't fully understand the world patricians live in. Even though Michele has a relationship with Farron, she can't know how they think. The concept of dominating the world is something scoffed at by anyone who's not in the ranks of the elite.

"The Keatings are already wealthy, Zyree. Denali wouldn't bother trying to conquer the world," Rykos argues.

"You're right. Patricians have enormous wealth and power. The only thing that gives them purpose is accumulating *more* wealth and power. Their lives are measured by how well they play that game, and Denali Keating is on the verge of winning it for good."

"I think we're going to need a better explanation than that, Zyree," Michele says.

"Okay, let's start from the beginning from an outsider's perspective. Everyone thought your attacks were nothing more than a series of isolated black swan events. They rationalize them away as desperate attempts to create mayhem by taking down the exchange. Nobody imagined they were interconnected as part of a larger goal."

"How do you know there's a larger goal?" Michele asks, her grin betraying the innocent attempt to throw him off.

"Because Denali Keating is involved. More than that, because you warned me about Haven's attack on Intercorpex. I'm guessing it was because his actions would somehow complicate matters for you."

Michele nods.

"What does any of this have to do with why Denali Keating has us locked up in his basement?" Rykos impatiently asks.

"I'm getting to that. Your plan disrupted patrician trading patterns enough to almost crash the market. The exchange was forced to close for the first time in its history. The outcry meant that a meeting with patricians and the regents was unavoidable. They needed to explain what happened and make assurances that the situation was under control. A weakened Intercorpex would want to do that in person to show strength. At that point, you became another loose end for Denali to tie up."

"We were expendable," Michele murmurs.

"Farron's domicile, taking my father to the Alamo to bait us, attacking us at NYU…it explains why he kept trying to kill you," Rykos says to her.

"It also explains his comment upstairs about me being hard to kill," she says before turning back to Zyree. "Do you think Denali knew that Haven would attack the meeting?"

"Haven knew the date and time, the security protocols, and managed to get a hold of enough explosives to obliterate a building the size of Assembly Hall. Denali didn't just know Intercorpex would be bombed. I think he ordered it."

CHAPTER NINE

RYKOS

Keating Family of the Gentez-Majorez Estate
Greenwich Geographic District
Southern Connecticut Municipal Corporation

I feel myself purge all the air from my lungs. That can't be true. There is no way a patrician would do that. They benefit most from the corporate world. The thought of any of them actively undermining the system is inconceivable. There must be another explanation.

"It took months to plan the Intercorpex attack," I say, struggling to come to terms with what everyone else has seemed to accept. "How could Haven know the meeting would be held in New York and not Geneva?"

The former chief inspector gives a little shrug. "Denali knew Raimius well. Maybe he assumed it was the obvious play if you want to show strength. He could also be working with other groups capable of an attack overseas if it came to that. Either way, Haven decapitated Intercorpex and the heads of the major patrician families. In one instant, he removed almost every obstacle in Denali's way."

"I don't understand how that helps him."

Zyree sighs. "Contrary to popular belief, patricians don't have carte blanche to do what they want. The Zurich Canon counteracts their influence. One of the new AG's first acts was to suspend it."

It explains an otherwise unexplainable act. Intercorpex needed a mechanism to control the patricians. The Zurich Canon provided that. Its suspension takes the governor off the engine. The elites are now playing a game that has no rules. That leads to a bigger question.

"Okay, yeah, but how would Denali know that it would get suspended?" I ask.

"The safe bet? The new Intercorpex administrator-general is in his back pocket. Lyris is an opportunist. It wouldn't surprise me if he struck a deal with Denali. That's why Chiana tried to kill me in the crypt and why I'm being hunted now. It also explains how he conveniently survived the Assembly Hall explosion."

It's pure speculation, but it makes sense. If Zyree is right, even about half of what he said, then they've been blind to everything. They thought they were one of the most powerful pieces in the game, but they were only the pawns.

"What about the corporations? Wouldn't they be able to step in?"

"Normally, yes, only America Incorporated has been in turmoil since Valen was replaced. Throw in this conflict with the qulis, and you get a recipe for inaction. By the time order is restored, who knows how much power Denali will have acquired. It's pretty brilliant, actually."

Dastardly may be a better description. Not that it matters. The conflict is written all over Michele's face. She has to be wondering how she didn't recognize any of this. I sure didn't. Farron never indicated that he was being deceitful. Were his lies that convincing, or did he not know what his father was up to?

No, he had to know. Denali needed him with Liberteum to report progress. That means Valhalla is compromised by now. The elder Keating might not know its location, but Farron does. He could march his men right down to it, and they would never know what hit them.

"I think I wanna throw up," Koltayne says.

He reached the same conclusion I did. "I don't suppose overpowering a guard and making a run for it will do any good?"

Zyree snickers. "We wouldn't get out of this house alive, much less off this estate."

"I refuse to accept that," I say, standing up and walking around the room. "We'll find a way out of here. Somehow. When we do, how do we stop them? Michele?"

She presses her lips together and shakes her head. No answers are coming from her. I glance at Koltayne, who looks like he may have been serious about throwing up. With pleading eyes, I turn to Zyree, who shrugs and lies back down on the bunk.

"Zyree, how do we stop him?" He's exhausted, but I sense something else. He doesn't have any fight left in him.

"We don't."

CHAPTER TEN

AMERICA, INC.

The White House
Corporate Governance District
Washington-Arlington Municipal Corporation

Joakeen, recently elected chairman of America Incorporated's board of directors following Hammond's suicide, is shown into the Oval Office. The VidLynk he had with Zeykala was short. He requested a face-to-face meeting and immediately left his office on Corporate Hill when she agreed. Whatever is on his mind, it's urgent, and he wants to keep it discrete.

Once the CEO of a major communications company, Joakeen was considered one of the front runners for chief executive officer before Valen filled the slot. The consummate networker, nobody was surprised when he was asked to fill a vacancy on the board of directors instead. He quickly became one of Zeykala's closest friends and staunchest political allies. His influence was a key factor in her being named interim CEO upon Valen's removal.

"You look like you've had a long day," Chairman Joakeen says, taking a seat on the sofa.

"Is that your way of telling me I look like hell?"

"It's my polite way of reminding you that you wanted this job," he says, sporting a grim smile. He's looking a little rough around the edges himself.

"Becoming CEO hasn't been everything I thought it would be," Zeykala admits, collapsing on the sofa directly across from him.

"No, I would imagine not. That's why I'm here. The board is nervous, Zeykala. I don't think you need a map and compass to point you to the reasons."

Without saying anything of value, Joakeen told her everything she needed to know. Zeykala nods at him, knowing that she's losing her power and influence over the members. Now, it's time to get it back.

"I appreciate the warning, but I didn't agree to this meeting because I needed to hear the obvious. There's a situation that requires your attention. The BCS identified members of Liberteum and chased them through the streets of Manhattan earlier this morning."

"I heard. If you had caught the terrorists, it would've been a big win…only you didn't get them."

"No, we didn't, and you need to know why."

Zeykala explains what she learned about the rogue Intercorpex inspector and the trap the BCS laid near the East River. He perks up when she describes how their agents were attacked by heavily armed helicopters before Liberteum rendezvoused with a boat and fled north into Long Island Sound.

"A boat, a helicopter…? Where did terrorists get those kinds of resources?"

"They didn't. They had help…from Denali Keating."

Joakeen leans back, processing that information. It sounds too unrealistic to believe. Patricians are societal elites. They don't wage wars against corporations.

"I'm aware of the rumors about the patricians building large security forces. Are you saying that a shareholder and one of the most powerful families of the gentez-majorez helped *terrorists* escape capture?"

"Farron Keating was with them. It's our belief that they've taken refuge at Denali's estate in Greenwich."

"That's quite an accusation, Zeykala. How certain are you of this?"

"Open BCS digital evidence file Keating One. Play the video clips in sequence," Zeykala orders her digital assistant.

The large display changes from the corporate logo to a video with a menu along the right side. It begins playing the scene from a drone and several static cameras in Glory of the Sphere Park. It stops when several men exit the conveyance, and facial recognition identifies Farron Keating.

The next series of videos shows the highlights of what transpired. Clear images of the helicopter attack are shown, zooming in on the tail rotor boom with a rendering of the Keating coat of arms. Video plays of the terrorists loading the boat with the same markings at the Ward's Island recreation center. Finally, a map overlay shows the path the vessel took into the Sound. The dashed line marks the route straight to the Keating Estate.

"Why would he attack us with helicopters that have his family's coat of arms on them? And that boat could have landed anywhere."

Joakeen is prudent to be skeptical. In this age, video can be spoofed with relative ease. Computers could have easily generated this footage. Everything that is seen on a display must be questioned. Zeykala grins. She is ready for that.

"Play the live drone feed of the Keating Estate."

The overlay is replaced with a streaming video showing the estate crawling with armed men. Joakeen shakes his head slowly as the camera pans over to the shoreline. The boat Liberteum fled in is moored at the dock.

"I don't know why Denali's men attacked us, but I plan on asking. I've ordered a cordon placed around his estate. Nobody enters or leaves."

"You don't have the authority to order that. It's a clear violation of the Zurich Canon."

Zeykala holds her hands out to her sides. "You heard Lyris's speech this morning. The Zurich Canon has been suspended. *That's* why I took this meeting. I want you to grant me emergency authority."

"You're putting me in a difficult situation."

She knows that. Corporations aren't permitted to take unilateral action against a patrician. That was yesterday's rule. It's a new day. This is not only the right course of action but the only one.

"Denali has put us into a difficult situation. We're in uncharted territory here, Joakeen. The exchange has been decimated. One of their own people is working with terrorists. The Zurich Canon has been suspended. Denali Keating has attacked our security forces, murdering many of them, and is harboring the most wanted fugitives in the world. We need to defend the interests of the corporation. A strong response will compel Denali to surrender the terrorists and explain his behavior."

Joakeen bites his lip and thinks about it for a long moment. Zeykala's frustration grows with each passing second. Why does it take so long for smart people to make obvious decisions? She's about to urge him on when he looks up at her.

"Does Talya know about this?"

"She isn't the CEO or the president of the board. We're the custodians of this corporation, and right now, we're being taken advantage of."

"You have my support. Do whatever you feel is needed."

"Thank you."

Zeykala rises and shakes his hand. Instead of letting go, he holds it. "Whatever actions you take need to work. The voices on the board that are calling for your dismissal are growing louder. Every moment this chaos lasts is a minute closer to a vote to replace you. You can't afford to lose any more support."

"I can't run this corporation with my neck under a guillotine, Joakeen."

She all but ensured he was named chairman. He needs to repay that favor. Unfortunately, that isn't something he seems to realize.

"That's the job. You dangled the blade over Valen's neck every day. You were appointed as an interim chief executive. The corporate charter is very specific about ascension to this office, and making your appointment permanent requires the language be changed first."

"Then get them to change it," Zeykala demands, pulling her hand out of his.

"That won't happen until this crisis abates. The board can and will replace you, regardless of my feelings on the matter. My advice is to end this insurrection quickly and efficiently," Joakeen says, pointing up at the display. "It's only a matter of time before I can't stop the board from removing you and appointing someone who will."

CHAPTER ELEVEN

THE PATRICIANS

Keating Family of the Gentez-Majorez Estate
Greenwich Geographic District
Southern Connecticut Municipal Corporation

The Keating Estate was designed to look like a medieval fortress because Denali knew the day might come when it would need to be one. Constructed from thick gray stone, it has a pair of octagonal turrets rising above the pitched roof to complete the image. He has always loved the view from the western turret. He can see a long stretch of shoreline and the tall buildings in Stamford. Facing to the southwest, Manhattan is visible on a clear day.

Farron and Commander Lacune are more interested in watching the BCS set up a thin cordon around the perimeter. Boats have moved into position off-shore, and a helicopter hovers off in the distance along with several surveillance drones. It's the most manpower and equipment he's ever seen the BCS deploy to one location.

"This is going to make the neighbors very unhappy," Denali mutters.

"I apologize, Father. They're here because of me."

"Yes, they are, but it was unavoidable. There was bound to be a coming out party, and now the day has arrived."

"So far, there's nothing special about their deployment," the commander adds, looking through high-powered binoculars. "They don't appear to be preparing to breach."

"They don't have the guts. They only aim to make sure we don't leave while the Pentagon decides how far to take this."

"Why does the BCS think they have the right to attack us?" Farron asks.

"They're in a state of martial law. It's a blank check to do whatever they want."

"I thought it was corporate law?"

"I prefer the old term. Corporate law, Corporate Hill, Corporate Hall, corporate this, corporate that…corporate, corporate, corporate. You'd think early executives would have shown a little originality back then."

Abbot emerges from the stairwell and makes his way over to them. "Sir, you have a secure VidLynk from the White House."

"It took Zeykala long enough. I'll take it down in the study. Commander, continue planning the defense. Ensure all secondary power supplies and redundant communications are ready in case they cut the utilities. If so much as a single agent steps foot on this estate, kill them all."

"Yes, sir. Consider it done."

Farron and Abbot join Denali on the trek down to the study. The VidLynk is activated, and a ragged-looking Zeykala fills the display. She looks terrible.

"Chief Executive Zeykala. I hope you're calling with an explanation as to why your security personnel are currently surrounding my estate," Denali says, seizing control of the conversation before she can.

"I think we are well past playing dumb, Denali, don't you?" the CEO fires back in a blatant breach of etiquette and protocol. "Your son aided and abetted the escape of Liberteum from Manhattan, and your security force attacked ours in the process. Now you're harboring those same terrorists at your estate."

There's no doubt the corporation has a solid timeline for the morning's events in Manhattan by now. Denying it would be futile. "That is all one hundred percent true, despite the corporate slant you are putting on it."

"Thank you for not insulting my intelligence by denying it. Those are the facts."

"Facts? My son was in peril because of the actions of your BCS," Denali says, turning to Farron. "I deployed my security services to protect his life. Those *are* the facts."

"He was aiding terrorists!"

Denali has no patience for her hysterics. Chief executive officers don't only run corporations – they're symbols that project their power and strength. Zeykala, with her temper tantrums, does neither.

"You are drawing conclusions without proper context, so let me educate you. Two years ago, we heard rumors that Liberteum was planning on attacking our interests. Farron began attending urch raves to infiltrate them. Once he earned their trust, it was only a matter of when the time was right to bring them to justice."

"You expect me to believe that?" she snaps.

The patrician grins. "I know this is embarrassing for you."

"I'm not embarrassed at all."

"You should be. We accomplished in one day what you failed to do for months. We have the two most wanted people in this entire sphere of influence in our custody – the leader of Liberteum and the Intercorpex chief inspector who helped destroy Assembly Hall."

"They would both be in *our* custody had you not intervened," Zeykala fires back.

Denali stifles a laugh. The best they could have done was kill them all, including Farron. That may have satisfied their bloodlust but would do nothing for his agenda.

"Do you honestly think Liberteum would ever throw down their arms and surrender to you?" Farron asks. "They killed hundreds of your employees. There's no chance they would go down without a fight. Trust me. I was there."

"The BCS would have killed Liberteum and lost you the opportunity you covet most," Denali adds.

"Which is?"

"The opportunity to parade Liberteum in front of your employees and show them what treason looks like," Farron explains. "To show them your leadership and how corporate justice works. I imagine, given the current crisis, everyone is losing faith in America Incorporated."

Denali puffs his chest out. Farron is learning. He's going to be a great patriarch of this family someday. The Keatings will know power surpassing any Roman Caesar, Russian czar, or American president. This family will be all of them combined.

"I demand you turn them over to us immediately. The BCS will receive them outside of your estate."

"Or else what?" Denali asks, leaning closer to the camera.

"We will take them by force."

Both patricians laugh. Denali even catches a glimpse of Abbot smirking.

"You are free to try. I promise you that the BCS is incapable of amassing a large enough force to seize this estate."

"You underestimate their capabilities."

"And you underestimate mine," he says, his voice growing more grave. "Why make the streets run red with blood when I'm willing to negotiate their transfer?"

Zeykala tries to remain defiant, but it's a façade. If the BCS attacks and fails, it would be humiliating. Negotiation is the low-risk play. Whether she can admit that to herself is another matter entirely.

"What are your terms?"

Denali glances at the time in the lower corner of the display. "Tell your security to hold their positions. I will dispatch my son to Washington tomorrow morning to negotiate with you directly. VidLynks are so…impersonal."

Zeykala scowls, clearly not willing to wait that long. Her impatience will be her undoing. She can reap the benefits of a successful negotiation. Can she stomach the failure of a direct assault? Denali doesn't think so.

"Tomorrow morning. Seven a.m. at the White House. Be prepared to prove your captives are still alive. Good day."

Zeykala disconnects without another word. That woman has no backbone. America Incorporated has never had a weaker CEO, interim or otherwise. The Baroness chose her stooge well for their purposes.

"That went much better than I thought."

"Father, since when does the corporation have anything we would want to negotiate for?"

"They don't. I just needed to buy time. Come up with a list of demands for tomorrow. Be creative and make it painful, but don't include anything Zeykala would be forced to say no to. You'll be taking the helicopter."

"I want the Intercorpex chief inspector with me. It will enhance our bargaining position."

"Not Michele?" his father asks, raising an eyebrow.

"No, she's way too valuable to let leave this mansion until the deal is done. Chief Inspector Zyree will suffice for our purposes."

"Very well."

"Father, why exactly do we need more time?"

Denali grins and clasps his hands behind his back. "To start spreading the wealth. I don't think it's fair to the rest of the world that America Incorporated is the only corporation struggling through a crisis."

CHAPTER TWELVE

LIBERTEUM

*Keating Family of the Gentez-Majorez Estate
Greenwich Geographic District
Southern Connecticut Municipal Corporation*

The titanium pins click as they recede into the heavy vault door. The four captives turn as it swings open. Abbot comes in pushing an ornate cart with a dinner service. He wheels it into the center of the room near the table and sets out folded white linen napkins.

Zyree picks up a fork and studies it. He gives the manservant an "Are you kidding me" look. Rykos stands and admires the bone china plates covered with sterling silver cloches and diamond-inlaid utensils. His eyes track to the open vault door. It's an open invitation for an escape.

"Is there a problem, Chief Inspector?" Abbot asks in his condescending British accent.

"You're serving hostages dinner on fine china?"

"You are not a hostage. You're a guest," he corrects. "Were you expecting plastic dinnerware? We're not savages."

"Ever been stabbed with one of your fancy butter knives, buddy?" Koltayne asks, grabbing one of them and holding it menacingly.

"Dispatching me might provide you with some temporary satisfaction, but it will ultimately do you no good. Even if you were to incapacitate me—"

"We wouldn't incapacitate you. We'd just kill you," Zyree clarifies.

"Even if you were to *kill* me and make it past the armed guards, we're currently surrounded by the Bureau of Corporate Security."

"You're lying," Rykos asserts. "They have no remit for that. It's against the Zurich Canon."

"Intercorpex suspended the canon," Zyree reminds him.

Abbot gestures theatrically toward the door. "You're welcome to see for yourself. I can predict how it will end. They're here for you, not us."

Rykos and Koltayne seem ready to take their chances. Zyree hates the idea of being the voice of reason. If Denali was the least bit concerned about their escaping, his unescorted and unarmed butler wouldn't have left the vault door wide open.

"Put the knife down, Koltayne," Michele orders, also believing that Abbot isn't bluffing.

"A prudent move, ma'am," Abbot says with a deferential bow of his head. Koltayne reluctantly slams the knife down onto the cart in frustration. "The BCS traced your escape here. Given their incompetence trying to catch you these past weeks, the Keatings were surprised they connected the dots so quickly."

"You're not afraid they'll attack this mansion to get us?" Rykos asks.

"I doubt they'll have much success with that. Besides, arrangements are being made. Your stay will be short."

"What kind of arrangements?" Zyree asks.

"High-level ones."

Zyree presses his lips together. He isn't surprised that Denali is brokering a trade. If their present situation is dire now, it's game over the moment they are remanded into BCS custody.

"If you're going to turn us in, it should be to the New York PSS," Rykos says. What he's driving at is obvious to everybody, including Abbot.

"You want Patrician Keating to turn you over to your father, I presume. Unfortunately, that's not a possibility. He's no longer the chief guardian of public safety and security."

"He was removed from his position?"

"Registrant Rykos, your father is dead."

Everyone turns to look at Rykos. People react differently to bad news. Some cry, while others lash out in anger. He is stunned. Abbot's words hit him with the force of a sledgehammer.

"Wh-what?"

"Oh, you didn't know? I truly apologize for the callous manner in which I delivered the news. I regret to inform you that Chief Guardian Teman was terminated earlier this morning at Rikers Island for crimes against the corporation."

Rykos becomes wobbly, and Michele grabs his arm before he falls. Koltayne pulls out a chair, and they ease him into it. He might not have been on good terms with his father, but no son is prepared to accept a parent's death. It's worse under those circumstances.

"And my mother?" Rykos asks in a near whisper.

"Chief Executive Ilaria?"

"Chief exec— What?"

"My, you all have been out of touch."

Abbot explains everything that happened while they were on the run through the streets of Manhattan. It's a revelation. What little information they had in Valhalla about the outside world came from AME News. They didn't report on any of this, of course.

Rykos just stares off into space during Abbot's recount of events. He is listening, but his mind is elsewhere. He could be wondering or even hoping that Abbot is lying. Zyree has been in this business long enough to know when someone is providing disinformation. He isn't.

"Where is my mother now?" Rykos mumbles, staring blankly at the wall.

"She was taken into custody by Director Virtari and moved to an undisclosed location."

Michele rubs Rykos's shoulder to console him. He doesn't respond, so she sits in an adjacent chair to look into his eyes. They're empty. The spark has left them. He stands and retreats to the corner, where he collapses to the floor with his knees up and his head buried between them.

"I will retrieve your plates in an hour," Abbot says. "Bon Appetit."

A heavy feeling descends over the room after Abbot departs. Michele and Koltayne look over at Rykos and back at Zyree as the heavy door is secured. There's nothing he can say. Apologies and condolences won't bring his father back.

Everyone in this room has faced struggles. Despite the odds, there was a sense of optimism about the future until the boat sailed up to the Keating Estate. They had cheated death only to walk right back into its clutches. Whatever Denali has planned for them doesn't include freedom or the promise of a better life.

The mood of the room is heavy. Zyree was betrayed by the organization he dedicated a life of service to. Rykos has lost his father, with his mother soon likely to share his fate. Koltayne has realized that he's on the losing team. And Michele, despite her years of planning and initial successes, knows that they will fall short of their ultimate goal.

Despite the loss of appetite, Zyree needs to force food down. Except for Rykos, the others join him in grabbing a plate. They eat in silence, all resigning themselves to the same conclusion: No path leads to the ending they hoped for.

CHAPTER THIRTEEN

NYCMC RESISTANCE

Chief Guardian Teman's Domicile
Upper West Side Geographic District
New York City Municipal Corporation

They paced themselves better than Ilaria thought they would. Alcohol is forbidden, so she expected them to have passed out drunk hours ago. Instead, they stopped at what she estimates were two drinks each and stopped to enjoy her domicile's view and amenities.

No restaurants are open while the city is under corporate law. Her babysitters were forced to cook the meager provisions stocked in the pantry. What they fed her was barely edible. To add to the insult, she had to eat off the plate when they wouldn't remove her restraints.

From the sounds coming from the living area, the two men settled in front of some stale AME programming after dinner. It wasn't long before the one-gallon jug of urch shine was reopened. They got a little carried away around midnight. Now, almost two hours later, they're hammered and bored. That's a dangerous mix.

She hears the telltale creak of the door hinges. It's showtime. Ryax stammers in, unsteady in his footing. He leans on the wall as he closes and locks the door behind him. Ilaria takes a deep breath to relax. It's time to get this over with.

"I told you I'd be back," he slurs.

"I was hoping you would," she says, shimmying off the bed and sauntering over to him. "It's been lonely in here."

"You mocking me?" he asks, grabbing her arms in a vise-like grip.

Ilaria guides her face toward him, and he edges away. She tries again with the same result. The third time is the charm. He lets her in, and she kisses him hard, working her tongue into his mouth. His grip weakens enough as she presses her body against him.

"Did that feel like I was mocking you?"

"You're playing games," he says, his stern look softening. "You hate us. We killed your husband."

"Yeah, you killed my abusive, cold, unloving husband. Teman was soft. Do you know how many late-night fantasies I've had about taking a big, strong man into my bed? Do you?"

"You're lying."

Ilaria turns and walks to the edge of the bed before facing him. "Then punish me. Call your friend in here if you'd like."

"He's busy," the agent says defensively.

"Then you get me first, so do it. Do *me*."

That was all the encouragement he needed. Ryax slides the zipper down on her tunic and yanks it off her shoulders. He tears open the thin, synthetic shirt she's wearing underneath and exposes her bra and midsection.

His scruff scratches her neck as he kisses her shoulders. His fingers struggle to unbutton her pants before he slides his hand down and probes her with his fingers. Ilaria closes her eyes and moans softly.

He spins her around violently and forces her head onto the mattress. She closes her eyes, expecting him to yank down her pants and mount her from behind. Instead, she feels the electromag cuffs disengage and fall from her wrists. Her arms are free.

"You won't regret that when you see what I can do with these hands," she says, rising from the bed and turning.

She kisses him as she unzips his uniform top and slides it off him. Ryax impatiently removes his second shirt, revealing bulging pecs and biceps. Ilaria coos as she runs her hands down his chest to his pants. She lets out a series of squeals as he grabs and massages her breasts as she furiously unfastens his trousers. She makes a show of kissing his chest as she pulls his pants and underwear down to his ankles. Ryax smiles, thinking he knows what's coming next. He doesn't.

Ilaria stands and kisses him again, grinding her chest against his. She reaches down and grabs his manhood, stroking it hard. With her other hand, she begins to massage his testicles. He closes his eyes and moans in delight.

"I want to ride you all night," Ilaria whispers in his ear.

She strokes him even harder. Ryax closes his eyes and tilts his head toward the ceiling. Seeing her chance, Ilaria holds his penis with one hand and clamps hard on his balls with the other. She digs her fingernails in. Shock registers on his face as he tries to pull away. It only makes things worse for him as she twists her hand and yanks down as hard as she can.

The sound of ripping flesh is satisfying. The high-pitched screams of a man in unimaginable pain pierce her ears as he trips over the trousers draped around his ankles. He tumbles hard to the ground, grasping at his genitals as blood pours onto the carpet. To add to the horror, she drops his scrotum in front of his face.

Ilaria hears a commotion in the living room. Two loud claps, followed by a third. She has only moments to prepare. When Mornym sees what she's done, the punishment will be worse than getting sexually violated.

She wrestles her tunic back on before rushing over to the nightstand. The bedroom doesn't have many potential weapons. The long, heavy aluminum reading light on the table has some mass and weight that may do some damage to her remaining tormentor.

Racing over to the door, Ilaria positions herself off to the side. Seconds tick by, and her heart pounds a quick cadence with ferocity. She inhales deeply and exhales slowly in a vain attempt to control her breathing. Then the doorknob jiggles.

The door is kicked open, and she takes a final breath. She prepares to swing the lamp, only nothing happens. There's no movement. No sound of alarm at his wounded colleague wailing on the floor of the bedroom. Nothing.

"Ilaria?"

She's startled at the sound of her name. The BCS agents never used it. And it sounds so familiar…then she makes the connection.

"Phylep?"

A man in a tactical uniform enters the room, and Ilaria clams up. The lamp is still at the ready.

"Whoa," he says, lowering his weapon. "We're the good guys."

Phylep steps into the room and looks around before whistling. He slings the weapon over his shoulder and looks at Ilaria in admiration.

"We're…uh…here to rescue you," he says with a smile before nodding at the man with him. "Not that it looks like you *need* rescuing. Remind me to never get you pissed at me."

The guardian raises his rifle and fires a round into the agent's forehead, putting him out of his misery. The yowling ceases, and silence once again reclaims the room.

"You should have left him screaming in pain," Ilaria laments.

"I could barely hear you over his crying. What exactly happened to…to tiny here?" he asks after noticing the diminutive size of the agent's penis and the severely damaged scrotum lying next to his face.

Ilaria tosses the metal lamp she's holding. She thought this would be much worse. The alcohol dimmed the agent's judgment enough. Other than needing mouthwash and a shower, it worked out for the best.

"He got what he deserved."

"Chief Executive, did he…?"

"No. I'm fine. Where's his partner?"

"Bleeding out on your couch with a bottle of urch shine in his hand and three holes in his chest."

Ilaria nods. "How did you find me?"

"Phylep, these guys reported in five minutes ago," the guardian says after checking the man's tablet and tossing it back to the ground.

"Good, then we'll have a decent head start. The guardians knew something went wrong after they lost contact with you at Rikers. They put together a rescue mission, and I offered some qulis to help. We have excellent knowledge of that facility. We were getting ready to go when the RTCC notified us that your Maester system had gone offline. Dzamko's, too. We figured they must have brought you back to Manhattan…for some crazy reason."

"Zeykala had a plan for me. Where are Dzamko and Deyago?"

"We're extracting Dzamko now. That's probably more of a fight than this was. I doubt he'll have the opportunity to rip a drunk agent's balls off. We have no idea where they brought Deyago and the others yet."

The guardian listens intently to his earpiece before leaving the room. Ilaria and Phylep follow him into the living area, where she sees another quli and guardian standing watch. Ilaria looks around. She knows this is likely going to be the last time she ever sets foot in here.

"We need to leave before we get company," the guardian says. "We don't have the ammo for a prolonged firefight."

They take the elevator down to the lobby and exit onto the street. Instead of heading south, they turn toward Central Park. It's not the direction she was expecting.

"Where are we going? I need to get back to One Guardian Plaza," Ilaria says. Being surrounded by heavily armed guardians is preferable to hiding beneath the massive park.

"We will get you there, but we need to meet up with some friends first."

CHAPTER FOURTEEN

AMERICA, INC.

PSS Emergency Operations Center (BCS Controlled)
Lower West-Side Office Building
New York City Municipal Corporation

The opportunity to rest comes only in short spurts during an emergency. What they are facing now is the worst crisis the corporation has experienced in decades. Virtari was in desperate need of a few hours to keep his batteries charged. Just because the BCS director prides himself on his ability to function without sleep doesn't mean he can go without it in perpetuity.

He rubs his eyes as he enters the main operations center. The message said this was urgent. Virtari scans the displays along the wall. Nothing of consequence seems to be happening. The only notable thing is the time on the LED clock, which reads just before three in the morning.

"This had better be good," he growls, getting the attention of the EOC shift commander.

He grasps his hands behind his back. "We've lost contact with the two teams holding Ilaria and Dzamko. It could be a communications error."

"I might believe that for one team, but not both," Virtari concludes with a sigh. "Dispatch fire teams to the two domiciles to check."

"They are arriving now. Patching the video in."

An agent puts a split screen from a helmet camera on the display. Teams enter both domiciles simultaneously. The footage is gruesome in each. On the left, an agent is on a sofa with holes in his chest. The other image shows an agent lying on the ground in a pool of blood. The quarters are searched and are empty. The left side of the screen zooms in on a half-naked agent lying face down on the ground. His scrotum is lying next to him. On the right side, another agent is slumped over a table with his forehead blown out.

Virtari's jaw tightens at the sight of his men. He knows it was the PSS, possibly with help from the qulis. None of the agents put up a fight, which means none of them were taking their assignments seriously. Alert sentries don't allow this kind of thing to happen. He expects better from those who serve in the vaunted BCS.

"Pull video from both buildings and find out who did this."

"Yes, sir."

Zeykala needs to start acting like a decisive chief executive. Denali Keating has negotiated himself into a standoff in Greenwich and limited their options. Had the order been issued to breach the estate, he could have ended this quickly. Now, they'll be ready for an assault, and he'll need a small army if that order comes.

Her decision to let Ilaria and Dzamko live can be added to Zeykala's growing list of mistakes. Moving them to Manhattan was stupid. Their rescue couldn't have been predicted, but the risk of it never should have been taken. All that's left is to clean up the mess.

"We have four subjects entering and five leaving Ilaria's building," an operator says.

"That's them. Where did they go?"

"They turned north toward Central Park. We can use static street surveillance to trace their route, but the cameras inside the park are offline."

Virtari nods. It's a smart play. They know the BCS doesn't have the assets in place to secure the park. Even if they did, there's a labyrinth of tunnels under it to shelter and hide in.

"Do we have drones reconnoitering the park?"

"Yes, sir. There are heat signatures scattered everywhere, but the largest concentration is here at Frisbee Hill. It seems to be the center of activity."

The thermal image shows people streaming in all directions. They are in large groups, heading down roads and paths to and from the gathering in the center. It looks coordinated. They know the limitations of these drones and are taking advantage of it.

There isn't enough light for standard video at this hour. Infrared and thermal can detect targets, but there's no way to positively identify them. Any heat signature could be Ilaria or Dzamko, or none of them at all.

"Very clever," Virtari says, almost admiring the tactic for its simple brilliance. "I guess there is such a thing as safety in numbers."

"Do you want me to mobilize teams to detain them?"

"With who? We don't have the manpower."

He could dispatch agents with heavy weapons to start mowing them down. They're all violating curfew and the action is permissible under corporate law. The heavy-handed action is decisive, and that's why Zeykala would have a fit. Leaked footage to the GlobalNet would be a major optics problem for her. While Virtari doesn't care to play political games, the CEO can still manage to make his life more miserable than she already is.

"Has the White House been informed of the escapes?"

"No, sir."

"Good. Don't report this. Bring up Ilaria's biographical information."

The display populates with her work history, housing assignments, family members, and known associates. Human Resources tracks everything. The database already lists Teman as deceased and her son as a known traitor. It also names the older child.

"Bring up the information on the daughter," Virtari orders.

"Varella…she attends Harvard, has stellar grades, no disciplinary action…."

"She's a poster child for the modern corporate executive. How did she end up in this family? Pull up her current location."

Leverage. It's one of his favorite words. If Virtari can't find Ilaria or Rykos, there must be a way to get them to come to him. The display shifts to a map, and he expects it to zoom in on the Cambridge area. It doesn't. Instead, a red dot pulses in lower Manhattan less than a mile from here. The director shifts his gaze to the two men for an answer.

"Varella is interning at the America Tower. Her shift is slated to start at nine, but with corporate law in effect…."

"It's all hands on deck there," Virtari says, checking the time. "Have a secure transport ready downstairs in four hours. I will meet with her there personally."

It's early, and she isn't going anywhere. This will be a long day, and he needs more rest. Virtari takes one last look back at Varella's image on the display. Ilaria put on quite the show at Rikers while trying to convince him not to terminate her husband. Now, he gets to see if she'll take the same approach with her only daughter.

CHAPTER FIFTEEN

THE PATRICIANS

Keating Family of the Gentez-Majorez Estate
Greenwich Geographic District
Southern Connecticut Municipal Corporation

The Queen's Army in London, Volga in Moscow, White Lotus in Beijing, and the Königreich in Berlin are to those corporations what Liberteum is to America Incorporated. The world calls them terrorists, but in reality, they're nationalists dedicated to fighting the corporate structure. What they are to Denali Keating is much simpler: useful idiots.

"How do you think they came up with these names?" the patrician asks Commander Lacune as they stare at the displays in the operations nerve center deep inside his Greenwich mansion. "Do you think they sit around in a huddle and think of something catchy, or does it happen organically?"

He shrugs. "A little of both, I imagine."

Their names have no bearing on what is about to happen. The question is only a means to pass the time. These missions were supposed to launch forty minutes ago, but the video shows nothing more than men sitting around.

"What the hell are we waiting for?"

"One of the teams isn't in place yet. Volga had a member get stopped by Russian corporate security. He talked his way out of it, but it has put them behind schedule."

"Is this putting the other missions at risk?"

"There is no immediate danger of discovery," Lacune assures him. "You wanted these attacks to be simultaneous, sir. The targets were all selected for that reason. Do you really want to move without the Russian contingent in place?"

Denali scowls. Throughout most of human history, few people have been actual witnesses to history. Most learned about current events from word of mouth. The printing press began a new era of information sharing, and then television made it faster and more visible. World-changing events like Pearl Harbor and the dropping of the atomic bombs on Japan were announced to the world through newspapers and newsreels.

That began to change at the turn of the century. Americans watched in horror as airliners crashed into skyscrapers on live television. The attacks on 9/11 weren't notable for the government response so much as how it made everyone bystanders to a significant historical event.

Corporations found new and more efficient ways to connect people to information. The speed at which information flows today leaves little time for the human mind to process it. The issue is that people see only what corporations want them to see. Despite everybody being connected, few will have a front-row seat for events that will shake corporations to their core and reshape the world. They will eventually learn the truth, assuming these terrorists ever get around to it.

"Can we speed this up?" Denali asks, fidgeting in impatience. "I don't want to wait any longer."

"You don't have to," the commander says, noticing the status link turned green on the Volga display. "All I need now is for you to give the word."

Denali grins. It has taken years to get to this point. Getting the required weapons and devices into the hands of these groups proved far more difficult than manipulating Liberteum was. It was a procurement and logistical nightmare. His security team required an inordinate amount of time to train and organize the groups. Everything is finally in place, and the time is here.

"Execute."

The commander smirks and sends the "go" signal that will set the men in motion. Denali inhales deeply and lets it out slowly as he checks the time – 5:07 a.m. Eastern Time. He makes a mental note of it.

Seventeen attacks against eleven major corporations will change this smug and arrogant world. They all watched from a distance as Liberteum took the exchange offline. They laughed at the incompetence of America Incorporated's security forces. Now, the war comes to them in a way they could never imagine.

The first discernible action comes from White Lotus warriors. They are the least trained of the groups but the largest in terms of manpower. Twenty-two separate five-man teams disembark from vehicles in Beijing, Shanghai, and Hong Kong and attack corporate centers, public places, mass transit, and high-volume foot traffic areas with heavy weapons.

The carnage is graphic. These men are Chinese clones of Haven. They hate everything and everybody and are relishing the opportunity to vent that hatred. Their murderous rampage is sparing no one.

The main display images shift to a new camera feed. Denali is about to protest until he sees why. Hundreds of people are convulsing on the ground in a packed London tube station. The image shifts again to Berlin, where massive explosions are rocking the city as sabotaged natural gas mains explode under crowded streets.

When the footage gets too shaky, the commander switches back to the feeds from China.

With nothing of interest happening in Moscow yet, Denali focuses on the Brazilian team. The force there is small but lethal. The presence of a mole inside the CEO's residence allowed for this special plan. The patrician has had more than one run-in with the arrogant bastard who runs that corporation.

The Brazilian commandos breach his compound with the help of the insider and begin their assault. They're now engaged in a vicious firefight somewhere in the residence. The assassination will either succeed or fail, but the bold attempt will be enough to get him searching for a deep hole to hide in.

A fireball erupts in Paris, marking the detonation of the truck bomb. On a separate display, a high-speed train derails as it pulls into a station in Delhi. Planting plastic explosives on the tracks is more than enough to send trains careening out of control. In the India Corporation alone, they sabotaged eighteen of them.

Denali glances over at the feed from Moscow. Still nothing. The feed from China goes dark. The men are offline or were killed. If the other White Lotus attacks were half as successful as this one he witnessed, China will be dealing with a substantial body count.

In London, the medical brigade responding to the attack on the Underground is pinned down by small arms fire. The groups who planted the nerve agent offered to sacrifice themselves and maximize casualties by ambushing anyone trying to render aid. The patrician couldn't believe how easy it was to manufacture the lethal gas. Fear is contagious, and the effect on the employees there will paralyze the UK Corporation for months.

"Sir, it looks like the Brazilian group managed to fight their way through the mansion, but the CEO escaped into a strong room. We can't get to him."

Denali shrugs. "Oh, well. Order them to burn the palace to the ground."

A white light flashes across the display of the Moscow feed. Denali smiles as he watches it turn into a hazy orange before finally dissipating. By the time they realize how special this attack was, it will be too late. This blast alone will usher in a new era.

"Moscow is successful," the commander informs him.

They were never going to get the archaic device to function as intended. There isn't enough expertise available to make it work. The mushroom cloud from a thermonuclear detonation would have been iconic, but the dirty version will still work for Denali's purposes. Radiation is an unseen enemy. Spread fissionable material far enough via an explosion, and it will continue to kill long after the smoke has cleared. They won't be working around Red Square for a long time.

"The attacks are complete, sir. Survivors are pulling back to their designated rally points."

"My compliments to you and your men on an outstanding job, Commander."

"Thank you, sir."

"I have some business to attend to regarding our guests. Monitor for any corporate response and send anything critical to me through Abbot."

"Of course, sir."

Denali exits the operations center and climbs the stairs to the mansion's main floor. Farron will need final instructions for his meeting in Washington with Zeykala. The information about what's transpired will rattle the world's corporations. The employees in these corporations will be terrified. Liberteum will be eliminated, but their legacy will continue to shape the world as he needs it to.

Everything about the day is going according to plan, but the journey isn't over. At least Denali can share good news on his conference with The Trust this afternoon. The rise of the patrician class to ultimate power is all but certain now.

CHAPTER SIXTEEN

RYKOS

Keating Family of the Gentez-Majorez Estate
Greenwich Geographic District
Southern Connecticut Municipal Corporation

I sit up in the bed Zyree vacated when they came for him a couple of hours ago. I knew he wouldn't be returning anytime soon and moved to the unoccupied cot. The lights are turned down but not completely off. Without the faint glow from the overhead LED, the windowless steel room we are imprisoned in would be pitch dark.

Most urches are used to sleeping on hard surfaces, so Koltayne opted to pass out on the floor. Michele is still sitting at the small table in the center of the room, looking a little ragged but otherwise wide awake. She must have been there all night, alone with her thoughts.

"I know you don't want to talk about it," Michele whispers, not wanting to disturb Koltayne, "but I'm sorry for what's happened to your parents. I'm sorry I got you into this mess."

"I got myself into it," I say, rising and taking a seat across from her at the table.

"I kidnapped you."

"Yeah, then you released me. If you have anything to apologize for, it's not putting a few more seconds on that timer when you blew up the subway station."

That feels like a lifetime ago. So much has happened since I was Liberteum's captive. Now, I'm their ally. My father was placed in charge of their apprehension, was tortured by Haven, and was killed by the corporation he served. My mother has gone from a housewife to a prisoner of the BCS. It all started that day.

Michele flashes a brief smile. "I knew you'd get out okay."

"I did. Then, I sought you out to help with my father. I volunteered to find you. If I had to do it all over again, I would."

The admission clearly surprises her. "Why?"

I shrug. "Honestly? I had a one-way ticket to mediocrity before we met. I went to Dinsmore Academy only because of my father's influence. I got okay grades, but I was on track for some middie position at a sub."

"Middie? Sub?"

"Sorry, it's a mid-level manager at a subsidiary corporation. I would have lived an uneventful life, gotten married, had a kid or two, and once I was no longer useful, they would have terminated me. That would have been my life. Only it really isn't a life at all, is it?"

"That's a matter of perspective, I suppose."

"Exactly," I say, shifting my weight in the chair. "I used to hang out in Central Park with my friend Balin. He was the one you knocked unconscious when we were fleeing the rave."

"I remember."

I nod. "We used to talk about what we thought was wrong with the world. It was treasonous stuff, which is why we always did it in private. We wanted to experience more from life, and that's how we ended up at the rave in the first place.

"After I was rescued, I told the lie you instructed me to tell. I was surprised that anyone believed me, let alone name me a 'hero of the corporation.' Because of that, I got into Harvard and started dating Mollae, who was, by far, the hottest girl in the school."

"What the hell kind of name is that?" Michele asks, trying to lighten the mood or get under my skin. I'm not sure which.

"What kind of name is Michele?" I fire back with a smile.

"An old one."

"Mollae only has time for the upwardly mobile," I continue. "I was on a career track that could have taken me to the highest levels of the parent corporation. It's most registrants' dream and the only reason she took an interest in me.

"The problem was that it wasn't *my* dream. Mollae and I were on a date in Central Park when Zyree ambushed me about the lies I told. Seeing him reminded me how miserable I was. When my mother asked me if there was a chance I could find you to help free my father, I didn't agree out of obligation – it was something I wanted to do. I wanted to be a part of something bigger. I believed in your father. I believe in you. I still want to make a difference."

"Yeah, some difference we're making," Michele says, looking around their subterranean prison. "I worked on Archimedes for years with my father. I never could have believed it would fail so spectacularly."

I understand her frustration. I can't imagine dedicating my life to a plan that has all but fallen apart. Most of her friends are dead, her hideouts compromised, and she is at the mercy of a deranged patrician with the rest of us. It's a sober reality check, but maybe one she needed.

"This was never going to be easy. We're four generations removed from lofty ideas like liberty and democracy. People have no concept of what they are. Corporatism is what they know, and most of them are comfortable with it."

"Deep in the soul of every person is a longing to be free," Michele says, imparting some ancient wisdom as she glares at me.

"And the foundation for all human motivation is food, shelter, and security. The corporation provides all three. People equate freedom with having those basic needs met. That's the hill we will need to climb…if we ever get out of here."

My sobering analysis isn't something she wants to hear. It needed to be said, but I probably should have picked a better time. Michele is already under enough stress. The idea that her grand plan to reshape the face of the world would be met with fierce resistance by the people she's looking to save isn't exactly motivational.

"I need to get some rest," she snaps.

I stand and grab her arm as she heads for the cot. She doesn't immediately pull it away and looks into my eyes. I brush a strand of hair from her face.

"I don't know what happens from here, Michele, but whatever does, know I'll stand by your side through all of it."

She forces a smile and nods. "Thank you."

Her getting some rest is going to have to wait. The large door opens, and Abbot enters. Two men follow, pushing a display on a metal stand that's also equipped with a camera and speakers. I look at Michele, who is thinking the same thing I am: This can't be good.

CHAPTER SEVENTEEN

AMERICA, INC.

The White House
Corporate Governance District
Washington-Arlington Municipal Corporation

The helicopter swoops over the South Lawn and lands on the grass. Zeykala scowls out the Oval Office window, wondering who the hell gave them permission for that. Patricians are already granted too many liberties to do as they please. Only arrogance precipitates the need to land on the grounds when there are a dozen helipads within a short drive.

Two men disembark and are escorted into the West Wing. She waits for the notification to pop up on her tablet announcing their arrival in the Charter Room. It's impolite to keep a patrician waiting even a minute, but she's done with theater. Three minutes later, Zeykala walks out of the Oval Office and across the hall.

Formal introductions are made once they gather around the conference table. Farron doesn't look the least bit interested in the pomp and circumstance. He's busy searching the faces of the various executives and staff members present in the room.

"Where is Executive Fiolla?" Farron asks after the mediator ends his pageant. "It's customary that the senior representative from corporate affairs is present for meetings."

"She's indisposed," Zeykala says as they take their seats.

"Very well. Let's begin. To set expectations for this meeting, assuming our conditions are met, Michele, Rykos, and Koltayne will be transferred into your custody. We're handing you the leader of Liberteum, one of her men, and a traitorous former hero of the corporation."

"We want Chief Inspector Zyree as well," Zeykala demands, glancing over at the stoic man seated next to Farron. "He murdered numerous BCS agents in Manhattan and must face justice."

"He is not a part of this negotiation. Intercorpex wants him for far worse crimes, and he will be turned over to them."

The CEO leans forward. "Then why bring him here?"

"To prove to you that they are all still alive."

"This only proves that *he* is still alive," she says, waving a dismissive hand and leaning back in her chair. "A proof of life video means nothing as well."

Farron nods at Zyree, who slides the next-generation tablet he's carrying across the table. "This tablet connects via secure VidLynk back to our estate in Greenwich. Have your people sync it to the room."

One of the staffers connects it to one of the large wall displays. When the connection is made, Zeykala sees a gray room with three people in it. Something catches their attention and they all stare into the camera.

The leader of Liberteum is not at all what Zeykala expected. The strikingly beautiful brunette looks more like a model than the leader of a terrorist group that has murdered their way through New York City.

"Michele, is it? I'm Chief Executive Zeykala. I have to say, for someone who caused so much trouble, you don't look like much."

"I'm sure your employees say the same thing when they watch your Oval Office addresses," she says, smirking.

Zeykala is almost amused at her insolence.

"And Registrant Rykos, a hero of the corporation, now revealed to be nothing more than a common thug. It's too bad you were so willing to waste such a promising career track." The look he returns is pure hatred. "What, no witty comeback?"

"You murdered my father and incarcerated my mother. We're beyond snappy repartee."

"I terminated your father for treason. Your mother will have the chance to atone for her subversion. You will not be so fortunate."

"We have to end up in your custody first," Michele says. "I doubt you'll be able to meet Farron Keating's demands."

"I guess we'll see about that. I'll be seeing the three of you soon." Zeykala signals to end the VidLynk and turns to Farron. "What are your terms?"

Farron taps a few buttons on the tablet before handing it across the table. The CEO begins to read the document but doesn't get past the first demand.

"Are you serious? A full pardon?"

"For all crimes, alleged and proven, past and present."

Zeykala shakes her head and continues reading. The rest of the list is just as bad: a promise not to seize or interfere with Keating interests, permission to maintain security personnel within the sphere in numbers to be determined, and on and on. Michele was right – she may not be able to meet his demands.

"This is not a negotiation. It's extortion."

Farron shrugs. "You need Liberteum's leader and the traitor Rykos far more than we need to give them to you. They are the keys to restoring order, making them valuable assets. To obtain something of value, you must be willing to pay the price."

Zeykala hates to admit it, but he's right. She does need them. That doesn't mean she can negotiate with a gun to her head. She needs to find some leverage.

"Let's talk about the price of your actions. Your security forces murdered our agents in Manhattan. What do you think the cost of that will be?"

"Your agents were shooting at *me*. Thankfully, they were missing…a lot. My father is willing to look past that. I'm less motivated to ignore that fact and would be thrilled to walk away from this table. These are our terms, Chief Executive Zeykala, and they are not negotiable. Yes or no?"

Zeykala feels her face burn hot with anger. This patrician's complete disregard for what his men did in New York is offensive. His actions are indefensible. Farron Keating isn't dumb and knows that no harm would have come to him had he not been consorting with terrorists. Yet, he is still audacious enough to walk into this and demand she absolve them of all their sins.

"I cannot agree to this."

"Then, there is nothing further for us to discuss. Good day."

"We can seize the traitors ourselves," the CEO blurts out as he stands.

Farron sits back down, amused. "That's the second time you've made that threat. Our response is the same: You can certainly try. I warned my father that coming here was a waste of time. You have nothing to offer other than empty threats. Liberteum is also wanted by Intercorpex, so perhaps their compensation will be more…generous."

Patricians are difficult to outmaneuver under favorable circumstances. The Keatings know the BCS isn't in a position to storm their mansion amidst an insurrection and reports surfacing that the world is on fire. Complicating matters, Intercorpex would certainly be willing to strike a favorable deal.

Virtari and his BCS aren't going to like this. Fortunately, they work for her, and she has no choice. The violence needs to be quelled, or the board will find someone who will quell it. Every potential successor will say they would have made this deal.

"I agree to your terms without condition."

"Excellent," Farron says, clasping his hands together. "I will have my people contact yours to make the proper arrangements once the document is signed."

"No arrangements are necessary. Once you receive the agreement, transfer Liberteum to the agents posted outside your estate."

"No, I'm afraid that won't do. We've already received too much attention because of your presence. We will fly our guests from our estate to a neutral location."

Zeykala scowls. His quibbling over this minor detail is infuriating. It's arrogance, plain and simple. Farron Keating couldn't do her job half as well on his best day. He's never run a large corporation. That takes the kind of gall only patricians possess.

"Fine. Where?"

"We'll transmit a suitable location to you. Oh, and one more thing, once that document is signed and authenticated, I want Executive Fiolla to contact me to secure the delivery instructions."

The CEO fails to squelch her grimace. "Why her?"

"We've had dealings before. Given the sensitivity of this transaction, I prefer to work with someone I'm familiar with."

Zeykala isn't buying that for one second. "I understand, but as I told you earlier, Executive Fiolla is indisposed."

"You're the CEO. Make her available."

"I would if it were in my purview. Fiolla is scheduled to be terminated for *subversion*," Zeykala says, stressing the word as she studies his face for a reaction. There isn't much of one.

"Subversion? I never would have guessed that. What a shame. Have someone from her office contact me then." Farron reaches his hand across the table. "Chief Executive Zeykala, it's been a pleasure doing business with you."

CHAPTER EIGHTEEN

AMERICA, INC.

Meade Human Resources Center
Seven Oaks Geographic Area
Baltimore Municipal Corporation

Fiolla is unshackled from her chair and given a bright orange oversized jumpsuit to wear along with plain undergarments and laceless shoes. Doffing the hideous clothing brings a foreboding sense of dread. Whatever is about to happen is going to be bad.

She doesn't have to dwell on it for long. Two agents barge in and escort her down the sterile corridor into another equally depressing room. Smaller than her last quarters, it features only a counter with a small sink, an overhead cabinet bolted to the wall, and an inclined medical chair positioned in the center of the room.

One of the guards politely asks her to sit, and she's secured to the apparatus by her wrists and ankles. She remains silent but is screaming on the inside. Something is very wrong.

"Leave us," a short, balding man orders after he enters the room.

The guards do as he commands. Whoever this man is, he wields a great deal of authority. He methodically checks her restraints, visually inspecting each.

"I'm Doctor Krevor. You must have questions about what is about to happen."

"Doctor? As in medical doctor?" Fiolla asks, her voice raspy from a lack of water. Noticing her difficulty speaking, he fills a cup from the sink's faucet, inserts a straw, and holds it in front of her face.

"That is one of my degrees, yes," he says as Fiolla quickly sucks down the water in the cup. "To fulfill my mandate, the corporation saw fit to ensure I was educated in medicine, psychology, and advanced research, among other disciplines."

"If I'm here for a physical, I just had one six months ago," Fiolla manages to say, summoning what little defiance she can muster. He's not here to check her cholesterol.

He lets out a sardonic laugh and then abruptly stops. "I reviewed your records. You are in excellent health. It will make my job easier."

"What job is that?"

"I extract information."

"Sounds like you're a sadist."

Krevor cocks his head. "You are a sassy one, aren't you? You may want to rethink that with me."

"If you don't like it, call the guards back in and have them beat me to death. It'll save the corporation the cost of the bullets."

The doctor presses his lips together in a frown. "I abhor physical violence."

He pulls an auto-injector from the cabinet and checks the vial. Setting the dosage on the small display, he jabs it into Fiolla's arm. He follows the first shot with two more using the same procedure, and she begins to get woozy.

"I have nothing to gain by cooperating with you," Fiolla slurs.

"You have nothing to lose either. I've had everything from high-level executives to hard-boiled corporate spies in this room. Each told me everything I wanted to know. You will be no exception."

Fiolla jerks her head away when he tries to affix something to her temples. Krevor grabs her face and holds it as he attaches the devices.

"There, that's better. Shall we begin? I'm Doctor Krevor. What is your name?"

"Minnie Mouse."

Fiolla feels a jolt like someone is stabbing her brain with icepicks. Her eyes open wide as she screams in agony. The stabbing sensation ceases, and she fights to catch her breath and regain her senses. She blinks several times and focuses on the doctor bending sideways into her line of sight.

"Oof. That looked like it hurt."

"Go to hell."

"You first, my dear."

He presses the button. The pain almost causes her to retch. It takes even longer for her to recover from the trauma.

"You're going to die today, Fiolla. There's no incentive for me to go easy on you. The process you're going through is called 'cognitive disassociation.' The drugs I injected you with work with the devices to suppress your conscious state and unlock your subconscious. I pioneered this method, and it took decades to master. The results are effective and much quicker than the truth serums that were once used for this sort of thing."

He makes a show of fiddling with the device in his hand. Fiolla can't help but stare at it. She knows what another push of the button will mean.

"The subconscious is incapable of deceit. It's a database of raw information stored as memories. Like hacking a computer, all I need to do is bypass the firewall your conscious erects and steal them. Allow me to demonstrate. I'm Doctor Krevor. What is your name?"

Fiolla doesn't speak. The doctor shakes his head and presses the button. The pain is excruciating. Screams morph into hysterical sobbing.

"Executive Fiolla," she hears herself say.

"Good, and where did you previously work?"

She squeezes her lips together tightly to restrain herself from speaking. Cooperation is not—

"The White House."

Fiolla's eyes open wide in horror. What the hell? She didn't say anything. She knows she didn't.

"I know you're still in there, Fiolla. You feel locked in because your conscious self is still close to the surface. That will change as we continue. You will drift further away from reality. Before you go, I want you to know you're a traitor and deserve every second of this and more."

He presses the button again. Fiolla screams but doesn't hear anything come out of her mouth. Krevor removes his thumb from the button and leans in. His voice sounds like she's underwater.

"By the time I'm done accessing your mind, you'll beg to get marched into the courtyard and shot."

CHAPTER NINETEEN

LIBERTEUM

The White House
Corporate Governance District
Washington-Arlington Municipal Corporation

Farron takes long strides across the South Lawn as he walks with a sense of purpose toward the helicopter. Zyree struggles to match his gait, still angry that the patrician sold out people he once called friends. It's worse that he struck a deal that benefits only his family. It's time to take a stand. To hell with the consequences.

"I'm not going with you, Farron," Zyree says, stopping cold as the patrician turns to look at him.

"The hell you aren't. Get in the helicopter, Chief Inspector."

"I don't go by that title anymore. If you're going to hand me over to Lyris, you might as well put a bullet in me now."

Obvir starts walking toward them, seeing trouble. Farron follows Zyree's eyes and waves his bodyguard off.

"I know what you're thinking, and I don't blame you. This isn't what it looks like. You took a leap of faith by jumping into my car in Manhattan. Take another with me now. Time is of the essence."

Zyree prides himself on being able to read people. Other chief inspectors were reliant on biocomps to gauge truthfulness. He likes to go with his gut. There is a determined fire in Farron's eyes that was absent before this meeting. If he's lying, it would be a world-class deception. Zyree nods and follows the patrician to the helicopter.

"Back to Greenwich, sir?" the pilot asks after they climb on board and don their headsets while he powers up the engines.

"No, head over the Potomac and then turn heading northwest. We're going to Darkshadow. Obvir will give you the coordinates after he establishes a VidLynk with my father."

"Roger that."

The display inset in the copilot's seat glows to life as the VidLynk connects. The conversation was sent only to Farron's headphones. Denali's pleased look is all Zyree needs to see to know he wouldn't like the conversation.

"Sorry about that. I had some administrative business to deal with," Farron says after the conversation ends and his father disconnects.

"How about you tell me what the hell is going on."

"My father wants to control the world and has a complicated but brilliant plan to make that a reality."

"Your father is a psychopath."

"Sociopath is a better word. I don't share his lust for power. I believe in Michele and what she stands for. I have no intention of letting her, Rykos, and Koltayne fall into the hands of the BCS, nor am I turning you over to Intercorpex. I'm asking you to trust me on this."

"Please don't tell me you're planning on rescuing them yourself."

Farron grins. "Why do you think I brought you along? We're going to Darkshadow to enlist help from old friends. We're tight on time, so we need to be convincing. Michele and Rykos will depart Greenwich at noon, and we have to make a stop and pick up someone first."

The patrician's strategic insight is surprising. He had a plan before coming here. It's only a little after eight. Four hours is more than enough time to launch a rescue mission, assuming that's what he really wants to do. Zyree thinks there must be more to this.

"Pick up someone? Does it have anything to do with the questions you were asking Zeykala?"

"She threw me a curveball. I didn't come down here to negotiate. We could have done that over a VidLynk. I came for Fiolla."

Zyree nods. That explains why her name came up twice. "Who is she?"

"My fiancée. Well, probably not anymore. It's complicated."

Farron gives the abridged version of his relationship with Fiolla, from how they met to how their relationship grew. Even without details, the patrician is right – it is complicated.

"A rescue is a drastic step for someone it sounds like you were using," Zyree concludes.

"I was using her, at least in the beginning. Then I—"

"Yeah, yeah, yeah, you fell for her. I get it. Look, rescuing Michele from your father is risky enough."

Risky is an understatement. It's the definition of the word "insanity." Attacking heavily armed BCS agents is not the act of a rational man. It's the stupid thing only a suicidal or lovesick man would do. Many would argue those two concepts are one and the same.

"Okay, fine," Zyree says as Farron remains silent. "But your sleek transport helicopter is armed with bottles of scotch, not the missiles and guns you're going to need."

"You're right. This helicopter won't get it done."

He points out the window as the pilot flies low over the runway of a small airfield before touching down on the tarmac. Ensuring there is no ground traffic, he taxis the chopper in front of a cluster of hangars.

A trio emerges from one of them as the pilot throttles down the engines. Despite their attire, they aren't security personnel. Farron and Zyree climb out of the sleek helicopter and are greeted by a mocha-skinned beauty who walks up and slaps Farron hard across the face. His head snaps to the right as the sharp sound echoes off the cavernous hangar. To his credit, he doesn't react.

"Zyree, please let me introduce Patrician of the Gentez-Minorez Sonneara Olivero," Farron says, rubbing his cheek. "Sonneara, this is Zyree, formerly a chief inspector with Intercorpex."

"Are you friends with him?" she asks in heavily accented English after muttering something in Spanish under her breath.

"I'm actually his prisoner."

"*Sé como se siente,*" she says, turning to walk away before stopping and gesturing. "*Vamanos.*"

Zyree looks at Farron for an explanation as they reluctantly follow Sonneara toward the largest hangar and her waiting associates.

"We dated for a while. It didn't end…well."

"What he should be saying is that he dumped me," she calls out from in front of them.

"Just when I thought things couldn't get more awkward today."

"Hold that thought," Farron mutters.

Introductions are made to Chyan Zhou and Akaito Nokagawa, the two patricians who were waiting with Sonneara when they landed. Farron is engaged in a stare-down with a mysterious fourth person standing in the hangar.

"Welcome to Darkshadow. We only have a small number of men between us, but you have our support," Chyan explains. "We're still working on bringing other patricians into the fold. Unfortunately, most of them are adopting a wait-and-see attitude. They're not eager to throw in with the son of the man possibly responsible for the murder of their loved ones at Assembly Hall."

"Not all of them were killed there. Some of them died before that attack," the mysterious man says.

Sensing Zyree's confusion, Sonneara is the first to cut through the tense silence. "This is Oriyon. His father, Yannen, was murdered by Denali along with two other patricians and dumped next to a bridge."

Zyree's jaw clenches. That clarifies things. He visited the site with Malkor and Chiana, the latter of whom took responsibility for the investigation. She never solved it. Conventional wisdom laid the blame on Liberteum despite his reservations. Nothing about that incident made sense as a terrorist act, and now he knows why.

"He eliminated your father because he was influential. The attack on Intercorpex was orchestrated to decapitate the heads of the rest of the families while he executes his plan. We're all that separates my father from his dream of controlling the world economy. I'm offering you the chance to avenge your father's death in the process."

"What about Intercorpex or the corporations?" Akaito asks. "Surely, they will intercede."

"Lyris is his puppet," Zyree says, "and the corporations are in turmoil. By the time they regain control and react to his moves, it will be too late."

"*Todo bien. ¿Cuál es el plan?*" Sonneara asks, prompting Farron to recite what needs to be done to stop his father.

The patricians listen intently, asking only the occasional question. There are a lot of variables that can't be accounted for but overall, it does give them a fighting chance.

"And you need our men to rescue these terrorists?"

"After he rescues his girlfriend," Zyree adds, making sure they don't lose sight of the lunacy surrounding that part of the plan.

"*Ay, bendito!* She'd better be worth it," Sonneara interjects.

"We don't have many men. I can't justify sacrificing them on something that reckless."

"Let me use the beast," Farron asks Oriyon. "It will level the field considerably."

"What's the beast?" Zyree asks.

"You were a chief inspector with Intercorpex?" Oriyon asks, getting a nod in return. "Then you're going to love this."

CHAPTER TWENTY

AMERICA, INC.

The America Tower
Manhattan Financial Geographic District
New York City Municipal Corporation

The double doors automatically swing open as the guest is announced. Virtari continues to look out the windows at the sweeping view of Manhattan from his seat in the high-backed executive chair. The magnificent skyscrapers gleam in the sunshine as their shadows hide the chaos gripping the city in the streets below.

"I was told to report here," the young woman says in a voice filled with confidence.

"You were. I've been looking over your personnel records. They're very impressive. You were top of your class at Dinsmore Academy. You have an impressive academic record at Harvard, and you've managed to land an impressive internship with the parent company. You're climbing a ladder that leads to becoming a prominent CEO someday, Varella."

"Thank you…sir," she says, her voice trembling. She was expecting a far less masculine voice to come from behind the desk in the New York CEO's office.

"The only problem is that you belong to a family of traitors," Virtari adds, spinning around to face her.

"Director Virtari," she says with a slight bow, the confidence ebbing into something more akin to a grave revelation.

"You recognize me," he says, surprised.

"Of course, sir. I make it a point to know influential people, and you're at the top of the list. You're the best BCS director the corporation has ever had."

Virtari grins. If her intent is to suck up to him, it's working. There's no hint of deception nor an ounce of fear in her eyes, even with two parents and a brother labeled enemies of the corporation.

"Do you know why you're here?"

"Not to discuss my resume. Since my father is dead, that leaves using me as leverage against my mother or brother, or maybe both."

The investment the corporation has made in her education is money well spent. Varella has an analytical mind to go with her cutthroat competitiveness. Virtari is actually impressed.

"Perceptive."

"Thank you. It won't work."

"Oh? Why not? You won't compromise your loyalty to them?"

Varella lets out a laugh followed by an amused smile. "No, it won't work because they hate my guts."

Virtari squints. He can understand her brother hating her. Sibling rivalries often have a profound negative effect on their relationship. To say that her mother doesn't care about her is counterintuitive.

"You expect me to believe that?"

"I wouldn't expect you to take my word for anything, sir. You're the head of the greatest investigative unit the world has ever known. Let me save you some time while they confirm it. My mother was always partial to Rykos. I was far closer to my father."

"I met your father once," Virtari says, steepling his hands. "I thought he was incompetent even before I learned he was a traitor. That's why I gave the order to terminate him."

"My father wasn't incompetent. My mother made him look that way. He was doing something critical to corporate interests, and all she could think about was herself. It was distracting, and he was suffering because of it. The termination put him out of his misery."

"And your brother?"

"Rykos," she says, approaching the desk, "was a waste of resources. He's a slacker who was never going to amount to anything in this corporation."

"He got into Harvard."

Varella bristles at the mention of her university. Some things cannot be faked, and fiery hatred is one of them. She detests her brother and doesn't think he's worthy of admittance to such a prestigious institution.

"Only because he lied his way into being named a hero of the corporation. Thankfully, he decided to join a terrorist group to die a horrible death instead of reporting for classes."

Virtari scoffs and stands, moving around the large, modern desk. Varella watches him through the eyes of someone who has confidence gained from knowing nothing but success in life. She's not what he expected when he summoned her.

"That's not what you expected to hear, is it?"

"I expected you to say what you said."

"But not to actually mean it. Director Virtari, my mother and brother are traitors. That will hang over me for my entire executive career. They've sabotaged a future I've worked hard to secure. If you want my help, all you need to do is ask."

"I'm not sure what you think you can do for me."

"Has Chief Executive Zeykala held you responsible for what's going on in the city yet?"

"What does that have to do with anything?" Virtari snaps. She struck a chord.

"I did a case study on her during my first year at Harvard. Zeykala is a ruthless opportunist who will do anything to enhance her standing. She won't take responsibility for the quli uprising. The board and the patricians will demand that someone takes the fall, and it won't be her."

"And you think it will be me?"

"Why else declare corporate law? She'll take the credit if you restore order. If you fail, then she has her patsy. Either way, she has the opportunity to remove the single greatest threat to her leadership: you."

Virtari is mildly offended that she didn't think he already recognized Zeykala's game plan. He was never under the illusion that their working together was a permanent arrangement.

"I didn't rise to my position without being one step ahead of my adversaries."

"Yes, sir, but you need to maintain focus on the security mission to be successful. That means you have a political blind spot."

"And that's something you think you can help with?"

"I have built personal relationships with a lot of executives in this city. I've studied Zeykala. I know my mother and brother. Most of all, I'm expendable. Tell me, Director, what's the downside?"

This woman is nothing if not audacious. Varella might be exactly the type of person Virtari needs to work with. Only he doesn't trust anybody this overtly political.

"The downside is the risk of you betraying me."

"Then I will find myself standing in the exact spot my father was in the last moments of his life. I will earn your trust. What can I do to convince you that my services will be invaluable?"

Virtari decides to see where this goes. "Start by telling me everything I want to know about your mother."

CHAPTER TWENTY-ONE

NYCMC RESISTANCE

Central Park
Central Park Geographic District
New York City Municipal Corporation

A drone buzzes high overhead, moving east to west. The BCS learned their lesson by staying well above the trees this time. They flew one low a couple of hours ago, and two guardians shot it out of the sky with their rifles. Since then, the drones covering the park have kept their distance, relying on the zoom capability of their on-board optics. Fortunately for Ilaria and everyone in the park, no camera ever invented can see through foliage.

Watching the drones is about all Ilaria has been able to do for the last several hours. The adrenaline rush from her rescue has subsided, leaving idle time to think about her current plight and limited future. Teman is dead. Varella hates her. Rykos was shot and is probably dead. She was captured and almost raped. Her future may only be measured in days, if not in hours. None of that is worth reflecting on.

Ilaria glances down at the baggy overalls and work shirt one of the qulis in the park gave her to wear. The clothing reeks of sweat and tobacco, the latter of which is forbidden in the sphere of influence. Not that those prohibitions have ever stopped the labor class. One of the advantages of not being a full employee is having a greater degree of freedom, or at least the benefit of corporate indifference. That was until Chief Executive Officer Zeykala's latest edict stripped it away from them.

"All the groups made it to their assigned destinations without incident," Phylep says after walking over to her.

"None of them were stopped?"

"No," he responds, smirking. "Either they don't know we came to the park or didn't bother trying to stop anyone from leaving. Their manpower situation might be more desperate than we thought."

"The BCS isn't designed for large-scale operations," Ilaria explains. "They always poached the PSS for their manpower-intensive actions."

"It took you guys long enough," Phylep says to someone behind them.

"We had to take the scenic route," Prano responds, walking toward them with Andanz beside him. Directly behind the duo is a welcome sight.

Ilaria's heart leaps as she rushes over to give Dzamko a long hug. It's hard to believe that she barely knew this man a few days ago. They've already been through so much together, and now there is more than just a passing familiarity between them; he feels like a friend she's known for decades.

"Are you okay? You look like hell."

"I'm as good as can be expected," Dzamko grumbles. "The BCS agents holding me weren't exactly gentle. Are…are you…?"

"I'm fine."

"She's better than fine," Phylep interjects. "She had already ripped an agent's ball sack off by the time we got there."

"It looks like we picked the right ally in this fight," Prano says in admiration.

Dzamko stares at Ilaria, part in wonder and part in disbelief. She shrugs. "It's a long story."

"I can't wait to hear it. What's the situation?"

"Constantly changing," Phylep says. "Right now, the BCS controls the Financial District, Times Square, and the west side of the island from Broadway to the river, including the tunnels and bridge. They withdrew from a chunk of Midtown from Thirty-Fourth Street to Forty-Second over to Park Avenue, including Grand Central Terminus. We believe some PSS loyal to Virtari are securing that area for them."

All eyes turn to Dzamko.

"It's probably Captain Freyker. He fancies himself a BCS agent. It wouldn't surprise me if he's seizing the opportunity to enhance his status by throwing in with the team he thinks will win."

"Dzamko, your men control all the East River Crossings except the Battery Tunnel."

"What about One Guardian Plaza and the NYCMC Executive Center?"

"The NEC is essentially empty except for the acting CEO… or the acting-acting CEO," Ilaria says.

"Who is it?"

"I don't remember his name. He hasn't done much of anything since he got there from what we've heard."

"And what about One Guardian Plaza?" Dzamko asks.

"The PSS garrisoned the building," Phylep confirms. "Qulis still control Astor Park with their help. Our men have teamed with yours and spread throughout eastern Manhattan to maintain a presence. We expected the BCS to make a move by now, but outside of the occasional patrol, they've held their positions."

"They're planning something," Dzamko says, rubbing the growth that's taken over his normally clean-shaven face.

"How do you know?"

"They don't have enough men or equipment in the city to put down an uprising of this size. They've secured river crossings for a reason."

"They're going to amass a large enough unit to take the city back by force," Phylep surmises.

"That's my guess. The BCS will use the tunnels to enter the island and head right for Guardian Plaza to take out the RTCC. When we respond, a second force will come from the north to box us in."

"We can't let that happen," Ilaria says, not feeling as good about their situation as she was a few minutes ago.

"No, we can't. Can you guys block the tracks leading to GCT?" Dzamko asks the three quli leaders.

"Sure," Prano says, a devilish grin crossing his lips. "Do you want disabled, damaged, or destroyed?"

"Disabled with a side order of damaged should work. Break it enough so the tracks are unusable but won't take months to fix."

"You got it. That sounds like your specialty, Andanz."

"I know just the guys for the task. Consider it done."

A drone flies overhead, and they all reflexively move farther under the cover of the large tree. The BCS has considerable capabilities despite being outmanned. Leveraging the PSS's drone fleet gives them real-time intelligence and helps uncover weaknesses. Or they can identify Ilaria and Dzamko if they're not careful.

"We need to get out of this park before the BCS decides to get bold," Prano says.

"And go where?" Dzamko asks.

"That's easy. Guardian Plaza."

The men all look at Ilaria like she's taken leave of her senses. Instead of withering under the intensity of their stares, she returns them. It's not a crazy idea at all.

"With all due respect, ma'am, that's ground zero when the BCS tries to take this city back."

"I know. That's why I need to be there."

"I have to agree with Phylep," Dzamko adds. "You won't be safe anywhere near that building."

Ilaria nods. Safety is a relative term. She's marked for death by the corporation and is living on borrowed time. She might as well make those minutes count.

"You guys risked your lives to save me. You're willing to die standing up for what you believe in. Well, I believe in it, too. I'll be damned if I'm going to hide in some basement while you fight in the streets when the storm comes."

"Ma'am, you won't be in a basement. The qulis can get you out of Manhattan across the East River. It'll be safer there."

"There is no place I can run to where they won't find me. I'm not going to live like that. America Incorporated made an enemy of me when they murdered my husband. Now, I'm going to fight the corporation and win, or I'm going to die and join him. Either way, I'm not running."

"Ilaria—"

"This isn't up for discussion, Dzamko. I've made my decision."

The constable doesn't like it one bit but is professional enough to know it's time to cease the argument. Ilaria knows they'll be revisiting this conversation in private at some point. It will be as fruitless for him as this one was.

"Can you guys get us downtown?"

Prano, Phylep, and Andanz take turns looking at each other. "Yeah, but it might take a while," Phylep finally says. "Some of these drones are armed, and conveyances make tempting targets. Nobody loyal to the corporation is driving while the city is under corporate law. We'll have to travel on foot to keep from drawing attention."

Ilaria claps her hands. "Then we'd better get started."

CHAPTER TWENTY-TWO

AMERICA, INC.

The White House
Corporate Governance District
Washington-Arlington Municipal Corporation

Zeykala greets Chairman Joakeen in the middle of the Oval Office. She nods at the executive secretary who showed him in, signaling the man to depart the room. Her guest waits until the door closes before he speaks.

"Thank you for meeting me, Chief Executive Zeykala. I know you're busy."

"Your request to speak in person sounded urgent. Why couldn't we have this meeting via VidLynk?"

"It's a sensitive topic," he says, taking the seat on the sofa she offers. "I signed an order to begin an executive search to replace you as CEO."

Zeykala is dumbfounded, especially since she knows each of these board members personally. Many are close, personal friends. She can't believe they'd betray her like this. She'd been warned but thought she would have more time.

"We're in the middle of a crisis! You want a change of leadership now?"

Joakeen eyes her cooly. "This is not my doing, but the board is nearly unanimous that we do something to halt this plummet toward anarchy."

The CEO fights to control her temper. Her allies are failing her. Now they're turning against her to cover their own incompetence.

"We are *not* plummeting toward anarchy. Nothing, and I mean nothing, could be further from the truth. Things look far worse than they are."

"Appearances are everything in corporate politics. You know that better than anyone, Zeykala. The board is under incredible pressure. They're questioning your competence because you haven't provided them anything to help your defense."

"So, their response is to replace me? And *you're* going along with it?"

"I warned you this was a possibility. Declaring corporate law was a mistake."

"How is that not an attempt to defuse the situation?"

"It's an admission of how far it's decayed. Then again, it's not as bad as it seems. Everything is under control, right?"

Zeykala doesn't bother responding.

"Your words don't match your actions. The feeling amongst the board members is that you don't know what you're doing. What would you be saying if you were still on Corporate Hill and Valen was sitting in this office?"

Her actions are being thrown back in her face. She led the charge to have Valen removed because of his ineptitude in dealing with Liberteum's attacks against Intercorpex in New York. Now, she's in the crosshairs.

"Who will the board be interviewing?"

"We are refining the list. Once that's complete, we'll start with the obvious candidates."

Joakeen's subtle smirk conveys that he knows why she asked. The importance of his answer cannot be understated. He's referring to the shortlist.

"Chief Executive Zeykala, the helicopter is ready for you on the South Lawn," her automated office assistant announces.

"Chairman, if you'll excuse me, I need to get to settle some business out of the city. Thank you for the advance notice."

"Of course," he says, shaking her hand. "I'm sorry it has come to this, Zeykala. I truly am. I will keep the wolves at bay as long as I can."

"Thank you."

Zeykala leaves her office and joins an agent in the portico. They step out into the Rose Garden on the way to the South Lawn and the waiting helicopter.

"Eight agents will escort you to your destination," he says as they walk across the grass.

"Seven agents. I need you to stay here and do me a favor."

"That's not protocol, ma'am," the burly man protests.

"I wouldn't ask if it were unimportant. The official shortlist for CEO prior to Valen's ascension is stored in the corporate archives. I can get the list myself, but I want to know the reasons they were all passed over. You guys keep dossiers on every executive. I need you to scour the BCS database and report on every skeleton you find in their closets."

Executive dossiers are privileged information that even the CEO of America Incorporated isn't entitled to see. The Pentagon shares only what it wants to. Fortunately, Virtari's dedication to secrecy doesn't match his lust for power.

"I'll get right on it," the agent says before heading back toward the White House.

Zeykala boards the aircraft, and it lifts off. She stares blankly out the window at the smoke plumes from structure fires dotting the northern part of the city. Washington is the cradle of America Incorporated. This metropolis was the first to have order restored after the collapse. An uprising of any strength here is unfathomable.

She leans back into her seat and exhales as an uncomfortable thought jars her. The board of directors may be right to question her leadership. She may not be being told how bad the situation really is.

CHAPTER TWENTY-THREE

THE PATRICIANS

Keating Family of the Gentez-Majorez Estate
Greenwich Geographic District
Southern Connecticut Municipal Corporation

A quarter to ten in the morning is early to be drinking, but a celebratory beverage is in order. Denali takes a long sip of scotch as he watches corporate public relations officers around the globe scramble to cover up his handiwork. From the exquisite red leather sofa in his study, he's relishing watching the world pretend it isn't crumbling.

Reactions to the attacks are predictable. The large display cycles through news reports from around the world. Each has spun the incidents in different ways, ranging from the implausible to the insane. Despite global communications capabilities, corporations are shockingly isolated from each other. These reports are seen only in their respective spheres of influence and by patricians. That is by design.

Decades ago, sensationalism and instant access to information led to the world's undoing. To protect against another collapse, the corporations chose to heavily regulate information to serve their own needs. That manipulation ranges from selective reporting of the truth to outright lies.

There is a vast difference between journalism and propaganda. The latter is a synonym for corporate news bureaus. Executives control the message, the message controls perception, and perception guides employee behavior. That formula was concocted even before the world imploded.

Covering up these attacks is going to be a challenge for them. China has ignored the carnage and blood-stained sidewalks altogether. Brazil has said their now-deceased CEO is ill and recuperating at the residence that burned to the ground with him inside it.

The UK has attributed the nerve agent attack in their underground to noxious fumes from a malfunctioning power generator. India is claiming the train derailments were caused by excessive heat warping the tracks. That's a monumental feat of nature in May, even on the subcontinent.

The rest of the corporations excused the attacks as accidents. What was seen by the employees cannot be unseen, and the truth will eventually come out. Trade representatives will report what really happened back home. Corporations will begin to exchange information, and once the scope of the attacks is fully understood, panic will set in. Then, the fun begins.

Stronger corporations will keep up the charade of lies and deceit the longest. That will stoke suspicion among their smaller, weaker, and less economically sound counterparts. Safety and security will once again be prioritized, and the means to provide it a new commodity. Supply and demand will create a market, and where imbalance exists, opportunity lives.

"Is there something you need, Abbot?" Denali asks after hearing him enter the study.

"Master Farron's helicopter has deviated from its flight plan. He is not returning to Greenwich."

Denali nods. "Did he head to Virginia?"

"Yes, sir."

"He mentioned last night that he might drop in on an associate there who may be of some use to us. It's nothing to worry about."

"Very well, sir," Abbot says, stopping to check the large display on the wall. "Does the world realize it's on fire yet?"

"They don't even smell the smoke in the air. Corporations are slow to recognize anything that doesn't conform to their worldview. Their level of incompetence is beyond understanding."

"Speaking of incompetence, Administrator-General Lyris has made contact several times already this morning. He seems desperate to speak with you."

Denali groans. Lyris has served his purpose. There is only one more thing required of him before the patrician can stop wet-nursing his ego.

"What's his problem now? Did he get a paper cut?"

"He claims the bureaucrats in Zurich are opening up an investigation into his being named administrator-general."

Lyris is a child doing a grown-up's job. He's inept, but the idiots in the administrative arm of the exchange are far worse.

"Did he say who is leading the investigation?"

"He was vague on that point, sir."

"Because he doesn't know. He's hearing rumors. Did the great leader of Intercorpex mention anything about opening the exchange for trading?"

"No, he did not."

Denali scoffs, turning his attention back to the corporate news stations. Even in Russia, the massive Moscow explosion is being treated like an accident. The corporation must have discovered the radioactive debris scattered everywhere by now. Their dishonesty will cost lives. The on-scene reporter seems oblivious to the silent killer working to sentence him to an early death.

"Is everything set for Liberteum's transfer?" the patrician asks.

"Yes, sir. It's not my place, but if the plan is to have Liberteum blamed for these attacks, why not take credit for capturing them and enhance your image around the world?"

"There is a bigger picture here, Abbot. I can't be tied to Liberteum in any way. Nobody must ever know they were here, and Farron's involvement with them must remain a secret."

"Do you expect America Incorporated to keep that secret?"

Abbot knows as well as anybody how the world's corporations work. Denali would stack him up against the best executives the world has to offer. He's right in suspecting that no corporation can be trusted to keep a secret unless it's one hundred percent in their interests to do so.

"Executives will be quick to assign blame when news of these coordinated attacks finally leaks. Executing the terrorists will be Zeykala's best course of action. By the time she leaks that they were in my custody, it will already be too late."

"Thank you, sir. I apologize for asking."

"Abbot," Denali says, rising from the couch and placing his hand on the man's shoulder. "You are my most trusted associate. I burden you with way more responsibilities than I should. You never need to apologize for looking after my interests. Go check on our guests and inform them they are taking a trip in a couple of hours."

He graciously nods and moves off. Denali settles back into the sofa and takes another sip of his mid-morning drink. Everything is coming together just as he planned.

CHAPTER TWENTY-FOUR

RYKOS

Keating Family of the Gentez-Majorez Estate
Greenwich Geographic District
Southern Connecticut Municipal Corporation

There are few things worse than being locked in a windowless steel vault in the bowels of a mansion. There is nothing to keep our minds occupied other than the thoughts about what comes next. Michele is getting antsy, and without any meaningful way to burn off that nervous energy, she's been pacing back and forth since breakfast was delivered. It's beginning to wear on my nerves.

"You're driving me crazy, Michele," I complain from my seat at the small table.

"I can't help it. I may live in the underground but I'm not used to being confined. You wouldn't understand."

"Really? Try spending a half year stuck in business law class."

"I'm not sure I could spend five minutes in any class."

She should consider herself fortunate. Dinsmore was nothing if not dull. Michele's father taught her everything she would have learned in a classroom and then some. She learned how the world really operates and has the one skill that matters most – survival. Not that it helps us in our current predicament.

"You're lucky."

"Yeah, lucky that we're prisoners who were betrayed by a friend and about to be turned over to a corporation dreaming up imaginative ways of killing us. Is that what you mean?"

"Okay, it was a bad choice of words, but your pacing won't solve any of that."

"How would you suggest I pass the time?" Michele snaps.

I raise my eyebrows and bob my head from side to side. I can think of some ways. Even the perpetually quiet Koltayne lying on the cot lets out a chuckle. Boys will be boys.

"Don't make me hurt you," Michele admonishes with a grin.

"Do you think Farron struck a deal with Zeykala?" Koltayne asks, turning the conversation to something more serious.

His betrayal is an open wound that may never heal. Even if Michele is given the chance to kill the bastard, his duplicity will always haunt her. He knows all of Liberteum's secrets. If he shared them with Denali, everyone in Valhalla is likely already dead. I don't point that out to Michele. Her mind is already in a dark place.

"Yeah, I do."

"What do you think will happen to Zyree?"

"His journey isn't any rosier than ours," I surmise. I know more than I want to about Intercorpex.

"'These are the times that try men's souls,' Michele mutters. "The summer soldier and the sunshine patriot will, in this crisis, shrink from the service of his country; but he that stands it now, deserves the love and thanks of man and woman.'"

"That's profound. Who said it?" I ask.

"Thomas Paine wrote it in the early days of the American Revolution," Koltayne says, getting a nod from Michele. I remember reading some excerpts of that. I have a favorite quote I still remember.

Our conversation is cut short when the heavy door unseals and opens. It's the first time that the noise hasn't caused me to jump. I'd hate to think I'm getting used to being imprisoned here.

Abbot walks in, escorted by a male security officer and female counterpart. Both have weapons holstered on their thighs. It's the first time that he's shown up with armed guards. It can't be a good sign.

"I trust your breakfast was satisfactory. You will now be escorted to our shower facility one at a time to clean up."

"What's wrong, Abbot?" I ask. "Are we starting to stink up your mansion?"

"I believe you all required showers before you arrived," he deadpans.

The man is remarkable. He even makes an insult sound polite.

"The clothes you arrived in have been mended and laundered," he continues. "They will be laid out for you. You will take all directives from the guards. Michele, we have assigned a female to escort you to make you feel more comfortable."

"Damn. I was looking forward to being ogled this morning."

Despite everything she's been through, she can still rock the sarcasm. It must feel good.

"We are not savages."

"What's the occasion?" I ask, unable to stifle my burning curiosity.

We were shocked when Chief Executive Officer Zeykala appeared on the display they wheeled into the room. They didn't bother making us presentable to be used as pawns for whatever game Farron was playing with her. I can't help but wonder why they are now.

"You're being freed."

We look at each other in disbelief. Abbot nods to the male guard, who escorts Koltayne out of the strong room. Without another word, Abbot leaves with the female guard, and the door seals behind them.

I sit back down in the chair. Michele sits next to me, remaining silent. She doesn't need to say anything because we're both thinking the same thing. Abbot has a way with words. Whatever is about to happen doesn't include being freed.

CHAPTER TWENTY-FIVE

AMERICA, INC.

Meade Human Resources Center
Seven Oaks Geographic Area
Baltimore Municipal Corporation

Located on the grounds of what was once known as Fort Meade, this termination center is one of the multiple facilities in the sphere of influence run by the Bureau of Corporate Security. Here is where those accused and convicted of serious offenses against the parent corporation spend their final days. The execution grounds are a bleak place located deep in the woods south of the main complex. It's the last journey the condemned will ever take.

"Welcome to the Meade Termination Center Execution Grounds, ma'am," an agent says after Zeykala exits the conveyance with her entourage.

"Thank you. Is everything ready?"

"Yes, ma'am. The terminee is already positioned in the yard. The men are standing by to execute the order."

Zeykala smiles. She can always count on the BCS to handle their business with professionalism and precision.

"Is she conscious?"

"She's still feeling the effects of her enhanced interrogation, so we didn't need to sedate her. She's conscious but not alert."

"I want to see her."

The demand catches him off-guard, but he stifles any objection. "Of course, ma'am. Right this way."

The CEO follows the agent into the nondescript concrete building that resembles an old military bunker. Unlike corporate buildings, there's no fancy marble façade or ornate exterior designed to impress visitors. Nothing about this structure masks its true purpose – death to anyone who stands against the corporation.

They enter a foyer with a staircase leading up to the second level. Doors on either side of the space lead to administrative rooms and break areas. Walking past the stairs, they travel down a corridor stretching fifty feet to the far side of the building. Two agents open a large steel door that leads out into the yard.

Zeykala has never been to a termination center. There isn't much to see. The yard is long and rectangular, with thirty-foot concrete berms running along each side and one twice as high in the rear. There are no fences or other visible passive security measures. They aren't necessary.

The bunker towers behind her with a long row of angled, tinted windows running the length of the building. Two turrets jut out from the corners, each manned by an armed agent. It's an imposing final sight for anyone unfortunate enough to find themselves staring at it.

Her BCS escort stands fast as she makes her way to the pedestal. A long sidewalk leads to a concrete pad that serves as the firing station. The men nod as she walks past.

Fiolla's feet are lashed together, and her arms outstretched by the apparatus she's secured to. Zeykala stares at her for a long moment, soaking it up. This is a sight she wants to remember for a long time.

"This isn't the way I planned it, Fiolla. You were meant to die on that MetroLev platform. Of course, your escape works out better for me. Now, I actually get to watch you die live instead of on a display."

Fiolla lowers her eyes at Zeykala's taunting. She's not only drugged up – she's defeated. Her once vibrant spirit is broken. It's joyous…and tragic.

"What, no witty response? None of your usual sass? C'mon, Fiolla, you're so good at disrespecting your superiors." Zeykala leans closer and stares intently into her eyes. "Nothing? Wow, they really did break you. It didn't have to be this way. I like strong women. It pained me to watch you tarnish yourself by being Valen's pet. I always knew you were capable of so much more."

Zeykala stands upright and looks around the execution grounds. "I recognized your potential when I took control. I was serious about keeping you in your position. You could have been an incredible asset. You swore that your loyalty was to the office of the chief executive and not the occupant. My mistake was believing you.

"I guess I shouldn't have been surprised that you tried to undermine me. Some executives are still loyal to Valen. Maybe they'll remember that their first allegiance is to the corporation once they learn of your fate."

Zeykala jabs the red dot painted on her chest. Nothing is left to chance when performing a termination by firing squad. Even with the agents' advanced training and the expensive optics on their rifles, they use the mark as their aim point. They won't miss it. She holds Fiolla's chin up.

"So, here we are. I'm here at the beginning of my reign as CEO, and you're at the end of your life. I won, Fiolla. I always win. You must die knowing that."

CHAPTER TWENTY-SIX

NYCMC RESISTANCE

One Guardian Plaza
Lower Manhattan Geographic District
New York City Municipal Corporation

It took everyone in the room a moment to recognize who walked in. The first guardian to notice Ilaria and Dzamko let out a cheer, and the subsequent applause in the RTCC became almost deafening. Executives get polite applause from employees at quarterly meetings. Her and the constable's return here is akin to Romans honoring a conquering Caesar. She finds the reception almost embarrassing. She doesn't feel like she's done anything to deserve it.

After a round of heartfelt embraces and hearty handshakes, everyone settles down and gets back to work. The BCS is in control of a significant part of the city, and they don't have any plans to combat them. There is a lot to work through as they gather around the console near the front of the room.

The worn-out battle captain has a handle on the situation and is briefing them with gusto, but Ilaria isn't listening with the intensity she should be. Her attention is drawn to a display on the wall with a split screen showing an anchor on one side and a static image of the NEC on the other.

It's not what she would have expected them to be reporting. Looting qulis and bloodied employees, yes, but a tame scene that feels more like business as usual? No.

"What the hell is AME News rambling about?"

"Who knows? It's been nonsense since yesterday," the battle captain says in a disinterested tone as his eyes follow hers up to the display.

"Nothing about corporate law or the quli uprisings?"

"Nope. Other than the scrolling warning about corporate law, employees have no idea what's going on. They've minimalized the impact of everything that's been happening."

Ilaria shakes her head. The media is the best tool to shape opinions. Employees are conditioned to believe without reservation what the parent company tells them.

People across the sphere of influence are bound to be scared. A lack of information will fuel rumors and stoke those fears. It's a mistake not to get ahead of it.

"Is that live video of the Executive Center?"

"Yes, ma'am. Based on the angle from the south, it's probably a long shot from the top of One Fifty-Six Broadway."

"Phylep told me the acting CEO is there. Is that correct?"

"Chief Executive Darnon. Yeah, he's in there…doing a whole lotta nothing."

Ilaria nods. So, it's Darnon. She would have expected either the sanitation or finance director to seize the reins. Darnon was always quiet about his ambitions. Somehow, he pushed his way past the loudmouths to realize his dream.

"Can you get him on a VidLynk?"

"Uh…sure. Stand by…."

Ilaria waits patiently for the connection to be made. Dealing with this the wrong way will earn her yet another enemy, and she already has enough of those. Despite the risks, this is a gamble worth taking.

"Executive Ilaria," her replacement says with a priceless look of surprise. "I didn't realize you were set free."

"I wasn't. I hear you're running the city now, Darnon."

"If you could call it that," he moans. "When you were taken into custody, I offered my services to Virtari to help him restore order."

"How did that work out for you?"

He waves a dismissive hand. "I was thanked and told to report here. They never made contact. I called the EOC this morning and was informed that Virtari was running the city and to stay here and look busy. Then the BCS agent ended the VidLynk."

Ilaria wants to gloat, but this isn't the time. She may have issues with Darnon's smug arrogance, but allies are allies. Darnon is disillusioned and looking for relevance.

"Don't take it personally. Virtari and Zeykala want the optics of a functioning leadership while we're under corporate law."

"I noticed. I'm being used. They'll toss me aside when this is over."

"Does the BCS have control of the building?"

"No, we're completely unguarded. Agents patrol the area once in a while but aren't on the grounds. What do you want me to do?"

It was the question she was hoping for. "Why are you asking me? You're the CEO."

Darnon presses his lips together. "The job is yours, Ilaria. It was yours when Safmor was killed, and it's yours now."

"In that case, I could use your expertise. Round up the remaining staff and come over here. This building is more secure. Dzamko will ensure the sentries know you're coming so you don't get shot by accident."

"Then we'll be over in a few."

"And Darnon? Cut the power to the building before you leave," she orders.

"Will do." The VidLynk disconnects.

"Ilaria? You know he tried to order the PSS to assault the qulis when he took over, right?" Phylep asks.

"No, I didn't, but it's irrelevant."

"Says you."

Ilaria places a hand on the distraught quli's shoulder. "I get it. I'd be pissed too, but Darnon learned he was powerless when the PSS refused his order. Then, the BCS hung him out to dry. That's why he gave control back to me."

"It sounds like you have a plan. What are you thinking?" Dzamko asks.

"Darnon knows the workings of the city better than any of us and has the respect and loyalty of the other executives. That could be useful when the time comes."

The lights go out at the NYCMC Executive Center, and the building is bathed in darkness. With the power manually cut off at the panel, the automated assistant can't restore it. Neither can the EOC. Within a few seconds, the video changes back to the anchor in the studio. Someone at AME News is paying attention. They know the broadcasting images of a dark building will not assuage employee fears. It also gives Ilaria another idea.

"Can you establish a secure transmission that can't be traced by the EOC?"

"Secure, yes. I can't guarantee it'll be untraceable. The Emergency Operations Center is designed to monitor all of the city's communications."

Ilaria pouts her lips. "We'll have to take our chances. See if you can contact Journalist Kassaya at AME News. Tell her I have a photo opportunity for her."

CHAPTER TWENTY-SEVEN

AMERICA, INC.

Meade Human Resources Center
Seven Oaks Geographic Area
Baltimore Municipal Corporation

Zeykala's words stab at Fiolla's heart, and the evil smile she's wearing burns her soul. This is what weak people do to appear strong. It might hurt more if Fiolla could feel anything. Her mind is sharp, but she's still locked inside her body. Comprehension is married to an inability to respond. Fiolla is watching what's happening like it's a movie – scenes play in front of her that she can't interact with or respond to.

The drugs administered during her interrogation had the desired effect. Doctor Krevor manipulated her mind after detaching it from the world. The process stripped Fiolla of everything that makes her human. Feelings of fear, sadness, and regret seem more like dull echoes than raw emotions.

Zeykala lets go of her chin and walks back toward the firing squad and then into the gray, lifeless building. A man begins to read from a tablet a few moments later. Fiolla hears the words without understanding them. It's the termination order. Nothing he's reading matters. The result is predetermined.

The armed men look so…peaceful. How can they be that way when they kill for a living? Fiolla felt guilty after killing two men determined to push her in front of a train. These men are indifferent to taking life.

She hears a muffled beating sound that no one else seems to notice. The sound grows louder as the firing squad raises their rifles. The order to fire will be the last thing she ever hears. Instead, they raise their heads and focus on something behind her. The beating sound…do they hear it, too?

The men don't know what to do. A roar overhead claws at Fiolla's eardrums, and she clenches her teeth as a strong wind buffets her from above. The men with the rifles evaporate before her eyes. Human beings are transformed into chunks of flesh and red mist. Sharp thumping noises overhead precede glass windows being blown out. The sound stops, and several wooshes are followed by explosions.

A shadow casts over Fiolla as the strong wind tugs harder at her clothing. She looks up to see the most monstrous machine she's ever laid eyes on. The sound and physical feeling…it's too much for her repressed consciousness to process. Overcome, she feels herself suddenly go limp.

CHAPTER TWENTY-EIGHT

THE PATRICIANS

Meade Human Resources Center
Seven Oaks Geographic Area
Baltimore Municipal Corporation

The pilot rears and puts them into a hover. The violent maneuver makes Zyree and Farron grab for anything to keep their balance in the cramped troop compartment. For such a large machine, the "Beast" is surprisingly nimble.

Anyone watching from the gallery is toast. The two guard turrets on either side of the bunker have been neutralized. The gunship is no longer being engaged by ground fire, so the only thing left to do is deny any remaining resistance a place to return fire while they land.

"Put a pair of rockets into the gallery," Zyree commands over his headset.

The nose of the ancient Mi-24 Hind dips and the weapons systems operator squeezes the trigger. Two rockets leap off the launchers located under the stubby wings protruding from the aircraft. They hit their mark with dramatic effect, sending a fireball cascading through the second floor.

For a machine designed more than a hundred years ago and built before the turn of the century, the Hind is every bit as lethal today as it was for the military that employed it. The pair of bulbous canopies for the pilot and weapons officer make it unsightly compared to its sleek modern-day counterparts. The twin machine guns in the nose, coupled with gun pods and rocket launchers, will make anyone in their sights forget about how the aircraft looks.

Muzzle flashes appear on both sides of the building, but they aren't aiming at the Hind. That could only mean they're trying to finish their mission.

"Put us down between those men and Fiolla," Zyree calmly commands the pilot as Farron looks on in horror.

"Do it now!" the patrician screams into his headset, his emotions running away with him.

Zyree signals to Sonneara's men who accompanied them. "As soon as we touch down, retrieve her and get back on board."

The three men nod and check their weapons. The aircraft spins parallel to the face of the building. Zyree mans the ninety-year-old belt-fed machine gun, ready to end anyone stupid enough to fire at this flying tank. Farron watches the remaining agents retreat around the side of the bunker as they land.

The three men jump out the starboard door. Making quick work of the rescue, they return with Fiolla. She's unconscious, but there are no obvious injuries. The way she went limp, Farron was sure she was hit. They lay her down in the back of the helicopter as the pilot pulls up on the collective and the stick, raising the armored beast out of the yard below.

"Now what?" the pilot asks over the headset.

Farron attends to Fiolla. He's been an emotional wreck since this attack began. Zyree is more than capable of directing the pilot to mop up here.

"How many rockets do we have left?" Zyree asks.

"Twenty-two."

"Good. Blow that building to hell and fire a couple at the spot where Fiolla was rescued from."

The pilot circles the aircraft, and the weapons operator does as instructed. The first two rockets obliterate the center of the yard, and the rest turn the bunker into a raging inferno.

"Do you want me to go around again?" the pilot asks.

"No, it's time to go. Farron?"

"I'm busy."

"Make yourself un-busy."

"She's injured!"

Zyree grabs the patrician and yanks him up, clocking him on the side of the head. "We need to go. Give the pilot a heading."

"Due north," Farron orders. "Obvir arranged a refueling point in southern New Jersey. Contact Darkshadow and get the coordinates from him."

"Roger."

Farron jerks away from Zyree and moves back to Fiolla in the rear of the aircraft. He's worse than a mother hen. She's only unconscious, but he's fussing over her like she's bleeding out. One of Sonneara's men pulls out an aid kit and checks her vital signs.

Out of the corner of his eye, he sees Zyree settle into the jump seat and stare out at the beautiful countryside. Farron has no intention of sitting on one of the cloth strap seats. The Russians weren't big on passenger comfort. It was designed for combat, so at least they don't need to worry about being shot down. With the armor this thing sports, the BCS will need to dig deep into their arsenal to find something capable of that.

* * *

The pilot powers down the engines while a ground team moves in to refuel the Beast. It's as loud as it is big, and it's nice to get a break from the constant noise. It's also an opportunity for the team to walk around the tarmac to stretch their legs. It's the first time Farron has left Fiolla's side since the rescue. Whatever he thought was going to happen with her after this extraction isn't coming to fruition.

"Is she okay?" Zyree asks.

"The medic says she's physically fine. Mentally and emotionally? No, I don't think so. Maybe it's the drugs…she won't even look at me."

"Give her some time. We cut that close. She was seconds away from death. That's a lot for anyone to process."

"I guess."

"Are you going to finally come clean about why you're doing this?" Zyree asks. It's a fair question. Five hours isn't much time to digest this seismic shift in loyalties. He never would have expected the son of a powerful patrician to disobey his father.

Farron stares back at the Hind. "I'm an elite, free to live as I saw fit. I didn't realize how the world worked until I met Michele and her father. They taught me that employees are nothing more than indentured servants. They are born, educated, trained to perform a specific job, and then die. That's not living."

Zyree nods in agreement. "No, it isn't. What are you prepared to do about it?"

Farron hasn't done anything that wouldn't eventually be forgiven by his father. Snatching Fiolla from the BCS isn't something he would fret over. The same can't be said about rescuing Michele, Rykos, and Koltayne. That's directly interrupting his plan.

"We're going to return Michele to Valhalla so she can finish what she started."

"Help her do what, exactly?"

Farron grins. "Free the world."

Zyree recognizes the meaning of the word "Liberteum." What he doesn't have is a straight answer as to how they plan on doing that. They hacked into Intercorpex and placed false trades on the wire. They managed to manipulate the trading system to force the exchange offline. Haven, once a member of the group, destroyed the exchange's headquarters in an explosion. What would the finale look like?

Farron expects Zyree to press for details, but that will have to wait. They are on the clock, and it's ticking. Getting up in the air and back to New York is a more pressing concern.

The assault at the termination center took only minutes, but an hour of flight time lies ahead. That's not taking into account the indirect route needed to avoid detection. If they miss the exchange and Michele is turned over to the BCS, they'll never get her back. This will all have been for nothing.

"Are we going to make it to the handoff?" Zyree asks.

"We'll make it," Farron assures him. "I'm not done with the surprises today."

CHAPTER TWENTY-NINE

AMERICA, INC.

Emergency Operations Center
Lower Manhattan Geographic District
New York City Municipal Corporation

There is something to be said for keeping your enemies close, especially when they claim to be an ally. Varella is an impressive young woman, but she's still the daughter of a man who failed the corporation and a woman who betrayed it and joined an uprising. Maybe she's the loyal employee that America Incorporated demands, and maybe she isn't. Time will tell.

"Most people are more impressed when they walk into this room," Virtari says, escorting her onto the Emergency Operations Center's main floor.

"You forget who my father was," Varella advises, looking around impassively.

"No, I haven't forgotten." It was a warning as much as a statement. "We can control the entire city from this room. Utilities, transportation, surveillance, communications… nothing is beyond our reach."

"Father always said that if the NEC was the brain and Wall Street the heartbeat of the city, this and the RTCC were its central nervous system," Varella says with a nod before turning her attention to a display in front of the room. "Is that a live feed from AME News?"

"Yes," an agent says from the terminal in front of them. "Why?"

Varella shakes her head. "Our employees are huddling scared in their domiciles watching AME News to understand why their lives have been disrupted. If this is the broadcast, then they're not being *shown* who the real enemy is or who is empowering them."

"So what?" Virtari asks.

"So, we should show them. How much surveillance video do we have of qulis creating havoc in the city?"

"Not as much as you'd think," the agent says. "Despite their aggressiveness, we aren't seeing the types of violent clashes we are elsewhere."

"Then start compiling what you have from other cities. A quli is a quli, regardless of where they live. Show the employees the most violent footage you can find to paint them as threatening our way of life. It will justify any actions we take later."

Virtari sneers. "I don't need to justify *my* actions."

"It's marketing, Director. You issue orders, and your men follow them. Bosses do the same with employees. The difference is that morale matters because it affects productivity; productivity affects profit; profit affects promotions. There's nothing senior executives care more about than their own reputation and career trajectory. Now, apply that to Zeykala."

The head of the BCS shakes his head. "It's not our responsibility."

Varella moves closer to the director. "Sir, we have a powerful tool that the qulis, the terrorists, and even the White House don't. This is corporate law, and AME News is under our control. Leverage that advantage to deliver *your* message to the employees. You have the sole authority to craft the narrative."

Virtari rubs his chin. She has a point. He has never concerned himself with the bleating of the sheep. The mission has always come first. This time, he is fighting multiple enemies, and one of them is in the White House. He should be willing to use all the advantages that corporate law offers.

"Then I guess you'd better get to work on putting that footage together," he says, eliciting a broad smile from the young intern.

"Attention in the EOC!" Everyone in the room to stop what they're doing. "We have an initial report of an attack on the termination grounds of the Meade Human Resources Center in Maryland."

"What kind of attack?" Virtari says, charging toward the front of the room.

"Details are sketchy," the agent advises, shaking his head as he scans the display in front of him. "Initial reports are an airborne assault."

"Airborne? Like a helicopter?"

"Unknown, sir."

"Casualties?"

"Also unknown."

"Target? No, wait, let me guess. Unknown. Start getting those answers," Virtari orders.

"Why would Liberteum bother attacking that facility?" Varella asks, staring at the screen.

"They wouldn't."

"Sir, we are getting an inquiry from the White House," an agent monitoring communications relays.

"Tell Zeykala that we don't know anything about the attack in Maryland yet."

"They aren't coming from the Oval Office. Her staff is wondering if we know whether Zeykala is still alive. She was present at the termination center at the time of the strike."

The blood drains from Virtari's face. That changes everything. This wasn't a random assault against a target with no strategic value. It was an assassination attempt.

"How would the terrorists know she was there?" Varella asks. "Her schedule is kept secret under corporate law."

"It is unless it was leaked by a traitor in the White House."

Virtari rubs his head. This will hamper their efforts. Not only are they combating a terrorist organization, a mutinous PSS, and riotous qulis, but now they're fighting themselves. It's the last thing they need right now.

"Have the Pentagon stand up a war room and set up a small task force to liaise with them," Virtari commands after turning to the agent-in-charge of the EOC. "We need to know if Zeykala is still alive. Move a contingent down there from Baltimore and interview every person on the ground. Then have the Pentagon analyze every shred of surveillance footage. Find me answers to who perpetrated this."

"Yes, sir."

Virtari grabs his arm. "Get me the White House schedule. I want to know who she's met with during the past forty-eight hours, VidLynk and in person."

He looks over at Varella, who offers a quizzical look. She may have sincere allegiance to the corporation or she could have been lying to save her life. Either way, she hasn't earned enough trust to be told who he thinks is behind this.

"The traitor doesn't have to be *in* the White House, just someone with access to it. I'll handle this. I believe you have work to do."

CHAPTER THIRTY

THE PATRICIANS

Keating Family of the Gentez-Majorez Estate
Greenwich Geographic District
Southern Connecticut Municipal Corporation

When the VidLynk connects, Denali is disgusted at what he sees. Lyris greets him with unkempt blond hair, red and puffy eyes, and a disheveled uniform. If the patrician didn't know better, he would think the head of Intercorpex has been crying. Scratch that. He knows he has been.

"Denali, I've been trying to reach you."

"I've heard. What news do you have?" the patrician says, preoccupying himself with an antique letter opener that serves no modern function.

"I'm under investigation from the bureaucrats in Zurich."

"That's it?" A confused look flashes across the administrator-general's face, causing Denali to shake his head. "Lyris, announce you are opening the exchange. Then do it."

"What?"

"Has your hearing not returned since the explosion?"

"Sir, New York City is under siege. America Incorporated is under corporate law. There are reports on the GlobalNet about other incidents around the world. With all this chaos, the market will collapse in a matter of minutes."

"It wasn't a suggestion, Administrator-General," Denali warns.

"They're already investigating me! It will guarantee my removal if I try to reopen the exchange."

Self-preservation is this man's default state. He has no concept of what real leadership is, which is why Denali chose him for the job. Unfortunately, he's forced to suffer with that choice for a little longer. Puppets sometimes forget they have strings.

"Your job is to oversee a marketplace. If you are unwilling or unable to do so, I have already warned you that I can find someone else who can."

"You don't care, do you?"

That gets Denali's attention. He wants to smack him for being weak and feeble, but he still needs the administrator-general in the fold. If that means massaging his fragile ego, so be it.

"Lyris, you are a man capable of solving your own problems. That's what makes you different than Raimius. It's why you're the perfect choice to run Intercorpex and why I made it happen."

"I won't do it," he says, shaking his head defiantly. "I can't open trading and put Intercorpex on a path that will lead to its destruction. Nothing has ever been clearer to me than this."

"'Can't' is the most popular word in any loser's vocabulary. Let me show you what 'can' looks like."

Denali nods at Lacune, who whispers commands into his throat microphone. Within moments, the operations center patches a second video feed to the second display. Abbot waves his hand to share the feed on the VidLynk with Lyris.

"What am I looking at?" the administrator-general asks.

"You don't recognize your own building?"

A woman and man are sharing an elevator when the car comes to an abrupt stop. Lyris leans in, studying the video on his own display. A look of horror creeps across his face.

"That…that's Nevala!"

"I would have thought you'd have recognized the woman you're sleeping with much faster than that."

Nevala looks at the man next to her, and he shrugs. She turns her back to him and opens the communications console in the car. It may be a fatal mistake. He looks at the camera and flashes a knife.

"Unless he receives additional instructions in the next thirty seconds, he will slit Nevala's throat. You will get to watch from your office as she bleeds out."

"You can't do this!" Lyris screams.

"I am doing it. Twenty-five seconds."

Lyris is searching for a solution. He'll never get to her in time, and even if he could, the elevator is between floors. There is only one way out of this, and the clock is ticking.

"Fifteen seconds. Is it that hard of a decision?"

"You're insane, Denali!"

"I would characterize myself as dedicated. You have ten seconds. Trust me, you don't want to wait until the last moment."

The man in the elevator begins to reach for his quarry. It may already be too late.

"I'll do it. Call him off!"

Lacune relays the abort command. The man places his hand on her shoulder before quickly tucking the knife back into his Intercorpex uniform. He points to the floor readout, which indicates that the system is rebooting. A moment later, the elevator begins to move. The woman is safe, but Lyris looks like he might pass out.

"That exercise was unnecessary. I've handed you everything you ever wanted on the proverbial golden platter. I made you the administrator-general of Intercorpex. You will hold that position for as long as you wish so long as you answer to nobody except me."

"If I don't do what you say, you'll kill those close to me?"

"Yes. And then I'll kill you, if necessary." His face hardens at the disclosure. "The man in the elevator is only one of the people I have in Intercorpex. All of them will carry out my instructions without hesitation. Do you understand?"

"Yes."

Lyris is processing the information, wargaming different scenarios in his head. He's forcing himself to believe what Denali is telling him. For his sake, the patrician hopes he does.

"You will announce that you are opening the exchange. Trading will commence in the next seventy-two hours. Let Zurich investigate you. Only the Regents had the authority to remove you from power, and they're all dead."

"I will take care of it, sir."

Denali smiles. That's more like it. "See that you do. I expect the next time we speak will be right before you head downstairs to ring the opening bell."

CHAPTER THIRTY-ONE

NYCMC RESISTANCE

One Guardian Plaza
Lower Manhattan Geographic District
New York City Municipal Corporation

So much has happened in the past two days that Ilaria can't help but feel overwhelmed. She fled to a nearby lounge area for a much-needed break from the tumult of the RTCC. The silence is welcome, but the memories that come with being in this place aren't.

Teman honorably served the PSS for his entire adult life. The guardians here were desperate to find him via his biojack after he was captured in a Liberteum raid, but they came up empty. That's why she sent Rykos off to find Liberteum. Ilaria didn't believe her son's story about what happened after he was taken at the rave. It didn't ring true.

A gentle rap on the door interrupts her thoughts. "Knock, knock. Are you okay?"

"Yeah, I'm fine, Phylep," Ilaria says, wiping her eyes as he sits on an adjacent sofa.

"You don't look fine. What's wrong?"

"Oh, I'm taking a rough trip down memory lane. I can't help but wonder what happened to my son. Teman shot him in the Old Saint Patrick's Cathedral crypt. He was taken to the NYU Medical Training Center afterward. That's all I know. I have no idea if he's alive or dead."

"He's alive," Phylep interjects, "or at least was as of a couple of days ago."

Ilaria's eyes open wide. "How do you know that, Phylep?"

"I met him before I met you. Rykos was recovering from his injuries, but he was alive and well."

"Met him? How? Unless…? I think you need to start from the beginning."

Phylep shakes his head. "We only have time for the abridged version."

He offers a brief explanation of his history with Michele, her father, and the group they founded. Teman assumed the qulis and Liberteum may be working together. He knew they mixed company at the underground raves but never would have been prepared for what she had just heard.

"You were working with terrorists?"

"If you believed in your heart they were terrorists, you wouldn't have sent Rykos to ask their help in finding your husband."

He's right, but that's not the whole story. "My husband was *tortured* under that church by Liberteum, Phylep."

"Yes, but you should know that the man who did that was one of their former members, and he *hated* Michele."

Defying the corporation and joining a quli rebellion has been trying enough. Now, Ilaria is being asked to distinguish between good terrorists and bad ones. What's next?

"Rykos said Michele is very beautiful."

Phylep closes his eyes and nods slowly. "That she is. She's also the most intelligent and driven woman I've ever met."

"Teman thought she was insane," Ilaria argues.

"Passionate is a better word. Michele's a visionary who knows freedom must be fought for and always comes at a cost. For the record, that sounds a lot like another woman who I recently met."

Ilaria may not have completely bought the corporate propaganda about Liberteum, but that doesn't mean she supports them. If Phylep is right, they may share more in common than she thought. It's an assertion the wife of the former chief guardian finds unsettling.

Another knock on the door interrupts the conversation. "Ma'am, we have a secure link to AME News set up for you in the RTCC. Kassaya is standing by."

"I have to head back to the park. Andanz and Prano need additional adult supervision," Phylep says, rising from the sofa with a smile before turning for the door. "I'll leave you to it."

"Phylep? Do you know where Liberteum is?"

"They fled the city about the time you went to Rikers. My guess is they went up to Denali Keating's estate."

"In Greenwich? Why would they go see a patrician?"

"Because Farron Keating is also a part of Liberteum."

The knowing smile makes her wonder who else is in this group, but he disappears before she can ask. She makes her way back down the corridor to the RTCC with more questions than answers. The revelations about Liberteum and the qulis, the bombshell about Farron Keating…it's a lot to digest. It's also going to have to wait. She has more pressing concerns – like finding a way to keep them all alive long enough to get answers.

* * *

"Hello, Kassaya," Ilaria says when she reaches the communications station in the RTCC.

"Ilaria? Where…I mean, how are you? I heard rumors that you were in BCS custody for subversion and treason."

"I was. Are you interested in hearing why?"

The journalist leans back in her chair. "Absolutely."

Ilaria walks her through the events starting with her promotion, the face-off against the BCS in Astor Park, Teman's rescue attempt and her subsequent capture at Rikers Island, the house arrest and rescue from her domicile. She leaves out the graphic parts in the name of propriety. While an independent woman like Kassaya might approve of ripping an agent's ball sack off, now's not the time to revel in it.

"That's one hell of a story."

"It's been a long couple of days."

"For the both of us," she says, leaning toward the camera. "Our reporting chain is different under corporate law. AME News is taking direction from Director Virtari. He just issued instructions for us to report non-stop on the quli violence."

"There isn't any."

"There is some in other cities, and what they don't have on video, they're going to make up. They have a narrative they want every employee to see and hear."

Video manipulation is not a new thing. Ilaria will never understand people's willingness to believe everything they see or accept it as fact without a shred of critical thought.

"Then we had better come up with a message of our own."

"I can't report anything you told me, as much as I want to."

They need an ally in the media if this rebellion against the corporation has any chance of succeeding. There must be a voice that rises above the constant drumbeat of propaganda pounding the airwaves. Unfortunately, Ilaria isn't willing to manipulate Kassaya into doing that. It would cost her life, making Ilaria no better than the corporate masters she once served.

"I understand. You're in a bad spot, and I'm not here to make it worse. I just wanted you to know the truth."

"The truth," she says, looking forlorn and weary. "I'm not sure I would even recognize it these days."

CHAPTER THIRTY-TWO

LIBERTEUM

In Transit

Sailing and now flying – it's been a day and a half of firsts for Michele. She stares out the windows at the ground passing below her. Being in the sunlight is a rare enough feeling, but humming above the treetops like a bird is almost surreal.

Patricians know a thing or two about style. The helicopter is not only fast but also luxurious. She thought the motion might induce nausea, but that's not the case. The same can't be said for Koltayne, who's looking a little green. Despite her hands being bound in front of her, Michele gives him a thumbs-up, and the weak one he returns is less than reassuring.

The aircraft drops altitude and flares, sending a wave of uncertainty through her. Nobody else seems alarmed, so she tries to relax. The wheels touch down on the ground, signaling the beginning of her end. Crashing would be a preferred fate to what awaits. The engines wind down, and the rotors slow their turning. The pilot and copilot remain seated while a member of Denali's security force opens the door.

"Get out."

There's no point in resisting his order. The three prisoners shimmy across the seat and out of the helicopter. Michele surveys her surroundings. The air is salty and there is a suspension bridge looming in the distance. They landed in the center of playing fields for various sports activities. Other than some small equipment sheds, there are no buildings close by and no cover to hide behind. It's the perfect spot for an exchange when two parties don't trust each other.

"Do you know where we are?" Michele asks Rykos as they are escorted toward two uniformed members of the BCS waiting next to their vehicle parked fifty yards away.

"That's the Commerce Bridge. We're at the Ferry Point Recreation Area and Park."

She recognizes the name immediately. It's the spot where Farron's father dumped the bodies of the patricians he murdered.

"Right on time," an agent in an ill-fitting uniform says.

"Did you expect anything less? Here are your prisoners," Denali's guard responds.

The agent looks Michele over, followed by Rykos and then Koltayne. "She's hot, but other than that, I don't know what all the fuss is about. These three don't look like much."

"Is our business here concluded?"

"So impatient," the agent says to his partner. "Almost. There's one more agenda item to attend to."

"What could we poss—"

The two agents draw their sidearms and fire simultaneously. Rykos, Koltayne, and Michele all jump at the unexpected bark of their weapons. The security officer's face is frozen in shock as he collapses to the ground with two holes in his chest. One of the agents strides over and fires a finishing shot into his skull.

The second agent covers them while his partner holsters his weapon and draws a knife. Michele readies herself. If they're going to fight, it's now or never. The odds are long, but it's better than waiting to have their throats slit. The agent grabs Rykos, who swings his bound arms at the man's face and misses. Instead of anger or contempt, the two men look amused.

"Settle down, buddy," the agent says, causing Rykos to pause long enough for the man to flick his wrist and cut the plastic tie that's binding his hands. He repeats the action on Koltayne and then on Michele.

"What's going on?"

"You don't recognize a rescue when you see one?" he asks, cocking a thumb over his shoulder.

Two men climb out of the conveyance, and Michele's temporary sense of relief at being freed is replaced by utter confusion.

CHAPTER THIRTY-THREE

THE PATRICIANS

Ferry Point Recreational Park
Throgs Neck Geographic District
New York City Municipal Corporation

Everything happened fast, out of necessity. When they swooped in on the BCS, the agents were quick to surrender. Then again, anyone staring down the cannons of an old Hind gunship would likely drop their weapons.

The agents were stripped of their uniforms and secured in the trunk of the conveyance. Knowing that they would be recognized instantly, Farron drafted their borrowed security personnel to play the roles of the waiting agents. The whole thing went off better than he had expected.

"Farron? Zyree?" Michele asks, her voice trembling in stunned disbelief.

"Who did you expect?" Farron asks as they walk up to the group.

"Not you."

Michele's glare burns with fiery hatred. Farron knows she still believes he betrayed her, and this rescue hasn't given her enough reason to think otherwise.

"Who are these guys?" Rykos asks, breaking the awkward silence.

"They're security personnel belonging to one of my associates," Farron explains.

"Associate...more like Farron's ex-girlfriend who still has the hots for him," Zyree can't resist clarifying, trying to lighten the mood before Michele decides to rip the patrician's throat out.

"They just killed your security guy," Rykos points out to Farron.

"He was my father's security, not mine."

"Is there a difference?" Michele says with a sneer, still searching for some understanding.

"A big one."

"What happened to the real agents?" Rykos asks.

"They're getting to know each other in the trunk," Zyree explains, pointing his thumb over his shoulder. "Would you believe they only sent two of them here to pick you guys up?"

"Who's the girl in the conveyance?" Rykos asks, nodding at the redhead in an orange jumpsuit, semi-conscious in the back seat. Zyree smiles.

"That's his current girlfriend. We had to rescue her, too."

Farron rewards him with a nasty glance before turning to Michele. "I know I have a lot of explaining to do, but now isn't the time. The BCS will figure out something is wrong before long and send a drone to investigate. I'd rather not be here when they do."

"I think we can spare a minute," Michele says, crossing her arms and standing firm.

"This story is going to take longer than a minute," Zyree adds with a snicker.

Farron doesn't blame her for being wary. He wouldn't trust anyone after what she's been through. It took long enough to convince Zyree. The former chief inspector has been along for this ride and probably still doesn't know what to make of it.

"Please, you're just going to have to trust me."

"If you won't trust him, Michele, trust me. If he wasn't playing it straight, I'd have shot him a long time ago."

Michele looks over at Rykos, who nods. "Fine. How are we getting out of here?"

"The same way you arrived," he says, nodding toward the helicopter. Both the pilot and copilot are guarded by two men who were hiding in the equipment sheds.

"Farron? What's the meaning of this?" the pilot asks after they reach the flying limousine.

"I'm repurposing family property for personal use. Fly us where we need to go, and then you'll be released to return to Greenwich."

"This is highly irregular. Your father—"

"Is not your immediate concern. The man with the gun is. Cooperate and be released, or we can shoot you and send flowers to your widows. What'll it be?"

It isn't a hard decision. The two pilots look at each other before nodding.

"Fire it up," Farron commands in a rare authoritative voice.

"Where are we going?"

"The only safe place left for you, Michele. I'm taking you home."

CHAPTER THIRTY-FOUR

AMERICA, INC.

The White House
Corporate Governance District
Washington-Arlington Municipal Corporation

Everybody shoots up to their feet when a battered Zeykala storms into the Situation Room. She's greeted with a mix of surprised looks and confusion from the executives around the table. Whether their shock is over her being alive or because she looks like she's been through a war is anyone's guess. Zeykala is busy wondering if any of them knew this was going to happen or helped plan it.

"Get me the EOC in Manhattan right now!"

"Ma'am, you should get checked out by medical first," one of her executives suggests.

Zeykala slams her hand down on the table and clenches her teeth. "Get me Virtari right *now*."

Tension settles over the room like a winter blanket. She doesn't need a doctor as much as she needs answers about who tried to kill her. A moment later, Virtari appears on the main display.

"Chief Executive Zeykala? I'm glad to see you safe and unhurt."

"Are you? You have a penchant for ordering assassinations, Director. I will ask you plainly: Did you just order mine?"

Virtari recoils slightly. "Ma'am, I may be a lot of things, but the leader of a coup isn't one of them."

"You'll forgive me if I don't entirely believe you."

Nerves are already frayed. It's one thing to have disagreements, but it's another to openly accuse the BCS director of subversion in front of senior executives. Not that Zeykala cares. She was almost killed today, and someone will be held accountable for that.

"Ma'am, you've had a very traumatic experience. You deserve answers, but to blame me for the acts of terrorists is—"

"Terrorists? Liberteum lives in the Manhattan underground. Somehow, you think they acquired an armored helicopter and flew it down the East Coast to Maryland? Is that the official BCS position?"

Virtari is hiding something. That's what Zeykala senses and she wants to know what. It would mean his head if he was involved in this attack. The loyalty his agents harbor for him will only go so far.

"You're right, ma'am. Liberteum's involvement seems implausible."

"That type of old military hardware can only belong to a patrician with no reason to kill me, another corporation who could never operate in our sphere of influence, or my own Bureau of Corporate Security. Which of those explanations sounds most plausible to you?"

"The BCS had *nothing* to do with the attempt on your life," Virtari assures her, fighting to restrain his own anger.

"Your CEO was almost assassinated, and you've failed to restore order despite your powers under corporate law…not a banner day for the BCS. Is there anything else you want to add on?"

Virtari lowers his eyes. She was attacking his ego but touched on something he's been desperate to hide.

"I'm waiting, Virtari."

"Chief Executive Ilaria and Constable Dzamko were freed from their confinement this morning. Their domiciles were attacked by qulis supported by the PSS. Four of my men were killed."

Zeykala closes her eyes and rubs her temples. Her ears are ringing, and she has a headache from the explosions that is only getting worse by the second.

"When exactly did this happen?"

He stands up a little straighter. "I was notified at zero-four hundred hours."

"Four a.m., and I'm just hearing about this now?"

"It's a developing situation."

There's nothing "developing" about it. Zeykala immediately resorts to the worst-case scenario. Virtari must have thought she'd be dead and he didn't bother telling her. Why else would he hide that they lost the leverage needed to help bring this corporation back under control?

"Has Liberteum been transferred to our custody, or have you managed to screw that up as well?"

"It's happening as we speak," Virtari assures her.

"Well, that's something."

"Ma'am—"

"Shut your mouth and listen, Director Virtari. I need results from you, not excuses. Get them for me."

Zeykala makes a slashing gesture across her throat, and the VidLynk cuts off. There's nothing more the BCS director can say. She understands his intentions, and now it's time to stop them.

She turns to the agent at the table. "Who's second in command at the Pentagon?"

The question puts the young agent in an uncomfortable spot. "Ma'am, we're under corporate law. Director Virtari cannot be replaced until the order is lifted."

"I didn't say I was replacing him. I asked who's second in command at the Bureau. Answer me."

"Assistant Director Craynak."

"Relay to Director Virtari that before the end of the day, I want to know who perpetrated that attack. If he can't deliver, I'm going to assume he's responsible."

"Ma'am, that's not enough time to investigate…,"

Zeykala storms out of the Situation Room while he's in mid-sentence. She doesn't care whether Virtari gives her an answer. This is about buying time. If Virtari can't be loyal, she will find someone who is.

* * *

Zeykala was correct in her assessment. Old military hardware isn't easy to come by. It's doubtful that Liberteum, or even most smaller corporations, could procure antiquated weapons systems. Patricians can, and if Virtari's intelligence reports are accurate, they have.

The incoming VidLynk from his agent stationed at the White House was marked "urgent." His men are trained not to be dramatic when relaying critical information. Emotion clouds judgment, and time wasted addressing communications that aren't as important as the messenger thinks they are is inefficient and distracting. This is not one of those cases.

"She's giving you until the end of the day to find out who orchestrated and executed the attack," the agent informs Virtari.

"Or else what?"

"I'm not certain. Chief Executive Zeykala asked who is second in charge. I tried to explain that she can't replace you while—"

"That won't stop her. Has Assistant Director Craynak been apprised of the situation?"

"Yes, sir. His response was…colorful."

Virtari smirks. "What did he say?"

"He called her some old terms I hadn't heard before. Something about being 'bat shit crazy.'"

The BCS director nods, knowing that sounds about right. "Keep him in the loop. I don't want him thinking I take his loyalty for granted."

"Yes, sir," the agent says, ending the VidLynk.

Zeykala is barking up the wrong tree with that old codger. Craynak detests the executives who run this corporation. There's nothing worse than an endless bureaucracy run by cretins. Craynak is a security professional, and that rarely mixes with politics. The CEO will learn that the hard way if it gets that far.

Virtari searches the Pentagon's investigations database and selects the case number for the attack on the termination center. The directory listing of video footage and eyewitness and agent reports is already extensive, considering the small amount of time that has passed. He opens the official summary when a pair of names jumps off the display.

"Farron Keating and Chief Inspector Zyree?"

Facial recognition from video footage of the helicopter's occupants is a one hundred percent match for both men. How did a disgraced Intercorpex inspector get caught up in this? And why would the Keatings be behind an assassination attempt? Killing the CEO of America Incorporated serves no purpose for a family that craves stability. Helping Liberteum escape New York and attempting to murder the chief executive are antithetical to their worldview.

Virtari leans back in his chair and rubs his chin. Something else is driving this. The dots aren't connecting. This report misses the mark with one key that would help most: motive. He annotates that in a comment and closes the file. Suspicions about the Keatings won't placate Zeykala. He needs to understand their ambitions, or she'll start to fill in the blanks herself and grow this into an even bigger conspiracy.

There is nothing to be gained by sharing this information with her until he knows the full story. If the CEO cancels corporate law to get rid of him, the board will replace her. Sharks are circling, just waiting for their opportunity to strike. Sparing Varella may have been the right move, after all. She seems cut out for this sort of political maneuvering.

He marks the investigation with instructions to keep it limited to bureau eyes only. Zeykala will get her answers when he's ready to give them to her. The Liberteum problem will soon be over. Once they're in BCS custody, he can demonstrate to employees how they deal with problems.

Then, they can release what they know about the patricians and send them slinking back to their gated estates to wait out the storm. The Keatings may have immunity, but the damage will be done. When the terrorists are dead, the patricians humbled, and Zeykala pacified, he's free to deal with the treasonous qulis. That problem will be easy enough to fix.

CHAPTER THIRTY-FIVE

THE PATRICIANS

*Keating Family of the Gentez-Majorez Estate
Greenwich Geographic District
Southern Connecticut Municipal Corporation*

The initial reports coming in from Maryland are surprising. Multiple sightings of a massive helicopter and countless explosions near a corporate facility make for interesting reading. More amusing is AME News's constant denials that anything is amiss when all signs point to the contrary.

If the reports are true, then this was a deliberate attack that Denali didn't have a hand in planning. If his White House sources are accurate, then someone took a shot at Chief Executive Zeykala. That's an interesting development.

Abbot and Lacune stride into the study with a purpose. Their timing is perfect. Maybe they have some answers.

"Have you heard anything about this attack in Maryland?" Denali asks as they reach his sofa.

The two men look at each other warily. "Farron did not return with the helicopter from Washington."

"He said he was going to lunch at Darkshadow for some asinine reason."

"Yes, sir, only he didn't go to the Darkshadow estate. He made it to their airfield and sent his transport back from there because he found alternate transportation."

Denali's brow crinkles. That sounds both ominous and vague at the same time. It makes no sense why he wouldn't return with the helicopter after his meeting.

"I don't understand."

"Farron participated in the attack against the Meade termination grounds," Commander Lacune clarifies.

"That's not possible," Denali says almost reflexively.

"I'm afraid it is, sir," Abbot reluctantly says. "The early-century Mi-24 Hind aircraft that conducted the attack was the same aircraft that ambushed the Liberteum transfer site fifteen minutes ago. Farron is now accompanying our former guests to New York City aboard our transport helicopter."

Denali's mouth hangs open. These men wouldn't lie to him, and there's no indication this is some ill-advised comedic undertaking. Farron is young and impressionable. He feared that Michele's ideological musings could influence him to join Liberteum's futile quest. Despite his misgivings, he always believed that the family would come first. There must be a deeper, more sinister reason….

"No, no, no…Farron would not do this. He must be in distress."

"We considered that. Unfortunately, it appears he's doing this willingly."

"He wouldn't do this to me!" Denali shouts, standing and flinging his crystal tumbler against the study's far wall.

Anger surges through him with the power of high-voltage electricity. Farron turned against him for what – some idealistic version of the world that couldn't stand the test of time? The experiment in democracy failed and was unceremoniously deposited in the trash can of history for a reason.

"Track him down, Commander. I want him brought to this estate. I don't care if you have to drag him back here."

"I will put our best people on it," he says with a nod before leaving.

Denali begins pacing the floor. Of all the meticulous plans and various courses of action to execute them, he never considered this development. There are no contingencies for treachery within his own family. Despite his son's idealism and affinity toward Liberteum, there was never a reason to expect he would act so rashly.

"Tell me, Abbot…why do you think Farron did this?"

Few things escape his servant's notice, which means Farron managed to keep his subversion very quiet. That's hard to do in society today. Everybody talks when the price is right. At least Abbot understands the concept of loyalty.

"I wouldn't presume to know why he would make such a poor decision. You have offered him the world. He had no reason to betray you."

"Even for Michele? I know he's quite fond of her."

"She is a beautiful enchantress with a warped view of reality, and Farron is an idealist. He is also old and wise enough to know better."

That doesn't make Denali feel any better. Farron has gone down a path that will get him killed. Even if he is brought to his senses and returned to Greenwich, the trust has been lost. That will change a great many things.

"His idealism comes from his mother. I should have told him about my plan much sooner. Thank you, Abbot. I want to be alone for a while."

"Please let me know if you need anything, sir."

A range of emotions runs through Denali: guilt, anger, shock, sadness…all of them competing for superiority. Regret comes from the back of the pack to take the lead. This plan was all for him…it would secure the family legacy for a dozen generations. He has betrayed the family and his own future. The path forward will be traveled with Farron at Denali's side. The course is as clear and irreversible. Nothing can stop him from seizing control of the world's corporations.

His son was groomed to take over the Keating empire since he was a small boy. When Denali created The Trust, it was done knowing he would step in to lead it someday. That reality is gone. Farron will need to live with the consequences of his actions. If he doesn't want to help rule this world, then he can suffer alongside the people in it.

CHAPTER THIRTY-SIX

RYKOS

Ferry Point Recreational Park
Throgs Neck Geographic District
New York City Municipal Corporation

The exfiltration from the park clearly took much longer than Zyree and Farron thought it would. It started with retrieving the woman in the orange jumpsuit from the back seat and practically dragging her across the field to the waiting helicopter. Farron offered to help Zyree, but she wanted nothing to do with that.

The men who posed as the BCS agents volunteered to stay behind and find alternate transportation to the Catskill Mountains airfield, where the armored helicopter Farron calls the "Beast" apparently flew to after they ambushed the BCS. I can't wait to see that thing.

That's for another day. The immediate task is getting Farron's girlfriend, if that's who she really is, into the helicopter. Given her state, it isn't the easiest of tasks. Once we get her seated, we load up, and Michele opts to sit next to her.

"Let me get that for you," she says, helping the woman with her seat restraint. After fighting with it for a few seconds, the restraint clicks. "There you go."

The woman offers a weak smile. "Thank you."

Farron and Zyree do a double-take. She must not have done much talking on the trip up here, if she spoke at all. The woman looks like she's been through hell and, despite the rescue, still won't even look at Farron.

"We've never met. I'm Michele. This is Rykos, and the quiet one over there is Koltayne."

"Fiolla," the woman croaks in a raspy voice.

I make eye contact with Zyree. Fiolla was likely administered all manner of drugs that are only now starting to wear off. It's also possible that her silence was a symptom of severe psychological trauma that Michele's basic kindness is beginning to heal. My guess is that she's only comfortable responding to another woman right now.

The two women seem to bond as we take off and head southwest. The flight to Manhattan is short, and we begin to fly over Central Park in a matter of minutes. The buildings and scenery are the same, but the city feels different, even flying above it. This is a much different place than it was when we climbed aboard the boat for the fateful trip to Denali's Greenwich estate. It's far different from the time I used to meet Balin here to complain about the state of the world.

"Where do you want me to land?" the pilot asks over our headsets.

"The closer to Valhalla, the better," Zyree says, getting a nod from Michele.

"How about there?" Farron asks.

"That'll work."

Just to the south of a large fountain and promenade that extends from east to west lies a small field surrounded by trees. Central Park's landscaping was constructed to provide the appearance of a wide open space amid an urban jungle. This clearing is the closest area to the southern edge of the park that's big enough to land in. We don't want to risk clipping the trees with our rotors.

The pilot expertly hovers, deploys the landing gear, and sets down gently on the grass. Content that the aircraft won't sink into the ground, he powers down the engine.

"Take off as soon as we disembark," Farron instructs the pilots.

I reach over Fiolla and open the side door. I sense something is wrong before I see it. Zyree does, too. He scans the tree line and signals everyone to stop. There is movement. We are not alone here.

"Uh-oh," Koltayne says, staring out the front of the helicopter.

"What?"

"Uh, sir?" the pilot says, also staring out the windscreen.

I poke my head between the pilot and the copilot. Men in PSS uniforms are swarming out of the trees with rifles leveled at the helicopter. The movement to our left must have been fire support teams moving into position. We're boxed in.

"Close that door, Zyree. Take off!" Farron urges the pilot.

"This isn't the Beast, Farron. We won't make it two feet off the ground if they open up on us."

"Do you have a better option?"

A dozen guardians form a semicircle in front of us, ready to open fire. Five men approach from each side, all with clear shots at the passenger compartment. Forget lifting off. We'll all be dead as soon as the pilot restarts the engine.

"How about it, Zyree? Any bright ideas?" Michele asks.

"Ones that don't get us all killed or involve surrendering? No."

One of the guardians signals us to exit. He pauses for a moment and then shows us five fingers…then four…then three.

"When that last finger falls, the game is over," I advise. "I suggest we follow orders and take our chances."

"You guys exit first," Farron commands the flight crew.

Everyone unbuckles their seatbelts. The cockpit doors open only a moment before Zyree opens the passenger compartment door. The pilot exits with his hands up as instructed, followed by his copilot. We all stare intently out the windscreen. The good news is they haven't been shot, and the PSS isn't being hyperaggressive with them. With the flight crew in custody, now it's our turn.

"Okay, now what?" Michele asks.

"Uh, Fiolla's gone."

We all turn back to Koltayne and then over to the empty seat Fiolla was sitting in. I peer back out the windscreen and watch her make her way around the front of the aircraft toward the armed men. She holds her hands away from her, but that will do little to stop them from shooting her.

The guardians shout orders that she seems to ignore. Fiolla makes her way over to the man who appears to be in charge. He pulls out his sidearm and points it right at her forehead.

I press my lips together and shake my head. "This isn't good."

CHAPTER THIRTY-SEVEN

LIBERTEUM

Central Park
Central Park Geographic District
New York City Municipal Corporation

Fiolla keeps her hands extended to show she is unarmed. The men are shouting at her, but she ignores their orders. Her focus is on their commander and the weapon he has pointed at her face. If she can't convince him that she's not a threat, this will be a short conversation.

Everything since her interrogation has felt like an out-of-body experience. Not that Fiolla has firsthand knowledge of that feeling. She was conscious of Zeykala's gloating but couldn't respond. She was aware of her rescue but couldn't react to the event. She felt like she was traveling in a conveyance set to auto-drive. Fiolla's mind was along for the ride but not in control. Now that her senses are returning, it's time to take charge. That starts right here, right now.

"Are you the one in charge?"

"Who are you?" the guardian responds.

"Are you the one in charge?" she calmly repeats. This is a battle of wills, and he needs to know she's not intimidated.

The man shakes his head. "Who are *you*? I won't ask you again."

"My name is Executive Fiolla. I was the corporate affairs liaison to the White House."

The guardian takes the measure of her appearance and narrows his eyes. "Was?"

"Yes, as in past tense. I was designated a traitor to the corporation by the chief executive officer herself and processed for termination at the Meade Human Resources Center by the Bureau of Corporate Security."

The look on his face as he processes that information is priceless. Direct honesty is rare nowadays. He is marrying facts in his head. Fiolla's confession about imminent termination explains the bright orange jumpsuit with the red dot painted over her heart. He lowers his weapon slightly.

"And now you're here. How did that happen?"

"It's a *very* long story."

"Probably not one I'll believe, either."

"I don't imagine you will, so let's get back to my original question. Are you in charge?"

"I'm asking the questions. Who's on that helicopter?"

Fiolla turns and checks the scene over her shoulder. Both pilots are standing outside, but none of the others are. Telling the guardian will cost her leverage. Not telling him will lose her what little rapport she's established. Fiolla tries to force through the remaining cobwebs and focus. Middle ground…she needs to answer the question without answering it.

"Some of the most wanted people in the entire sphere of influence. Who do you report to?"

"Director Virtari," he croaks.

His tone gives him away. Detecting deception is a skill Fiolla quickly learned while working in the White House. She's heard enough fiction come out of the mouths of career executives to know when a novice is lying.

"I don't think you do. The man is a pig, and you know it. Who do you really report to?"

He stares at her through narrow eyes. The guardian doesn't want to betray his true allegiance, but he's also smart enough to realize that this is a weird situation. All he needs is a little reassurance.

"Look, we're not armed and wouldn't survive a firefight with your men even if we were. You have nothing to lose by telling the truth, and that may change the complexion of everything that happens today."

He stares back at the helicopter and nods. "We report to Chief Executive Ilaria and our acting chief guardian, Constable Dzamko."

His chest puffed out as he said those words with a great deal of pride. That causes Fiolla to smile. She became acutely aware of who she was traveling with once they got airborne. Now, it's time to put that knowledge to good use.

"Excellent. Do you have communications with them?"

The question earns her a suspicious look. "What do you think?"

"Please get them on the line. One of the men on that helicopter is someone I'm sure your CEO will want to hear from."

CHAPTER THIRTY-EIGHT

RYKOS

Central Park
Central Park Geographic District
New York City Municipal Corporation

We were escorted to a copse of trees to get us out of the open. Drones are circling overhead, and the BCS might already know we are here. If they do, they aren't acting on the information. Either way, it'd be dumb to tempt fate.

Central Park is a strange place for the PSS to be manning a command post. In my father's time as chief guardian, I never once heard about them basing an operation in the park. They have done sweeps, but they were always coordinated through the Real-Time Crime Center or a mobile command truck. I guess nothing is normal in this city right now.

"Nice job setting this up," I whisper to Fiolla as a guardian fires up the secure communications console.

"Thanks. It felt good to do something useful."

"It took a lot of courage to confront guardians pointing rifles at your head. You must have been convincing."

"I'm finally starting to feel more like myself. And I didn't make it this far to die now," Fiolla says to me with a wry smile.

"Can I ask you a question? What happened in Washington?"

Fiolla smiles weakly at Michele. "You mean, why was the corporation going to kill me?"

"I apologize for asking, but it's strange to me. Farron said you worked at the White House, so I know you're a big executive."

Michele could never appreciate how big an honor it is to get that posting. She doesn't know how hard it is to reach that level in the corporate ranks. Preparatory school and the right university education only put you on the management path. Then you have to walk the walk. It takes a lot to get noticed and find your way to the parent company, much less a position in the White House. Fiolla is a rock star among corporate executives.

"We are supposed to be loyal to whoever sits in the Oval Office. My loyalty was reserved for its previous occupant, not its current one. Zeykala discovered I was working with Chief Executive Valen behind her back. Collusion wasn't enough to haul me in front of a tribunal, so she ordered the BCS to follow me to a MetroLev station and push me in front of a train."

"That sounds a little extreme even for the parent corporation," I conclude. "What were you doing for Valen?"

"That's a long story, but he's in more danger now because of it than we are."

"I hope to hear the story sometime if you decide to stay with us," Michele concludes.

The offer surprises Fiolla. She reflexively crosses her arms and presses her lips together. Michele has never been a corporate employee, but her father likely taught her a thing or two about recognizing negative body language. Life in the underground must have provided countless opportunities to hone that skill. The leader of Liberteum overstepped her boundaries.

"I'm sorry, Fiolla," Michele says, lowering her eyes. "I didn't mean to make you uncomfortable."

"No, it's just…you have to understand, Liberteum has always been the enemy. I know you as the leader of a terrorist group that threatened my whole way of life. You don't know how many security briefings and meetings I've heard about or participated in. Only…."

"They aren't the evil killers they are portrayed as," I say, helping her reach the conclusion I did long ago. "I struggled with the same dilemma."

There is a long, awkward pause in the conversation. There isn't much more I can say to Fiolla and nothing that Michele can add. Years of indoctrination won't be overcome in one conversation under the shade trees in Central Park on a beautiful spring day.

"Isn't this the point where you're supposed to say, 'because I'm not a terrorist?'" Fiolla finally asks.

"No, because I am one, at least from the corporate perspective. I want to destroy a system that represses everyone who serves it except the most fortunate. And I have killed people. I am also responsible for the deaths of others. If those are the criteria I'm judged against, then I'm every bit the monster you've been told I am."

I study Fiolla's face. Whatever she was anticipating Michele to say, that wasn't it.

"That was…more honest than what I'm used to hearing," the former executive says with a smile.

"Living as an urch is hard enough," Michele offers. "We don't have time for word games when we spend our lives trying to survive."

Fiolla nods her understanding. "Is brutal honesty how you enlist people for your cause?"

"The idea of freedom sorta sells itself," I add, causing the corner of Michele's mouth to curl. Fiolla tries to suppress a grimace, and I cock my head. "You don't agree?"

"Living as a corporate executive is hard enough. We don't have time for idealism when life is reduced to climbing the corporate ladder."

Oh, I like this woman. She's quick-witted. Most of the executives I have met are stiff and dull. Fiolla has a spark that's exceedingly rare in the mundane corporate world.

"Maybe we're not as different as you think we are," Michele concludes.

"That depends. Have you ever been used by a man you thought you were in love with?" Fiolla asks, turning to watch Farron, who is talking with Zyree and some guardians a few dozen feet away.

"No, but I was used by his father," Michele says, getting the quizzical look from Fiolla she was probably expecting. "That's *my* long story. Let's just say that he's in more danger than we are because of it."

Fiolla lets out a slight laugh at hearing her words. The commander tells us that we're ready. I take a deep breath, but there's one more thing I need to say first.

"Fiolla," I say, turning to her. "It's not my business, and I'm not in the habit of defending Farron Keating, but if he was only using you, would he have risked everything to save you?"

Fiolla turns to Michele, who shrugs. "It's a fair point."

CHAPTER THIRTY-NINE

NYCMC RESISTANCE

One Guardian Plaza
Lower Manhattan Geographic District
New York City Municipal Corporation

The priority VidLynk request from their team in Central Park caught everyone by surprise. It wasn't a routine status update. That was made clear when the commander on the ground specifically asked for Ilaria.

Dzamko didn't like the sound of that. He liked it even less when the guardian in command explained they had some people in custody and that one of them requested the conference. He wore a grave expression when he warned that the team could have been compromised and that this could be a setup.

He may be right, but the BCS will eventually learn that she's at One Guardian Plaza, regardless. Teman once said that to a hammer, everything looks like a nail. She doesn't want to look for conspiracies and traps around every corner. Establishing this communication doesn't risk their mission or their security.

It takes only a couple of seconds for the technician to establish the video. It's not the commander of the team on the display. She blinks twice, not believing what she sees.

"Rykos?"

"Hello, Mother."

"I thought…I thought I had lost you," Ilaria admits as a wave of relief washes over her. "I heard you'd been shot. Are you okay?"

"It was touch and go for a while, but I'm fine," Rykos assures her.

"How did you end up in Central Park? I thought you left the city with Liberteum."

"We did. We came back by helicopter," he deadpans, eliciting a look from Ilaria that speaks volumes. "We have a lot to catch up on, so I'll explain later. What about you? CEO?"

"It's not as impressive as it sounds. I started working for Chief Executive Safmor right before he was killed at Intercorpex…you weren't involved in that, were you?"

Ilaria braces herself for the answer. After watching her husband get executed, being taken captive by the BCS and almost raped, and even staring death in the face standing with the city's qulis, nothing would be more devastating for her than the news that her son was responsible for the murders of over a thousand people.

"No, that was Haven's doing. He was working for Denali Keating."

"What?" Dzamko and Ilaria say at the same time.

"Yeah, it was a shock to us as well. It's also why Denali imprisoned us. Technically, we were his 'guests,' but I don't think he locks his visitors in a basement vault. He was about to hand us over to the BCS when Farron and Zyree swooped in for the rescue."

"That explains the helicopter that landed in Central Park," Dzamko says.

"Who else are you with?"

"Michele, Koltayne, Farron Keating, former Chief Inspector Zyree, and Executive Fiolla from the White House."

Ilaria looks over at Dzamko, who raises an eyebrow. Rykos is full of surprises.

"So, the leader of a terrorist group and one of her men, the son of a patrician who held you captive, a disgraced Intercorpex chief inspector, and a woman who works for the parent company? That's quite the crew."

"Fiolla *used* to work for the parent company, Constable. She was slated for termination. It's another long story. Before you ask, I don't even know all of it yet. Anyway, while we were in Greenwich, I was told Father was terminated and you were in BCS custody. It appears that wasn't true."

The RTCC quiets. Every set of eyes settles on Ilaria. Everyone here knows what happened at Rikers.

"They were both true, Rykos. Your father is…he's gone."

Her son closes his eyes and nods in understanding. He might not have been close to Teman, but no child is ready to hear of a parent's death. For Rykos, that's especially true considering the pains he took to save his father after his capture.

"Your mother and I were apprehended by the BCS trying to rescue him at Rikers Island," Dzamko interjects. "We, in turn, were rescued by the qulis."

"The qulis?"

"I believe you might be acquainted with one of their leaders," Ilaria says with a smirk. "Phylep was one of the guys who rescued me."

"Small world," Rykos says with a grin.

"Sir," a guardian interrupts, addressing Dzamko. "We have reports of a BCS team entering Central Park from the west."

"It's probably a reconnaissance team," the constable hypothesizes.

"They may have figured out that we were on that helicopter and want to see if we're still here. We need to go. We have a place to hide out and only need to get there."

"Where?"

"Midtown. It's better if you don't know the exact location."

Ilaria wants to know, but he's right. It may be better if she is in the dark. She'd much rather him with her at One Guardian Plaza, but this place won't be any safer for him. It's likely more dangerous.

"The parent company has declared the NYCMC in open rebellion," Dzamko says. "They're going to make a move to squash that. Manhattan is a mess right now, but my guardians can get you and your friends where you need to go."

"Thank you, Constable. Mother, this is going to sound like an odd request, but I think we should work together to stop the BCS."

Despite Phylep's assurances about them, Ilaria isn't ready to associate with terrorists. The hunt for them ripped her family apart and cost her husband his life. Michele may not have been directly responsible for that, but the leader of Liberteum bears some of the blame.

"We'll talk more about that when you arrive wherever you're going. And Rykos?" she asks before he disconnects. "I love you. Please watch your back and don't do anything stupid."

"I love you too, Mother," he says before smiling. "And no promises."

CHAPTER FORTY

AMERICA, INC.

Emergency Operations Center
Lower Manhattan Geographic District
New York City Municipal Corporation

Virtari watches the video in the briefing room without speaking or reacting. The agent walks him through how they uncovered the information. When the agents at the exchange failed to report in, a drone was sent to investigate. Their conveyance was found abandoned at the park with a body next to it, and a small team was dispatched to investigate.

The two agents were unharmed but were stripped of their uniforms, bound, and secured in the trunk. Anger wells up in Virtari's chest. He normally would have had two dozen providing security. Unfortunately, thanks to Zeykala, they're stretched too thin. The BCS isn't manned to handle a rebellion of this scale, and now his men are getting killed because of it.

"Sir, we checked the surveillance camera footage and found this."

The display changes to a series of still camera and video shots of a large attack helicopter. Virtari doesn't need an abacus to put two and two together.

"Has it been tracked?"

"It headed northwest over the Hudson Valley and into the Catskills before we lost contact. Liberteum and some of the team on that gunship left Ferry Point in Denali Keating's transport helicopter. We tracked it to Central Park."

"Is it still there?" I ask.

"Uh, no, sir. It lifted off about fifteen minutes after it landed and headed northeast across the Sound."

The men in the room brace for Virtari's reaction. As angry as he is, lashing out will solve nothing. These escapes require damage control, and he needs his agents on his side to effect that. This loss in leverage and Zeykala's near-death experience in Maryland are the excuses she needs to dispose of him.

"Get a VidLynk established with Denali Keating. I want to know why he double-crossed us."

"Right away, sir."

Virtari has no idea what Keating has to gain by freeing Liberteum. What he does know is they're loose in Manhattan again. In the spectrum of outcomes, this is one of the better ones. Had they fled to a rural area, finding them would be next to impossible. Instead, once they have full control of the city, they will tear it apart until they locate and eradicate them.

"How close are we to full muster?"

"About eighty-five percent of our roster is at the staging area, sir."

"I want the attack plan on my tablet for approval within the hour," Virtari orders.

"May I speak to you in private, please, sir?" Varella requests. He dismisses the agents, and she turns to him once the door closes. "What are you doing, Director?"

"Executing my authority to pacify New York City."

"Sir, with due respect, AME News hasn't even begun to run our video packages yet."

Virtari leans forward and steeples his hands. "I'm responsible for the security of this corporation, and I'm going to restore order in the corporation's largest city. I will make an example out of those who resist as a warning for the rest of the sphere of influence. That is the end of the discussion."

"I'm not saying you shouldn't take back the city by whatever means necessary. What I'm saying is you should wait until people realize that you have cause to do it."

This is the problem with young executives. They are too cautious. When given the choice, they opt for inaction over getting concrete results every time. That's what happens when you worry more about your career than the interests of the corporation you serve. It seems to be what they are teaching at Harvard these days.

"Did you fall and hit your head or something? A quli uprising and the declaration of corporate law is all the 'cause' I need."

"It's not. Employees aren't seeing one and don't understand the other. We need AME News to *show* them what's going on."

"You're trying my patience, Varella," Virtari says, rising from his seat. Varella follows suit.

"You asked me to coordinate a message…*your* message. The corporation has convinced employees to believe in the system, but they're still permitted to have opinions. Bulldoze the whole city if needed, but if it isn't viewed as justified, they will look at Zeykala, and she will point her finger at you. What do you think will happen then?"

This woman knows how to get under his skin. As irate as Virtari is about Ilaria, Liberteum, and the attack on Zeykala, he may be even more annoyed that Varella could be right. Corporate politics is a nasty business.

"I'll give you until tomorrow morning. Then I'm deploying my men."

"That won't be enough time," she protests as he makes for the door.

Virtari rewards her with the coldest glare he can muster. "Have AME News air the packages on a continuous loop. Then they can stream video of the BCS coming to the rescue of our employees in Manhattan because that's what's going to happen at oh-seven hundred tomorrow. Other cities experiencing quli uprisings will follow, so you had better get to work."

The negotiation is over. Orders have been issued. Varella needs to learn when to shut up and do what she's told. She's not an executive and isn't running anything yet.

"You want to be a hot shot, Varella," Virtari snaps when she shakes her head. "Prove you belong here. Make this happen. If you can't, I'll find someone who can. I've watched the best and brightest executives in this corporation do far more with less time."

CHAPTER FORTY-ONE

THE PATRICIANS

Nothing fills the emptiness left in the wake of betrayal. When someone you trust stabs you in the back, the blade cuts into your soul. Denali is struggling to keep his emotions in check. This was not an ordinary betrayal. It was from his own flesh and blood.

Emotional reactions lead to inevitable mistakes, and Denali cannot bear the cost of one. Not when he's on the cusp of achieving everything he set out to do. What's done is done. Farron made his choice, and he must live with the consequences. Denali needs to focus on finishing his mission.

"Sir, you are receiving an urgent secure VidLynk request from the New York Public Safety and Security Emergency Operations Center. I believe it is directly from BCS Director Virtari."

Denali nods. There is only one thing this can be about. "Go ahead and connect us, Abbot."

"We had a deal, Denali," Virtari says, skipping the usual deference to patricians when the display glows to life. "No more games. I demand that you release Liberteum into our custody."

"I don't have them."

"You're a liar!"

Denali excused the disregard for protocol. Virtari is under incredible stress under his current circumstances. News of the botched transfer was bound to unleash his colorful side. The patrician will not, however, ignore the blatant disrespect of having his integrity questioned.

"Do not dare presume you can challenge me like that! Director, you know by now that the helicopter transporting Liberteum met your agents at the rendezvous as planned. You also know that it continued to Manhattan before returning here to Greenwich. I'm sure you've connected the dots."

"Your forces attacked my men on the Upper West Side and allowed Liberteum to escape. My men were ambushed by an Mi-24 Hind attack helicopter that we have confirmed your *son* was aboard. That same helicopter attacked the Meade Human

Resources Facility in Maryland and tried to assassinate our chief executive officer. Now, Liberteum is missing. Connect those dots and see what's about to happen next," he threatens. "I have all the reason in the world to pound your glorious estate into dust."

"We both know it wouldn't be that easy, so spare me the empty threats and hyperbole. We were pardoned for the assault on your men, and if I didn't want to agree to the transfer, I wouldn't have. As for the other attack, my son has done some things that I do not condone. Trust me when I say that he will face the repercussions when he returns to Greenwich."

Virtari doesn't look like he's buying that for a second. "Do you take me for a fool, Denali? You're in material breach of the agreement you made with Zeykala. We spared you from an attack on your compound in good faith after the fiasco on the Upper West Side. I will not make that error again."

Denali takes a cleansing breath. Men like Virtari are volatile and fluster easily. He was never suited to run America Incorporated's Bureau of Corporate Security. He's too emotional for the job, and that makes him easy to manipulate. It's time to drop the hammer on the arrogant bastard to remind him who he's dealing with.

"You didn't make that decision, Director, Chief Executive Zeykala did. My guess is she cut you out of the loop on that decision because you never would have supported it. Am I wrong?"

Virtari doesn't respond, and he doesn't have to. The BCS doesn't believe in negotiating. There is no doubt he would have paid the steep price to eliminate Liberteum by storming this mansion. That action would have horrified executives who dedicate their careers to placating patricians. It would have caused the BCS irreparable harm.

"America Incorporated is under corporate law, meaning you're responsible for everything that happens in this sphere of influence," the patrician continues. "An attack on my compound will spell your end. Of course, I'm sure that will make Zeykala very happy."

"Don't for an instant think she's calling the shots," Virtari sneers. "If the board takes administrative action on her, she won't even be CEO for much longer."

Denali fights to hide his surprise and stifle the resulting smile. That's news to him. Virtari should never have divulged that and could be lying. But, if it's the truth, it could impact his plan in unforeseen ways. He files that away in the back of his mind for later.

"Let me be straight with you," Denali says, shifting to another tactic. "I don't know what happened during the hand-off or how my son is involved. What I do know is where Michele and her Liberteum terrorists are likely going."

"How would you know that?"

"They were in my custody, remember? I was listening to their conversations."

Surveillance is pervasive in modern society. It also makes disinformation believable. Denali's lie provides a convenient cover for how he really learned Valhalla's location. Farron's involvement with Liberteum must remain a secret for as long as possible. He's making that challenging enough with his antics.

"Where?" Virtari demands, likely expecting Denali to withhold that information until a concession is made. Not this time.

"St. Patrick's Cathedral. They have a stronghold either in the church or an access that leads to it from there."

"You're lying. We've combed through that building countless times. There's nothing there."

"Then I suggest you search it again, Director. Do it more *carefully* this time. Perhaps the cardinal can help. He has been in league with the terrorists for years."

The director's gears are turning. For a man who lies for a living, he is remarkably easy to read. Denali is keenly aware that he may have sacrificed his son by relaying that information. The young man made his decision, and that may be one of the consequences. The fallout of his relationship with Liberteum won't matter in a few days.

"Even if we find them there, it doesn't square things between us, Denali."

Virtari disconnects the VidLynk in another serious breach of protocol. It doesn't matter. Dealing with the BCS's insolent director is a small price to pay to get what was needed. By the time they're done chasing Liberteum in Manhattan, it will be too late for Virtari, Zeykala, and the rest of the corporations to stop what's coming.

Denali turns to Abbot, who is patiently standing against the back wall. "Get a message to the Baroness. Tell her I need to know what the hell is going on down in Washington. If Zeykala is about to be replaced, I should have known about it."

CHAPTER FORTY-TWO

LIBERTEUM

St. Patrick's Cathedral
Midtown Geographic Area
New York City Municipal Corporation

The trek south on Fifth Avenue was a stroll down memory lane. Zyree was running for his life on this very street only a couple of days ago. So much has changed since then, making the shootout with Chief Inspector Chiana and the BCS feel like a lifetime ago.

"We're here," Michele says, turning to their PSS escorts and thanking them.

Zyree looks up at the ornate stonework on the hulking front of one of the world's most prominent cathedrals. Rykos smirks at him. It must have been killing the kid to keep this secret.

"You've got to be kidding me. Liberteum's base of operations is in another church?"

"Sort of," Michele says with a mischievous smile, walking up the short stairs leading to the center set of large oak doors.

They enter the narthex and proceed into the nave via another set of doors. The sanctuary is splendid, with high arches creating a cavernous space filled with natural light from the windows above. The group walks down the center aisle before being greeted by the magnificently dressed Cardinal Michael Castellano.

"Hello, Emissary."

"Michele! I'm so happy to see you well, my child," he says, giving her a warm embrace. "And Rykos, you're looking much better than you did the last time I saw you."

"Thank you, Your Eminence. I feel much better."

"And Farron Keating…I did not expect to see you back here."

"There is much to explain, Your Eminence," Farron says, acting as contrite as anyone has ever seen him.

"Yes, I'm sure there is. Koltayne," he says with a nod, getting a shy one in return. "I'm afraid I don't know your other guests."

"Emissary, this is Zyree, a former chief inspector with Intercorpex."

"Ah, yes, the fugitive who created quite a stir in this area. I'm happy to see you were spared from the unfortunate fate the authorities had planned for you."

"Me too," Zyree says, still a little in awe of these recent developments.

"And this is Fiolla, a former executive from the White House." The cardinal gives Michele a puzzled glance before turning his attention back to the redhead dressed in the loose orange garb. "We live in strange times, Your Eminence," she says.

"Indeed, we do. It is very nice to meet you, Fiolla."

"How are you doing, Emissary?" Michele asks, placing a hand on his shoulder.

"The quli uprising in the city has given me many souls to pray for. I ask the Lord for peace, but fear there will be much more violence before He answers that prayer."

"I'm afraid you may be right."

"In the meantime, I'm pleased to inform you that there have been no security agents snooping around of late. Valhalla is very much secure."

"That's good, but I don't think it will last. I fear we are placing you in grave danger."

"I do the Lord's work, Michele. If His will is that I must sacrifice my life, He will call me home when my work on this Earth is done. I know you are eager to retreat to Valhalla, but someone here has insisted on seeing you. Please follow me."

Zyree and Michele share an apprehensive look. Few people know about Valhalla, and the qulis would have greeted them with the cardinal. Even more concerning is that nobody is supposed to know they're here.

They move past the high altar and transept into the chapel at the rear of the sanctuary. Michele takes tenuous steps as they travel along the curved wall. Zyree takes a deep breath, preparing for the unexpected. He isn't prepared enough to see a man in an exoskeleton admiring a statue of the Virgin Mary.

"He insisted I bring you to him when you arrived. He's annoyingly persistent."

"Ortan? I thought you were dead!" Zyree exclaims, brushing past Michele and the Emissary to embrace him.

"The news of my death has been greatly exaggerated."

"Mark Twain," Michele says, earning a knowing smile.

"I knew there was a reason I liked this girl," he says. "It's a pleasure to finally meet you in person. You're even lovelier than you are on a display."

Ortan blushes a little after paying the compliment, causing Zyree to smirk. Being a recluse in a windowless data center on a sparsely populated island would make anybody socially awkward. He must like her. Ortan's not the warm and fuzzy type.

"Thank you. That's very sweet of you to say."

"How did you…I mean, you said that security was coming for you, and I heard there was an explosion at the data center."

"They did come for me, and there was an explosion. Fortunately, I anticipated the former and planned the latter. The hardest part was getting to New York. I was forced to use non-standard transportation to cross the Atlantic and sneak into the city undetected."

"Non-standard?" Rykos asks.

"Some of my clothing may smell like swordfish."

The pungent smell aside, seeing Ortan opens up new possibilities. The man has unequaled access to information. With him in the fold, maybe they can finally get some answers about what's happening around the world.

"Do you know what's going on with Denali Keating?" Zyree asks.

Ortan glances at Farron. "I've been in the dark since leaving Iceland. I didn't even know that America Incorporated was losing control of its cities until I arrived to find a dock full of angry longshoremen."

"We'll get you caught up when we reach Valhalla," Michele says.

"I'm ready when you are," Ortan says, lifting a suitcase-sized valise that was resting next to him.

"What's that?" Rykos asks.

"My clean underwear."

Zyree doesn't take that at face value but knows not to press for the real answer. It's likely some techno-wizardry that Ortan packed for emergencies.

"The entrance is uncovered. I will secure it once you begin your descent."

"Thank you, Emissary," Michele says.

"Descent?" Zyree asks, figuring their hideout was underground without thinking about how deep.

"Valhalla refers to the place where half of those who die in combat are guided by Valkyries to continue their service of Odin in the Einherjar. This stronghold is accessed via a long spiral staircase," Ortan adds, using a matter of fact tone that causes Rykos, Farron, and Michele to look at each other in a mix of amazement and concern. "I have chosen to call it the 'Stairway to Heaven.'"

"Let's hope not," Zyree mumbles under his breath.

CHAPTER FORTY-THREE

RYKOS

St. Patrick's Cathedral
Midtown Geographic Area
New York City Municipal Corporation

I stop short of the entrance to the Archbishop's Sacristy. The desk has been slid over to the vestment cabinet from the center of the room and the carpet is pulled back. The well-disguised mosaic tile entrance to Valhalla has already been opened. Koltayne disappears into the darkness and Zyree is helping Ortan manipulate his exoskeleton to get a feel for the ladder that leads into the void at the top of the "Stairway to Heaven," as Ortan coined it.

"What's wrong, Rykos?" Michele asks, noticing my reluctance.

"I'm not going with you." That was harder to say than I thought it would be. This isn't an easy decision, but one I was sure about until the time came to tell her.

"What do you mean?" she asks, walking over to me.

"I can't go with you."

"I don't understand."

I guide Michele away from the cardinal's changing room and office. The last thing I need is everyone offering reasons why I shouldn't go. Convincing Michele that this is the right decision will be hard enough.

"I don't know how to explain this, so I'll say it plainly. I'm going to One Guardian Plaza to meet my mother."

"You're leaving me?"

The wounded tone in her voice hurts me. "It's not like that."

"Then tell me what it's like."

"You can't fight the BCS and Denali Keating at the same time. You need help, and I'm going to secure some for you. There's an opportunity to work with my mother, the PSS, and the qulis. I need to be there to broker that arrangement."

"You can do that from here."

"Maybe, but there's another mission you gave me. The time has come to start the process."

Michele lowers her eyes. She may be regretting having told me why I was taken after that raid on the urch rave. She wanted me to be the face of Liberteum back then and needs me to be it now more than ever.

"Rykos, a lot has changed since then. You don't need to convince the people anymore. We lost the chance of earning their support when Haven leveled Intercorpex."

I shake my head. "I don't believe that, and I don't think you do, either. We *need* the people's support. If we have lost it, I'm the best person to help earn it back."

She looks away from me, not wanting to accept this. I'm not finding this any easier. We have come a long way since I was her prisoner on Broad Street.

"There has to be a way that doesn't require you to leave me here by myself."

"Zyree can keep you safer than I can. You also have Ortan and Fiolla, along with the rest of Liberteum. You aren't alone, Michele."

She grabs my hands and holds them. When she lifts her head, I can see the tears forming in the corners of her eyes. I've never known her to be weepy about anything. She wasn't this emotional after losing her father or after my father shot me. I'm at a loss for what to do. I know what the moment demands, but I'm afraid of making a mistake.

"That's not why I don't want you to leave."

Caught up in the moment, she reaches up and kisses me. Our lips press together softly, and it's…wonderful. She pulls away slightly, only to begin again more aggressively.

I pull her closer as the dam holding back our feelings crumbles. What started out for me as a crush has become much more. Michele isn't an object to conquer and hasn't been one for a long time now. She's a woman I want to be with for all the right reasons. It explains why I don't feel guilty about kissing her so passionately in a church. It's also what makes this decision to leave so difficult.

We finally separate, and she hangs her head. I lift it gently and find myself staring into her watery eyes. I see pain, desperation, and fear…but also a glimmer of hope and promise of things to come. She's the strongest woman I have ever met, but also the most complex.

I wipe away a tear as it begins a slow roll down her cheek. She's right. A lot has changed. The world has changed, and so have I.

"Stay. Please," Michele pleads.

"Leaving is the last thing I want to do. But if I'm being given a choice between spending my final days hiding in a subterranean cave and helping you fight to make this a better world that we can grow old in together, I choose the latter."

"There are no certainties that any of us will survive to see a better world, Rykos."

"You knew that when you launched Archimedes. You pressed forward anyway. Now, I'm as invested in it as you are. A lot of people are. Let's finish this amazing thing you started, and what happens, happens."

She nods, albeit with a great deal of reservation. Something in my peripheral vision catches my eye and I notice Fiolla watching quietly from just inside the sacristy. I guess our private moment wasn't as private as I thought.

I start to leave, holding onto Michele's hand until our arms stretch to the point where they can no longer keep contact. My heart aches, but I won't be deterred. I will be with Michele again, in this life or the afterlife. Whichever world it ends up being, it will be far better than the one we find ourselves saying goodbye in.

CHAPTER FORTY-FOUR

LIBERTEUM

St. Patrick's Cathedral
Midtown Geographic Area
New York City Municipal Corporation

Fiolla just witnessed love in its rawest form. Two people with obvious feelings for each other finally set their vulnerabilities aside and let the walls keeping them apart come crashing down. It's something she's always longed for. More important to her than a career or lofty executive position was someone to share her life with.

That person was going to be Farron. Trust is the bedrock that any relationship is built on. It was a challenge since he was a patrician and she was an executive. After all the deceit, trusting him will never be a reality. It doesn't matter that he saved her life. There will never be a happy ending that includes Farron Keating in the picture.

Fiolla retreats to the sacristy after watching Rykos walk back up the aisle. She patiently waits for Michele to return. When she does, it's in a desperate struggle to hold back her tears.

"Are you okay?"

"I'm fine," she says, her voice cracking. "Where's Farron?"

"He already went down."

Michele nods at Fiolla. "Okay, are you ready?"

"Am I your hostage, or am I free to leave?"

It's not an unwarranted question. Fiolla has only recently regained her senses. She was completely numb during the rescue and was only beginning to regain control of herself during the trip to Manhattan. She has been with this group by default. She has no idea if she is free to leave them.

"You're not a prisoner, Fiolla. You are welcome to stay with us, but I won't try to convince you. The men down there believe in something deeply and know they're risking their lives for it. I won't ask you to do the same."

"Do you want me to stay?"

"Only if it's for the right reasons. But if you do decide to go, make sure it's because you want to, not because you're running away."

She doesn't need to elaborate on what she'd be running from. Everyone recognizes the tension between her and Farron. Their problems will only be exacerbated in the cozy confines of their subterranean base.

"I feel like I'm suffocating around Farron. I have a lot of conflicting emotions. Some distance between us may help me figure things out."

Michele sighs and presses her lips together. "Distance can be overrated."

"You've never been in love before, have you?"

Michele doesn't answer, but she doesn't have to. Her body language speaks volumes. She's fallen for Rykos despite how hard Fiolla thinks she's fought it. The pair reminds her a little of Romeo and Juliet: two people from different worlds brought together amidst chaos and forced to leave each other with only the hope of being together again someday. There's even a member of the clergy involved in that story. She hopes it ends better for Rykos and Michele than it did for their literary counterparts.

"I don't have much experience with relationships. I also can't imagine what you've been through these past couple of days. Yet, here you are. You have a resilience that reminds me of Freya."

"Who's Freya?"

"She was a very close friend of mine," Michele says, staring off down and left and smiling slightly as if recalling a good memory. "She took the task of hacking public safety's EOC during the first attack on Intercorpex. It was a dangerous mission with a low probability of survival, but she insisted on being the one to do it. The PSS captured and killed her. She sacrificed herself for all of us and the cause, but I miss my friend. You have her strength."

Fiolla is only beginning to comprehend the depth and breadth of Michele's pain. She has endured so much. A bond is growing between them, but that will only make things harder later. She looks toward the open door and the cavernous sanctuary beyond it.

"It's not safe for you anywhere, including with us," Michele concludes, moving to the heavy stone doorway that leads to their hideout. "I can't guarantee your safety. I also can't fix the broken heart Farron left you with, but I do know that distance won't resolve that either. If you decide to stay, I can only promise that we'll deal with them together."

There is sincerity in her voice, her words, and her eyes. It's rare to see that down in Washington. It's a city where most people talk, fewer listen, and nobody means what they say. Fiolla looks toward the door once more and then back at Michele.

"The decision is yours, Fiolla, but you have to make it now."

CHAPTER FORTY-FIVE

NYCMC RESISTANCE

One Guardian Plaza
Lower Manhattan Geographic District
New York City Municipal Corporation

America Tower is a corporate nerve center and a valuable piece of real estate. Because of its height, there isn't a place in this city they can't monitor with the right optics and sensors. Not wanting to bother the guardians in the RTCC, Ilaria found an open workstation to monitor the BCS agents deployed around the gleaming skyscraper. There is an ulterior motive…it's also where she thinks her daughter may be hiding out.

Dzamko is nowhere to be found. One of the guardians huddled around the holographic generator at the front of the RTCC said he stepped out to deal with an issue on the perimeter. He didn't indicate it was anything that serious, but there was something strange in the way he answered the question.

Her concerns subside when he strides back into the room with a purpose. It's not a loud entrance, but it is a commanding one. Every set of eyes follows him through the center of the oval as he approaches Ilaria.

"What's wrong?" She was almost afraid to ask that question, and her heart beats wildly in anticipation of the response.

"I have good news and bad news, ma'am. The bad news is that we had an infiltration of our perimeter that's been handled."

"Okay…what's the good news?"

"We can officially close out one of our missing person reports."

The mischievous smile he flashes her is disconcerting. Dzamko doesn't play games like this. He nods over his shoulder toward the door just as Rykos walks in. Ilaria's heart leaps. She runs around the workstation and through the oval to hug him. It's been too long since she got to do this. She doesn't want to let him go, so she doesn't.

"Mother, this is starting to get a little embarrassing," Rykos says as the embrace drags on.

"There's nothing you need to be here for, Ilaria," Dzamko says as she holds her son's face in her hands. "Go spend some time with Rykos. I'll summon you if anything important happens."

"Thank you."

They make coffee in a small break room and relocate to comfortable sofas in a lounge a couple of floors below the RTCC. They have a lot to catch up on. Rykos recounts the story about finding Michele, running from Chief Inspector Zyree, the firefight at the crypt, and what he remembers from the showdown at New York University. His account of the running gunfight in Manhattan and subsequent incarceration at the Keating Estate is equally compelling.

Ilaria doesn't say much. She's amazed and thankful he's still alive.

"You've lived a lifetime since I last saw you."

"I hope not. It was close to being cut short too many times already."

There's a big difference between the boy she sent off to rescue his father and the man sitting across from her now. Ilaria always wondered if someone could grow this much as a person in such a short time. The question is now answered. There's passion and determination in Rykos's eyes that he never displayed as a registrant at Dinsmore Academy.

"Teman told me from his hospital bed that he shot you."

"In Father's defense, Haven scrambled his mind. I don't think he knew what he was doing."

Ilaria cocks her head. "It's a little weird to hear you defend him."

"It wasn't a pleasant reunion, but he was being tortured by a sadistic maniac. I had to forgive him."

"You said this man…Haven…did it? And that he's the member of Liberteum who blew up the patrician meeting at Intercorpex?"

"Ex-member. Haven never believed in Michele or her cause. He was a psychopath bent on revenge, pure and simple. Her father kept him under control, but once he was killed during the Broad Street raid, the dog was let off the leash. Michele told me when I was recovering that he killed employees for sport during his escape from Old St. Patrick's and almost wiped out a SpeedRail full of people. That was all before he detonated his bomb at Intercorpex. I wasn't sad to hear Zyree killed him."

"The BCS killed Haven," Ilaria says, shaking her head. "We were told Zyree was working with him."

Rykos smirks. "That's not how it happened. You didn't become the rebellious CEO of this city by believing the parent company's narrative."

"Touché."

He's right. Ilaria has learned not to believe anything she sees on AME News or explanations uttered by the executives in Washington. Maybe Rykos is brainwashed…or, more likely, everyone else is.

"How exactly did you become CEO, anyway?"

Ilaria shares her own long, sordid story. He listens intently about the events following the bombing, the killing of the BCS agents at the protest, the fight to save his father, and her subsequent capture and rescue. She doesn't hold back about how she feels about corporate security or the men who serve in it.

"It sounds like we have a common enemy," Rykos says, sipping his coffee.

"That's the same thing I told the qulis in Astor Park."

"That seems to have worked out well."

Ilaria presses her lips together and shakes her head slightly. "They weren't terrorists."

"No, but the qulis have worked with Liberteum for years. They built Valhalla."

"Valhalla?"

"Liberteum's operations center."

"They have an operations center?"

He nods. Another of her preconceptions is shattered. She imagined them living in filth and squalor in some subbasement somewhere because that has always been the corporate narrative. To characterize their base as an "operations center" is jarring. That's a feeling Ilaria is starting to get used to.

"Is that why you're here? You want me to work with Liberteum?"

Rykos leans back into the sofa. "You're the CEO of the NYCMC, Mother. That choice is yours. I'm here to make introductions. Understanding the truth about Liberteum and its goals will help you make an informed decision."

"Truth," Ilaria muses. "There may be nothing more elusive on this planet. I know what Phylep has said about Michele and what you've told me, but I'm still not comfortable with the idea of working with them."

"First, we try, then we trust."

"Okay. How can I reach Liberteum?"

"You can't. Michele will contact us. You only need to decide if you're willing to answer the call."

CHAPTER FORTY-SIX

AMERICA, INC.

The White House
Corporate Governance District
Washington-Arlington Municipal Corporation

Stress has been a by-product of the business world since before the Industrial Age. Employers seeking efficiency and productivity push employees to their breaking point. This relentless grind for more takes a mental and physical toll. From its earliest days, America Incorporated invested in medical advances to relieve symptoms of stress and fatigue to maintain employee health. Relief comes in the bottle of capsules sitting on Zeykala's desk.

She pops two pills into her mouth and swallows them down with some water. The effect won't be as immediate as an injection, but considering she was almost assassinated three hours ago, the CEO doesn't trust anyone to come near her with a needle.

This is the first real breather she's had since returning to the White House. It's been one fire to douse after another. Corporations are falling apart, and now rumors about overseas attacks are circulating. The growing instability around the globe is unprecedented, at least in this era.

The BCS hasn't provided any answers about what happened in Maryland. The only plausible explanation for their silence is that investigators are dragging their feet. They don't want her to know the truth, and that makes them complicit in the assassination attempt.

Zeykala turns her attention to the AME News coverage. The reporting has changed since the last time she paid attention. Her eyes narrow.

"Reports of violence across the sphere of influence are inundating public safety officials," an on scene reporter says into the camera. "Even the BCS, with their expertise and resources, is struggling to stifle the violent attacks from these riotous laborers."

The broadcast cuts over to a surveillance recording of some anonymous street. What plays next is more graphic than anything ever witnessed on this network.

"In this disturbing video obtained by AME News, a gang of quli thugs viciously attacks a group of employees trying to return to their waiting families after making a trip out for food. Unfortunately, Los Angeles isn't the only city suffering from unprecedented levels of violence, and all this is happening despite the CEO's recent declaration of corporate law. Reporting live from Los Angeles—"

"Get Jenizee in my office right now!" Zeykala commands her automated office assistant.

This report isn't designed to sway employee opinion – it's meant to convince the board to remove her. Zeykala seethes as she waits for the public relations liaison's arrival. Two minutes later, the doors swing open, and the frazzled woman rushes in.

"What the hell is AME News reporting?" Zeykala asks, standing and pointing at one of the displays on the wall.

"I saw it too, ma'am. I was in the middle of drafting a report," Jenizee says, hoping to placate her.

"You're writing a report? The Oval Office is two hundred feet from where you work! Why are they reporting this? I left specific instructions about what I wanted broadcasted."

"The chief editor received a new directive about coverage from Director Virtari."

It's just as she thought. Virtari's murder attempt failed, so now he's moving on to character assassination. Zeykala exhales sharply. If he wants a war, that's what he'll get.

"I want this garbage removed from the airwaves immediately."

The liaison hangs her head. "I'm afraid I can't issue that order, ma'am. We're under corporate law. Media control falls to the Director—"

"Of the Bureau of Corporate Security. I got it. You're dismissed, Jenizee." The woman scurries out, and Zeykala folds her arms as she contemplates her next move. Despite Virtari's powers under corporate law, this breach of trust cannot go unchecked. "Contact the New York City Public Safety and Security Emergency Operations Center."

The VidLynk is established within seconds, and an agent's face fills the screen. "Yes, ma'am?"

"Get me Director Virtari."

"I'm afraid he's not in the facility, ma'am. He's overseeing our troop mobilizations across the river. I can forward this VidLynk to his tablet."

Zeykala nods, too angry to speak. His absence should dispel any notion that he's taking a personal interest in the assassination attempt investigation. That makes sense, considering he's likely behind it.

"Uh, I'm sorry…his tablet is not accepting VidLynk requests."

The CEO disconnects in anger. It takes brass balls to refuse contact from the Oval Office. They reached an accord long ago that cooperation was in both of their interests. Now that Virtari has tasted power, he wants her gone and has made a new enemy today because of it. Zeykala didn't rise to this position by being passive. The BCS director is about to find that out the hard way. If he wants to terminate their arrangement, he'll face the consequences.

CHAPTER FORTY-SEVEN

LIBERTEUM

Valhalla
Midtown Geographic Area
New York City Municipal Corporation

Intercorpex security personnel are trained in techniques to combat sleep deprivation. To Liberteum's credit, they do just fine without any training. Zyree chalks that up to motivation and a sense of purpose. But the adrenaline high from the rescue and trip to Valhalla is finally waning, and everyone eventually needs rest. This is the calm before the storm, so now is the time.

"We will set up Fiolla in the main bedroom," Michele says to Zyree after returning to the main operations center from the quarters. "There's a bunk room farther down the hall on the right if you need to crash. We should sleep if we can."

"There's something we need to discuss with you first," Adiz says in his usual whiny voice as he stands from his terminal. "This cyborg really thinks I'm going to give him access to OdinNet. It's never gonna happen."

"You guys named your network OdinNet?" Ortan asks with a dramatic mock laugh. Adiz tries not to look offended and fails.

"It wasn't my idea," Jasper mumbles under his breath.

"When did that become your decision to make, Adiz?" Michele asks.

Adiz has been an invaluable asset to Liberteum since joining them. He refined the plan to disrupt communications and tap the wire to steal the login information. They never would have gotten this far without him.

The downside is his propensity to be a pain in the ass. He knows he's overstepped his bounds but isn't intent on apologizing. His face contorts into a cartoonish mix of confusion and anger as Michele stares at him impassively.

"You can't possibly be considering this! We have to safeguard the integrity of the network."

"If I remember correctly, Ortan compromised our firewall with ease a few days ago. If he wanted to do it again, I don't think there's much we could do to stop him."

"There's nothing to be gained by his involvement."

"Everything is to be gained," Zyree chimes in. "Neither of us has earned your trust yet, but Ortan is an invaluable resource, a good friend, and you're lucky to have him here."

"I wouldn't have let you within a mile of this place if I was in charge!"

The leader of Liberteum folds her arms. "And that's why you're not in charge."

"Michele, be reasonable," Adiz pleads. "He could compromise everything."

Zyree studies her as she considers both sides of the argument. That's the trait of an excellent leader. Michele is guarded, and rightfully so. This facility didn't remain a secret because she was cavalier with information about its existence. But she is also open to new possibilities.

"What do you think, Jasper?"

"He's with me," Adiz snaps.

"Is your name Jasper?"

The senior hacker fumes at the admonishment but holds his tongue as all eyes turn to the junior colleague.

"Ortan should only be allowed network access while one of us is present. Otherwise, I have no objection."

"This is ridiculous! He's our enemy! He worked for the very exchange we fought to bring down. Friends died making that a reality, including Freya."

"You won't score any points by invoking her name, Adiz. She was my friend…and she despised *you*."

"I understand your reservations," Ortan says, punctuating the tense silence. "I'd be equally apprehensive if our roles were reversed. But I trusted you to help my only friend. I'm asking you to trust me to help you in return."

Ortan's simple, heartfelt words have the desired effect. "Give him administrative rights to the network, Adiz."

"You're going to get us all killed."

Michele quickly grabs the hacker by the throat and squeezes. Despite being taller and stronger than she is, Adiz has no luck breaking her grip. The more he flails, the tighter she squeezes. She moves her face close to his but says nothing until he ends his resistance.

"I was always told urches were too slow and stupid to make it in the real world," Fiolla whispers in Zyree's ear. "She's neither."

"I made the same assumptions. I've reevaluated all of them in the short time I've known Michele."

"You work for me, Adiz," Michele says with steel in her voice and fire in her eyes. "I value your opinion, but never undermine me. If you can't accept my decisions, I will lock you in the bunk room. Nod if you understand."

Adiz complies, and she releases her grip.

"Fine," he says with a rasp to his voice after fighting to recover his breathing, "but I'm going to watch every move this freak makes."

Adiz storms off back to his terminal, rubbing his throat. She watches him go with a shake of her head. Zyree isn't sure if it's out of disgust, anger, or disappointment. Maybe it's all three.

"I apologize for that."

"What's his problem?" Ortan asks. "Did he not get enough attention from his mother growing up?"

"It's as good a theory as any," Michele says, eyeballing him across the room before turning and placing a hand on Ortan's face. "I'm trusting you. Please don't betray that trust. The last couple of days have been hard enough."

Michele and Fiolla walk out of the operations center toward the bunk rooms and small kitchen. Ortan looks as if he's going to melt. Whether Michele did it intentionally, the affectionate touch just earned her a friend for life.

"Rykos is going to be jealous," Zyree chides.

"She must really like you," Jasper adds.

"Why do you say that?"

"She didn't threaten to kill you. Come on, I'll help you plug in."

Ortan hefts the aluminum suitcase he was carrying onto the counter. Glancing at a curious Jasper, he disengages the latches and opens the lid. The hacker's mouth drops open. Even non-techie Zyree raises his eyebrows in surprise. It's definitely not a case full of clean underwear.

"My God, look at this thing. Is that all RAM?" Jasper asks, pointing.

"The latest prototypes, as are these solid-state drives."

"There has to be more computing power in there than our whole network," he admits.

Ortan scoffs. "There's enough computing power, storage, and memory in here to run Intercorpex."

"Uh, is this what I think it is?" Zyree asks, leaning in for a closer look.

"Elves don't travel outside of Iceland, Zyree. This hardware supports the advanced decryption algorithms I created."

"What sort of algorithms require that much storage and power?" Adiz sneers from across the room.

"Good ones."

Ortan hands Jasper a fiber cable that he dutifully connects to a switch that routes the traffic between workstations. He sits down and cracks his knuckles before typing in some commands. Zyree checks the clock on the wall. It's a few minutes shy of six, and he's wondering if the BCS dare try a nighttime assault.

"How long will it take for you to get set up?"

"Are you in a rush, Zyree?"

"To die, no. To know what's going on in the EOC? That's another story. Can you find out what the BCS is up to?"

"It's a heavily encrypted network," Jasper warns. "We had to send somebody on-site to access it. You won't get in."

"Oh, I'll get in."

"Yeah, right," Adiz mumbles from his workstation.

Ortan rolls his eyes and starts working his magic. Zyree leans in, and he stops typing. "This won't go any faster with you looking over my shoulder. Go play with Fiolla or something."

Zyree grimaces and pats him on the shoulder. "I'm going to forget you said that."

CHAPTER FORTY-EIGHT

AMERICA, INC.

Titan Executive Airfield
Meadowlands Geographic Area
Bergen Municipal Corporation

The armored trucks halt in front of a row of hangars at the Titan Executive Airfield located across the river from Manhattan. Despite the aggressive warnings from agents manning the EOC that it was too dangerous for Virtari to leave the command post, the trip was uneventful. All is lost if he can't travel to New Jersey through corporate-controlled territory without fear of attack.

"Director Virtari! Welcome, sir," Agent-in-Charge Arnauld says from the entrance. "I'm pleased to report that our preparations are on schedule. If you'll follow me, I can show you what we're working on."

The director nods, and they enter a small office area in the hangar that is buzzing with activity. Ilaria and her band of misfits kicked over the hive, and these men are itching for payback. He's never seen a more focused and motivated group of people.

"I see you had no trouble procuring the required space."

"Nobody flies while we're under corporate law. The current tenants were more than happy to lend us their space and moved the corporate jets onto the tarmac so we could utilize the hangar lighting to complete our tasks."

"Show me."

Arnauld walks around the long counter that serves as a passenger check-in area and down a light gray corridor that leads to a set of steel doors.

"Are the ground unit commanders here yet?"

"No, sir, but they should be momentarily."

Arnauld swipes his biojack over a scanner. The set of double doors leading to the main hangar swings open. Virtari's eyes adjust to the bright light of the cavernous space and his head bobs in appreciative nods. He expects the sight before him, but it's still impressive.

Rows of drones brought over from public safety's Queens Air Operations Center are being overhauled by an army of technicians. Three rows are complete, with subsequent rows of drones in various states of disassembly.

"You've made significant progress in the short time allotted. These drones don't look very intimidating, though."

"PSS drones are meant to be surveillance platforms. It's been a challenge turning them into weapons systems. Eighty percent will be retrofitted to carry at least some armaments by morning. They won't win any design contests, but they'll be deadly."

"And the other twenty percent?"

"They'll be tasked with target acquisition for the others. We're updating their core processors and operating software, along with installing more robust transmitters for communications. They can identify threats, acquire targets, and execute attacks with minimal human intervention."

"Can the PSS regain control of them?"

"No, sir. They're designed to operate on a closed network. Commands are transmitted via a secure channel from the EOC. Even if the uplink is somehow compromised, the encrypted command key is uncrackable. These are serviceable, but let me show you the muscle."

They exit the hangar and walk over toward the adjacent one. Identical to the previous structure, this one houses the modern BCS drone fleet. Virtari has never seen so many of them in one place.

He traces his hand over one of the behemoth quadcopters and admires the subdued America Incorporated and BCS logos on each side of the flat black fuselage. The front of this thing is all business, bristling with four machine guns and two grenade launchers. It's a flying mass murderer, and he's about to unleash it.

"What's this?" he asks, pointing to a set of scales painted on the camera's visor.

"Oh, that…it's an inside joke, sir," Arnauld sheepishly says. "When He broke the third seal, I heard the third living creature saying, 'Come.' I looked, and behold, a black horse, and he who sat on it had a pair of scales in his hand. It's from the Book of Revelation."

"The Third Horseman of the Apocalypse. It's fitting. I like it."

Arnauld is visibly relieved. "We've used these drones in the past to secure events and protect cargo vessels against piracy. They've never been this heavily armed."

"Will that affect their loiter time?"

"Unfortunately. The weight of this ammunition is an issue. These drones will require frequent recharging and rearming during operations."

"I hope you don't intend to bring them all the way back here to do that," Virtari says, concern dripping in his tone.

"Only drones that are damaged or lose signal will return to base. We have mobile supply depots that will trail the vanguard to rearm and charge the drones. That should cut turnaround time by more than half."

"Excellent. Now show me the crown jewels."

They move to the next hangar. As impressive as the last two were, nothing compares to the four gleaming white aircraft housed there. The BCS has maintained and upgraded these antiques for years. It wasn't easy keeping the executives in Washington in the dark at budget time, but the result is worth the effort.

The design is based on an MQ-9 Reaper. The corporation destroyed the former U.S. Air Force's most advanced drone fleet after the collapse, but they forgot about the ones in mothballs. Intercorpex frowns upon these weapons, but desperate times call for desperate measures. The decision to keep these available for emergencies showed incredible foresight.

"We've updated the communications gear, targeting system, and engine with modern technology. The aluminum skin was swapped for carbon fiber to make the craft lighter and able to carry more cargo. And by cargo, I mean death. We armed them with Hellfire missiles, Paveway Two laser-guided bombs, and Joint Direct Attack Munitions we pulled from the weapons stockpile. The best part is that the Reapers will operate at higher altitudes, so there is no direct threat to them from the ground."

"You have to love pre-collapse technology. They sure knew how to kill each other back then," Virtari gushes. "Do they require operators?"

"No, sir, they're fully autonomous. Ground personnel can prioritize targets based on real-world intelligence, but this thing will seek and destroy anything it's instructed to."

The agents in charge of the ground operation arrive, and introductions are made. He knows Bruzik and Flandyr but not well. Rarely does the BCS ever mobilize for an operation of this size.

"I called you here to issue this directive personally to ensure there is no ambiguity. You will relay it to your men and enforce it at all costs. Understood?"

"Yes, sir."

"Good. From this point forward, the use of deadly force is not only authorized but expected. Anyone on the streets of Manhattan who is not wearing our uniform is a target. Employees have been directed to stay in their domiciles. If they're out on the streets for any reason, they'll regret not listening. No explanations, no quarter, and no mercy."

"This includes the PSS?"

"Our enemies are clever, Flandyr. Terrorists donned BCS uniforms to gain access to Intercorpex with a truckload of explosives. The qulis likely have access to

PSS uniforms and may use them to wreak havoc. No defection of PSS personnel is permitted. If guardians try to surrender, shoot them anyway."

"And the contingent that secured Grand Central Terminus for us? I hear Captain Freyker has been supportive of our efforts."

Virtari grimaces, having forgotten about them. The first to respond to the shootout in the train station following the bombing of Intercorpex's headquarters, they have held that ground while pledging their allegiance to the BCS. When push comes to shove, will they be willing to place that loyalty over their fellow guardians?

"Bruzik, when your column reaches Grand Central, dispatch a couple of squads to round up the guardians and take them to a secure location. Then, thank them for their service and execute them."

"Yes, sir."

Virtari needs men who follow his orders. This is no time for second-guessing or half-measures. He studies their faces for signs of dissent and finds none.

"Gentlemen, we are in the middle of a struggle for the future. The fate of our corporation is at stake. Whether this rebellion is a footnote in history or something more rests on your shoulders. Failure is not an option. The operation commences at zero-seven hundred tomorrow. Ensure your men are ready."

CHAPTER FORTY-NINE

THE PATRICIANS

Keating Family of the Gentez-Majorez Estate
Greenwich Geographic District
Southern Connecticut Municipal Corporation

The Crucible is one of Denali's favorite rooms in the mansion. It earned its moniker after establishing The Trust and setting up these holographic meetings. A "crucible" is a ceramic or metal container used for melting metals at very high temperatures. It also can refer to a place where diverse elements interact to create something new. It was for that second definition that he chose the name.

The Trust is going to reshape the world. It took considerable persuasion to bring its members to the table and it will require even more to keep them there. It's a challenge Denali is simultaneously welcoming and loathing. His peers may not know it yet, but their names will be whispered in awe and reverence by future generations.

The Crucible is meticulously decorated in a medieval theme. A large, working stone fireplace with a wood beam mantel and hearth dominates the far wall. The window is covered in a large, ornate curtain, and authentic tapestries drape the walls. Replica broad swords, shields, maces, and morning stars hang between them. There is even a stand for halberds and lances in the corners.

Sconces, pedestal candles, and an antique chandelier suspended from the rafters of the vaulted ceiling provide the lighting. There are few trappings of modern technology in the room, save one.

Several holographic images are already present around the rectangular table. Despite the blue hues the members are manifested in, this technology offers a superior personal touch that VidLynks can't offer. It *feels* like they are in the room.

Denali sits and waits patiently, knowing his hologram is present in each of the twenty members' estates. Elites express impatience with everyone except other patricians. Offending his peers is counterproductive to his mission, and he speaks to call the meeting to order only when the other patrician families join.

"Denali, I assume you called this meeting to discuss the attacks happening around the world," Quinlin Wexler says, firing the opening shot.

"I don't want to spend our precious time discussing them, Quinlin. These are troubling times, and I want to act to prevent a calamity. It's time we consolidate our forces and deploy them to combat corporate instability. The elites acted too late to prevent governments from falling. I don't wish to see history repeat itself."

"The calamity you speak of is of your making," Reagul Madera sneers. "Even America Incorporated is struggling to maintain power because of it. You were only supposed to weaken them. Instead, the sphere of influence is on the verge of wholesale revolution."

"You're overstating the capabilities of the qulis."

Reagul grins. "Or you're understating them."

"The Trust was created to enhance the power of select families of the gentez-majorez, not neuter the corporations that enrich us," Maddizain McMillan adds, piling on more dissent in her high-pitched voice.

"You don't need to remind me why I created The Trust. You were all brought in with the full understanding of what would need to happen before our dream was realized. This is a step in that process."

"We were made aware of that after the fact, if I recall," Quinlin argues, to the amusement of the others.

"I told you that this world needs to be reborn. Corporations and Intercorpex must be reminded of our families' sacrifices instead of allowing them to continue stripping our power. You all agreed to this reset."

"You mentioned nothing about this level of violence," Maddizain argues.

"Or the tactics. Radiological and chemical weapons, senseless mass murder…I didn't sign up for this," Quinlin concludes. "And when they find out that we orchestrated the whole thing?"

"Do you plan on telling them? I sure don't. So long as you all maintain your silence, outsiders will never know."

"Secrets cannot be kept in perpetuity."

The holographic faces around the table are apprehensive. Denali cannot allow The Trust to fall apart. Not now. Not when he's this close to the finish line.

"Ladies and gentlemen, we have come to a crossroads. Events have transpired that we cannot undo. We only have the power to shape the future. What side of history do you want to be on? The strongest and the smartest will lead the world into the new century as corporations falter. That responsibility is ours, just as it once was with those who preceded us."

"This situation is different, Denali. Our forefathers responded to a crisis," the usually quiet and reserved Wynstin Dupon argues.

"One that they planted the seeds of. Let's be honest. It wasn't the world's plumbers, teachers, and clerks who plunged the globe into financial ruin. It was the bankers, economists, and politicians drawn from the upper class. We saved the world that we almost destroyed."

"This is still an intentionally manufactured crisis."

"Yes, Quinlin, it is. Will you stand by and watch as corporations and Intercorpex slowly erode your power and influence? You're an avid historian with unsurpassed knowledge of the old books. How many times have you waxed philosophical about the shame people must have had watching Nazi Germany rise to power in Europe?"

"Denali, your passionate argument is admirable, if somewhat misguided," Maddizain interjects. "We share the same end goal, or we would not have pledged ourselves to The Trust. However, you must understand our reluctance to embrace the chaos this is causing."

The patrician leans back in his chair. This is a problem. Maddizain has natural leadership ability and the McMillan family is among the most respected among patricians. Where she goes, many members of The Trust will follow.

"I appreciate your input, but it's not reluctance I sense – it's fear. You're afraid of losing everything. I understand, but that's the outcome if corporations and the exchange have their way."

"That's only speculation," Wynstin argues.

"You have asked us to bear a great deal of responsibility," Aris Fontanbleu says, weighing in for the first time.

"The burden weighs most heavily on me. The Keating family will pay the steepest price for failure."

He nods. That's a big win. Aris commands respect as one of the oldest patricians. He had a close relationship with Valen yet was among the first to recognize the benefit of The Trust. While Maddizain is a leader, Aris is the wise elder who remembers the darkest days of the collapse. His advice is gospel, and consent to this operation is crucial. Denali just received it.

"My fellow patricians, our fate rests in your hands. I have asked for your support in helping to quell the chaos and bring stability to the world once again. The timing is critical, my friends, so I must press for a decision. We will reconvene at six tomorrow morning Eastern Time for your answer."

"And if we decide not to participate? If the members of The Trust join me in the belief that you have gone too far?" Maddizain asks.

"Then the corporations win, and you will watch from the cozy confines of the McMillan Estate as the wealth and power your family has spent lifetimes amassing vanishes before your eyes."

CHAPTER FIFTY

LIBERTEUM

Valhalla
Midtown Geographic Area
New York City Municipal Corporation

Fiolla slips into the fresh clothing Michele laid out for her. She almost feels human again. The loose-fitting garb issued at the termination center was the opposite of her executive tunic in style and comfort. That's by design. They waste no opportunity to make a terminee feel uncomfortable.

"How do you feel?" Michele asks as Fiolla smooths out the new clothing.

"Much better. The clothes are great. Thank you. And the shower was amazing."

"The qulis didn't take many shortcuts when building this place. Good water pressure is needed to get the grit of the underground off your skin. You look good, Fiolla. The clothing suits you. Something's not right, though."

"Really?" Fiolla says, looking herself over. The urch goth clothing is even more form-fitting than corporate executive garb. What could be wrong with it?

"Yup, and I know what it is. May I?" Michele turns Fiolla around and begins weaving her long red hair into a single braid like hers. "This is the style down here, and it's functional for the underground. There we go."

Fiolla smiles as her host ties off the braid with a black elastic band. "I love it, thanks."

"You're welcome."

"If you had told me three days ago that I would be dressed in urch goth two hundred feet below a Manhattan landmark and having my hair braided by the leader of Liberteum...this is all a little surreal."

"I know the feeling. It's no stranger than my hosting an Intercorpex chief inspector, a White House executive, and a world-class cyber security expert."

"I guess we've both had some twists and turns on our journey."

"We do live in interesting times."

Fiolla recognizes the expression. It was first used by the British diplomatic service in China circa 1936 when it was attributed as a native curse on their enemies.

In business circles, executives utter it when they want to politely tell someone to go to hell. She's certain that Michele doesn't know that modern usage.

"Where did you get these cosmetics from?" Fiolla asks, changing the subject. "I wouldn't have expected there's much of a demand for them in the underground."

"I only ever wore them at raves. You can get almost anything on the black market down here if you own some slugs and know the right people. At least, that used to be the case. C'mon, let's show you off to the boys. It'll be fun watching their tongues hang out."

Fiolla never considered herself someone who could make men do that. She only wanted a career, a husband, and a family. The modern dating process, with its digital matching engines and compatibility profiles, is cumbersome and artificial. That was why Farron was so appealing. Their first meeting felt less…constructed.

The duo walks out of the sleeping berths and into the main operations center. Farron is talking to Zyree in the middle of the room and is the first to notice Fiolla. Their reaction to her new look is something she's never experienced.

"Wow…Fiolla, you look…."

"Amazing," Zyree finishes for him, earning a harsh glare. Everyone is gawking at her.

"Thank you, Zyree," she says, embarrassed at the attention. "This place really is impressive, Michele. I never would have guessed you guys possessed this kind of equipment."

"We count on being underestimated to stay a step ahead of our enemies."

Michele omitted the human element of their intelligence network out of respect. Fiolla is aware that Farron used her to siphon information to them, and the wound from that betrayal is still open. The thought makes her freeze in place.

"Speaking of staying ahead of our enemies, what's the status across the river?" Zyree asks the hackers seated at their workstations.

"Still static."

He shakes his head. "I half expected the BCS to use the cover of darkness to attack. Maybe Virtari doesn't want to risk it. Night optics are useless in a well-lit city like New York."

"I need to speak to you," Fiolla says before pulling Michele brusquely by the arm toward the planning table.

"What's wrong?"

"Your systems are impressive, but I know you guys relied on human intelligence. We did, too. You know that Liberteum was on the corporate radar even when you were inactive."

"I figured that was a possibility."

"You also know I was close to Chief Executive Valen, right?" She nods. "He was successful because he was always two steps ahead of his rivals and never afraid to be creative in solving problems."

Fiolla looks around the operations center to ensure nobody is eavesdropping on their conversation. There is more than the typical concern and curiosity, but everyone has maintained a respectful distance, including Farron.

"Where are you going with this, Fiolla?"

"Valen confided in me after he was removed from power. He explained that he arranged an operation with the previous BCS director to dispatch several highly trained agents to the New York City underground to live as urches."

"Why did he tell you this?" Michele asks with nervousness in her voice.

"He needed me to do something for him that he couldn't risk doing himself."

"Do what?"

Fiolla sighs deeply. "Relay a message to the mole who infiltrated Liberteum."

CHAPTER FIFTY-ONE

NYCMC RESISTANCE

One Guardian Plaza
Lower Manhattan Geographic District
New York City Municipal Corporation

The only easy day was yesterday. If that adage holds true, Ilaria will need what little rest she could manage last night. Not that it came easy. A peaceful night's sleep isn't possible in high-stress situations. Still, it was better than nothing.

She needs to know what's happening. After a quick shower and pouring a cup of coffee, Ilaria makes her way into the RTCC. Some of the faces are the same. Others assumed the duties of operators working here yesterday. The constable is exactly where she expects to find him near the inner ring of workstations.

"How'd ya sleep?" Dzamko asks without looking up from the display.

"Who says I did? Every time I dozed off, the idea of opening my eyes to a room full of BCS agents jolted me awake. What about you?"

"I don't worry about BCS agents around my bed. We won't make it that easy for them. But I'm too wired to sleep. So is your son. He hasn't stopped since he got here."

Rykos is hovering over the holographic generator with a mixed group of qulis and guardians. They appear engrossed in whatever they're working on. She's never seen him so enthusiastic.

"What's he doing?"

Dzamko smirks. "Why don't you let him explain?"

Taking the constable's advice, she wanders over to the holographic generator and listens to Rykos coordinating…something. The holograph is of Manhattan, complete with remarkably detailed 3D renderings of all the structures. Red dots hover over intersections on the side of the city they control. They aren't incidents or BCS incursions, and there doesn't seem to be any tactical value to the locations.

The group clams up when they finally notice her standing there.

"You're supposed to be resting, Rykos. Since you aren't, what am I looking at? Are these red dots checkpoints?"

"I couldn't sleep. And no, the red dots are more important than that."

"Your son approached us with a problem," Prano explains. "Emergency services were suspended after Zeykala imposed corporate law. With no goods moving into or out of the island, food stocks must be getting low."

"I asked if we could set up locations to distribute food, supplies, and medications for employees trapped inside their domiciles."

Ilaria studies the holograph again. The red dots are all in heavily residential sections of the island. The points provide easy access for the people while maintaining a level of security. She's impressed.

"That's brilliant, Rykos."

"I can only take partial credit. These guys liked the idea and ran with it. Prano helped mobilize the qulis to deliver food and medicine, and the guardians helped procure medical professionals to deliver first aid."

"And all these places are up and running?"

"Twelve have been set up with twenty-seven more coming. Most of them are small, so we're looking to scale up to accommodate expected demand."

Ilaria flashes a smile of motherly pride at the amazing work. Rykos has matured twenty years since she last saw him. Gone is the maverick who only cared about himself and his own needs. Now, he's tireless in his effort to help others.

"Great job, guys, really. I won't get in your way," she says before moving back over to Dzamko. "Wow."

"I thought you'd like that."

"Dyllon, you're looking a little rough around the edges," she says, turning to her trusted corporate affairs representative.

"Yes, ma'am. I was busy arranging trucks for the supplies. Then I helped marshal resources for Darnon when we had a sewer problem on the Upper West Side and a manhole explosion in Harlem."

"Was it the BCS?" she asks Darnon when he joins them.

"We ruled it out. It's hard to keep the city together with what's going on. Failures are bound to happen. We're addressing them the best we can."

"You both are doing great work, thank you. Why don't I take it from here? You guys go get some rest."

"Thank you, ma'am, I think I could use it," Dyllon says, wasting no time turning and heading out of the RTCC.

"I can last a little longer," Darnon argues.

"I know you can, but today isn't going to be any easier than yesterday and I need you fresh. I'm relying on you to help keep this city in one piece, and you can't do that if you're about to fall over."

"Call me if you need me," he says, following Dyllon out of the room.

"Darnon's gone from trying to take your position to being behind you one hundred percent," Dzamko opines. "Letting him handle infrastructure issues was a master stroke."

"He's a capable executive, even if I find his personality grating. I knew he would be valuable."

When Ilaria offered her job to the municipal executives in that Corporate Hall conference room, she was serious. Darnon stepping up when she was captured at Rikers was either naked ambition or unwavering dedication to the municipal corporation. This was a test of his loyalty. She's pleased that he passed it because she doesn't need any more drama.

There has never been a crisis this severe at any point in corporate history. This is not the Catharsis or the Pirate Wars. What started as a protest has turned into an insurrection, and they are all staring down a lethal enemy determined to restore the status quo.

"Do I dare ask what the security situation looks like?"

"Well," Dzamko says, scratching his head, "the BCS pulled back from their forward checkpoints last night. They're concentrating along the West Side Autoway."

"Why would they cede ground?"

"I don't know. The move makes no tactical sense, and that has me worried."

"Stay on it. Have we heard anything from Rykos's friend?"

"Not a peep. I would have thought Liberteum would have reached out by now."

That's another area of concern. Rykos said they would contact them, but Ilaria assumed it would have been last night. He doesn't appear alarmed at the radio silence, but she's beginning to wonder if something bad happened.

"Me too. Keep me posted."

CHAPTER FIFTY-TWO

LIBERTEUM

Valhalla
Midtown Geographic Area
New York City Municipal Corporation

Michele is sick to her stomach. There's been so much betrayal already. Narik turned on her, then Haven, Denali, and even Farron, before she learned differently. The remaining members of Liberteum have been with her for so long that she can't comprehend any of them stabbing her in the back. It's just not possible.

Her first reaction is emotional. She wants to lash out at Fiolla and tell her she's mistaken. But she can't. A blind man could see that the White House executive has been through a lot. It would have been easier to keep this information to herself. There is just no upside to her lying, but it is a possibility.

It could be a corporate ruse or another of Denali Keating's games. Either of those situations is plausible despite not matching the events that have transpired. They couldn't have known that Fiolla would end up here. Still, it's easier for Michele to believe this is another ruse than to face another betrayal of one of her own.

She surveys the room. The mole could already be dead. She has lost dozens of men since Broad Street. The handful of guys who have lived in Valhalla for years can't be corporate spies. It must be someone with the required access to communicate and cover their tracks afterward. That leaves her most trusted hackers.

There's a way to get to the bottom of this. Ortan is a stranger, just like Fiolla is. But that could also be an advantage. She decides to settle this before she loses her sanity.

Michele walks over and puts her hands on Ortan's shoulders. "Are you busy?"

"Not for you," he says, matching her hushed volume. "What's up?"

"I need you to check something for me. Can you access our logs and find out who went to a specific GlobalNet site?"

"Too easy. Which one?"

Michele nods at Fiolla, who joins them and provides Ortan the name of the site Valen gave her. His hands are almost a blur as he gesticulates his way through their file structure before stopping. "Are you sure that's the correct site?"

"Positive," Fiolla confirms.

He looks back at his display. "Okay, then, not so easy."

He makes a couple of gestures, and the lights in his suitcase start blinking wildly. A moment later, his display changes to a status bar that moves rapidly from left to right. He leans back and puts his hands on the top of his head.

"What are you doing?"

"Rebuilding and indexing and your shared network drives. Ah, there it is. All right, what do we have here? Okay…the log was deleted."

"Is that normal?"

"Yes and no. Logs are only kept for a short time, but what isn't normal is how or why this one was deleted. Someone destroyed it with a cyber shredder."

"I'm not following," Michele admits.

Ortan swivels in his chair. "Whenever a file is deleted, it never really is. The spot it occupied on the drive needs to be overwritten several times for it to be completely gone. A cyber shredder does that. Fortunately, I have a tool that can rebuild almost any deleted file. Someone didn't want this log found. I suppose that's why you asked me to check."

"Yeah, it is. Who deleted it?"

He makes a tap gesture with his finger, and the username comes up. Michele shouldn't be surprised, but she is. They all turn at the same time to find Adiz standing behind them. Maybe he was curious or concerned about what they were doing. Whatever his reason, now he's alarmed.

"How could you?"

"How could I what?" he snaps, taking a step closer.

He notices the output on the display. When he recognizes the log, his reaction is immediate. He dives back toward his workstation and gropes under the counter before anyone can stop him. Michele trips over his chair and loses balance as it spins across the back of the operations center. By the time she regains her footing and raises her head, a gun is pointed at her face.

Adiz moves his finger to the trigger, not bothering to waste time with idle conversation. Ortan swings hard in his swivel chair with his leg extended, and the exoskeleton makes a heavy thud when it strikes the traitor's shin. He whelps and jerks his arm as his finger pulls back on the trigger.

The unexpected noise causes everyone to jump. The gunshot was deafening in the tight confines of the room, but Michele still heard the telltale snapping sound a bullet makes when it barely misses you. That was too close.

Adiz begins to recover from the blow to his leg. He wheels his weapon around at Ortan. Michele is about to lunge for him when another muzzle reports from the opposite side of the room. The round catches Adiz in the shoulder and spins him. Losing his balance, he crashes into the workstation behind him.

Michele surges at him, knocking his gun to the floor. It's within grasp, but as he reaches for it, a black, high-heeled boot comes crashing down on the top of his hand. Fiolla squats and retrieves the weapon as Michele pins Adiz down and inserts her thumb into his shoulder wound. He screams out in pain before she eases the pressure.

"This will only get worse for you if you resist, you bastard."

Zyree walks around them with his weapon trained on Adiz's face to retrieve the gun Fiolla is precariously holding. Anyone who was sleeping no longer is, and the operations center fills with everyone in Valhalla.

"Did I miss a team-building exercise or something?" Jasper asks, seeing his antagonistic colleague bleeding.

Rage overcomes Michele. She wants to kill the bastard right here, right now. Nothing would be more satisfying to her than pulverizing him to death with her fists. It's what he deserves.

"I know what you're feeling, Michele. I've been there," Zyree says quietly. "Let him up. I've got him."

Fiolla places her hand on Michele's shoulder. The touch is comforting. She isn't alone in this fight. Both of them know something about betrayal. It helps her settle her runaway emotions. Adiz gets one last shove before she turns to Ortan.

"Thank you. You saved my life."

"And you saved Zyree's. Let's call it even," he says with a wink.

"Will somebody tell me what's going on?" Jasper asks.

"Adiz is a mole Chief Executive Valen planted in Liberteum," Fiolla says. "He's been working for America Incorporated the whole time."

"What?"

The news hits the newcomers to the room like a bomb. The men down here consider themselves brothers. Like Michele, they'll take this disloyalty personally.

Adiz says nothing. Despite the pain, he defiantly stands and glowers at Fiolla. To her credit, she doesn't wither under his stare. If anything, she grows bolder by the second.

"Unlike you, I was performing my duty to the corporation."

"And I'm doing my duty to the people repressed by it."

"You're a traitor," Adiz says with a sneer.

Fiolla takes a step toward him. Farron moves to intervene before Michele holds him back with her hand. She slowly shakes her head. This is between the two of them.

Fiolla gets in his face. "I don't think you should throw that word around so nonchalantly, considering what you've done."

"Go to hell."

She smiles. "You first."

"Secure him in the spare bunk room," Michele says, not wanting to see his face any longer. "We'll figure out what to do with him later."

"If you don't bleed out from that wound first," Zyree says to Adiz. "Move."

Zyree ushers him out of the operations center. Fiolla is shaking despite the strength she showed. Michele takes her hands.

"Thank you. Adiz could have killed us all."

"I'm so sorry to be the one who had to tell you."

"It's better that I find out now than later. If you'll excuse me, I'd like to be by myself for a few minutes."

Michele leaves for the cozy confines of the bedroom and locks the door behind her. She struggles to hold back the onslaught of tears. Her whole world feels like it's crashing. It's like the Keating Estate all over again. The emotions are too familiar, and she doesn't know how much more she can take.

CHAPTER FIFTY-THREE

AMERICA, INC.

Emergency Operations Center
Lower Manhattan Geographic District
New York City Municipal Corporation

The status reports all read the same way, so there's no point in continuing the torture. Virtari tosses his tablet on the table and runs his fingers through his hair. They are losing control of cities across the sphere of influence. The qulis are emboldened by their inability to regain control and are becoming more aggressive as the situation deteriorates.

The news from the White House isn't any rosier. Zeykala evicted all BCS personnel from the executive mansion. It's not the smartest move given the state of affairs, but irrational thinking is that woman's hallmark.

He needs a victory. This attack on Manhattan must succeed. With Intercorpex crippled and other corporations rumored to be facing the fallout of attacks against them, the world feels like it's careening down a dark path. America Incorporated can only help once order is restored. That starts today.

Varella's knock on the office door interrupts his foreboding. "Can I bother you for a minute, sir?"

"You already are. What do you want?"

"Video packages aired on AME News all night. Several more are queued for this morning, but we're running out of material. We need a fresh angle."

"You're going to get one in another forty-five minutes. These stories are driving Zeykala nuts, so they must be effective. Good work," Virtari says, issuing a rare compliment.

She beams. "Thank you, sir. There is one more thing. How strong is your relationship with Zeykala?"

The question commands the director's attention. "She evicted my men from the White House because she thinks I'm behind her assassination attempt, so what do you think?"

"Were you behind it?" Varella deadpans.

Virtari wants to take offense to the question. Then he thinks twice. If this young woman thinks he's ruthless enough to be capable of that, it may serve his purposes later.

"No. The investigation into who was is ongoing."

"You know damn well who it was. Tell me," Varella presses.

The director smirks. "Farron Keating."

"That's not the name I expected. I assume you haven't told Zeykala the truth behind Liberteum's escape because it will lead to accusations that you're working with him."

"You're a quick study, I'll give you that. Why did you ask about my relationship with Zeykala?"

She takes that as an invitation to park herself in the chair across his desk. Virtari would normally find that sort of behavior grating, but the young woman has something to say. Given his current standing with the CEO, he decides to hear his "political advisor" out.

"I came across a report that the board of directors is thinking about replacing her, and that poses a problem for us. Zeykala has stood by you despite the mounting pressure. Her successor will view that as a mistake not worth repeating."

"She's not standing by me. She thinks I tried to kill her."

"And you have done nothing to challenge that assumption. If America Incorporated is going to weather this current storm, it'll be because you both guide us through it. You need to make amends."

Virtari leans back in his chair. This has become a decisive moment. He can let Varella into the inner circle or leave her outside looking in.

"What I'm about to tell you is never to be repeated. Utter a word, and it will be the last that ever escapes your mouth," he says, getting a nod. "Zeykala became an executive because of her talent, but she's CEO because of me. It wasn't my choice to work with her. You don't make friends running security for a company this size. I've done unsavory things during my time at the Pentagon, and she threatened to reveal my activities to Valen if I didn't cooperate with her. That man hated my guts and would have used any excuse he was given to remove me."

"She blackmailed you?"

"Right out of the executive playbook, isn't it? There is no trust between us."

"And that's why she's convinced you're behind the Maryland attack."

Virtari steeples his hands. "In hindsight, it would have been easier if I had killed her."

"Maybe not," Varella says, leaning forward in her chair and pressing her hands together in front of her mouth to match his body language. "We have an opportunity. No chief executive will admit they can't move the world by themselves. You can't tell her she needs you, so you need to show her."

"Care to explain how?" the director asks as she rises from her chair.

"I'll get back to you on that, sir."

"This better not be about replacing Zeykala with you."

"It's not, but would that be so bad? I *understand* your value. Any BCS director would rather have an ally in the Oval Office who appreciates his work over someone who blackmailed him."

Varella departs the office, and Virtari checks the display on his desk. A smile creases his lips. He hates to admit it, but she's starting to grow on him.

CHAPTER FIFTY-FOUR

LIBERTEUM

Valhalla
Midtown Geographic Area
New York City Municipal Corporation

Fiolla slides into the seat at the counter like she's sneaking into a conference late and doesn't want the speaker to notice. It was of no use. No sooner does her backside hit the chair than Ortan stops working.

"I'm sorry, am I distracting you?"

"You smell good."

It was an awkward response. It's rare to hear comments about your personal appearance in a professional environment. When lewd comments occurred, they were from sexists and charlatans like Virtari. This isn't a corporate office, Ortan is not a sexist, and the compliment isn't unwelcome. It's just rare.

"I'm sorry," Ortan says, regarding her sheepishly, "I didn't mean to make you uncomfortable. I haven't had a woman's company in a long time. I've forgotten how to act."

Ortan's honesty and vulnerability are a refreshing change of pace. He has a charisma about him, but it isn't the cocky showmanship most top executives display. It's a quiet confidence that comes from knowledge and experience, even if it doesn't extend to working with the opposite sex.

Zyree mentioned in passing that Ortan lost the use of his legs in an accident. She wonders if that's why he's a recluse who plugs into the world instead of living in it. It's a plausible explanation, but probably not the whole story. Whatever happened to this man runs deeper than that. She's only too chicken to ask.

"What are you watching?"

"I have a front-row seat to the world unraveling," Ortan says, pointing at a display. "The GlobalNet has been buzzing with rumors of terrorist attacks across the world. I've heard of everything from mass murder to assassinations to train derailments to possible chemical weapons. There's even suspicion that the bomb that detonated in Moscow had a radiological component."

"That's horrible!" Fiolla glances over her shoulder and leans toward him. "These guys...."

"Aren't involved," he assures her. "The worst part is the attacks have started again. This is footage from Paris, Moscow, Shanghai, Beijing, Tokyo, and Rome. There are others I haven't accessed yet."

Each scene is more horrific than the last. The attacks are varied in their method of execution. The one thing they all have in common is unmistakable: a lot of people are dead.

"I accessed surveillance feeds once I learned what was going on. Corporations aren't publicizing these events, but I know they occurred within minutes of each other. There's only one man capable of that precision who has the proper motive."

"Denali Keating. No wonder Farron is all out of sorts. I can't imagine being stuck two hundred and fifty feet below the ground while my father maims and murders people around the world. What do you think of him?"

"Who, Farron? He's a mystery to me."

"To both of us," Fiolla admits. "May I ask you a question? You're friends with Zyree. Does he trust Farron?"

"Trust is a strong word, especially with a former chief inspector at Intercorpex. He's naturally suspicious. But once you earn his trust, you have it for life unless you break it. Unfortunately, too many people recently have, so he's guarded."

"He sounds like a good man. How long have you known him?"

"Only a couple of months. We met in Iceland right after the Secaucus data center attack," Ortan says, causing Fiolla to raise an eyebrow. "I'm not exactly a people person, as you can probably tell. Zyree is the closest thing I have to a friend in this world, even if he's only a recent one. You like him, don't you?"

She blushes. "I don't know what to think or feel right now. My world has been turned upside down. I'm still trying to figure out who I can trust."

"If it makes you feel any better, we're all in the same situation."

"You trust Michele, though, right?"

Ortan thinks about that for a moment. Fiolla is growing closer to the woman she's been conditioned to view as an enemy. The hesitation makes her wonder if that's a mistake.

"She helped Zyree escape certain death when she didn't have to. He was her enemy. I had leverage on her, but it felt like something she wanted to do. I'm inclined to give her the benefit of the doubt."

"You know, she hasn't asked a single thing from me since I've been here. No requests for inside information, or intelligence, or anything. I thought she was keeping me around to use me for something, but that isn't the case. I'm not used to that and am afraid I'm missing something."

"I'll tell you what. If you watch my back, I'll watch yours. And we'll both watch Zyree's."

"Deal," Fiolla says, warming to the odd computer expert.

"Watch my what?" Zyree asks, coming over to them.

"Fiolla was just saying how cute your butt is," Ortan says, causing her face to turn bright red in embarrassment.

"I did not!" Fiolla says with a pleasant laugh that sounds good coming from her.

The episode with Adiz rattled Michele but somehow brought those in Valhalla closer together. It's as if a bad energy was removed, allowing everyone to relax. Zyree is happy to see Ortan and Fiolla opening up to each other.

Michele joins the party at the workstation. The required routing and encryption were established yesterday, but they all needed rest. Today will be long, but this introduction can no longer wait.

"We're ready, Ortan."

"You up for this?" Zyree asks.

"As much as I'm going to be," Michele assures everyone before exhaling.

He wants to make a joke about her meeting her future mother-in-law, but it's not the right time. Michele has enough to deal with without the added pressure that comes with that realization. And he isn't supposed to know about her romantic interest in Rykos. She thinks it's still a secret down here.

CHAPTER FIFTY-FIVE

RYKOS

One Guardian Plaza
Lower Manhattan Geographic District
New York City Municipal Corporation

The call finally came. I was beginning to wonder if something was wrong in Valhalla. Without a way to contact Michele, I had to wait for Adiz and Jasper to establish communications. When the VidLynk came in, the energy level in the RTCC went off the charts.

My mother and Dzamko join me at the communications terminal while Phylep hovers behind us. The request was for me, likely so I could make the necessary introductions. The constable looks like he ate some bad sushi. He's not at all in favor of this. My mother is being more open-minded, or so it appears.

"It's good to see that you found your way downtown without getting lost, Rykos," Zyree says when the VidLynk establishes.

"I'm not the one who needed a biocomp to tie my shoes, Zyree," I retort, not able to restrain myself from engaging in the playful banter to lighten the tension.

"You could have used its help to up your game with that girl you were courting in Central Park."

"What girl?" my mother and Michele both ask at the same time.

I clench my jaw. The chief inspector did that on purpose. "Don't make me come up there and knock you unconscious...again."

Fiolla lets out a short laugh, and Michele lets a rare smile cross her lips.

"You knocked him unconscious?" Dzamko asks me.

"It's a long story. Zyree, Michele, Fiolla, this is Constable Dzamko, the acting chief guardian, and this is my mother, Ilaria, the acting CEO of the Municipal Corporation of New York City."

"It's nice to finally meet you, sir, ma'am," Michele says with a deferential nod, catching both of them off-guard.

The last thing my mother expected was respect from the terrorist who kidnapped her son. She's probably wondering if I'm in love with her. Seeing her now, she must know there's a physical attraction. I hope she doesn't ask publicly because this VidLynk is already awkward enough.

"Likewise, Michele, although I must admit it's a little weird to hear myself say that. I need allies in this fight, but I didn't expect them to come from a group my husband was hunting."

"That makes two of us," Dzamko grumbles, still not in love with this idea.

"My apologies, Michele. The constable promised to play nice on this call," my mother interjects before I can. I know all too well the look she's giving him. I saw it enough growing up.

"It's all right, Chief Executive Ilaria. He has undoubtedly lost good men because of Liberteum. I've lost good friends because of the PSS. Under most circumstances, we'd have no business having this conversation. In this case, we have a common cause and a mutual enemy."

"Yes, here we are," Dzamko mumbles again, earning a second glare from my mother. He's playing with fire.

"I understand your hesitation, Constable," Fiolla interjects. "I've had to take a similar leap of faith. My name is Fiolla, and three days ago, I was working in the West Wing of the White House."

"Wait! Fiolla…were you the executive who was working with my husband during his search for Liberteum?"

That gets Michele's attention. Mine as well. It's a small world.

"Yes, ma'am. I knew your husband, although not well. I'm very sorry to hear about his termination. You have my sincerest condolences. He deserved far better."

"Thank you."

"Constable, everyone here has been on a different side. We all have history with each other," Fiolla says, looking at Michele. "There are regrets, and there is pain. We were all doing what we thought was best at the time, but those times have changed. We're up against a corporation determined to kill us to maintain a status quo that aims to keep the people under their thumb. We have a unique opportunity to stop that, but it requires us to set aside the past. If we don't, it will be the people who suffer most."

There's a long silence after Fiolla finishes her unexpected monologue. My mother waits for Dzamko to process her words. I give her credit – most executives would pile words on top of hers to convince him. She remains silent because she respects his opinion and won't dictate what it should be.

"You must have been very good at your job, Fiolla," Dzamko says to everybody's relief. "If we're going to work together, we should share information. The situation hasn't changed much in the past twelve hours on our end."

Dzamko goes on to explain the BCS's strongholds in the city and how they pulled their agents back to the river early this morning. He describes the quli medical and food distribution points and the areas their joint forces are guarding.

"What we don't have are eyes on the other side of the Hudson," I say, knowing what Valhalla is capable of. "The BCS retreat isn't random, but we don't know what they're planning."

"Ortan, can you get eyes on Secaucus?" Zyree asks.

"Sure, let me just…uh, uh-oh."

"What is it?" a chorus of voices asks.

"You should see for yourself. I'm sending the raw footage over to your display in the RTCC."

"He can do that?" Ilaria asks me, getting a wry smile in return.

Ortan puts the video on one of the wall displays. Heavy tracked machines with large cannons on rotating turrets lead columns of troop carriers toward the tunnel. The surveillance feed from the south river crossing shows the same thing. This is not good.

"What the hell are those things?" I ask, gawking at the metal beasts.

"M1 Abrams main battle tanks," Michele says, studying the video. "They were the armored backbone of the United States Army's ground attack forces before the collapse. Those look like A3 or A4 variants."

I'm a little in awe. The girl knows her military equipment, but that shouldn't surprise me. The old history textbook her father gave me is probably one of dozens she had access to. All eyes turn to her in amazement and she notices the sudden attention.

"I did a lot of reading about old wars, including Desert Storm and Iraqi Freedom. The books had pictures."

"I thought all military weapons were destroyed," my mother says.

"The BCS quietly kept a stockpile in case of emergencies," Zyree interjects. "Most corporations did. It makes you wonder what really happened to the nuclear arsenal."

"The good news is we know they're coming," I say, trying to be optimistic. "The bad news is that any direct action against them will be laughingly one-sided. Can the qulis seal the tunnel, Phylep?"

"We don't have the explosives for that," Prano says.

I look at Michele on the VidLynk, and she shrugs. "Everything we had was at the Motorpool. My guess is Haven used it against Intercorpex."

"It's a moot point," Zyree says. "The BCS pulled back this morning to protect the tunnel entrances. Even if we had the means, we'd never reach those tunnels."

"We have another problem," Ortan interrupts, bringing up another feed. "This is a shot of the airport."

"That's a lot of drones," I observe gravely. Things just went from bad to worse.

"*Armed* drones. Look under their wings," Michele says, pointing.

Dzamko looks at me and then at my mother. The realization is settling in that our newfound alliance may be a short-lived one. The BCS isn't playing around.

"We'll hold them off as long as we can," the quli says.

"You'll be exposed if you're in the open. The missiles and bombs those drones are carrying aren't filled with confetti," Zyree warns.

"Buy us as much time as you can, Phylep. Teams of guardians will support you. Just keep your men out of sight as much as possible."

"Yes, sir."

Dzamko and Phylep go about their business, and the room that had been paying close attention to our conversation now begins to buzz with activity.

"Michele, Rykos can stay in touch with you as things are about to get hectic here. We'll do our part to stop their advance, but our capabilities are limited. We're going to need a solution that doesn't rely on force, and I'm afraid that's going to fall on you."

"We'll do our best, ma'am."

"I know you will," my mother assures her, "but if you don't succeed, we won't be alive in an hour, so good luck."

"You too, Chief Executive Ilaria. I think we're all going to need a lot of it."

The VidLynk disconnects, and she turns to me with a smile plastered across her lips. "I can see why you like her. Let's get to work."

CHAPTER FIFTY-SIX

THE PATRICIANS

Keating Family of the Gentez-Majorez Estate
Greenwich Geographic District
Southern Connecticut Municipal Corporation

The holograms around the table in The Crucible look at each other as if they're physically present. The Trust only functions because it lacks a leader. Patricians are fickle about taking orders. This group was conceived as a modern incarnation of the Knights of the Round Table. Everyone is an equal with an equal voice, although stronger personalities wield more influence.

There is a downside. The lack of a leader to steer the group and drive the conversation makes decision-making painful. Camelot had a King Arthur, but Denali is apprehensive to fill that role more than he has. The result is that his peers are waiting for another to step up and speak. That nobody has is a bad omen.

"Have you reached a decision?" Denali asks, finally deciding to end the torturous silence.

"We have," Quinlin says. "We understand your wanting to protect the power of the patricians. However, we cannot condone your actions. You were less than forthcoming about your plans when you asked us to form this cabal."

"I see."

The decision is shortsighted. Denali didn't explain the full scope of his plan because they never would have agreed to it. These people are soft and content to sit back and watch as corporations make them irrelevant. Then, they would have the audacity to complain about it later.

Patricians might retain their fortunes, but wealth without power and influence would mean this is the last generation of useful patricians. Families would eventually lose their wealth and be relegated to the history books with dinosaurs, democracy, and other extinct things.

"Unfortunately, we agree that there is no choice but to continue down the path you started us on," Aris Fontanbleu decrees in his typical shaky voice.

"Make no mistake, Denali," Maddizain says, noticing his relief. "We have grave concerns about this."

"I will take it a step further," Reagul interjects. "I don't *trust* you."

The heads turn to gauge their host's reaction. Denali wants to rip his throat out. Reagul is a snake habitually on the wrong side of the Zurich Canon. His lecturing anyone about trust smacks of hypocrisy.

Unfortunately, Denali needs his forces. He needs all their forces. These people aren't here because of their charm or financial reserves. They were selected because each maintains a sizable security force that Denali needs control of.

"I appreciate all of your support. I apologize for not being more forthcoming with you about my intentions. I take full responsibility for the breakdown in communication."

"As well you should," Reagul mutters.

"We heard there were more attacks against corporations," Wynstin says, eager to move on.

"Things are moving quickly now. Corporations are panicking, and their desperation will continue to grow. Those not directly affected are reacting to the unrest. The Caribbean and Sub-Saharan Africa corporations are already on the verge of failure."

"What do you need from us? How do we deploy our forces?" Maddizain asks.

"We will extend an invitation to assist in stabilizing the situation. Offer corporations use of your security forces for the duration of this crisis and see if there are any early takers."

Everyone knows what this step means. What was once theory and speculation is now real. Patricians are on the cusp of a global takeover, and their feet are starting to get cold.

"Corporations are not going to just invite us in," Quinlin argues.

"The primas are sidelined, and Intercorpex is incapacitated. Corporations that don't maintain a large security force will need manpower. I believe they will agree if it means maintaining order and their grip on power. There is no downside to accepting our help."

"I will make my offers immediately," Aris says.

"As will I," Wynstin confirms.

The men and women around the table begin nodding in agreement. Even Reagul seems resigned to follow suit. Denali represses the smile from growing any wider across his lips. Things are moving along nicely.

CHAPTER FIFTY-SEVEN

LIBERTEUM

Valhalla
Midtown Geographic Area
New York City Municipal Corporation

Everyone knows the BCS is going to make a move. That prompted Michele to open Valhalla's armory. Zyree is impressed with the array of weapons. He's even been the target of ones just like them at Broad Street. It's another journal entry into how surreal life has become.

While everyone else draws arms, Zyree watches video feeds across the city with Ortan. There is no system this man can't find a way to access. He is so wrapped up in watching the display that he doesn't notice Koltayne, Farron, Fiolla, Michele, and Jasper gathering behind him.

"Is it as bad as it looks?" Michele asks, getting his attention.

"It's worse," Ortan says, posting the map to the overhead display and pointing at it. "The southern column emerged from the tunnel and is heading down Church Street. I'll give you three guesses where they're going, but you'll only need one."

"One Guardian Plaza. Are they leaving troops behind?"

"Small teams are securing major intersections. Otherwise, they're going to strike with their full force."

"And to the north?" Michele asks, her concern over Rykos evident in her tone.

"They came out of the northern tunnel and rumbled through Times Square down Forty-Second Street. I thought they would stop at Grand Central Terminus, but they rolled past it and are turning up Fifth."

"They're heading right for us," Michele concludes.

"They know where we are," Zyree concludes.

Everyone in the Valhalla operations room ceases their conversations and turns to stare at him. The news isn't surprising, but still unwelcome. It's the worst possible development, and he doesn't have answers as to how to stop them.

"How could they know?" Fiolla asks.

"The BCS could have had us under observation when we left Central Park. Or Denali Keating gave us up to them. The how doesn't matter. They're coming."

"Can we throw them off the trail?" Michele asks, grasping for ideas.

"They have actionable intelligence. If we were spotted walking naked down Broadway, those tanks would still level this cathedral."

"Then we run," Farron concludes. "We leave before they get here and live to fight another day."

"And go where?" Jasper argues. "No place in this city is safe, assuming we escape before they get here."

"We can't help Ilaria and Rykos if we flee Valhalla. I won't abandon them. I can't."

Michele presses her lips together. This is personal for her, and it seems everyone knows why. She fights the urge to correct herself, but there is no surprise on anyone's face. Apparently, her budding relationship with Rykos isn't much of a secret.

"Michele, we can't help them from here, and fighting those things is a lost cause," Farron pleads, pointing at the video streaming to the display. "If we stay here, we die."

"Fiolla, Zyree, Ortan…you guys didn't sign up for this," Michele says, turning to address the group. "If you want to go, leave now. Farron, you can join them. The same goes for the rest of you here. I won't ask anything more of you, but I'm staying."

"Michele, that's suicide."

"Jasper, I grew up in Valhalla. This is my home. If my time ends today, it will be standing right here, finishing what we started."

She's still emotional over Adiz's betrayal and likely worried about Rykos. Everyone here hates the idea of losing to Zeykala and Virtari. She moves to an adjacent workstation and begins studying the surveillance feed from Fifth Avenue. The armored column is slowly lumbering north. Time is short, and she turns to Ortan, who hasn't budged from his chair.

"Don't look at me like that. I'm not built for running."

"Me neither," Fiolla says from behind him, crossing her arms for effect. "I'm done with that. It's time to fight. Tell me what you need me to do."

"You didn't abandon me in my time of need," Zyree says, grinning. "Besides, Ortan is helpless without me."

"Psssh," the computer expert snorts.

For the first time, Michele feels like she has a team she can count on. Absent is Adiz's whining and Haven's psychopathic behavior. Even with an opportunity to leave, the men and women here are choosing to stay. Thomas Paine's words she quoted to Rykos in Greenwich have never ringed truer: "These are the times that try men's souls: The summer soldier and the sunshine patriot will, in this crisis, shrink from the service of his country; but he that stands it now, deserves the love and thanks of man and woman." There is indeed nothing stronger than the heart of a volunteer.

Koltayne and Jasper smirk and nod, as do the smattering of others who call Valhalla home. That leaves Farron as the only one left to decide. The others are ready to do their part, and once again, he finds himself on an island.

"I need to deal with my father."

Michele nods in understanding. "Yes, you do."

"I need you for that. I didn't snatch you from the jaws of the BCS to let you die today fighting a pointless battle."

"Then you have a problem because I don't think it's pointless, and I'm not leaving."

Patricians are used to getting their way. Even Farron has that arrogant mindset once in a while. Not this time. He doesn't look like he wants to argue with the leader of Liberteum. Her mind is made up, and he's powerless to change it.

"Okay, then make me a promise."

"What?" she snaps.

"When this is over, if we're all still alive, you'll help me stop my father."

Michele extends her hand. It's not a gesture urches are known to engage in. Handshakes are vestiges of the corporate world, not the underworld. Farron understands the symbolism and shakes her hand.

"Deal."

CHAPTER FIFTY-EIGHT

AMERICA, INC.

The White House
Corporate Governance District
Washington-Arlington Municipal Corporation

Stress sweat is a thing. Even though executive tunics are made using top-of-the-line moisture-wicking materials, no fabric ever conceived can alleviate Zeykala's perspiration. After working straight through the night, she could use a long hot bath.

That's not a possibility, so the CEO settles for a trip up to the Residence and a five-minute shower. Since she isn't permitted to live there yet, she needs to avoid Valen. Fortunately, there's no shortage of bathrooms in the mansion. Life will be easier when human resources finally moves him out.

Zeykala returns to the Oval Office feeling refreshed despite her lack of sleep. There is a never-ending list of people to talk to and a litany of fires to put out. The sensation of being energized is short-lived when she sees who's waiting for her.

"You had a rough day yesterday."

This woman is insufferable. There is no way she ever sipped tea while comfortably ensconced on the sofa when Valen occupied this office. That Talya Bettancourt thinks it's permissible now is infuriating and disrespectful.

"You came to Washington to point out the obvious?" Zeykala asks as she checks for the latest updates on her tablet.

"No, I'm here because you've let this sphere of influence spin out of control. Cities are falling apart. I heard that qulis may actually control Detroit and Cleveland."

"They don't, but the chaos shouldn't surprise you."

"Excuse me?" Talya asks, setting down her cup in its saucer on the coffee table.

"No, I don't think I will. You forced me to issue that stupid order integrating the qulis. Everyone knew how they'd react, which is why Valen pushed back on you. I hate to admit it, but he was right. I never should have done it."

"You were elevated to this position because of *me*. You owe *me*."

"And yet here you are, accusing me of incompetence."

"It's not an accusation, Zeykala. You've made a mess of things."

"So you keep saying. Of course, everything that's gone wrong was because of someone else's poor decisions. Director Virtari, you, Chief Guardian Teman…we wouldn't be in this position if I followed my instincts and ran this corporation as I saw fit."

"Don't flatter yourself. You're not that good. Talent didn't earn you this job."

Politics is perception. The rise of corporatism as a viable political system didn't change that. Talya is convinced of her worldview. Facts and rational arguments won't change it.

Zeykala doesn't need another war to fight right now. Her political survival hinges on subduing the qulis and destroying Liberteum, which she can't do while arguing with Talya Bettancourt in the Oval Office.

"I owe you a lot and will be forever grateful for the doors you opened for me, Talya."

"There better not be a 'but' following that," she says with a sneer.

"There is. I am the chief executive officer of America Incorporated. You are the largest shareholder and prima patrician. I appreciate your input in that capacity, but I don't take orders from you."

Talya shakes her head and rises from the sofa. "I thought you were a capable executive who understood how the world works, but I was wrong. Promoting you to this office was a mistake."

"Spare me, Talya. This conversation is getting tiresome. If you want to get rid of me, then do it."

"I didn't figure you to be a quitter."

Zeykala knew the comment was coming, but it still makes her angry. Placating Talya will only lead to the unwise demand. The more she capitulates, the worse it will become. That is no way to run a corporation.

She has a lot of influence as prima, but it isn't absolute. The permanent appointment as CEO rests on her extinguishing the flames of this insurrection. Once that is done, it will be easier to take care of Talya, Virtari, and anyone else who conspires against her.

"I have work to do. Show yourself out," Zeykala commands.

The automated assistant opens the door to the Oval Office. Talya doesn't protest the brusque treatment as she uses the door. She knows the strings to this marionette have been cut. The next move is hers to make.

CHAPTER FIFTY-NINE

NYCMC RESISTANCE

One Guardian Plaza
Lower Manhattan Geographic District
New York City Municipal Corporation

The secure VidLynk that comes in from the Emergency Operations Center marked for Ilaria's eyes only gets everyone's attention. She thought maybe it was Valhalla spoofing the IP address of the sender, but the technician confirmed it was legitimate. Everyone in the room is thinking the same thing.

"Why would the EOC be contacting me?"

Dzamko shrugs. "Surrender demand?"

He knows the BCS doesn't know the meaning of the word mercy. If they want anyone here alive, it's to make a public spectacle of their terminations. A surrender demand is pointless, and they must already know that.

"Connect it."

The camera view is narrow enough that little of the RTCC can be seen behind Ilaria. She doesn't want whoever this is to know who's here or in what numbers. The few advantages they have must be protected.

Ilaria gasps when the VidLynk connects. "Varella!"

"Hello, Mother," her daughter says, tears streaming down her cheeks.

"What are you doing at the EOC?"

"I was in the America Tower. The BCS picked me up and brought me here," she says, stifling sobs.

"Are you okay? Have they hurt you?"

"I'm okay. The agents haven't done anything to me, but...they have Rykos."

The comment catches Ilaria off-guard. She turns to Dzamko, who looks confused as hell.

"They have him? How? How did they find him?"

"I...I don't...One of the agents said Liberteum was captured last night trying to leave the city. They're all dead. They said Rykos will die too if you don't surrender."

"You've seen him? Rykos?" Ilaria asks, her voice cracking.

"They let me see him. They're torturing him. He's hurt bad, but he's alive. Oh, Mother," she adds before unleashing hysterical wails.

"Varella, look at me. Are you sure it was him?"

"I'm positive."

"I don't understand how they could have him," Ilaria says, fighting tears as she covers her mouth. "Rykos can't be there."

"They have him…I saw him. They have both of us," Varella says, growing even more emotional.

Ilaria wipes the fake tears and presses her lips together. "You're lying."

"Mother, I would never lie about that. Why won't you believe your daughter?"

"Because, Varella, Rykos is standing right next to me."

He takes position alongside his mother and faces the camera, grinning at Varella's shock. Stories of siblings despising each other have existed since biblical times. Her children take the concept to a new level. For once, Rykos has the upper hand.

"Hello, Sis. How's my torture there going?"

"Rykos…you're at the RTCC," Varella says, the tears having suddenly stopped.

"It turns out that I am. Your performance would have almost been convincing if everyone didn't already know that you're a pathological liar."

"Well played, Mother. You should know that I serve the corporation. My duty is to—"

"Yeah, yeah, yeah, whatever," Ilaria says, waving a dismissive hand. "I know the ridiculous corporate pledge of loyalty shtick. Put Virtari on. I'm sure he's there."

Varella steps aside, and Director Virtari comes into the frame. Despite having his ruse uncovered, he's still wearing a smug expression. The man knows no humility.

"Ilaria, to your daughter's credit, she said this wasn't going to work. I thought it was worth a shot."

"I figured you were behind this. The question is, why bother?"

Virtari takes a deep breath and looks around before turning his focus back to the camera. "Neither of us wants the streets of Manhattan running red with blood. I don't want people to die for no reason."

"And marching my daughter in front of a camera to manipulate me is your idea of preserving life?"

"I don't negotiate with traitors. Since my little ruse didn't work, I'm forced to resort to a different tactic."

Virtari grabs Varella and yanks her close. Holding her by the throat, he places a gun to her temple. The abrupt action takes her by surprise. Confusion in her eyes is replaced by fear. She didn't see this coming.

"I've already killed one person you love in front of you. I'll do it again."

The emotions Ilaria endured at Rikers rush back. She despises Varella's decisions, but she's still her daughter. A mother will always love her child. She can't bear to watch this monster murder another member of her family.

"Be sensible. We both know how this will end. Whether we regain control of the city today or tomorrow, the outcome is certain. You're going to die, as will the traitors helping you. The question is, how many innocents will join you? We'll start with your only daughter."

Virtari presses the gun harder into Varella's temple. A tear rolls down her cheek – a real one this time. He's not bluffing. Her life means nothing to him, leaving Ilaria facing an impossible decision.

CHAPTER SIXTY

LIBERTEUM

Valhalla
Midtown Geographic Area
New York City Municipal Corporation

The intersection of Church and Chambers was the logical spot for an ambush. Once the column reached that point, they had their choice of routes to One Guardian Plaza. Guessing wrong would mean Dzamko and Phylep would have to redeploy their men, and halting their advance was already a long shot.

The crossroads is dominated by tall buildings on the corners. Stopping the column there would force them down narrower side streets. That would break up the formation into manageable chunks. It would also reduce the effectiveness of the drones flying air support. It was a good plan. Too bad it didn't work out that way.

The PSS first engaged the column with the heaviest weapons available. The qulis did their part, descending on them in a clever assault. The agents were forced to find protective cover from the hail of gunfire. What happened next was both predictable and tragic.

The tanks engaged the qulis with their cannons. One of the buildings the laborers were fighting from was reduced one to rubble. Missiles streaked in from overhead drones and obliterated the barricade, forcing a hasty retreat. The guardians and qulis are now on the run, with heavily armed drones stalking them like giant killer mosquitoes.

"This is going to be a massacre," Zyree moans. "Ortan, is there any way to hack into those drones?"

"Sure, but you need to consider the consequences. Once they learn we have that capability, they'll kill the power to the city. Without Valhalla's network, we'll lose any advantage we have."

Ortan doesn't toss in any jokes about the OdinNet moniker, which he's been mocking all night. He's serious about this. Even a socially awkward recluse knows this struggle is between life and death.

"What about the tanks?"

"They're pre-collapse dinosaurs. There's no internal system that I can access that will make a difference."

"So, we can't hack the tanks. We'll be discovered if we hack the drones, and if we don't do anything, they'll annihilate us, and it won't matter anyway," Michele summarizes.

Her conclusion is accurate. Every attack plan ever devised through millennia of recorded history has a flaw. This one is no different. They only need to find it.

"Can you shut down the EOC?" Zyree asks.

"Shut it down?"

"Losing the video feeds will hamper their command and control. Without power, they have no communications, and without communications…."

"They'll lose control of the drones."

"Won't they just reestablish communications from somewhere else?" Jasper asks.

"It gives the qulis a chance to escape," Michele says. "Do it."

"Ortan, can you make the power failure look like it wasn't a hack?" Koltayne asks, causing everyone to stare at the normally quiet bodyguard.

"I like the way this kid thinks. Uh, yeah, I can do that."

"How? The critical systems are heavily encrypted," Jasper argues.

"No system is completely isolated. It's all about knowing how to bypass countermeasures."

"You don't have the computing power," the Liberteum hacker continues to protest.

"Psssh," Ortan dismisses. "You don't drive a nail with a wrench. When you have the right tool for the job, anything is possible."

Ortan has a flair for the dramatic. When he makes his final gestures, he isn't even watching the display. Fifteen seconds later, Jasper's mouth hangs open. He has full access to the EOC's network.

"How did you do that?"

"Magic. The EOC is a nerve center and I'm going to use its capabilities against it. I can sever power to the entire block and cause an electrical surge to take the standby generators offline. It will take them a while to figure out what happened."

"Perfect," Michele says, impressed.

He taps his finger in the air without looking at his display.

"I hope they have candles."

CHAPTER SIXTY-ONE

AMERICA, INC.

Emergency Operations Center
Lower Manhattan Geographic District
New York City Municipal Corporation

The VidLynk suddenly goes dead as the EOC plunges into darkness. Emergency lighting clicks on as Virtari pushes Varella aside. The room is completely offline. Not a single display is glowing. Then, the emergency lighting cuts out. The only light comes from the battery-operated exit lights above the doors.

"Damn it! What the hell is going on?" Virtari barks.

"We have complete power loss, sir."

"Yeah, no shit. What happened to the emergency generators?"

Nobody has an answer to that question. Several agents activate torchlights, and their beams slice through the darkness. At least Virtari can see the clueless faces of the agents.

"Somebody get me answers! This place has mobile command centers, right?" the director asks the nearest agent.

"I believe so."

"Don't believe. Confirm. If it does, get one fired up and contact our columns. I need to know what's happening."

"On my way."

Maybe the room will come back online, but it's not worth taking the chance. This could be a simple mechanical failure, but the timing is suspicious. That the emergency power also went down has sent the director's conspiratorial mind down a dark path.

An agent hands Virtari a torchlight, and he shines it on a shaken Varella. She's trying to compose herself and failing. Boo-hoo.

"You were going to kill me."

"I would kill my own mother for this corporation. Sacrifices need to be made if order is going to be restored. If you aren't willing to do the same thing, then you're not the executive you think you are. You're still alive, so stop your sniveling."

"Has my assistance been worth that little to you?"

"I saw an opportunity to end this, nothing more."

Varella shakes her head. "I told you it wouldn't work! My mother hates me."

"She's still a mother, and that's a powerful bond. Children are a weakness. I was willing to exploit that one if it meant regaining control of this city."

Reality is sometimes cruel. Executives and employees are expendable. The men and women who serve it come and go, but the corporation is forever. It's a harsh lesson everyone eventually learns.

"You're the daughter of traitors, Varella. I spared you so you may serve me in life or in death if I deem it. Do you understand?" She nods. "Good, now let's get back to work."

"Sir, the entire block is without power," an agent rushes to inform him. "It's not localized to this building. The generators appear to be offline due to a power surge."

"Did the qulis take out the grid?" Varella asks, recovering from her traumatic experience.

"If it was just the power, I'd say yes. Losing the power *and* the generators in the middle of a VidLynk with your mother? That can't be a coincidence. Something else is going on."

"Sir, we are powering up a mobile command center and established unsecure comms with the columns. They're proceeding but have slowed without air support."

"What?"

"The drones returned to the airfield when the uplink went down. They were programmed to take their commands from here."

Virtari rubs his forehead in frustration. He never would have thought the EOC would have been this vulnerable to attack. Somehow, Liberteum managed to knock them offline. Underestimating them is a mistake he's tired of making.

"How many command trucks are down there?"

"Three."

"Get them all staffed. We're abandoning the EOC. I'm done with this place. Send one to the New Jersey staging area. Have the second rendezvous with the southern column. Primary operations will go with me in the third truck."

"Where are you going, sir?" the agent asks.

"To church."

CHAPTER SIXTY-TWO

LIBERTEUM

Valhalla
Midtown Geographic Area
New York City Municipal Corporation

The EOC is now blind and powerless, but Michele has all the views she needs of the bad news heading their way. New York City has ten times more surveillance cameras than it does people. Every angle of every inch of street, sidewalk, and pedestrian lowline in Manhattan is monitored. Thanks to Ortan, they watch BCS agents dismount their transports in high-definition as their tanks assume positions around the cathedral.

"This won't even be a fight," Michele says, despondent.

"Isn't this place impregnable?" Fiolla asks. "It's so deep underground."

"It's tough to locate but not impossible to access. The Alamo was our stronghold."

"Alamo? You mean Old St. Patrick's?" Zyree asks.

Michele nods. "And that fell easily once they found it. Valhalla is meant to be invisible. Now, we have a spotlight on us."

"I never would have found that access," Fiolla argues.

"They'll find it. They will tear this place down stone by stone if they need to. It won't matter if it takes months."

Michele grimaces at Zyree. "We can't fight them or wait them out. We'll have to outthink them."

"Good luck with that," Jasper says under his breath.

"No, Michele is right," Fiolla interjects. "Ortan can hack into anything. America Incorporated is a monolith, but it has sensitive pressure points. If we find the right one and squeeze, it will force them to pause."

"Until they cut our power or data connections," Ortan says. "We're dead in the water without either."

"They'd have to black out all of Manhattan," Jasper adds.

"They wouldn't hesitate to do that," Zyree concludes. "Not for a second."

"One problem at a time, guys," Michele says. "I know how we can stop the BCS attack. We finish Archimedes."

"That's such a great name," Ortan compliments, nodding at her.

"But you already took down the exchange," Zyree says.

Michele remembers that she never had the opportunity to brief the former inspector on the rest of the plan. She takes a deep breath and exhales deeply.

"Archimedes has three phases. The first two were designed to halt trading on Intercorpex. We started by severing a critical link between data centers."

"Secaucus. The explosion there forced the NOC to transfer over to a less secure point-to-point microwave communications system to appease the patricians," Ortan clarifies.

"Which Haven intercepted using an old satellite dish. We needed to know how exchange messages were formatted. With that knowledge, we fabricated messages and inserted them on the trading circuit."

"That's why you chose the old Broad Street Station," Zyree concludes. "It had nothing to do with its proximity to the exchange. It was converted into a utility hub. You had the perfect spot to stay invisible while accessing the cables below Wall Street."

"I can guess the next part," Ortan volunteers. "You tapped into the fiber optics, but that was only one of the two Intercorpex trading circuits. You needed to disable the other one and used some disturbances in the city to mask the true objective of taking it out."

The explosions were in residential or other random areas. They weren't targeted at busy transit hubs or populated areas. It took a while for them to uncover what was impacted. That second circuit was the common denominator.

"It has the added benefit of being a plausible reason why the market was going haywire. We needed to cause volatility on the IGI to force patricians to access their trading accounts. Once they did, we captured their personal login information."

Only the gentez-majorez can trade on the Intercorporational Global Index. Some try to accumulate shares to gain a majority stake in a corporation and become prima. Others use volatility to increase their fortunes. Whatever the reason, nearly every patrician was buying and selling that day.

"You defeated modern security with an old-school phishing scam," Ortan says, appreciative of the cleverness Liberteum displayed.

"Wait!" Fiolla interjects. "This was all part of a single plan? The corporation looked at those as isolated incidents. Nobody in Washington ever connected the dots."

"Black swan events," Zyree says, shaking his head. "Surprise incidents that have a major negative effect and are incorrectly rationalized after the fact with the benefit of hindsight. We rationalized them as desperate terrorist attacks."

Fiolla's head must be swimming. She grew up in a world that convinced employees that executives were the best and brightest in society. They are nearly infallible, and her working for Valen must have done little to change that mindset. He always came across as in control. It must be a shock to learn that they were all duped by urches they consider inferior.

"We were counting on that. The second phase was to create a distraction and use the account information we captured to place trades directly from patrician accounts. We knew it would force them to shut down the exchange."

"And it did."

"The distraction was blowing up Old Saint Patrick's Cathedral and a running gunfight in Manhattan?" Zyree asks.

"No, that was the fallout from my rift with Haven. I went with Rykos to the Alamo to help retrieve his father. We were there when the stronghold was discovered."

"So, you were there," Zyree says, amazed. "I was on that raid. My colleague tried killing me in one of those crypts."

Michele forces a smile. "It looks like the Glory of the Sphere Plaza wasn't the first time our paths crossed, Zyree."

A heavy silence grips the room. Every single person down here was involved in the events of that day in one way or another. Some of them were on different sides. It makes their presence in this subterranean base together that much more surreal.

"So, the final phase was leveling part of Intercorpex and killing patricians?" Fiolla asks.

"No, that was my father's idea," Farron interjects, joining in on the discussion. "He was working with Haven on the side to advance his own agenda."

"The point of a distraction is to shift focus, not invite more unwanted attention. Our original plan was to disrupt power, communications, and transit systems throughout the city."

"You were going to hold a fire sale." Ortan is clearly enjoying this.

"A fire sale, as in selling goods at a heavy discount?" Fiolla asks, eliciting snickers from the hacker.

"No, a fire sale as in 'everything must go,'" Jasper says. "It's hacker lingo for an attempt to disrupt multiple computer systems simultaneously."

"We could have created disorder and chaos while keeping it largely bloodless. Haven and Denali had other plans."

"I know what you're thinking, Fiolla," Zyree says, studying the apprehensive look on her face. "Here's something that might change your perception. Michele contacted me with Haven's location before he detonated that truck bomb. We came within a whisper of stopping him. The warnings we sent Intercorpex and the BCS were acted upon too late."

Fiolla's mouth hangs open slightly. That story was likely never reported to the White House. The BCS would have covered up their incompetence. Even more stunning is the realization that Michele was willing to sacrifice the success of her plan to save those people.

"If you didn't think taking down the exchange would create change and destroying it wasn't part of the plan, what is phase three of this Archimedes plan, and how can it help us now?" Zyree asks, breaking the silence.

"We're going to seize control of Bytecoin."

CHAPTER SIXTY-THREE

THE PATRICIANS

Keating Family of the Gentez-Majorez Estate
Greenwich Geographic District
Southern Connecticut Municipal Corporation

The quli uprising was a surprising development. Denali almost wishes Haven were still alive to add to the chaos in the city. He was a rabid dog and would have been useful in stoking the fires of dissent. His only real failure was leaving Michele and the rest of Liberteum alive. Not that he gets all the blame. Even Denali fumbled his chance to be rid of the devilishly resilient terrorist leader. Now, it's on the BCS to do what he and Haven couldn't.

That's an opportunity begging to be seized. Subduing the qulis and chasing Liberteum will keep them preoccupied. The turmoil gripping major cities will take weeks to subdue. By then, the global power shift will be irreversible. America Incorporated was the only corporation in a position to stop him. With them looking inward, they won't even see what's happening around the globe until it's too late.

"Pardon the interruption, sir," Abbot says, walking into the study. "Commander Lacune wanted me to inform you that the BCS has commenced their attack on Manhattan."

"Very well. Keep me informed of their progress," Denali says, rising from the sofa to stretch his legs.

Abbot notices the empty coffee cup and refills it from the service. He glances up several times as he pours. "There is the question of your son's whereabouts."

Denali shouldn't be bothered by that. He turned his back on his own father, so hoping his son dies a painful death is justified. Unfortunately, part of him still does care despite his best efforts to exorcise that feeling.

"He wasn't at the brownstone or his domicile. That means he was stupid enough to go with Liberteum."

"There is a chance that is not true. Our people are scouring the city. It's not an easy task, given the current situation. Unfortunately, there is no sign of him."

"He's under St. Patrick's with Liberteum," Denali concludes. "Once the BCS surrounds it, he's as good as dead."

Farron had obscene wealth, a top-notch education, the finest possessions, unlimited travel, beautiful women…Denali ensured he had all the trappings that come with status and privilege. In a few short days, Farron would have been handed the world on a silver platter. Then, he threw it all away, and for what? Loyalty? A bankrupt ideology?

"Sir, your actions will ensure your family's legacy for generations. Without Farron—"

"I'll have three idiot nephews who can assume control of this empire upon my death. With the right mentoring, one of them might adequately carry on the Keating legacy."

"Of course, sir."

Abbot doesn't believe that for a second. He knows the limitations of that branch of the family tree. Fortunately, Denali doesn't plan on departing this Earth anytime soon. He has years, if not decades, to groom an heir to the global empire he's about to inherit. It may take that long, considering the aptitude of those three idiots.

"There is one more thing. The board of directors is considering replacing Chief Executive Zeykala with someone more…competent."

"I've heard. They are desperate. All of the corporations are."

Russia and China are reeling from massacres, the United Kingdom is trying to calm their employees in London, and India is struggling to get their employees to work after the transit attacks. None are watching what's happening on the global stage, nor will they reach out to America Incorporated to enlist their help in stopping it.

When you can't see the forest for the trees, you don't see the fire coming at you. Corporations will turn to the patricians for help out of necessity. Survival comes before all else. If The Trust doesn't lose its nerve and follows through on its commitments, Denali will be waiting with open arms.

"Is there anything more I can do for you, sir?"

"Has Lacune located the attack helicopter my son used in the attack on the termination center?"

"No, sir, I'm afraid not."

"Order him to keep searching. I want to know what patrician families are helping Farron."

The other families of the gentez-majorez and -minorez aren't a threat, especially against the combined manpower of The Trust. They would be a nuisance at worst. What's disconcerting is not knowing that a minor family possessed that level of weaponry. It's an unwelcome surprise.

The patrician takes a deep breath as Abbot shows himself out of the study. In the next seventy-two hours, the world will be on its knees. A new era will be ushered in, and Denali Keating will have done what Adolf Hitler, Genghis Khan, Alexander the Great, and Julius Caesar couldn't do. He will become the most powerful man who has ever walked this Earth. The Keating name will be etched in the annals of history for all eternity. The thought causes him to smile.

CHAPTER SIXTY-FOUR

LIBERTEUM

Valhalla
Midtown Geographic Area
New York City Municipal Corporation

Stunned silence. That's the best way to describe the operations center in Valhalla. There are a lot of things Michele could have named as Liberteum's target. Corporate governance, key industries, trade…the list is too long to articulate. The very last thing anyone would have guessed is Bytecoin.

Currencies have been around for millennia. Coins once made of precious metals morphed into paper money backed by gold reserves. That changed again in the 20th century when governments adopted fiat currency that could be manipulated. Corporatists didn't want to make the same mistake. As the new world governance took hold, a decentralized digital currency became the medium of exchange. Governed by Intercorpex, Bytecoin is the lifeblood of the world's economy.

"You're going to destroy the global financial system?" Ortan asks.

"We don't intend to destroy anything," Michele explains. "We wanted to force change by ransoming the one thing global corporations can't do without."

"Currency."

"I don't understand," Fiolla says, thrown by the revelation.

"I do," Zyree interjects. "Intercorpex relies on physical infrastructure to operate. They need circuits to communicate and data centers filled with servers running matching engines to complete trades. Authorities would assume terrorists could only attack physical targets. They would never recognize a threat to infiltrate a decentralized financial network."

Michele nods. Zyree was closer to understanding what they were up to than she anticipated. He only needed one or two pieces to put the puzzle together. Would that have been enough to stop Liberteum if he were still working for Intercorpex? It's questionable. He wasn't looking in the right place. Regardless, she's glad he's on their side now.

"That's a brilliant ruse," Ortan says in admiration. "Nothing was mentioned about Bytecoin at Intercorpex before I became persona non grata."

"Okay, so you want to ransom the currency system…to do what?" Fiolla asks.

"Free the world," Zyree explains, causing Michele to crack a smile. "That's what Liberteum means."

There's another long silence as the group digests what they've been told. There are undoubtedly a lot of questions about what a free world looks like, but the BCS has entered the cathedral, and time is short. They need to wrap this up.

"The world's CEOs will never change how they do business based on sporadic attacks. They need a compelling reason. Losing control of the financial network gives them that reason."

"Michele, you don't understand executives. Even if we somehow manage to control Bytecoin, the corporations won't bargain with us. They'd rather see the world in ashes than give up their power."

"That is why we need the support of the qulis and open-minded employees. There is power in numbers. We're already seeing it," she says, pointing at the map of Manhattan. "My plan was to have someone take our message directly to the people."

"Rykos," Zyree concludes, causing everyone to stare at him. "That's why you took Rykos after the raid on that urch rave."

Fiolla nods slowly. "A hero of the corporation and son of a chief guardian would have a profound influence on our employees."

"Especially now when his mother is working with the qulis to confront the BCS," Farron adds. "It might be the only advantage of this uprising. His words will resonate even outside of New York City. The people are brainwashed to be dependent on the system. If he can convey an alternative form of governance that satisfies those needs, they will listen."

That is not what Michele had in mind when she took Rykos following the raid. Her father was a long proponent of having someone on the outside acting as their messenger, but finding the right person felt like a daunting challenge. Then, she met Rykos. A lot has happened since then, and to get him to stay, she even argued that having a messenger was no longer necessary. Now, she realizes she was wrong and he was right to leave to fill that role.

"Let's back up for a second. How are you planning to gain control of Bytecoin?" Ortan asks Jasper.

"Take a look for yourself."

Ortan looks at Jasper's work as he brings up the code on his display. The computer expert nods as he scans the lines and then smiles before leaning back in his chair.

"This is absolutely brilliant work, Jasper," he says, eliciting a broad smile.

"I know it's not there yet, but I think we're close."

Ortan mouth opens slightly as he clenches his teeth. "No, you really aren't."

"What are you saying, Ortan?" Michele asks, not liking the direction this is going.

"I have some bad news about the last phase of Archimedes, Michele. It doesn't stand a chance of working."

CHAPTER SIXTY-FIVE

AMERICA, INC.

The White House
Corporate Governance District
Washington-Arlington Municipal Corporation

It feels good to stand up for yourself. That's the thought rattling around Zeykala's mind. She is invigorated after showing some backbone to her former patron. Most executives are wary of patricians and quick to fold under their pressure. She knows that feeling all too well. But this is her corporation now, and enough is enough. She refuses to be Talya's or anyone else's slave.

"Chief Executive Zeykala, you're late for the crisis meeting in the Executive Conference Room," the automated administrative assistant warns after the prima patrician departs the office.

"Tell them I'll be with them momentarily."

The time has come for Zeykala to assert her authority. The executives of their subsidiaries are challenging her. Parent company executives are questioning or defying her. Corporate security arranged an assassination. Change is in order, and that starts now.

Instead of heading down the hall, she takes the stairway to the sublevel and strides into the Situation Room. This place has seen a lot of history. It's about to see some more.

"Ma'am, I didn't know we had a scheduled briefing," her newly appointed Pentagon liaison says, standing from his seat at the table.

"We don't. Have all Bureau of Corporate Security been removed from the White House?"

"Yes, ma'am. They are maintaining a small presence in the mansion for Valen, but they have departed the West Wing and left the grounds."

She looks at the live feed from New York being beamed into the room. Virtari's operation to retake the city is underway. Good. Now is the time to make her moves.

"How many men are assigned to Valen's detail?"

"Nine, rotating in three eight-hour shifts."

"Make sure they stay in the residence. I don't want them to set foot outside that mansion unless they are heading for their conveyances."

Zeykala leaves the Situation Room with her first legitimate smile in days. She's half surprised the agents obeyed her order. It almost would have been more fun to instruct Washington Public Safety and Security to escort them out. That would be a slap in the face.

She returns to the main floor and strides into the Executive Conference Room. Once called the Cabinet Room, this is where the president of the United States used to meet with the heads of important government departments. It's like entering the lion's den. Each of these executives aspires to have her job someday. Some want it sooner.

"I apologize for my lateness. These are extraordinary times. I trust you have all been informed of the current situation."

Zeykala gets a smattering of nods from the dozen CEOs around the table and verbal affirmations from those joining via VidLynk.

"Ma'am, we asked for this meeting because we all find ourselves in precarious positions. Productivity has all but stopped because of your corporate law order."

"To build on what my esteemed colleague is saying," another executive says, "no productivity equals no revenue. We are beyond measuring the economic impact of this crisis and are standing on the precipice of a complete economic meltdown."

"And you are somehow under the impression that I'm aware of that?"

"We don't know what the White House staff is communicating to you. There is no manufacturing, transportation, or retail. It will take months to recover from the supply chain interruption if we recover at all. You need to end this crisis."

"A plan is in place to restore order. Until then, the stores are all well stocked, and we have excess inventory—"

"They were, and we did. As in past tense. The rioting has taken a toll."

"The mad rush to the stores once this crisis is over will ensure what remains gets picked clean."

"We can replenish but restarting production and getting goods to market will take time."

"And until that happens, we will have a whole other crisis to deal with."

"Not to mention, we are close to defaulting on global trade agreements. Other corporations are in as bad or worse shape than us. That's the only thing keeping our contracts in force."

The rapid-fire comments spewed from around the table almost sound rehearsed. They are really piling on. It's not some nefarious plot to make things appear worse than they are. Everything they are saying is one hundred percent accurate. A litany of challenges faces her once she moves beyond the current crisis.

"Ladies and gentlemen, you are the chief executives of our major subsidiaries. I trust you will find a way to make it happen."

"It's not that easy."

"Bringing this crisis to a close isn't any easier. You all understand what will need to be done when corporate law is lifted. I will rely on all of you to put your expertise to good use. You can count on whatever support you need from the White House. Now, if you'll excuse me."

Zeykala doesn't make it two steps before the CEOs start acting like petulant children when their mother drops them off at daycare. The hollers from the room demanding her attention rise above the cacophony of grumbling and general griping.

"Ma'am, we didn't come here for a three-minute pep talk."

The sardonic tone commands her attention, and she wheels to face the red-faced executive. "No, you came to Washington because you heard rumors that the board of directors is replacing me and you want your names included on the shortlist."

The room goes from chaotic chatter to stone-cold silence in the blink of an eye. They're stunned, and it is not because of the veracity of the accusation. They know it's a fact and are embarrassed that their actions are so transparent.

"Rest assured, the board may elect to do that. You may get your chance to lobby board members for this office. But I'm still here, and you will follow my directives. Anyone found busy politicking and not minding their respective companies during this crisis will be relieved from their duties and terminated. I hope I have made myself clear."

The threat has the desired effect. The executives share uneasy looks, but there are no further challenges. Zeykala strides out of the conference room, wearing another smile. There's nothing more that needs to be said. The BCS is gone, and the executives are put in their place. That's two problems down in ten minutes. She's on a roll.

CHAPTER SIXTY-SIX

LIBERTEUM

Valhalla
Midtown Geographic Area
New York City Municipal Corporation

Michele checks the surveillance video from outside the cathedral. The BCS has established a perimeter but has yet to storm the church. They're waiting for something, and that can't be good. The delay is better than the alternatives, but the clock is definitely ticking.

She turns to Ortan. "An explanation would be useful here. What do you mean Archimedes won't work?"

He leans back in his chair and frowns. "All systems processing financial transactions are protected by a program called Archangyl. It's not exaggerating to call it the perfect anti-intrusion defense mechanism. It's also the closest thing in the world there is to an actual artificial intelligence. It learns, adapts, and combats threats without human input or intervention. You never would have penetrated it without detection. Jasper's code would cripple a normal network, but Archangyl isn't vulnerable to this kind of attack."

The news carpet bombs her optimism. She has heard of Archangyl but never believed it was that foolproof. She looks at Jasper, hoping he has a counterpoint or some brilliant plan to circumvent that system. He doesn't. He looks defeated.

"What you're saying is all this work was for nothing?"

"You had a better chance of sprouting wings and flying than you did hacking Archangyl the way you planned."

"How do you know that?" Michele asks, grasping for anything that doesn't relegate her grand plan to the colossal failure category.

Ortan bites his lip before exhaling. "Because I helped write it."

She didn't see that coming. The man has skills, as he has already demonstrated multiple times. To think he wrote the program installed to defend the most critical computer system on the planet is mind-blowing.

"You wrote Archangyl?" Jasper asks, exacerbated.

"Part of it. I was the lead developer on a six-man team that spent years designing, testing, and implementing the system. I'm the only one of us still alive."

"What happened to the others?" Fiolla asks.

"What typically happens in this world when someone becomes expendable? I saw it coming. We finished testing, and Archangyl went into production. Then, things began to change. I felt something was wrong and took precautions. Then, they came for us. One senior developer died of a heart attack, and another of hypoglycemia. The other three junior developers died in a fall down the stairs, drowning in a swimming pool, and by carbon monoxide poisoning from an old heating unit. All of that happened within two days. For me, it was a traffic accident."

Everyone reflexively stares at his exoskeleton.

"I was crossing a street when I was struck by a conveyance. I was the lucky one. My teammates lost their lives. I only lost the use of my legs."

"Your own bosses tried to kill you?"

"We have more in common than you think," Ortan says, smiling at Fiolla. "You can say that's why I have trust issues."

"Why would they do that?" Jasper asks. "It seems like a waste of incredible talent."

"You were a security risk," Zyree concludes, getting a nod from Ortan.

"They were afraid we coded backdoors into the system. The only way to ensure one could never be exploited was to eradicate the coders. Our primary task was completed. We weren't needed anymore."

"That's messed up," Koltayne says.

"Welcome to the Corporate Age."

"What happened after the accident?" Michele asks. Accident doesn't seem like the right word to use given the circumstances, but it was the only one she could come up with.

"I wasn't killed, so someone was sent to finish the job. I was recovering in a medical center when an ICX inspector slipped into my room. It fell to him to ensure I didn't live to see another morning. He didn't agree with his assignment and spared me. He reported to Intercorpex that the job was done and stashed me in a different facility under an alias until I healed. Then he hid me away in the last place anyone would ever look."

"Iceland."

Ortan nods. "My cover was as a network architect, and I was good enough at it that nobody asked questions. My real job was to help him with investigations, internal audits…stuff like that. He became a prominent inspector and rose through the ranks quickly."

"Jurghen?" Zyree asks, not believing where this story is going.

"The chief of security for Intercorpex," Ortan explains for the benefit of the others, "and Zyree's boss."

"Former boss. That's why he sent me to see you in Iceland after the Secaucus attack. You two have a history. He knew you could help find answers."

"That he sent you to me was all I needed to know about how much he trusts you. I never got guests. It was too risky."

"Did you put one in?" Michele asks. "A backdoor to Archangyl?"

"No. If any of the others did, I never stumbled upon it."

"So, we're back to square one?"

Zyree knows there was a reason for telling this story. Ortan has a purpose in everything he says and does, even if it takes him a while to get to the point. He likes being dramatic, probably because he hasn't had much practice with it in person over the years.

"Are we back to square one, Ortan?"

He grins. "I said Archangyl couldn't be hacked. I never said it couldn't be controlled. Archangyl doesn't require human input to function, but he listens to his sister."

The realization hits Zyree with the force of a train. "Huldufólk?"

"You didn't think actual elves worked for me in Iceland, did you, Zyree?"

He feels stupid. The Icelandic elf he said ran his computer systems is the system itself. That's how he managed to get information so quickly. His computer is a clone of the world's most powerful program.

"What's Huldufólk?" Farron asks.

"I actually only took one precaution in preparation for my demise – I made a duplicate of Archangyl's source code. When I started the job in Iceland, the data center provided all the processing power and memory I would ever need. Over time, I taught the program how to play offense instead of defense."

"Ying and yang. That's why it's his sister," Jasper muses.

"Exactly. Archangyl recognizes the code as a sibling. I found out by accident that he listened to her and would do anything she asked. With the combined strength of Huldufólk and Archangyl, there isn't a computer system on Earth I can't break into and control."

Michele always thought that hacking into the Bytecoin system was a pipe dream. Her father was far more optimistic and brought in men like Jasper to make that plan a reality. Over time, she shared in his optimism and became convinced that it could be done. This conversation has become a rollercoaster, and Ortan has given her a fresh adrenaline high.

"So, where is this program now?" Michele asks.

Ortan grins like a magician who just made a rabbit appear out of thin air. He runs his hand over the suitcase he brought. "Plugged into your network."

CHAPTER SIXTY-SEVEN

AMERICA, INC.

St. Patrick's Cathedral
Midtown Geographic Area
New York City Municipal Corporation

The reappropriated PSS mobile command center stops at the airtight perimeter established around the hulking cathedral. Virtari knows his men have secured the surrounding buildings to search for any escape tunnels. Hundreds of ground sensors are being placed to monitor the area, and drones track activity overhead. Liberteum is not going to escape this time.

Four tanks are on site, with their turrets rotated and cannons trained on the cathedral. These BCS agents probably hope they don't find the terrorists. They can't wait to see these ancient fighting machines open up on the stone structure.

The streets are deserted. As with the vanguard, the command truck met no resistance in Midtown. The qulis and PSS down south were bold to face down his agents when they were outmanned and on foot. He bets they're rethinking that strategy now.

"Where are we, Bruzik?" the BCS director asks the column commander when he jogs over.

"We've scanned the entire structure with thermal. The only heat signature in the building is located in the sanctuary. We think it's probably the cardinal."

Virtari nods. "Send the men in to secure the building."

"Yes, sir."

Bruzik barks at his team leaders, and agents pour through the three front doors. St. Patrick's was the ninetieth-largest church in the world. After the collapse of world governments, it moved up to forty-five. Even with this amount of manpower, it will take a few minutes to search for threats and secure the entire building.

"Talk to me about the special items."

"The ground penetrating radars are unpacked and waiting. If there's a terrorist nest underground, we'll find it. As for the special package, I thought it was prudent to leave it on the truck until we know we need it."

"The building is clear, sir," the team leader reports. "Cardinal Michael Castellano is being held in the sanctuary."

"Commander Bruzik, begin your radar search," Virtari orders. "The access to Liberteum's stronghold is hidden here somewhere. Be ready to deploy the special package. The terrorists will fight like badgers to protect this place, and I don't want to waste lives."

"Yes, sir."

Virtari walks up the short set of stairs and through the heavy oak doors into the narthex. He takes a moment to admire the centuries-old architecture. Cathedrals like this have a special mystique about them. Employees whisper when they enter as if the Lord Himself is present. Of course, the place has a much different feeling with the presence of over a hundred heavily armed agents.

The cardinal is clad in full religious regalia and being guarded by two men on the main altar. The ornate garb is overkill considering conducting church services is forbidden under corporate law.

The man doesn't protest the BCS presence. There is no objection to their actions or whining about his treatment. The cardinal knows he's about to meet God. Virtari is happy to make the introduction if he doesn't cooperate.

"Where are they?"

"Where are who, my son?" the cardinal says.

Virtari punches him hard on the chin. The shot would have laid most people out, and had it not been for the burly agents arresting his fall, this "man of God" would have been no different.

"You are hiding Liberteum here. Rest assured, we will not leave until they are found. Help us locate them, or you will die."

"You dare desecrate this house of God and then expect my help?"

Virtari punches him again. The clacking sound of knuckles against the flesh of his cheek is satisfying as it echoes in the cavernous room. Clergymen rank only below patricians in terms of their insufferability.

"You have already desecrated it, Your Grace."

"I do the Lord's work. I protect his flock from the wolves."

"Protecting the flock is my job, not yours. You have gone astray. There is evil in the world, Your Grace. You are protecting the wicked, and now it is time to atone for your sins."

"I will meet God with a clear conscience."

Virtari scoffs and picks up a gold chalice from the altar to study it. Christ was a simple carpenter. He wonders what the Almighty would think about the men entrusted with His Church drinking out of such an ornate instrument. He would ask the cardinal, but his opinion on the matter is irrelevant.

"How many people have died in the name of their religions?" the director asks, twirling the chalice in his hand. "Hundreds of thousands? Millions? Tens of millions? Judaism, Christianity, and Islam have all done unspeakable things in God's name. Religion is the greatest mass delusion in human history. It's a relic of a bygone era. Our corporate founders showed an incredible lack of foresight for not abolishing it after the collapse. It ranks among their greatest mistakes."

"You can take people's freedoms easier than their faith, Director."

"The moment the people traded citizenship for employment, they had no further use for either."

Virtari tosses the cup, and it skitters across the floor. The clinking sound reverberates off the arched stone buttresses supporting the vaulted ceiling. The cardinal stares at him without passion, emotion, or hatred.

"The corporation needed the Church," the cardinal interjects. "People turned to their religion more than ever during the dark days following the collapse. They never would have accepted corporate rule without our blessing. You claim that keeping religion was the founders' worst mistake. Ours was allowing the corporations to take over in the first place."

"What was the alternative? Ah, I almost forgot. People of faith prefer persecution because they believe suffering brings them closer to God. What kind of god would let that collapse happen in the first place?"

"One that bestowed upon us free will to make our own choices."

"Yes, of course, the great paradox that is 'free will.' It's a convenient argument. It's almost like having no God at all, isn't it?"

"His will be done."

"He willed the collapse of governments? He willed hundreds of millions to die when anarchy descended over us? Or, maybe it was His will for corporations to rise and intervene. I've read the Bible and know what happens in the Book of Revelation. We saw famine, disease, and death sweep across the land. Corporations saved humanity, and God became irrelevant. After that happened, the world stopped being His kingdom and started being ours."

"The Lord has established His throne in the heavens, and His sovereignty rules over all," the cardinal mutters before looking at Virtari. "Psalms."

The BCS director didn't come to this place for a sermon. The clock is ticking, and he knows he's not going to get what's needed from this man.

Virtari scowls. "If you say so. I'm already tired of your preaching. This is the only chance I'll give you to save your soul, Cardinal Castellano. And your life. The longer I need to search for Liberteum, the worse it will be for them. Tell me where they are, or they will learn the meaning of Hell on Earth. The decision is yours."

"Corinthians, five-ten."

"What?"

"For we must all appear before the judgment seat of Christ, so that each of us may receive what is due us for the things done while in the body, whether good or bad."

Virtari nods. It's not the answer he wanted, but it's the one he expected. "Have it your way. Tell him I said, 'Hi.'"

CHAPTER SIXTY-EIGHT

THE PATRICIANS

Keating Family of the Gentez-Majorez Estate
Greenwich Geographic District
Southern Connecticut Municipal Corporation

The second wave of planned attacks is underway. Denali planned to enjoy the show from the comfort of his study, but there are more displays and better information down in his command center. This is too important not to be involved in on a personal level.

The next series of attacks is designed to complement the first round in the targeted corporations. This time, they're even deadlier and more devastating. The world will shake from the trembling of corporate executives trying to deal with this crisis. Their panic will become Denali's opportunity.

Early successes are no prediction of future results. Despite planning for every contingency, nobody can fully control outcomes. Most operations are going off without a hitch, but there is one major exception.

"You're connected, sir."

"What the hell is going on over there?" Denali demands when the secure VidLynk glows to life.

"White Lotus is refusing to participate in the next wave of attacks. They're claiming that the number of casualties in Beijing is making it necessary to begin consolidating their forces."

"Goddammit!"

"I'm afraid it gets worse, sir. Their regional commanders won't move forward with the transportation attack in Hong Kong or the port assault in Shanghai."

Denali fights to control his temper. The follow-on attacks against the United Kingdom, Chinese, and Russian parent corporations are critical. America Incorporated is on the precipice of a civil war, and one of those three corporations is most likely to fill the power vacuum. He can't let that happen.

For negotiations to succeed, corporations must feel helpless. A single attack against China, regardless of the body count, won't push them to the table. They have weathered far worse in their history before the dawn of the Corporate Age. The Chinese must be brought to their knees for talks to commence.

"Commander, White Lotus is failing me. We've already had coordination issues with the Volga in Russia. I can't abide a failure of this magnitude."

"Sir, I've done everything I can to convince them. I explicitly told their leader that if White Lotus loses their nerve, we will make sure the Chinese Ministry of Corporate Security knows where to find them."

"And?"

"Their leader thinks we're bluffing. He doesn't think you would risk allowing their capture. He was rather insistent about that."

He's right. It was a bluff. There's a palpable fear of security forces in many corporations, and China is no exception. If anything, they're the gold standard of ultimate corporate control. The capture of any member of White Lotus could jeopardize Denali's grand plan. Turning them over to authorities isn't an option. Neither is surrendering to their demand.

As soon as the rat knows the cat won't pounce, he'll take all the cheese. This is a ploy to claim their share of power. White Lotus wants a role in shaping the new world. They're about to find out how insignificant they are.

Denali mutes the microphone and turns to Lacune. "Is the secondary protocol for White Lotus in place?"

"Yes, sir, but what about the second wave of attacks?"

"Forward your control of the risk response protocol to this workstation. Prepare to accelerate the final phase against China Incorporated. We're done playing around over there."

"Yes, sir."

"Commander, there is nothing more you can do there," Denali advises the frazzled liaison half a world away. "Leave the building and do it quickly. We will confirm on the security feed that you're clear."

He disconnects the VidLynk and the display returns to the image of the Keating family coat of arms.

Denali returns his attention to bombings, shootings, and mayhem around the world at schools, corporate training facilities, medical centers, shopping areas, and transit hubs. It's amazing how sloppy and complacent these corporations are. They had the power to stop this and failed miserably to identify the threat, let alone be in a position to deter it.

The pre-collapse world may not have been perfect, but at least they tried. The rise of terrorism in the decades before governments drove the world off a financial cliff necessitated hearty intelligence capabilities and a robust response force to deal with these kinds of incidents. They coined the relative peace after the Second Pirate

Wars as "Pax Corporicana." This is what happens when you start believing your own propaganda.

"He's clear of the area, sir."

Some obstacles you can climb over. Some you simply move. Others you destroy. Denali swipes his hand to call up the protocol and taps his finger in the air to initiate the sequence. He likes bombs. They are easy to build, and remote detonators mean he can be involved in the action. It's amazing the kind of havoc one can create from thousands of miles away.

His display switches to a surveillance feed of a square on the outskirts of the city. The image is still and serene until a bright light punctuates the darkening evening sky. A hazy orange fireball emerges and cascades high into the night sky. With one twitch of his finger, the White Lotus problem in Beijing has been solved.

"Confirm the safehouses in Shanghai and Hong Kong were also destroyed. Have our man on the ground rendezvous with the Alpha team for the final phase."

Lacune nods and relays instructions to the other security personnel. Denali turns his attention to the events unfolding in the United Kingdom and Russian corporations. They will soon face a crisis similar to America Incorporated. China will follow them into chaos or be destroyed in the process. Either way, the world is falling into his hands.

CHAPTER SIXTY-NINE

AMERICA, INC.

The White House
Corporate Governance District
Washington-Arlington Municipal Corporation

It's been a full day filled with an exhausting mix of dealing with a snotty patrician, ambitious subsidiary executives, and Zeykala's own security. The problem is, it's only a quarter after eight in the morning. The day has just begun. When she walks into her office, she knows the hits will keep on coming.

It is rare when someone is allowed in the Oval Office with the CEO not present. One exception is Prima Bettancourt, and she exploits that privilege far more than is appropriate. The other is the chairman of the board of directors. With an office just up the street on Corporate Hill, there isn't much reason for him to come here. Yet, here he is again.

"How did your meeting with the executives go? I hope it was better than your conversation this morning with Talya Bettancourt."

"You're well-informed," Zeykala says, not meaning it as a compliment. Conversations in the Oval Office used to be private. "It went fine, although you probably already know that, too. We're seeing each other a lot lately, Chairman Joakeen. What brings you to the White House?"

"My duties."

"Ah, yes. The move to replace me while we're still facing a crisis and toiling under corporate law."

Zeykala offers the chairman a seat on the sofa, which he declines. That's interesting. Whatever purpose this meeting has, it is going to be brief.

"I warned you it would come to this. I'm here to escort a possible successor to Corporate Hall for vetting as your replacement."

Zeykala has seen the shortlist. She knows that half the executives she just met with are on it. The board will want quick action, not a lengthy interview process. Their first choice will speak volumes about their intentions.

"Who?"

"I hope I'm not interrupting," Valen says, striding through the open Oval Office door with a BCS agent behind him.

Zeykala's mouth hangs open. The former CEO is the last man she expected to walk through that door. This guy will not go away. He wears an amused grin as he notices the ridiculous look of shock on her face.

"You can't be serious?" Zeykala asks, turning to the chairman. "He was *removed* from office for incompetence!"

"I see you already gave my successor the good news."

"The board believes his removal may have been hasty," Joakeen explains. "He's at the top of the shortlist, and they've requested to see him. If the interview goes well, your status as temporary chief executive will be stripped, and Valen will be reinstated to lead this corporation."

Joakeen is being polite about the circumstances of Valen's removal. He is well aware that Zeykala was the driving force behind his removal at the behest of Talya Bettancourt. Now that she has lost the prima's support, Talya is wielding her influence with the board to get them to reconsider their decision.

They will admit to the mistake of removing Valen and shift the blame for the current crisis to her. It won't be a hard sell. With the prima providing them the necessary cover, the outcome is assured. Zeykala will be nothing more than an unfortunate footnote in the corporate record.

"Valen, wait for the chairman outside the office," the CEO demands, expecting to need to argue about the request.

Instead, he grins and leaves without saying a word. He's enjoying this and doesn't need to gloat about it. That will come later.

"Joakeen, you need to do something about this."

"I wish I could, but my hands are tied. You damn well knew that crossing Talya would have consequences. Our employees are demanding action, and the world is demanding stability. Nobody will think she isn't justified in having you removed."

"She is the one who set these events in motion!" Zeykala screeches.

"It doesn't matter. History is written by the victors, and those are usually the people with the most power and influence. I'm sorry. I truly am. But I have my marching orders from the board, and there is nothing you can do to stop it."

Joakeen exits the office, leaving Zeykala to stare out the window at the Rose Garden. This day started off promising and went to hell quickly. She never thought Talya could have moved so quickly. The only way she could have convened them that fast is if it was planned before she visited the White House. Zeykala is running out of cards to play. She needs to go all in or be pushed out of the game forever.

CHAPTER SEVENTY

LIBERTEUM

Valhalla
Midtown Geographic Area
New York City Municipal Corporation

For Zyree, Ortan's revelation about controlling an artificial intelligence program is one of a long list of surprises that started with the moment Chiana tried to kill him in that crypt. Zyree has been on a rollercoaster with this crew, but Michele is the one feeling the ride's effects most. He has watched her go from despondent to optimistic to despaired to elated in the span of one conversation.

"Okay, guys, we need to finish this later because we have a problem," Zyree says, catching movement out of the corner of his eye and focusing on a video feed from outside the cathedral.

"What is it?" Michele asks, leaning in with Fiolla, as both notice the sudden alarm on his face.

"The agents outside the cathedral are prepping explosives."

A human chain is formed from the back of the truck to the sidewalk directly in front of the cathedral. The devices are small or, at least, smaller than Zyree would have expected. If placed in the right locations, they could bring down a stone structure, but he is wondering if they have a different idea in mind.

"You don't really think they'd destroy St. Patrick's?" Jasper asks.

"Collapsing the church on top of us would seal us in here for good."

"It would trap us, Farron, but they need us dead," Zyree argues. "They can't know we don't have an escape tunnel leading out of here."

"It's more than that," Fiolla adds. "Zeykala and Virtari will need to parade our dead bodies in front of employees and the other corporations to prove they are back in control. They can't do that if we're buried alive."

She's right. They could use AI to digitally create footage, but nothing beats the real thing. There must be no doubt that they are dead. Even if they convince employees, lingering doubt will be left. Liberteum has proven elusive in the past.

Conventional wisdom was they were eradicated until Michele launching her Archimedes plan proved otherwise.

"They aren't unpacking enough explosives to bring down this cathedral. Those are breaching charges. The BCS is going to blow a hole in the floor once they find Valhalla's access."

"They could just knock," Koltayne muses.

"That is their idea of knocking, my friend," Zyree responds, patting the young fighter on the shoulder.

"Why are those men in strange suits?" Fiolla asks, pointing at a different feed.

Ortan switches over to it, and they gawk at the display. Men dressed in baggy, sealed plastic suits are unloading cylinders from the back of a truck. That they are using oxygen tanks for breathable air isn't lost on anyone.

"Gas," Zyree says with a sigh.

"The stuff used for crowd dispersal?"

"No. There would be no need for them to don protective hazmat suits for that. Those barrels must contain a chemical nerve agent like sarin or VX."

"Where the hell did they get that from?"

"It's probably either left over from the pre-collapse days or pilfered from stockpiles in the Middle East," Farron concludes. "They have tons of it buried in caches over there."

"I thought corporations banned chemical weapons," Fiolla says.

"They banned tanks, too," Zyree counters, pointing at the screen. "It's corporate law. The BCS has thrown out the rulebook."

That's the most unnerving conclusion. Corporate law is a desperate measure and not one that is taken lightly. It essentially changes the way the entire corporation operates. There are no guardrails. There is no due process through the human resources department. Anything goes, including using weapons that nobody thought still existed.

"Nerve gas? That's overkill, isn't it?" When it comes to the BCS, Michele likely knows it isn't. She probably needed to hear herself ask.

"They've learned from their mistakes. Virtari is taking the threat you pose seriously. They need you dead, so they brought along one of the most horrific ways to achieve that goal."

"Wait a second! Gas disperses upward. We won't be affected down here." Jasper is desperate for any glimmer of hope.

"Nerve 'gas' is a misnomer. It's really an aerosolized liquid that's heavier than air. If agents release that into the void below the cardinal's office, it will cascade down the Stairway to Heaven and settle at the lowest level."

"Which just happens to be this room," Michele concludes.

"They still have to find us," Jasper persists.

"The entrance to Valhalla is beautifully disguised but won't escape discovery during a search with ground-penetrating radar. Once they know there's a void, they'll blow it open with those breaching charges and recon it with small drones. Cameras will spot the stairs, prompting the BCS to pump in the nerve agent."

"Can we seal the doorway?" Michele asks.

"If it's a persistent chemical, it won't do any good. There is no weather, temperature fluctuation, or humidity down here. The chemical will take forever to break down, and we'll starve to death long before it does. Not that the BCS will wait for that. They'll send drones to identify and pierce any barrier we erect. One pinhole will do the job."

The men and women in the operations room fall silent. Everyone is out of ideas. The woman most invested in Valhalla has no plan to defend it. The place was designed to be invisible, not impenetrable. With the curtain pulled back, they are dangerously exposed. The only shot they have at survival is being proactive with their defense. If the BCS are permitted to use that gas, the game is over.

"Okay, now that we have a depressing list of challenges, what are we going to do about them?" Ortan asks, appealing to the only man in the room trained in combat tactics.

"Start working your magic with Huldufólk and Archangyl. I think I need to…."

Zyree starts to say something and then stops. The team waits for him to finish the sentence. He has an idea, but it's a long shot, at best. Even with better odds of success, he already knows they're not going to like it.

CHAPTER SEVENTY-ONE

AMERICA, INC.

St. Patrick's Cathedral
Midtown Geographic Area
New York City Municipal Corporation

There's nothing more to gain by his being here. Virtari issues Commander Brudzik some final instructions before climbing into the back of the mobile command center. He's satisfied with the troop deployment, measures taken to cut off any escape, and the plan for eradicating the terrorists. Liberteum is finished. He needs to move on to the other problem.

The convoy moves out, led by one of the four tracked armored beasts. They don't need all of the tanks to guard the cathedral, and the BCS director isn't taking any chances. The PSS and qulis are a more formidable threat than the terrorists. As they grind down a cross street, he laments not taking two of the tanks.

Virtari passively watches the multidirectional scanning displays as they cut over from Fifth Avenue to Third and then head south. The convoy has plenty of firepower, and drones are scouting overhead. This route may be the most direct approach to One Guardian Plaza, but it's also the riskiest. They're technically behind enemy lines if one can imagine such a thing in the heart of Manhattan. The qulis are out there observing this movement. The question is whether they have the balls to hit this column. He doubts it. It's suicide, and even the idiots in the labor class must understand that.

"Drones have spotted activity to our front," a technician announces.

Virtari checks the displays again. They're in the section of town called Cooper Square, where Third Avenue merges into Bowery. It's an area with a massive quli presence. He wouldn't have picked this spot for an ambush, but it does make sense logistically.

"How's the road ahead? Any barricades?"

"No, sir, it's clear."

"Then go."

An explosion rocks the command vehicle, causing Virtari to lose balance and hit the metal flooring. Heavy machine gun fire rips through the command vehicle above his head. The thin aluminum-plated sides are not meant to protect against large-caliber weapons. Men manning the terminals in the back of the vehicle begin to fall. Had he not lost balance, the director would have been one of them.

"Stay down! Deploy and return fire," an agent screams into his radio.

The concussive shockwaves from a series of smaller explosions pummel the command vehicle again as agents respond with bursts from their weapons. The rear of the command truck begins to fill with acrid smoke from burning wires and circuit boards. An agent covers his mouth with a towel and jumps on the communications gear.

"Attention all units! Command One is taking hostile fire at Third and Bowery! We're abandoning the vehicle. Out."

He grabs the director and manhandles him to the truck's rear exit. Agents provide cover fire as they evacuate to an open area between Third Avenue and where Cooper Square bends back north. It's a bad place to be.

"We're pinned down!" Virtari shouts as gunfire stitches the concrete no more than ten feet from him. "We can't stay in the open like this."

"They have us boxed in on three sides. There's no place to go!"

The tank fires its cannon and blows a chunk out of the corner of the far building. The fire coming from it is silenced, but there is plenty more coming from rooftops and floors of buildings around them. Virtari scans the sky, searching for his guardian angels. They are the only hope to fight back the horde of qulis and guardians raining lead down on them.

His wish is granted when the two machine gun drones scream down and engage targets on the rooftops. The flying weapons platforms are finally returning to service in large numbers following the power loss at the EOC. Bolstered by the air support, agents assume firing stances and pump rounds into adjacent buildings to the left and right. Suppressive fire should mitigate the lack of cover. It doesn't. Three of them fall in the withering crossfire they are caught in.

"Hit the surrounding buildings with every missile we have!" Virtari shouts at the convoy commander.

"Sir, there are employees in them! Missiles will destroy these buildings and kill everyone—"

"It's an order, Commander. Do it!"

The agent barks into the radio, relaying the order seconds before getting hit. Virtari drags him closer and applies direct pressure to the wound as he hides behind the severely wounded agent. Bright flashes precede the loudest sound he has ever heard. The concussion knocks the air from his lungs as the square becomes obscured with thick smoke. Debris rains down on his men as the buildings around them erupt in massive fireballs.

The roar of gunfire slows and then stops, ushering in an eerie silence punctuated by men's screams and the ringing in Virtari's ears. Agents move with their rifles up, checking on the dead and wounded. The tank traverses its turret left and pierces the stillness with one last deafening roar.

"We need to get out of here and link up with the southern vanguard before they decide to come back," the convoy commander says before turning to an agent who rushes over. "Load the wounded. We'll triage them when we link up at Guardian Plaza. The command vehicle is lost, so leave it here."

"Yes, sir."

Virtari takes cover in a troop carrier as the wounded are loaded. Some have minor injuries, but others aren't so lucky. The ambush took a heavy toll. The engines start, and they continue their southerly trek. Drones are sweeping the avenue ahead of them, engaging anything that remotely looks hostile.

He finally relaxes when the shot-up convoy reaches the BCS perimeter around One Guardian Plaza. Agents swarm the vehicles to assist the wounded. Virtari dismounts and is directed to the command vehicle after refusing treatment. The abrasions and bruises he has are nothing compared to what most of those men are suffering from.

"Medical transports will evacuate these men back to New Jersey," Flandyr says after hustling over to the director. "Are you okay, sir?"

"I'll live. What's the status?"

"We eradicated the perimeter the guardians set up. The survivors fled back into the building. We've surrounded the structure and are holding position. We sent a surrender demand to the RTCC, but it was ignored."

Virtari shakes his head. Ilaria must know she can't win. Even if she is too dumb or blind to see what's happening, guardians must be telling her the reality of what she's facing. Why sacrifice their lives for nothing?

"Let's get their attention. Have the tanks punch a few holes in the building to demonstrate our intent and then open the front door."

Commander Flandyr relays a series of commands, and the steel giants elevate their cannons. A moment later, they unleash hell. The armored beasts don't have a high rate of fire, but there is no disputing the results. The headquarters of the PSS was architected to resemble a medieval bastion, but it's a façade covering a typical steel structure. The tanks level their guns and send a final volley at floor level. When the dust clears, the foyer is cracked wide open.

"Prepare the heavy weapons assault team."

"Sir, wouldn't it be easier to have the drones level the building?" Flandyr asks, staring up at the looming structure.

It would be easier, but it's the same challenge they have with Liberteum. Ilaria needs to die, and AME News needs to broadcast footage of her corpse onto every display. It's the only way to bring this uprising to a swift end, and they can't spend weeks sifting through the rubble to find them.

"You have your orders, Commander Flandyr. Send the men in. I want everyone in that building not wearing a BCS uniform dead. Don't bother with prisoners. They don't deserve mercy or quarter."

"Yes, sir."

A machine gun opens fire from atop One Guardian Plaza, causing the agents to seek cover behind the command truck. A missile streaks over their heads and strikes the rooftop of the northwest corner of the PSS building, blowing it straight to hell. Incoming fire from the building behind them rakes the ground as the nearest tank swings its turret and fires. A drone swoops in and strafes the buildings to the left and right of the explosion. Whatever Ilaria has planned to stop the assault is no match for the firepower Virtari brought to the party.

The end for them is near. A stream of men makes for the exposed lobby of the bastion. It is only a matter of time. Nothing is going to stop his small army from taking this building and killing everyone inside.

CHAPTER SEVENTY-TWO

LIBERTEUM

Valhalla
Midtown Geographic Area
New York City Municipal Corporation

Fiolla can feel the tears forming in the corners of her eyes. Zyree's plan isn't crazy…it's suicidal. There will be dozens, if not hundreds, of agents up there. He can't fight them all off. Nobody could.

"Zyree, are you sure you want to do this?" Michele asks, breaking the long silence.

"No, I'm sure I *don't* want to do this. But we need to take the fight to the BCS when they uncover Valhalla's access. It's our only chance. Unless one of you has a better idea."

Everyone's eyes immediately move to the floor, searching for anything better than what Zyree proposed and coming up empty. Fiolla wants to be selfish. She wouldn't want him to go even if it increases their chances of survival twofold. His being here is comforting, and she needs that.

But he is an honorable and courageous man who won't cower down here and hope for the best. If he's going to die, it'll be fighting. Archimedes is Michele's thing. He's going to do his part.

Michele doesn't like the idea any more than anyone else. Fiolla appeals to her with her eyes, willing her to order him to stay. She can stop this. She can refuse to send him to his certain death. Instead, she looks at Zyree, clenches her jaw, and nods.

"Good, it's settled."

Zyree turns and disappears down the hallway. Fiolla stares at Michele, trying to mask her disappointment…and fear.

"I'm sorry," Liberteum's leader whispers. "I know you wanted me to stop him, but it's his decision to make. I have to respect that."

The choice is a mistake, and it's going to get Zyree killed. Fiolla storms off after him.

"Fiolla, where are you—"

"Not now, Farron," she says, brushing past him.

Of all the people in this room, the two of them have the most unfinished business. She will clear the air with him when she's ready and not a moment before. He doesn't immediately respond to her presence when she walks into the small arms room. It's a good thing because she has no idea what to say.

"Are you here to talk me out of this?" Zyree says as he dons body armor and struggles to adjust the straps on the side.

"Would it do any good?" Fiolla asks, turning him so she can pull the strap through the plastic buckle and stow the excess strap. "You don't strike me as the type who second-guesses his decisions. I'm just making sure you're doing this for the right reasons."

"You've seen what the BCS has up there, Fiolla. You know the odds against us. What more reason do I need?"

"Your partner lost his life," she says with a sigh. That gets his attention. "Ortan told me the story. He also said he thinks you feel guilty because of it."

"Malkor sacrificed himself to save me in the tunnels leading away from Grand Central Terminus. There's no doubt that I'd be dead if it weren't for him. He was a good man. That would make anybody feel guilty."

"And now you think you need to sacrifice yourself?"

"I don't expect you to understand," he says, picking up a rifle.

She places her hand on it. "When I was on the run, I found myself in the middle of a quli protest in Washington. I clearly didn't belong there dressed in an executive tunic, but a man I met said he would help get me out of the city. When the BCS found me, he stood between me and the agents. He tried to protect me…and they shot him for it. He sacrificed everything for a stranger wearing the uniform of a corporation he detested. So, yeah, I know a little about someone making a sacrifice that you don't feel you deserve."

There's anger in her voice. Fiolla is tired of overcoming assumptions. People see her as a spoiled executive who never faced real adversity. It couldn't be more untrue, and she's done being taken for granted.

"I'm sorry, I didn't—"

"Forget it. We both want to honor the sacrifices made for us, but that doesn't mean we should throw our lives away trying."

Zyree begins stuffing magazines into the pouches secured to his vest. "Loyalty is admirable, but it's also an Achilles' heel. I placed mine in the wrong people, and they tried to kill me. When I needed help, Ortan stepped up. Michele is a terrorist who risked her life to rescue me. They're both in that room out there. They're the people I believe in…that I'm loyal to now. They are who I will fight for…and die for if need be."

There is a passion in his words that Fiolla hasn't heard in a long time. He's not running away or trying to alleviate guilt over the loss of a friend. He believes in his heart that he needs to do this. He's on a mission to save his friends.

"Okay."

"Okay?"

"Yeah. I understand the concept of misplaced loyalty more than you know. I was loyal to my corporation, and they tried to kill me for it twice. I was loyal to my CEO, and he betrayed me. I was loyal to a man I wanted to marry who lied to me."

"And betrayed his father to rescue you from the most powerful security organization in the world. Farron may have lied to you, but he risked everything to save your life. I'm not one for defending patricians, but every minute I'm here, I'm reminded that not everything is what it seems."

"Do you trust Michele?"

"She's given me every reason to."

Programming is hard to overcome. Fiolla was conditioned to believe that Michele and Liberteum were enemies. Zyree actually fought them…twice. His belief in her is an almost unfathomable evolution. It makes this man that much more remarkable.

"Promise me you'll be smart and not waste your life. You're a good man, Zyree. Right now, the world needs to hang onto every good man it can."

"The world needs to, or you?"

Fiolla blushes in embarrassment. "Both."

Zyree slings a black bag over his shoulder and hefts his rifle. She doesn't know this man well and can't expect him to have feelings for her. At least, not like the ones she's starting to feel for him. He stops and faces her when he reaches the door. Fiolla forces herself to look up at him, wishing the single tear rolling down her cheek had stayed put for a little longer.

"All right, now I get it."

He wipes her cheek with his thumb and brushes the hair out of her face. The gentle gesture and warmth of his touch make her heart flutter.

"Get what?" she awkwardly asks in a whisper.

"Why it was so easy for Farron to fall in love with you."

CHAPTER SEVENTY-THREE

NYCMC RESISTANCE

One Guardian Plaza
Lower Manhattan Geographic District
New York City Municipal Corporation

The building finally stops shaking. Ilaria climbs to her hands and knees after being knocked off her feet by the violent explosions. Strobe lights slice through air choked with dust, and the piercing sound of the wailing fire alarm tears at her eardrums. The overhead lighting in the RTCC stops flickering as guardians manning the workstations retake their posts.

"Is everyone okay?" she shouts, struggling to her feet.

Another explosion rocks the building, but it's farther away than the last. It does nothing to alleviate everyone's frayed nerves.

"What the hell was that?" Phylep asks, articulating the question in everyone's mind.

"The tanks opened up on the building," a guardian shouts from the inner ring of terminals. "We have damage to floors seven, eight, fourteen, fifteen…the northwest roof, and the main entrance. Fire alarms have activated."

"Yeah, no kidding. Turn them off!"

Ilaria covers her ears to fight against the shrill noise. A guardian silences the alarm but not the accompanying strobes. She'll take that trade right now.

"That's one way to announce your intentions," Phylep grumbles. "I guess trying to take Virtari out was a bad idea. All it did was make him angry."

"I doubt it mattered. He's always angry."

"Fire suppression is active on four floors. The blazes are contained."

Fires are the least of their problems. There are hundreds of guardians and qulis ready to fight, but it won't matter if they smash the building to dust using tanks and drones. It's their best course of action if Virtari wants to avoid BCS casualties. Fortunately, the director of the BCS is a showman who would trade hundreds of his men for the spectacle their tribunals would provide. At least, that's what Ilaria is banking on.

"Attention in the RTCC! BCS agents are advancing toward the building's foyer."

The main display has been knocked offline. The smaller ones to either side are functioning, and one of them shows heavily armed men outfitted in body armor and heavy shields bounding for the entrance.

"Ma'am, we reestablished contact with one of our overwatch teams. They were forced to withdraw after the other positions were taken out by drones."

"So much for that idea," Ilaria moans. "All right, listen up, everybody. So long as they have men in this building, the BCS won't risk using their tanks or drones. Your chief guardian means to fight them floor by floor. Let's give him as much support as we can. I need one or two pairs of eyes watching the BCS on the perimeter. Everyone else needs to monitor internal surveillance and relay information to our fighters."

"It looks like they want to take you alive," Phylep concludes.

She nods. "Let them come."

"Every second they waste trying to take this building will give Michele more time to pull off a miracle."

Ilaria wants to be optimistic, but there isn't much to be positive about. These are the best people this city has to offer, but nothing they can do will stop the BCS. It's up to a woman who, until only a day ago, she considered to be a terrorist and an enemy. Now, all their lives are in her hands.

"Do you think she can do it?"

Phylep shrugs. "Let's hope so."

"Attention in the RTCC! Qulis are advancing toward the BCS perimeter from Astor Park."

He checks the camera footage and grimaces. "They aim to fight."

"Yeah, and it will turn into a bloodbath," the guardian says, a morose tone to his voice.

He knows what's about to happen. They all do. Courage doesn't stop bullets. Nothing they are armed with can take down drones or penetrate armored vehicles. Any fight would be laughingly one-sided.

"Get me in contact with Liberteum," Ilaria orders. "They need to know that we're running out of time."

CHAPTER SEVENTY-FOUR

AMERICA, INC.

Command Truck Outside One Guardian Plaza
Lower Manhattan Geographic District
New York City Municipal Corporation

The back of this truck is filled with displays showing aerial drone views and street camera footage. One is tuned into AME News and whatever corporate propaganda they are showing. The remainder are BCS feeds from Detroit, Los Angeles, and Chicago, showing violent quli resistance. Despite the BCS's best efforts, laborers have taken control of whole geographic areas. It's as bad as it gets.

The agents in the back of this truck are exhausted. Not only are they responsible for this operation, but they have to monitor the entire sphere of influence. It's a massive job when everything is falling apart.

"Sir, you should take a look at this," one of the agents says.

"What's the problem now?"

"We're getting some strange reports from patricians that their financial transactions aren't being processed. Others are having issues accessing their accounts."

"How is that our problem?" Virtari growls. "Intercorpex monitors the Bytecoin network."

"Yes, sir. It just...it feels like what happened before the exchange went offline. I don't think they know whether to contact Geneva or Wall Street, assuming they can get through to either."

"Bytecoin is handled in Geneva. Patricians should start there."

The agent nods and starts drafting a message. It's another entry on the ever-growing list of reasons this world is going to shit. Fortunately, Bytecoin is someone else's problem. They have their own, and solving them depends on Virtari's success in Manhattan.

"We need to talk," a woman's voice says from behind Virtari.

He didn't hear Varella climb into the back of the truck. She's not supposed to even be here. After closing down the EOC, she was sent to their staging area in New Jersey. Apparently, she had other ideas.

"How the hell did you get here?"

"I hitched a ride with a logistics convoy. You need me by your side, and you need to see what I have to show you."

"Not now, Varella."

"Are you personally running this operation?" she asks. "Because if you aren't, you're micromanaging your people. I *need* to show this to you. Your future may depend on it."

Varella turns and climbs down the stairs leading out of the command truck. Virtari shakes his head, wondering if this woman is going to be the death of him. She is waiting outside the command trailer with a tablet and holds it out to the director, who snatches it out of her hand. He scrolls through the document without saying anything.

"Zeykala is about to get removed by the board of directors. You know what that means."

"I don't have time for this, Varella," he says after scoffing. "What the hell am I reading?"

"A report from Meade Human Resources Center. Before Executive Fiolla was set to be terminated, you ordered her interrogation. Do you remember that?"

"Vaguely. So what?"

"You'll remember it in the future as the most brilliant decision you've ever made. This is the doctor's report on his findings. It's a must-read."

What started as Virtari placating the obnoxious young woman has developed into legitimate interest. The report has all the intrigue and riveting twists of an old spy novel. The more he reads, the more engrossed he becomes.

"This can't be right."

"I already confirmed its legitimacy."

The comment was more disbelief than a question of authenticity. The doctor used enhanced techniques, and he knows from briefings that the method is foolproof. Fiolla wasn't capable of lying or withholding information. Unless the doctor fabricated her statements, this report is beyond impeachment and the most damning proof of treason he's ever read.

"How do you feel now about my interrupting you? You wanted leverage, and now you have it."

Virtari hands the tablet back to her. "Keep this between us for now."

"Why? You can use this to save Zeykala before the board acts."

"They won't make an official move today. I need you to develop some action plans on how to best use this. Be prepared to brief me when this operation ends."

"Will do."

She opens a new document on the display and goes to work. She's nothing if not driven. It's yet another character trait that will serve her well in this world. He never would have seen that report without Varella's snooping. She may be an opportunistic snake, but she is proving invaluable. Virtari's glad he didn't kill her back at the EOC.

"And Varella? Nice job."

She beams as she moves to a safer place to continue her work. This is as close to a war zone as anyone has seen in decades. Virtari shouldn't even be standing in the open. The perimeter is a flurry of action as men begin clearing One Guardian Plaza. They are only a step away from restoring order to the city. Once Liberteum is located and this nascent resistance movement destroyed, he has what he needs to handle business in Washington.

CHAPTER SEVENTY-FIVE

THE PATRICIANS

Keating Family of the Gentez-Majorez Estate
Greenwich Geographic District
Southern Connecticut Municipal Corporation

Abbot barges into the study and rushes over to his employer. In all his years of service to the Keating family, not once has he ever displayed this sense of urgency. Something is very wrong. Denali can only hope it's not about Farron.

"Sir, we have a rather substantial problem. We have lost access to our financial accounts and cannot make transactions."

A myriad of things can go wrong with any plan, no matter how meticulously it's developed. The number of variables increases exponentially the more complex the plan. Even when there are hundreds of contingency plans ready, it's the unexpected developments that pose the biggest threat. Farron's betrayal was one of them. Liberteum's escape was another. Of the news he could expect Abbot to deliver, an issue with the global financial network was not on the list.

"What?"

"We are unable to make transactions, and all of our accounts are inaccessible."

Denali flashes him a look of disbelief and walks over to the workstation on the antique desk behind the sofas. To rule out any issues in Manhattan, he selects an account in Europe. After authenticating to gain access, nothing happens. He checks another account and then a third with the same result.

"This isn't possible. Have you contacted Intercorpex?"

"Immediately. Geneva claims there is no problem, but they were frazzled. I checked with the staff of other patricians, and they are experiencing similar problems. We've contacted Washington for insights, but they aren't taking VidLynk requests."

It's corporate law, so that part isn't surprising. Even in normal times, the world's largest and most powerful corporation is slow to respond to anything. It's how they let Intercorpex get bombed and how their labor force began taking control of whole cities. The lack of cooperation from Intercorpex is more concerning.

"Get our access back, Abbot. Somebody has answers. In the meantime, ready the reserve vault."

"You should know that our reserves are almost depleted."

"I know. Just get it done."

He nods and heads for the door. Financial networks are the most protected on the planet. Denali has lived too long to believe in coincidences. The odds of a random global financial network failure at the same moment the BCS is attacking Manhattan are exceedingly small.

Occam's razor states that *"Among competing hypotheses, the one with the fewest assumptions should be selected."* That would seem to point to some failure in Bytecoin's systems. However, Liberteum hacked into Intercorpex not once but twice. That was once thought impossible. The idea of them somehow seizing control of Bytecoin cannot be completely dismissed.

He should have eliminated Michele when he had the chance. All it would have required was his walking down to the strong room and putting a bullet in her head. It would have been better if Haven had done the dirty work as he was supposed to. She never should have been alive long enough to make it to Greenwich, much less manage to escape back into the city.

Denali presses the communications button. "Commander? Prepare my helicopter. I need to take a trip south later this afternoon."

"Yes, sir. It will be handled immediately," Lacune confirms.

It's pointless to reflect on what is going on with Bytecoin or why. Preparing for the ramifications of that is more pressing. Secondary is the opportunity it presents. If the financial system is offline, it provides him a myriad of options to explore. Regardless of how this situation develops, it's time to drop in on the Baroness.

CHAPTER SEVENTY-SIX

LIBERTEUM

St. Patrick's Cathedral
Midtown Geographic Area
New York City Municipal Corporation

There are two good reasons why Liberteum rarely emerges from their subterranean stronghold. The first is that reducing movement limits their exposure and reduces the chances of getting caught. The second is that these stairs are a bitch to climb. The Stairway to Heaven, as Ortan calls it, is narrow, dark, long, and claustrophobic. Zyree wouldn't want to make this climb often, either.

He climbs the spiral stone staircase as quietly as possible and must have been more silent than he thought. That, or Koltayne is fast asleep. The young sentry was sent up here to keep an eye on things following the discovery of the BCS's chemical unit. He doesn't react to the former chief inspector's presence at the top of the stairs.

"Hey."

The kid nearly jumps out of his skin. "Jesus, Zyree. You scared the hell out of me. What are you doing here?"

"You didn't think I was going to let you defend Valhalla by yourself. Where are they?"

"I hear footsteps and scraping in the sacristy like they're moving furniture," Koltayne says, looking up. "I think they realized there is a void down here, so I moved closer to the staircase in case they decide to blow a hole in the floor."

"Good thinking."

"What's going on down there?"

Zyree presses his lips together and gives a quick shake of his head. "Last-ditch efforts."

Zyree doesn't doubt Ortan's abilities. But even if they do seize the financial system, getting anyone in Washington to listen to their demands is a crapshoot. Regardless of his thoughts on possible negotiations, Zyree pledged to keep the BCS away from Valhalla as long as possible. That's what he's going to do.

A grinding sound and vibration confirm Koltayne's suspicions. The cathedral floor is thick, but the two-inch drill bit punches through. When it retreats, a thin beam of light from the room above punctures the pitch darkness of the void.

"Move back," Zyree whispers.

They retreat a few steps down the spiral staircase to ensure they're out of sight. The BCS will use a snake camera to recon what's down here. Then all bets are off. If they go straight to the nerve agent, they're screwed. He's hoping they don't see the stairs and that they want positive confirmation before breaking that stuff out.

The waiting is painful and only ends when a sharp blast caves part of the ceiling in. The dust from the crashing debris chokes the air and blocks the beams of light struggling to cut through from above. If they are going to act, now's the time.

"You ready?" Zyree whispers.

"Not really," Koltayne confesses.

The two men climb the final steps up the spiral staircase and ease along the wall of the void. The hole the BCS blasted in the floor obliterated the ladder leading up to the sacristy. The cleverly disguised access hatch is also gone. A tactical ladder is lowered, and an agent quickly starts to descend it. Zyree waits until he's at the bottom and turns before firing three rounds into his head. If the agents wanted confirmation, now they have it.

The initial weapon report and sound of their comrade collapsing to the ground causes several men to peek over the rim of the opening. That's a mistake. Koltayne and Zyree drill several of them with headshots before anyone can return fire.

Zyree scampers below the open ceiling to the far end of the void to draw their fire. The maneuver works. He has their undivided attention but is now pinned down without any cover or concealment. It's not a good feeling.

Koltayne reaches the body of the dead agent and secures a grenade. He pulls the pin and lets the spoon fly off, counting in his head before tossing it up to the floor above. The men have no time to react before being shredded.

"Now what?"

"Reinforcements are coming, and we're sitting ducks down here. We go up and fight."

"After you," Koltayne says, not wanting anything to do with being the first up that ladder. Zyree doesn't blame him. He's not keen on it himself.

He climbs up enough to level his rifle at the top. An agent charges in from the sanctuary, and Zyree pounds a shot through his forehead. He does a quick scan, finding the sacristy empty except for the bodies mutilated by the grenade. He pulls another grenade off one of the dead agents and rolls it out the door. It detonates, causing several men to howl in pain. Wasting no time, he climbs the rest of the ladder and rolls onto the floor.

Zyree moves to the door and engages several men moving through the nave from the cathedral's entrance. Koltayne joins him on the opposite side of the sacristy entrance and watches the area leading to the Lady Chapel. He fires at targets of his own when they appear. Agents are everywhere and all converging on them.

Targets appear faster than either can engage them. Men are scrambling between the pews that provide them decent concealment but no effective cover. Wood does little to stop high-powered rifle fire. Several agents learn that the hard way when it costs them their lives.

A coordinated volley of fire forces Koltayne and Zyree to retreat behind the sturdy stone walls. Koltayne drags over an assault pack from the closest dead agent and begins digging through it.

"How good's your throwing arm?"

"I would have made a great starting pitcher for the Yankees back in the day."

Zyree accepts a couple of fragmentation grenades. The men nod at each other, activate the devices, and launch them into the nave and the sanctuary. The concussions shake the cathedral and blow out countless stained-glass windows.

"Is there smoke in that bag?"

Koltayne retrieves four cylinders. He and Zyree toss them and watch as a cloud of dense white smoke pours out of each. The high vaulted ceiling will mute the effect, but it serves their purposes in the short term.

"Take these," he says, handing Zyree ear defenders. It's a good call. Security forces are in love with auditory weapons that debilitate anyone not wearing them.

"Let's go."

They leave the office and move across the sanctuary to the altar. The aggressive move surprises the agents. The BCS's fire is unaimed and inaccurate, but theirs isn't. Koltayne might be shy and quiet, but the man can shoot.

Movement is life in combat. So is positioning. The agents taking cover in the nooks and crannies along the sanctuary's walls are forced to withdraw now that they've lost control of the altar. Koltayne picks off two pinned down in the north transept and reloads as Zyree engages targets fleeing toward the main entrance with a fresh magazine in his rifle. With the firing and the hissing smoke from the grenade ceasing, an eerie silence fills the space.

"They'll be back in force. We can't be here when they return."

"We can't abandon Valhalla's entrance," Koltayne protests.

"The biggest threat is the nerve agent. They won't use it so long as there is active resistance. There is too much risk that one of those canisters gets punctured and kills everyone. We need to stay alive, and we won't if we fight from here."

"All right. You have an idea?"

Zyree looks at the shattered windows above the cathedral. "Yeah, we take the fight outside. Is there a way out of here that doesn't require going through a door?"

"There's a maintenance area under the church that runs between the transept and the crypt access. It's how we tried to disguise that void."

Zyree takes a deep breath as he looks around. It's a good but not great option. They need to come at them from an unexpected direction. Emerging from the cathedral into a heavily armed perimeter won't likely end well.

"You guys like tunnels. Anything that will get us past their perimeter?"

"None that I know of. That's why we relied on the Emissary."

Zyree nods. So much for that idea. "The maintenance area it is."

CHAPTER SEVENTY-SEVEN

RYKOS

One Guardian Plaza
Lower Manhattan Geographic District
New York City Municipal Corporation

It's a desperate scramble up the stairs. We stop at the tenth floor and yank the door open. Two guardians take positions to provide security. I take a knee and try to catch my breath. The BCS is moving quicker than I thought it would.

"We've lost control of floors two and three," the guardian solemnly reports to the RTCC over his headset as he rests next to me. "Roger. Rykos, Constable Dzamko has been wounded."

I close my eyes and take a breath. "How badly?"

"No details yet. They just received the report upstairs."

Casualties are mounting as the BCS methodically clears the lower floors. They had already lost a dozen men when the tanks overran the perimeter, and their cannons destroyed the foyer. The guardians are fighting hard, but we're overmatched. This is not a fight we can win. At best, we're delaying the inevitable.

"They've made it to the seventh floor in the A and C stairwells."

"Shit," I say, shaking my head. "The seventh floor? So fast?"

"They're taking heavy casualties, but replacements are filling the ranks as fast as they fall. It looks like they're bypassing floors now."

"They want to get up to the RTCC," a lieutenant says when he joins them. "They mean to cut off the head of the snake. Without command and control, we'll never stop them from taking the building."

I nod. "All right. We need to find a way to slow them down. Lieutenant, tell everyone to choke the stairwells with as much debris as they can. Desks, bookcases, chairs…whatever they can find. Make the BCS struggle for every inch of ground they take."

"With the stairwells clogged, we won't be able to retreat," he warns.

"If they make it to the RTCC, there will be no place left to retreat to. Tell the RTCC to coordinate with teams at the other stairwells and have them do the same. Go."

Men and women around us leap into action. Chairs are the first obvious items, but a few guardians start lugging heavier items toward the door. The radio operator explains the plan to the RTCC and gives a thumbs-up to us. If the same is happening on the floors above us, we are trapped on ten. It's a desperate measure but should buy some time. I hope it's enough. Ten was my sister's lucky number. I don't want to die on this floor.

"Rykos, this won't hold them forever."

"We don't need forever. We need more time than we have for someone to deliver a miracle. Do we still have guardians on the fourth, fifth, and sixth floors?"

The guardian shrugs. "Probably."

"Let's try to reach them. If we can coordinate assaults on the stairwells, we may be able to make the BCS pay for leaving those floors untouched."

"It's suicide."

I can't blame the lieutenant for being discouraged. He's a realist, and nothing about this situation gives us much to be optimistic about. Our time is up.

"We fight and risk dying now or sit back and die for sure later. I know what choice I'm making," I say, clapping him on the arm before slinging my rifle and joining the guardians in wheeling chairs toward the stairwell.

CHAPTER SEVENTY-EIGHT

THE PATRICIANS

Valhalla
Midtown Geographic Area
New York City Municipal Corporation

The sound of a muffled explosion thunders down the spiral staircase like a bass drum. Everyone turns their heads at the sound. The faint staccato of gunfire that erupts in its wake can only mean that the entrance to Valhalla has been breached. It's up to Zyree and Koltayne to hold off the BCS, and the odds aren't in their favor.

"We're out of time," Farron says. "The BCS has a small army outside this cathedral. It's now or never, so I hope you're ready, Ortan."

"I'm as ready as I'm gonna be."

"Michele, we have an incoming call from the RTCC," Jasper announces.

A jolt runs up and down Farron's spine. They are under siege but don't have the luxury of being deep underground. If they are being overrun, this could be Ilaria or Rykos telling them it's over.

"Connect it."

Ilaria comes up on display. She looks shaken, and the haze in the air and strobe lights in the background are ominous signs.

"Chief Executive Ilaria, are you okay?" Michele asks.

"The BCS hit us with their tanks and missiles from their drones. We are taking a beating. They've already entered the building and are fighting their way up to us. Rykos is helping to hold them off, but it's only a matter of time. If you have something in mind to stop them, it needs to be now."

There is desperation in Ilaria's voice. Michele seems to relax at hearing that Rykos is still alive.

"We actually do, Ortan?"

"Hold on. I have Zeykala, but I'm still isolating Director Virtari's biojack."

"Do we need them both?" Jasper asks.

"Absolutely," Fiolla says. "Virtari has operational control of the whole sphere of influence under corporate law. You won't get anywhere with them separately."

Farron nods at the young hacker, who seems satisfied with the response. "Good to know."

"Let me deal with Zeykala," Fiolla says after turning to Michele and getting an apprehensive look. "I know what you're thinking. I need you to trust me. You don't know her like I do."

Michele looks at Farron. He understands her concern. Fiolla was an executive who hasn't earned a lot of trust here yet, and she's emotional. But if anyone knows what the woman is capable of, it's Farron.

"Let her do it."

"Got him!" Ortan barks. The man is a magician with a computer. "I'm going to conference in the RTCC but mute them and hide their attendance. I just need to isolate the circuits, make the connection, and…. Hello!"

"What the hell!" Chief Executive Zeykala asks as she shoots out of her seat in the Oval Office.

"Who are you?" Virtari barks as he is conferenced in. "This is a secure network!"

"Secure? You call this secure?" Ortan mocks, enjoying the moment. Farron smirks, wondering if he's recording this to capture the shocked look on their faces for posterity.

"You're a dead man!"

"I don't think you're in a position to make threats, Director."

"Then you're not paying attention—"

"Shut up, Virtari!" Zeykala bellows. "You're Michele, right? The last time I saw you was on the VidLynk from Denali Keating's estate."

"A lot has happened since then."

"Apparently."

"Too bad it's all about to end for you," Virtari interjects, seizing control of the conversation back from his boss. "My men found your secret entrance. We know where you are."

"I suppose that's only fair," Michele says, grinning. "We know where you are as well."

"I have control," Ortan whispers. "Ready on your command."

"Director Virtari, I'm going to give you one opportunity to pull your men back before I start killing them."

CHAPTER SEVENTY-NINE

AMERICA, INC.

Command Truck Outside One Guardian Plaza
Lower Manhattan Geographic District
New York City Municipal Corporation

Virtari folds his arms across his chest. He doesn't respond to threats, especially empty ones. If Liberteum was capable of anything more than parlor tricks, they would have done it hours ago. There is no tactical advantage to waiting for your front door to get kicked in.

"Do you think hacking into our communications network changes anything?"

"Have it your way. Kind sir, if you please," she says to her hacker.

Nothing happens. That isn't surprising. This is nothing more than a desperate bluff.

"Uh, what the…. Sir, I've…I've lost control of our drones," a technician informs him as he works furiously at his terminal.

Virtari leans over and checks his display. The drones are highlighted in red. That's not possible. They can't all go offline at once. He glances back at the display to see the smug hacker grinning. Liberteum must have found a way to interrupt their connection. If that's the case, they should be able to reestablish it.

"We no longer control any of them!" the agent says in a panic.

"Calm down. Is it a communications issue?"

"No, sir, it appears that…they're being reprogrammed with new target priorities."

"How is that…? What are the drones targeting?"

He looks at Virtari with fearful eyes. "Us."

A piercing sound rips through the air. The concussion from a nearby explosion rocks the command vehicle. Virtari stares at the display in amazement. Two more missiles streak in and find their targets. Three tanks are destroyed and on fire. Men in the plaza seek cover wherever they can. There is no place for anyone in the command truck to go. That just as easily could have been them.

"Having some technical issues with your drone fleet, Director?"

Zeykala stares impassively at the camera. Her director of corporate security has a much more fiery look in his eyes. "How the hell did you break into our drone network?"

"Magic," Ortan says with a great deal of flair. "Say goodbye to that squad about to enter the building."

Virtari looks at the display as a drone swoops in. His men don't react. Why would they? There is no reason to believe they don't control the drones overhead. The machine guns open up, belching fire from their muzzles at their cyclic rate. The men fall where they are standing. Body armor can't withstand that caliber round or that volume of fire.

The director balls his hands into fists. "You can't stop my men from finding you or destroying your guardian and quli friends. I will kill them all without mercy."

"We thought you might say that," Michele says, an unnerving calm in her voice. "Look out the back of your truck."

Every agent in the command vehicle turns his head in unison. A black drone with machine guns and a set of subdued scales hovers fifteen feet from the door. The Third Horseman of the Apocalypse, except the technician at the hangar was wrong. As Virtari stares down the barrels of its machine guns, the awesome sight on the hangar floor is now an ominous one. This is now Death, The Fourth Horseman.

"I'm prepared to die," Virtari says, not wanting to relent.

"How noble. I'm happy to arrange it."

That was a bluff. The director isn't ready to die. He needs to stall until they can wrestle control of the drone fleet back. Or find a way to crash them so they can't be used against them. It doesn't appear that the technicians in the truck are having success doing either.

"They're desperate, Virtari," Zeykala screeches. "We can end this right now. Stay the course. We're on the verge of a great victory for the corporation."

Michele laughs, but she isn't the one who responds to the chief executive's insane comment.

"You're awful willing to sacrifice the life of your BCS director, Zeykala. I wonder why that is."

The strong, confident, and somehow familiar voice came from off-camera. When the woman it belongs to steps into the picture, Virtari learns how he recognizes it. Despite his best efforts to hide his surprise, the director's mouth hangs open. Zeykala is the only one more stunned than he is.

CHAPTER EIGHTY

LIBERTEUM

Valhalla
Midtown Geographic Area
New York City Municipal Corporation

Their shocked faces made it worth the wait. For the first time in Fiolla's life, she feels like she has the upper hand on her tormentors. The student has become the teacher, and now school is in session. That's enough to cause a smile to cross her lips.

"Fi-Fiolla?" Zeykala stammers, not believing what she's seeing. "You're supposed to be dead."

"Add that to your list of failures."

"You're with Liberteum?" Virtari asks, equally dumbfounded. Fiolla turns and smiles broadly at Michele.

"It turns out that the terrorists aren't the ones who have tried to kill me…twice."

The enemy of my enemy is my friend. Fiolla never thought too much of that adage. It has relevance in the business world, but her field was corporate communications. She negotiated while others set strategy.

She understands it now. In her case, it's more than an alliance of convenience. Fiolla is genuinely beginning to like Michele. She likes Ortan. She really likes Zyree. She feels better and more alive with these people than she did with anyone in the corporation.

"Farron Keating's attack on the Meade Termination Center…."

Fiolla fights the urge to look at the patrician lurking outside the camera's view. It's better if Zeykala and Virtari don't know he's down here. It would make for an interesting reaction but now isn't the time.

"Was to rescue me," Fiolla finishes. "Had he known Zeykala was there, his primary mission might have changed somewhat, but oh well."

"Farron Keating was responsible for the attack in Maryland?" Zeykala asks. That must be news to her.

"Why would he want *you?*" Virtari asks.

"Easy there, Director," Fiolla warns. "I'm not pinned against a wall on Corporate Hill with your hand on my throat. I'd hate to lose control of my temper and have that drone erase you from existence. Now, my friend Michele made a request that I suggest you honor."

For a long moment, Virtari stares at the drone hovering outside the door. To illustrate the point, Ortan trains one of the guns directly on him. He has no other option if he values his life and turns to his agents in the command vehicle.

"Have everyone hold their current positions. Assume a defensive posture in One Guardian Plaza and hold the perimeter at St. Patrick's."

"Virtari! Don't you dare stop this assault!"

"Do it," he commands his agent, ignoring the CEO.

"Wise move, Director," Fiolla says, not one hundred percent certain he would give that order. Score one for self-preservation over company loyalty.

"You can threaten Virtari all you want. It changes nothing," Zeykala spews.

"I'm not surprised you feel that way. It's obvious to everybody that you only care about yourself, and killing the BCS director helps you. So, in the spirit of inclusion, we conjured up a special surprise."

Ortan can't help but snicker as he works. The holographic America Incorporated corporate logo behind Zeykala gets replaced by Liberteum's torch. Fiolla turns to Michele, who smiles, equally amused.

Zeykala is less than thrilled. She looks around the room as the images on the displays ringing her office are replaced with burning torches. Ortan must have changed every display in the White House.

"Or this?" Fiolla says when she gets a nod.

The lights in the Oval Office go dark. The only illumination in the room comes from the displays and the torch holograph. Ortan makes a couple of gestures, and the lights begin flickering on and off violently.

"I hope you don't suffer from seizures, Zeykala," Fiolla can't resist saying.

"How about some music to set the mood?" Ortan adds.

Fiolla expects some crazy techno-electronic garble to fill the speakers. Instead, the voice of her automated administrative assistant comes on. "Playing Tchaikovsky's *1812 Overture*."

Zeykala glares at them as the music begins to play. Words aren't needed. The hatred in her eyes and the rage on her face speak volumes.

"As you can see, we have control of the White House's computer systems as well," Michele says, folding her arms.

CHAPTER EIGHTY-ONE

AMERICA, INC.

The White House
Corporate Governance District
Washington-Arlington Municipal Corporation

The lights and logos were bad, but this music is about to drive Zeykala over the edge. Whatever their faults, Liberteum has displayed a capability she was never told about. The computers that run the White House are heavily encrypted. Their managing to hack into them is astounding…and downright scary. When the lights begin to flicker in sync with the music, she's seen enough.

"Enough!" Zeykala shouts, holding her hand up. "You've proven your point."

Michele makes a slashing motion across her neck. The music stops, but the office illumination remains off, causing the emergency lights to activate. The room is cast in eerie shadows, but it beats having to deal with the strobes.

"Neat trick," the CEO says, trying to claim the initiative in this conversation. "But that's all it is."

"Oh, it's much more than that. As of twenty minutes ago, we assumed control of the global financial network."

"I don't think so," she dismisses. "Bytecoin is protected by Archangyl. Even your hacker can't break into that."

Fiolla smiles. "One of your many flaws is a failure to see the big picture. Why would I say we control it if we don't? If it's proven to be a lie, we would lose all our leverage. Right, Virtari?"

The BCS director doesn't say anything. He's trying to avoid drawing attention while his men fight to regain control of their drones.

"What about you, Zeykala? You know what? Don't answer that. Let's have a demonstration that hits closer to home…like your personal financial account. Let's take a peek, shall we?"

Zeykala is about to protest when it pops up on the side display. To her horror, it is her account. Logically, there is no way it can be faked. But it must be.

"Wow! Michele, did you know that executives made this much Bytecoin?"

"It seems exorbitant to me. We should reset it to something more in line with our illustrious CEO's real net worth," Michele says, playing along with Fiolla.

Zeykala watches as a series of debits are made to the account. The transactions post on the right-hand side as the balance approaches zero. Mocking her, they leave a single Bytecoin. Her tablet chirps, and she retrieves it from the desk. The alert informing her that the account balance is a lone Bytecoin is authentic.

"We have control of all global financial transactions and banking accounts for the world's employees, executives, and patricians."

"I don't believe you. If you could crash the financial system, you would have. So, go ahead and do your worst."

"Wait…are you saying you want us to shatter the global economy and plunge everyone into another dark age? Some executive you are. Well, if that's your wish…."

This can't be happening. It's just not possible. But if the terrorists can take down Bytecoin…the consequences are unthinkable. There needs to be a way out of this.

"Stop. What do you want?"

Fiolla looks at Michele. The former liaison for corporate affairs is leaving it to her new boss to make the final decision, just as she should. This episode is going to serve as notice that she's going to be a nightmare to deal with in the future if they don't eliminate her.

"Simple. End your siege of St. Patrick's Cathedral and One Guardian Plaza. Pull all BCS agents and America Incorporated executives out of the Municipal Corporation of New York City and pause all security operations across the sphere of influence. Once you have made those good faith moves, we'll discuss what comes next."

"And if we don't?"

"Then Virtari gets turned into cat food, and you'll be responsible for the destruction of corporatism as a viable political and economic system."

"Me? I don't think so," Zeykala argues.

Fiolla shakes her head. "You know better, Zeykala. Who do you think the people will blame for this when the truth comes out? Liberteum for making good on their threat? Or you for failing to agree to a simple request that would have prevented it?"

She's being outmaneuvered. Every tactic Zeykala tries walks her into another trap. They cannot let Liberteum and the traitor Ilaria live to see tomorrow. Order needs to be restored, and this is their best chance. But it would be reckless to risk the world's financial system.

"Michele, the BCS is trying to get their drones back," a man off-camera informs them.

"Tsk, tsk, Virtari," she taunts, nodding at a hacker seconds before a loud noise bombards the room's speakers. The view of Virtari on the display is replaced with a smoky, dusty haze.

"Virtari! Virtari!"

When he struggles back to his feet and comes into the camera's view, he's covered in blood and brain matter. Liberteum must have killed the other agents in the truck with him. The CEO covers her mouth at the shock of the gore.

"Damn it! Give the order, Zeykala," Virtari pleads.

"Yes, give the order," Michele parrots. "Or are you that desperate to hang onto your power?"

Zeykala doesn't answer the question. She feels the rage building, and it's clouding her judgment. All she can think about is revenge. Liberteum is going to pay for this. Fiolla is going to pay. Anyone standing against her is going to pay.

"Since timely decision-making isn't your thing," Fiolla says, "we'll give you ten seconds to decide the fate of the world: ten, nine."

"We're sure she can count, right?" the hacker mocks.

"Eight, seven...."

"I can't believe she's actually thinking this over," Michele says, causing Fiolla to raise an eyebrow.

"Five, four...."

"Damn it, Zeykala!" Virtari barks.

"Three, two...."

Zeykala clenches her fists and closes her eyes. "Order your men out of the city, Virtari."

CHAPTER EIGHTY-TWO

INTERCORPEX

St. Patrick's Cathedral
Midtown Geographic Area
New York City Municipal Corporation

They emerge from the maintenance area under St. Patrick's with predictable results. The bullets snap like popcorn as they whiz past Zyree's head. He dives into the garden planted between the cathedral and Fiftieth Street and crawls up to the short wall that separates it from the sidewalk. Koltayne joins him as rounds pelt the stone barrier and rip over their heads.

He hazards a glance over the wall and almost has his head shot off. Stone chips pepper his face as bullets ricochet around him. They're pinned down and aren't going anywhere.

"We're in trouble!" Koltayne shouts. He's right. Zyree led them right into a kill zone.

"Yeah, no shit."

"Why aren't they advancing?"

Zyree looks up. "They're waiting for a drone. Why put your men in harm's way when a machine can do the dirty work?"

"That's not reassuring, Zyree. We need to find a way out of here. I'm not about to get killed by a flying trash can."

Two small explosions erupt on the street. Men shout at each other and shift their fire. Ten seconds later, the street quiets. Zyree pokes his head over the wall and sees four dead agents and a man twenty meters away with a contraption connected to a backpack. It's a strange weapon, but considering he killed four agents with it, nobody will argue about its effectiveness.

Two more agents materialize on their flank. Zyree climbs to his knees and drops the first. Koltayne is on his feet and kills the second. The man turns to them and nods.

"Come on," a woman with him shouts, gesturing them over to a building entrance on the far side of the street.

Not wanting to take the chance of getting pinned down again, they hop over the short wall and sprint across the street. The man with the strange backpack weapon lets loose as they get closer, sending agents near the rear of the cathedral behind cover.

Zyree and Koltayne duck into the building and move around the sturdy stone receptionist counter in the foyer. The man reloads his contraption with a long string of what looks like nails while they reload their weapons.

"We're safe here for the time being," the man says. "Some guys from my shop are dropping Molotov cocktails from the office buildings on Fiftieth and Fifty-First. That's keeping their asses off the side streets. You guys PSS?"

"Liberteum," Koltayne answers.

"Both of you?"

"I'm new. My name's Zyree, and this is Koltayne. Who are you?"

"I'm Bouthe, and this is my wife, Nanchai. Brycek and a few others are around here somewhere."

"Is that what I think it is?" Koltayne asks, pointing to the heavy backpack and modified tool connected to it.

"Nail gun," he says, tapping it with a great deal of pride, "modified infantry-style. I'm a carpenter, so I use these every day. I amped up the compressor's air outflow on this one to give it more range and velocity. I added a shoulder stock for stability and rigged the tip so that I only need to pull the trigger to fire. I picked off an agent from fifty meters this morning."

"That is…as cool as hell. And that?"

Nanchai's weapon is more complex. She's clearly an electrician. A thick cord connects her form-fitting backpack to the device in her hands. The front has about a dozen sets of barbed prongs sticking out of it. It's not as intimidating as Bouthe's, but Zyree bets it packs a punch.

"It's an electroshock weapon with a range of about twenty-five meters. These prongs shoot out in pairs and lodge into the skin. Over fifty thousand volts are delivered through microfilaments connected to the high-capacity battery pack on my back. I can also get up close and personal with it to not waste barbs."

Zyree smirks. Necessity is the mother of invention. The BCS has top-of-the-line rifles and body armor. This guy weaponized a nail gun, and his wife built an old-school taser. There's no doubt about it – he would fight next to the qulis any day.

"What were you guys trying to do?" Nanchai asks. "Other than get yourselves killed."

"You can say we're winging it. We're trying to keep agents out of the cathedral. What about you guys?"

Bouthe shrugs. "We don't have much of a plan."

"You have one now. We need your help to neutralize those tanks."

"Tanks?" he asks with a puzzled look. Nanchai shrugs.

"Those tracked behemoths with all the armor and big guns on them."

"Oh, tank. What idiot named it that?"

"Who cares, Bouthe? Look, I may be a little crazy, but trying to take them out is suicide."

"I agree with my wife…for once."

"I understand, but the BCS pulled out of the church. Liberteum will be trapped if those tanks open fire and that cathedral comes down. I'm not going to let that happen, so we're doing this with or without your help."

This won't be easy even with four of them. They will have to fight through the agents on the ground, somehow get access to the tank, kill the crew, and then figure out how it works. Guerilla-style tactics are a safer option, but that won't do much for Michele, Ortan, and the others in Valhalla. They need a difference-maker, and a tank serves that purpose.

The couple looks at each other, speaking to each other with their eyes and facial expressions. Bouthe looks at the two men. "All right. Let's do it."

"I hate being the cynical one," Koltayne says, "but how are we going to take out armored vehicles with these weapons?"

"You're not going to like this. There's only one tank guarding the rear of the church. If we can force ourselves inside and commandeer it, we can use it to take out the other two near Rockefeller Plaza."

Koltayne looks at him like he has a head injury.

"Do you know how to operate it?" Nanchai asks.

As an Intercorpex inspector, Zyree has had some of the world's best training. It was inclusive and comprehensive, covering every skill that would be needed in the field. What it didn't cover was how to use antiquated military hardware. Zyree may understand the fundamentals of how a tank works, but he's clueless about how to operate one.

"Sure. I also know it takes a crew of four."

"Fine, but I get to drive," Bouthe demands.

"You ain't driven in over a decade, and you sucked at it then," Nanchai argues, slapping him in the chest.

"Maybe because I had you naggin' me the whole time I was tryin'—"

"Guys! My friends are in grave danger, so can we focus, please?" Koltayne interrupts. He's right. They've already wasted too much time.

"Okay, so do you have a plan to capture one of those things?"

Zyree frowns. Not really. "Yeah. Kill the bad guys in it and try not to die in the process."

Bouthe and Nanchai share a wary look. "I think we were hopin' for sumtin' more specific."

"That's all I got. We hit the agents on the ground and improvise from there."

"You sure you're not a quli?" Bouthe asks as his wife laughs.

Zyree returns the smile. "Let's go."

"Wait, wait, wait!" Koltayne insists. "Do you hear that?"

Everyone stops and listens. Other than some distant shouts and the occasional Molotov cocktail exploding, there's nothing.

"I don't hear nuthin'," Nanchai says.

"Exactly."

Now Zyree gets it. The constant staccato of gunfire has stopped. No tank rounds are being fired. It's as if someone pressed the mute button on the battle raging outside.

He walks over to the storefront and peeks out the shattered window. Rifles are still out and pointed, but the agents are no longer engaging targets. The others join him at the window when a man charges in through the rear. They all turn, and Zyree almost shoots him until Bouthe puts a hand on the former inspector's rifle and lowers it.

"It's okay, he's with us. Brycek, what's goin' on?"

"The BCS agents are starting to load up in their transports. I think they're leaving! We're gonna follow and see where they're headin'. Maybe we can pick off a few on the way. Comin'?"

"Let's roll, honey. We have work to do. These bastards ain't gonna walk off this island as easily as they walked in. Zyree, Koltayne, it's been a pleasure."

"Stay safe, you two."

"What fun would that be?" Nanchai says with a wink before she and her husband head out onto the street.

"Koltayne? How exactly do you think that relationship works?"

He shrugs. "The couple that fights together stays together?"

"That's as good a theory as any, I suppose. It makes you look at marriage in a new light, doesn't it? Come on. Let's get down to Valhalla and find out what the hell is going on."

CHAPTER EIGHTY-THREE

RYKOS

One Guardian Plaza
Lower Manhattan Geographic District
New York City Municipal Corporation

I needed someplace quiet with a view. The undamaged section of One Guardian Plaza's roof seems like a good place to watch what's going on in the streets below. We were minutes from being overrun on the tenth floor when the BCS stopped shooting and held their positions. I didn't believe the RTCC when they radioed to tell us that our enemy was pulling out of the city. Part of me still doesn't believe it, which is why I'm up here seeing it for myself.

I stopped by the infirmary before coming up here. There were too many wounded, and I feel almost guilty about surviving the ordeal unscathed. Dzamko wasn't so lucky. I can attest that getting shot is no fun, but I've never seen someone so angry about it. Fortunately, the wound in his shoulder isn't fatal, and he's already back on his feet. If there is any solace I can find in today's events, it's that the good men and women lost today didn't die in vain.

"It looks like your girlfriend came through," my mother says, coming alongside me as the tanks and troop carriers slowly withdraw back toward the river.

"Michele isn't my girlfriend," I argue.

"Sure."

"She's not."

"Right," my mother says with a smirk.

She raised me and has always had a sense of when I was less than truthful. It's how she knew I was lying about what happened during my kidnapping and what I told the corporation when I returned. In this case, it's not a lie. It's closer to being a sin of omission. I don't really know what's going on between the two of us, and I don't want to discuss it with my mother.

"I thought you didn't like Michele."

"I never said that. I said I was apprehensive about the idea of working with terrorists."

"And now?"

She smiles. "Let's just say I'm warming up to it."

There is no denying that Liberteum saved us. The BCS wasn't more than an hour away from wiping us out completely. Had Michele failed to hold the financial system hostage, none of us would be alive to admire this view. I can't wait to hear the full story about that negotiation.

"You know, Rykos, I don't think 'terrorist' is a good description of her."

"No, it's a lousy one."

His mother turns to face him. "Is she the one who taught you how to shoot a rifle?"

Alarm klaxons sound in my head, and I search for a way to dodge that question. "Not exactly. It's just something I learned to do."

"Out of necessity?" she prods.

"Something like that. Where are you going with this inquisition, Mother?" I can sense that she's trying to do this carefully.

"You know, when you went off to fight with the guardians, I was scared I would lose you again. I don't think I can handle that."

"Are you telling me I shouldn't have?"

"No. We're all doing what we must now. I am telling you to be careful. I'm also not ruling out the idea of covering you head-to-toe in bubble wrap next time you decide to fight the BCS."

"Yes, because puffy plastic will do a lot to stop bullets."

She smiles. "Maybe they'll be laughing so hard they can't shoot straight."

I can't help but chuckle, and my mother joins in until the laughter causes tears to stream down our cheeks. It's not that her comment was that funny, but we haven't had anything to laugh about for a long time. The emotional release feels good.

I start shaking my head when I regain my composure. "You know you don't need to worry about me."

"I'm your mother, Rykos. I will always worry about you. It's like breathing. It happens without me having to think about it."

"Does the same apply to Varella?"

It's a touchy subject neither of us has had time to talk about since her deceptive VidLynk with Virtari. I have no idea whether he pulled the trigger. If Varella is alive, she may be walking back to New Jersey with that convoy. Or, maybe she's already there. There's no way to know.

"She's my daughter, just as you are my son. Like you, she made a choice. It just so happens that Varella's decisions are taking her down a far different path than yours."

"Did you expect something different?"

I watch my mother's face contort. She doesn't know how to answer that. Varella is working with the man who forced her to watch his father's execution. She either doesn't know that or doesn't care. Her career comes first, and she values it more than her family.

The last of the BCS vehicles disappears in the shadows of the buildings as they head toward the Hudson. It's a pyrrhic victory. They know we're no match for them. We will never have the firepower they can bring to bear. If we're going to win this battle for humanity, it won't be with weapons of war.

"It won't be the last we see of this army," I say, changing the subject. "When they return, the massacre will be far worse."

"Maybe, but we'll stand for what we believe in despite the incredible odds against us. The way ahead is through courage and the conviction of those beliefs."

"I never thought I would hear you talk that way," I say, impressed.

"Seeing what was about to happen to the qulis and watching your father die forced me to open my eyes. I didn't like what I saw. I only hope other people see the truth about corporate rule before it's too late. This generation will only ever have one opportunity like this."

I nod. "Do you know Liberteum uses a torch as its symbol? Michele says it signifies the enlightenment that guides us down the path to freedom. Liberty's flame burns inside each one of us. We only need people to discover it and recognize it for what it is."

I was a complainer when I was a registrant. Balin and I would go to Central Park and gripe about the system and how people are seduced by it. But that's all it was. Words have power, but they are empty without action.

"More people will be against us than for us, I'm afraid," my mother warns. She's right, but that isn't the most important takeaway.

"It is not in numbers, but in unity, that our great strength lies; yet our present numbers are sufficient to repel the force of all the world." Mother stares at me like I'm speaking an alien language. "Thomas Paine's *Common Sense*. I did a little reading when I was recovering from my stomach wound. Michele only has old non-fiction lying around. That quote stuck with me."

"You read now? Wow! Michele is more remarkable than I thought," my mother says.

I drape my arm over her shoulder. "You have no idea. In fact, she reminds me a lot of you."

CHAPTER EIGHTY-FOUR

AMERICA, INC.

Tunnel Entrance
SoHo Geographic District
New York City Municipal Corporation

The men aren't dejected or defeated, but they are confused. They were winning, and they knew it. Comrades fell, but they honored that sacrifice by bringing the corporation to the cusp of victory. Then, they were ordered to stop and then retreat. It's an order they followed but likely resented. Even for a group as dedicated as the BCS, morale will take a hit.

That's why Virtari posted himself at the entrance to the tunnel leaving Manhattan. He wanted the agents to see him. He wants them to know he is still with them and is proud of what they were about to accomplish. Unfortunately, politics got in the way. It doesn't matter that his life hung in the balance...or so he keeps telling himself.

Virtari may be lucky to be alive, but he doesn't feel fortunate. The implications of Zeykala's decision will take time to fully understand. Historians will quibble for decades about whether her choice was the correct one. The cost is more than he can bear. They now live in a world where the corporation doesn't control its largest city.

Fixing that will be harder than it was this time. Liberteum, the qulis, and the PSS will have time to fortify Manhattan with them gone. The next assault will be against a prepared defense and without the element of surprise. The human cost of that urban fighting will be astronomical...and tragic.

"Sir? You've been summoned to Washington," the agent with the tablet next to him says. "Chief Executive Zeykala requests your presence in the Oval Office immediately."

"I bet she does," he grumbles.

"Shall I arrange your transport? We can have a plane waiting for you at the airport."

"Thank you. Tell operations that I'll be on the tarmac in a half hour."

To say his relationship with Zeykala has turned frosty is an understatement. With the pressure of her imminent removal, she'll be even more condescending and inflammatory than usual. The worst part is she's going to demand answers that he can't provide.

There's a difference between withholding information and not knowing it in the first place. Virtari kept the truth from her about the attack at the termination center so he could use it as leverage. That tactic backfired spectacularly. This situation is far different, not that she has reason to believe his denials now.

Liberteum hacked into their communications and the secure drone network. Somehow, they seized the impenetrable financial system. Learning how they did that is at the top of his to-do list. To put down this rebellion, they must neutralize their control of those systems.

"I don't want to talk to you right now," Virtari says, feeling Varella lurking behind him.

"Be pissed at my mother and brother, sir, not me."

He wants to shoot her in the head right now. If it weren't for the nagging thought that she might prove to be a future asset, he'd do just that.

"Your sass is going to be your downfall."

"And your anger yours," she fires back. "They played their best hand, and we lost, but we still hold most of the chips. A favorable outcome is guaranteed."

She's a typical executive. None of them have a clue about security. All they can offer are empty platitudes as they see the world through rose-colored glasses. Any fool would see that the outcome is far from guaranteed, and that makes her worse than a fool.

"I don't share your optimism."

"You need to be cynical. That's why you're good at what you do. Seeing opportunities in bad situations is mine."

"It doesn't take a cynic to understand what this failure means. Did they not teach you about scapegoats up at Harvard?"

"Zeykala may be replaced but there are many ways to make it difficult for Valen to replace you if she is. Your immediate problem is Liberteum."

"You mean your brother's friends?"

"We know where he is," she says, ignoring his barb, "and that presents an opportunity. We need to get back control of the financial system. The fastest way to do that is to get someone on the inside."

Virtari turns to look at the young woman. "How do you expect to do that? Are you going to go in there and reason with your mother?"

"No, we've already established that Rykos would shoot me on sight, and my mother would watch with a smile on her face."

"Maybe I should send you in there then."

"As tempting as you may find that, you'd lose the chance to hear how we can get to them. All it takes is sending someone who you already know you can count on to get the job done."

"Who?"

Varella grins. Any doubts about her making a good executive someday are fading in Virtari's mind. She's fearless, confident, and brilliant at using whatever leverage is available to get what she wants. In this case, it's dangling something almost irresistible in front of him.

CHAPTER EIGHTY-FIVE

LIBERTEUM

Valhalla
Midtown Geographic Area
New York City Municipal Corporation

The boys return to Valhalla with great fanfare. They look like they've been through hell, but they're alive and still on an adrenaline high. Fiolla rushes over to Zyree and hugs him hard, holding it for longer than is customary. Koltayne settles for high fives except for Michele, who embraces him.

"You're okay? You're both okay?"

"We're fine," Koltayne says. "It turns out the chief inspector here is pretty good in a firefight."

"You expected something less?" he asks, slapping him on the shoulder.

"Being a chief inspector for Intercorpex isn't the same as a general leading a Roman legion. I always thought you guys were too pretty to get your hands dirty."

"It helps when my battle buddy is a badass who knows how to throw a grenade. You did good work up there, Koltayne."

The young man grins and nods at Zyree. "I'm going to go clean up."

"I don't think I've ever heard him talk that much," Michele says, watching him disappear down the corridor after another round of congratulatory handshakes and slaps on the shoulder.

"Adrenaline will do that. We watched the BCS pull back from the cathedral. What happened?"

"Ortan took over their drones and the financial network. We threatened Virtari, and Fiolla blackmailed Zeykala to force the BCS to withdraw outside New York City."

"I'm going to need to hear the full version of that story. I never would have thought they'd agree to that."

"I was just as surprised as you. Thank you for protecting us."

"It was touch and go for a while there. I don't know if we really did anything meaningful. The BCS pulled back before we were going to seize one of their tanks."

"That's a story I want to hear. I'm glad you're okay, and I don't think I'm the only one happy to see you," Michele whispers. "You might want to leave that last part about it being touch and go out of the narrative until this is over."

She winks at Zyree and moves away so he and Fiolla can talk. She likes him, and he likes her. Even an urch who has never in her life had a meaningful relationship with a man can see that.

So can Farron. The pained look on his face tells the story. Michele can't help but feel a little bad for him. He took an incredible risk by rescuing her. Unfortunately, the feeling of betrayal is powerful. She understands that firsthand.

"Michele?"

"Yeah, Koltayne, what is it?" He looks a lot cleaner than he did a few minutes ago.

"I was hoping Zyree would tell you, but…the Emissary. He's…."

He doesn't need to finish that sentence, so she doesn't force him to. He earns another hug and, this time, a kiss on the cheek. It took a lot for Koltayne to tell her that. He knows how close she was to the Emissary.

"Go get some rest, Koltayne."

"I know that look you have, Michele. No way am I letting you go up there alone."

She nods, and they bound up the spiral staircase faster than ever before. Michele stops in the void below the archbishop's sacristy to catch her breath. The cleverly hidden access has been blown away and is completely open to the room above. She checks its stability and places her foot on the bottom rung of the tactical ladder when she's grabbed by the arm.

"Stay here," Koltayne insists. "Let me check it out first. Just because we *think* the BCS left doesn't mean they didn't leave someone behind to take a shot at you."

He climbs up the ladder and disappears into the room above. Zyree is more than a friend to Koltayne; he's now a role model. The quiet, shy kid she convinced to leave Haven and join them as they fled the Alamo is becoming a full-blown badass. It's an impressive transformation.

"It's clear. I'm going to scout around the perimeter. The Emissary is next to the altar."

Michele climbs the ladder and surveys the damage to the majestic building. It's worse than she thought, but at least it's still standing. Zyree and Koltayne had quite a firefight in here. The Emissary is lying face-up with a clean hole in his forehead. At least it was quick. There are no obvious signs of torture. Thank God for that.

"Thank you, Emissary," she whispers, closing his eyes. "Go in peace."

Michele sits next to the Emissary and wishes Rykos were here. He always knows the right thing to say at times like this. Her feelings for him have bubbled to the surface. She's been trying to ignore them, but they're unavoidable. The loss of the Emissary is hard, but losing Rykos would have been harder. That's not something she's used to dealing with.

Michele has lost friends in this struggle. Through it all, she steeled herself for those losses and walled off the inevitable emotion that came with them. It's the only way she could find the strength to press on.

Now the Emissary is gone. Her father is gone. Freya is gone. Many of the men and women who began this journey with her haven't made it this far. More are sure to follow, including her new friends who stood with her against incredible odds. Can she bear their deaths before this ends? Can she bear to lose Rykos?

Her emotions can no longer be held back. She pulls up her knees and buries her head under her arms, sobbing uncontrollably over the body of a man she once considered a second father.

CHAPTER EIGHTY-SIX

THE PATRICIANS

St. Patrick's Cathedral
Midtown Geographic Area
New York City Municipal Corporation

Farron makes the long climb up the spiral staircase into what's left of the Archbishop's Sacristy. The access looks nothing like it did, courtesy of the BCS and the hand grenades Zyree and Koltayne tossed up here. The spent shell casings littering the floor are a lingering testament to the battle that raged only a few hours ago.

Debris is everywhere, and he has to watch where he steps entering the sanctuary. The first conversation with an emotional Michele was awkward. This one will be worse. Farron makes his way to the far end of the transept with a sense of foreboding about what comes next.

That assumes Fiolla will come. This won't be an easy conversation for her, either. She feels betrayed, and Farron understands why. He is about to give up on waiting for her when he hears the echo of footsteps behind him and turns to see his fiancée decked out in black with her long red hair woven into a single braid.

"I was told you wanted to see me."

Farron nods. "I did. I wanted to say goodbye before I left."

Fiolla doesn't react. The cold response hurts but isn't completely unexpected. Now he knows what it feels like. Even if Farron didn't have to face his father, leaving would be the best for both of them.

"Is that it? Or were you waiting for me to get emotional? Because I think you've played with my emotions enough."

He lowers his eyes. "That was never my intent, Fiolla. Someday, I hope you believe that...and forgive me."

"Where are you going?"

"My father is suffering from a delusion that he can be the supreme leader of the world. He's going to bring the corporations and other patricians down one by one until there is nobody left to conquer. I need to go to Virginia to muster support to stop him."

Not that getting out of this city will be easy. The BCS will maintain a tight perimeter around it, and Farron will be apprehended on sight if he's spotted. It's a risk worth taking.

"Is that why I'm here? You wanted to tell me about your noble quest?"

Fiolla crosses her arms against her chest and bites down on her lower lip. At least she isn't walking away like he thought she would. Maybe she wants to hear this. Maybe it's closure for her. He needs to say this to help ease his guilt.

"No. This is about the story of us. It started with our chance meeting that night in Washington. Only it wasn't a chance meeting. I arranged for it to happen."

"I don't think I want to hear this," she says, fighting back the surge of tears that comes with knowing that part of your life was built on a lie.

"I know, but you need to know the truth. You made it easy to be interested in you. You are intelligent, articulate, passionate, and obviously beautiful."

"Everything a man could ever want in a fake relationship."

Farron lowers his head again. "It wasn't fake, it was business. I needed information and the access that you could provide. All I had to do was help you out in return. Since I knew what was happening in the world better than your bosses did, I justified it as a fair trade."

"So…this was a business transaction? Damn it, Farron, I fell in love with you! Didn't you feel any guilt for that? Did my feelings not matter at all?"

"Not at first, but that's where our story takes a turn. The more time we spent together, the more I began to…."

Fiolla holds a hand up to stop him. She doesn't want to hear those words. Not now. Everything that happened before the BCS tried to push her in front of a MagLev is irrelevant. For her, this is about the present and the future.

"Did Michele know you were using me?"

The question throws him a little. "No. She knew I had a source inside the White House. She didn't know who it was or in what capacity."

"Nobody in Liberteum knew?"

"Narik Covington did. He had a gun to Michele's head in the operations center when I sent you to see his father. That's how Michele eventually learned who you were and of our relationship."

"Did Narik know you wanted to marry me? Or did you not share that lie?"

"The promise of marriage was a lie at first. That changed—"

"I don't care when it changed! Don't you get it? You *used* me!"

"Yes, I was using you. Yes, I lied to you. Yes, our relationship was a farce, but the more time I spent with you, the more I realized how much you filled the hole in my life. I always looked at women as things – something to fill a sexual desire or bring to a gala to impress others. It was different with you. For the first time in my life, I found myself beginning to care about someone other than myself."

"Oh, so now I'm supposed to fall into your arms because you had a moment when you weren't a complete egotist? Forgive me for not expressing my undying gratitude that the great Farron Keating actually developed feelings. Too bad it was far too late. Your actions helped put me in that termination center in the first place!"

Farron cocks his head. That conclusion makes no sense. He didn't order her death and didn't even know about it until he met Zeykala at the White House.

"What are you talking about?"

"Farron, you can't possibly be that naïve. Valen knew about us, you idiot. He's a master manipulator who earns people's trust and then exploits their secrets. I learned that the hard way. He kept our secret to convince me that I could trust him. In return, I was obligated to help him pass messages. He knew what would happen if the board found out about the covert operation to infiltrate Liberteum, and he needed to cover it up. He used me to get what he needed, same as you did."

"Fiolla—"

"No! Don't try to explain it away. I endured all of this because of you. If you had just stayed out of my life, none of this would have happened!"

Her anguish over the betrayal has morphed into anger over what transpired. Her suffering may be traced to the day they met, but Farron doubts she would be any happier if she were currently working for Zeykala. Not that the argument will score any points with her. That's not how this works.

"You have every right to be angry with me."

"I don't need the permission of a high and mighty patrician for that."

"No, you don't. I know I can never make up for the things I've done. I can't rewrite the past. If I could, believe me, I would. I didn't realize until it was too late how hard I fell in love with you."

Fiolla winces. Those were the words she always wanted to hear. They are the same ones he said but never meant. Now that he does, all the damage his lies and deceit have caused make them irrelevant. It's a Greek tragedy playing out in the modern age.

"I'm in love with you, Fiolla. I know you don't trust me and never will. All I know is that I'm a better man because of you, and I need you to know before I leave how sorry I am for everything."

Farron takes a step closer to Fiolla, who fights the urge to move away. She closes her eyes as he leans in and gives her a kiss on the cheek. Without another word, he turns and leaves, knowing that this will haunt him for the rest of his days. If there is a silver lining, it's that there may not be many left after confronting his father.

CHAPTER EIGHTY-SEVEN

AMERICA, INC.

The White House
Corporate Governance District
Washington-Arlington Municipal Corporation

The notification that Virtari was en route to the White House was a pleasant surprise. The BCS director has been avoiding her calls, and she half expected the same treatment following the VidLynk with Liberteum and the subsequent withdrawal of the assault troops.

It was a difficult decision to make, and the order wasn't given to spare Virtari's life. She would gladly sacrifice him to regain Manhattan and quash the rebellion there. What she couldn't risk is the economic meltdown if Liberteum does have control of the financial network. All indications are that they do. If there is a silver lining, it's that the problem is about to become Valen's.

Virtari enters the Oval Office with a fresh-faced young woman behind him. She's attractive, but more than her looks, she walks with confidence. Even more than the man accompanying her, if that's possible.

"You don't look so good, Zeykala."

"I didn't summon you to Washington for you to point out the obvious, Virtari. Who the hell is she?"

Zeykala is less annoyed at Virtari's pointless observation than she is at his toting an aide behind him. The director of the BCS is known to be a loner. He rarely travels with anything resembling an entourage.

"This is Undergraduate-Intern Varella. She's attending Harvard and was on an assignment in the America Tower when corporate law was declared. Now she's working for me."

Virtari is a world-class chauvinist and is the last person anyone would expect to have a female working for him in a professional capacity. To the director, women are playthings. That makes Zeykala's rise to chief executive so satisfying.

"Working for you? Since when?"

"Recently. It turns out that Varella is the daughter of your least favorite CEO."

"My least fav—? You're Ilaria's daughter?" Zeykala screeches, too tired and frustrated to hide her disdain.

"Unfortunately. It's a great honor to meet you, ma'am. I've long admired your accomplishments."

Varella extends her hand, but the CEO stares at her as if she is a leper. What is Virtari thinking? How could he have the audacity to bring her here after what's happened today?

"Is this one of your sick jokes?"

"Not at all. Varella has been extremely helpful to me and I think she will be to you as well."

Zeykala waves her hand dismissively. "It's too late for that."

"That's the kind of defeatism I wouldn't have expected coming from a woman who single-handedly turned around the fortunes of Phytostat. When you became its CEO, you took it from three straight down years to sixteen straight quarters of growth, the last five in double digits."

"The last six were in double digits. The records shorted me one. Unfortunately, that was a long time ago."

"It was a very impressive run, either way. America Incorporated is a meritocracy, and your accomplishments are what landed you on the board of directors. Your leadership in the face of Valen's ineptitude is what landed you here."

The hint of a smile creases Zeykala's lips. Varella is sucking up to her, and it's working. Despite the disdain she holds for Ilaria's family, it is nice to meet someone appreciative of her previous accomplishments. It almost doesn't matter that her motives aren't exactly genuine.

"I'm starting to see why you like her, Virtari. Unfortunately, it does nothing to change the current situation. I'm getting removed from this office. The board is a whisper away from reinstalling Valen, and there's nothing I can do about it. You are to begin briefing Valen on the situation in the sphere of influence. He will reassume his duties as chief executive immediately following the board's vote tomorrow."

"I will handle it."

"I'm sure. You should know that the first thing Valen will do after having me removed from this building is sack you."

She knew pulling back the New York assault would have consequences. It gave the board the reason they needed to replace her. How Valen managed to get back into their good graces is anyone's guess.

"As Varella predicted. She's been right about many things since she began working for me. It would be a crime against the corporation if this woman doesn't end up running it someday."

"Is that so?" Zeykala asks, not in the mood to talk about future successors to an office that is rightfully hers.

"It is. She also believes that the fate of this corporation hinges on our ability to work together. Too bad we can't. You treat me like your servant, and that no longer works for me. For us to survive what's coming, we must respect each other and our roles."

Zeykala clasps her hands behind her back and rocks on her feet. "Go on."

"You know now that I didn't try to assassinate you. If you're willing to make a fresh start, I can share something Varella found – something that may change both our fortunes."

Virtari was coerced into working with her. It was a tactic that made perfect sense at the time but has fed Zeykala's paranoia ever since. If he's offering an alliance, she'd be a fool not to take it. It offers a better opportunity than what awaits her when Valen returns. She can't defeat Liberteum if she's no longer serving in this office.

"What did you find?" Zeykala asks Varella, engaging her in conversation for the first time. The question is greeted with a respectful smile.

"The key to your survival."

The CEO's eyes narrow at the dubious claim. Varella thinks she's a shrewd businesswoman and a capable future executive. It's more likely that she's an opportunist who is climbing the ladder by undercutting her competition.

"Expound."

"Our interrogation of Fiolla paid dividends," Virtari interjects. "With what we learned, neither of us will have to contend with Valen again."

Varella takes a step back. She may be an opportunist, but she also knows her place in the pecking order. Her stock just went up a point or two. This is now a negotiation between Zeykala and Virtari.

"What information do you have?"

"I'm afraid it's not that simple. I'm willing to work with you, but words are words. I need something in return."

He rattles down a list of demands without the aid of a tablet: more agents, more lethal equipment, a larger budget, greater control and flexibility, and most importantly, the complete revamping of cyber operations. Most of it isn't new. She's heard it all before.

"You've wanted to militarize the BCS for a long time, Virtari. As wily as you are, you didn't conjure up the idea to use this information as leverage."

Zeykala shifts her gaze to Varella, who's still standing off to the side. She meets her eyes with a confidence reserved for the most competent executives. She's fearless for someone still at Harvard and not yet tested in the real world. That will serve her well someday.

"As I said before, she's been of great assistance," Virtari adds.

"Ma'am, if I may?" Varella asks, stepping forward. "I've had the luxury of working with one of the greatest security minds in generations and studied one of the most ambitious and successful executives in decades. I'm humbled to find myself standing in the same room as you both. Your core competencies are opposite but complementary. You would be unstoppable if you could work together instead of plotting against each other."

"What makes you think I'm working against him?" Zeykala asks, a little too defensively.

"That's what I would do to a colleague whom I didn't trust. But circumstances have changed. Valen's ascension is a nightmare for both of you. The time for scheming and infighting is over."

It takes a lot to impress Zeykala. It's hard to believe that this is the daughter of the traitorous Ilaria and incompetent Teman. There had to be a mix-up at the medical center when she was born.

"What's in this for you? Don't tell me you're doing this just for the good of the corporation."

"I want a seat at the table to learn from the best. Then I'm going to use that knowledge to sit in this office someday."

The honest answer is refreshing. Zeykala and Virtari look at each other in silent agreement. There is a lot to work through, but they may be on the road to a very productive relationship.

"All right. Let's say I agree in principle to Virtari's terms. How do you suggest we handle Valen?"

Varella grins. She has her seat at the table. The CEO only hopes she knows what that means moving forward.

"What any great chess master would do with his opponent's queen: find a way to take it off the board."

CHAPTER EIGHTY-EIGHT

THE PATRICIANS

Somewhere Over Maryland

Denali stares out the window at one of his heavily armed helicopters. For most of his life, an escort wasn't a necessity in most corporations. The patricians are the revered elite. After decades of stability after the Pirate Wars, the world is a safe place. At least, it once was. Now, things have changed.

The pilot switched off the cabin illumination for this journey. It's an unneeded security measure, but the darkness has helped the patrician focus. This may be one of the most important meetings in his life, and he needs to be zeroed in.

There's an old saying that goes, "Proper planning prevents poor performance." That's true in all endeavors, especially the one he embarked on. Trouble financing his grand plan was on Denali's risk register. He never thought the trouble would result from Liberteum hijacking the financial network, but rumors are swirling that they did. The issues and opportunities that present are a subject for another time. He needs to ensure he succeeds in this upcoming negotiation.

The blackness of the night and the murky ocean below reflect his mood. The overseas attacks are having the desired effect, but he has underestimated corporate resolve. Even with overwhelmed security, the smaller corporations have still not reached out for help from patricians like he thought they would.

Only one corporation needs to swallow its pride and take the plunge. Once their plea for help is answered, others will notice and follow suit. It will eventually happen, just not fast enough. The Trust will not demonstrate unlimited patience with this plan. Assurances that Denali made must be met.

More disturbing is what's happening in this sphere of influence. America Incorporated is supposed to be in chaos but still in control. The former is true enough, but the latter is a question mark. The withdrawal of the BCS from New York could easily start a panic. That serves his purposes in the short term, but if America collapses, the world will follow. No one can rule over an anarchy.

That's what gives the most credence to the rumors that Liberteum controls the financial network. What else would compel Zeykala and Virtari to withdraw when victory was at hand? Another hour would have spelled the end of the nascent resistance movement. Liberteum would have been sealed had the BCS chosen to collapse the cathedral on top of them. Instead, they can claim victory.

Revolutionaries controlling the beating heart of the global economy is more than an inconvenience. He needs his accounts back. Had he known that Michele possessed the capability to hack an impenetrable network, she'd still be rotting away in the strong room. She's more astute an adversary than he gave her credit for.

Thus, the opportunity. Liberteum is significantly weaker without Haven. Michele has the ultimate weapon to use against the corporations with little or no means to protect it. If he can wrestle that control from her, nothing will stop him from fast-tracking his plan. He would lead the new world order with completely unchallenged power.

Michele's desperation to survive may have simultaneously been a tactical victory and a strategic blunder. Her whole mystique is predicated on the perception of her as a terrorist wanting to destroy the system. Having that power and trading it for a simple withdrawal makes her look weak and indecisive.

If she won't use the power she has, nothing will keep the jackals at bay. Everyone will want what she possesses and conclude her bark is worse than her bite. It's only a matter of who makes the first move, and he needs leverage to do it. Everybody cares about something. Even a "terrorist."

"Sir, we're on approach," the pilot informs him.

The massive estate fills the cockpit's windscreen. His plotting against Michele can wait. This meeting with the Baroness is the priority.

"Excellent. Have our escorts wait off the coast. This shouldn't take long."

"Yes, sir, I will relay the instructions."

He makes an arc around the property, with the glorious mansion to starboard and the dark waters of Chesapeake Bay to port. The helicopter crosses over a dock and the small spit of sand that serves as a beach and recreation area. Accent lighting marks the paths and sidewalks that lead to the pool, gardens, greenhouse, and outbuildings that dot the property.

Strobes come to life on the raised concrete helipad. The aircraft flairs as the gear extends, and they touch down. The pilot powers down the engines as a couple of staff members materialize on the sidewalk leading up to the mansion for what should be a very interesting meeting.

CHAPTER EIGHTY-NINE

INTERCORPEX

Valhalla
Midtown Geographic Area
New York City Municipal Corporation

The adrenaline high is starting to subside. Everyone left in Valhalla is busy watching the BCS retreat from the city. Koltayne and Michele are tending to the Emissary's body. Farron and Fiolla are likely engaged in a very uncomfortable conversation. Zyree doesn't like the idea of them getting back together. She'd regret it, although he is hardly impartial and would never tell her that.

Ortan finally stands and stretches. He looks around the operations room like he's about to start shoplifting before walking over to the planning area.

"Can I talk to you for a minute?" Ortan asks. "Some place where the walls don't have ears."

Zyree eyes him suspiciously. "Valhalla isn't that big, and I'm not climbing your 'Stairway to Heaven' again."

He nods to the side, and they trade the operations room for the small kitchen. It's empty, but you wouldn't know it, given how he's acting. Part of Zyree appreciates his paranoia, but almost everyone is gone, and he needs to get on with this.

"Did I do the right thing?" Ortan whispers.

"The right thing?"

"Zyree, I handed Liberteum the master key to the entire world. With Huldufólk and Archangyl working together, there's no door they can't open. They can run the world, or they can destroy it, and both would be easier than changing it."

It's a legitimate concern. Power corrupts, and you never know how a person or group will wield it until they are tested. Michele passed her test. She could have taken down the financial network regardless of whether her demands were met. She didn't. That means something.

"Does this group ever look for the easy way to do anything?"

"No, but I'm far more comfortable with ones and zeros than nouns and verbs. I understand computer logic better than human emotion. I need you to be my compass. You're the only person I completely trust. Even if that extends to Liberteum, others now know we have this capability."

"You're afraid it makes us more of a target?"

"Aren't you? There isn't a corporation on this planet that wouldn't kill for this power. Denali Keating is already bent on controlling the world, and he knows by now. Holding the currency network hostage is a stay of execution. Everybody will come after us. Valhalla's location is no longer a secret, and we don't have the manpower to stop a determined attack."

Ortan is quirky by nature, but there is fear in his eyes. It's a little unnerving.

"We have an island full of qulis and guardians between us and them."

"Are you willing to bet your life on that being enough? Would you be willing to gamble the fate of the world on it? It's only a matter of time before people come for what we have."

He has a point. Zyree doesn't appreciate the awesome power of these systems. That means the time for reveling in this small victory is over. They need to start planning for what comes next.

"Do you have any ideas?"

"I do, but you're not going to like it."

He explains his plan, and Zyree wonders if his friend is suffering from a concussion. There's bold, and then there's stupid. Some of it is the former, while most of what he just said falls into the latter.

Now Zyree knows why he was so secretive about Huldufólk's existence. He's right. Liberteum has control of two systems that could radically alter the trajectory of society. Everyone is going to want what they have. Unfortunately, if it goes wrong, the game is over.

"Michele is going to hate this idea."

"A good plan today is better than a perfect plan tomorrow. So, unless the two of you have a better option, this is what we have to do."

CHAPTER NINETY

NYCMC RESISTANCE

One Guardian Plaza
Lower Manhattan Geographic District
New York City Municipal Corporation

There is almost a festive atmosphere in the RTCC. The past couple of days have been a nightmare for the men and women here, and they deserve the chance to celebrate. The BCS pulling out of Manhattan is all the reason in the world to be elated. There is also a long road ahead to keep them out of the city and put this place back together. One Guardian Plaza has certainly seen better days.

"Attention in the RTCC!" a guardian bellows. "We have secured the EOC."

A cheer is followed by enthusiastic applause. Everyone is enjoying the moment except for one person. Dzamko looks like he's about to attend a funeral. He hasn't said much since returning from triage. His wound will heal, although the same can't be said for many of his guardians. Maybe that's what has him rattled.

"You don't look very happy, Dzamko," Ilaria says. "I know you lost men and women, but you could at least afford a little smile."

"I will mourn the losses later. This feels too good to be true."

"I understand, but we faced death a couple of hours ago. Life is measured in small victories. Enjoy this one."

A guardian comes up to them, studying her tablet and unsure whether she should interrupt. Ilaria gives her a nod.

"Ma'am, the West Side accesses across the river have been secured. We also took control of the America Tower and established a perimeter around Intercorpex's Wall Street NOC."

"Good. What about the BCS?"

"They mustered across the river in Weehawken and Jersey City. Smaller contingents are in Yonkers and Long Island. There have been no reports of any agents remaining behind."

"I never thought they would actually withdraw," Dzamko grumbles.

"Apparently, the White House took Liberteum's threat seriously."

"The White House may have, but Virtari didn't," Deyago said, nodding at the female guardian, who returned to her post.

"Deyago! Where have you been?" Ilaria asks, throwing her arms around him and giving him a bear hug.

"They had us locked up in an import-export office on Houston Street. Then they left. It looks like I missed a lot."

"I'm glad to see you alive and happy to have you back. We thought the worst."

"I'm fine. Before coming here, a group of us swung by the executive center. We ran into some guardians investigating a security breach. I went with them, and we caught a man snooping around."

"BCS?" Rykos asks, joining the group.

"Guardian Deyago, this is my son, Rykos," Ilaria says as the two men shake hands.

"Yes, but he's not an agent, or so he says."

"If he looks like a duck and quacks like a duck…."

"Normally, I would agree with you, Constable. This guy was unarmed, and there's something off about him."

"Like what?"

"It's best if you see for yourself," he says, beckoning for them to follow.

It's always something. The BCS was given very clear instructions by Michele. Only a fool would risk testing her resolve. With all the guardians in this area, why would they risk breaking the agreement over a futile intelligence-gathering mission?

The lock-up is buried deep within the bowels of One Guardian Plaza. Crime is not prevalent in this city, so the cells only have ever housed the occasional captured urch or unfortunate employee who ran afoul of company leadership. The windowless rooms are brightly lit and feature nice beds and bathroom facilities. In lieu of the steel bars, thin yet incredibly strong plexiglass dividers separate the cells. Electrifying them dispels any notion of escape.

"He says he's a BCS deserter, although I'm not convinced of it. He claims he was pressed into service and brought up here to assist in the attack."

"If that's true, their manpower situation must be far worse than we realized," Dzamko says. "Do you think this deserter will cooperate with us?"

"He hasn't said much since we took him into custody," Deyago says, "but you can ask him."

They turn the corner to see a young man standing there. Ilaria recognizes him instantly. Young and handsome, he isn't someone you easily forget. As surprised as she is, nothing compares to the shocked look on her son's face.

"Balin?"

"Hello, Rykos."

CHAPTER NINETY-ONE

LIBERTEUM

St. Patrick's Cathedral
Midtown Geographic Area
New York City Municipal Corporation

This is a quiet place. Michele needed to be alone, and the roof of the northeastern ancillary building on the grounds of the cathedral seemed like the perfect place. The only person who knows she's here is Koltayne, who is somewhere nearby but otherwise giving her space. Unfortunately, someone has found her.

Michele tries to dry her cheeks when she hears the approaching footsteps. Tears pour again, retracing the path of the ones before them. Any attempt to stifle them is futile. She'd rather not let anyone see her cry, but if someone does, she's happy it's Fiolla.

"Do you mind if I join you, or would you rather be alone?" Fiolla asks.

"No, it's okay. How did you find me here?"

"Koltayne. He said you wanted space, but I thought you might want to talk. It's nice up here. Peaceful."

"It is. I've never spent this much time above ground in my life."

"You've never been out of New York?" Fiolla asks, sitting down next to her.

"I had a brief stay in Denali Keating's basement. Other than that, no. I've never seen mountains or the ocean or the desert. I've never seen most of this city. I never realized how remarkable it is."

"You should see it from the top of one of the skyscrapers when you get a chance. The skyline is amazing. Too bad it hides a city filled with untrustworthy people."

"Are you talking in general terms, or was that comment targeted at someone in particular?"

"Both...neither...I don't know. Can I ask you a personal question? Have you ever been in love?"

Michele blushes. She hasn't had time to sort her feelings out. A month ago, the answer was a definitive no. Now? Love isn't something she's ready to deal with.

"There's not much room for that when you live in the underground," Michele half-heartedly says. "For urches, life is about survival."

"You didn't answer the question," Fiolla says with a pleasant yet probing smile. "You don't have to. I saw how you reacted when Rykos left."

Michele doesn't respond. There's no defense she can offer. Fiolla saw them kiss in the sanctuary. Everyone knows by now that she cares for him. But love? It's an unfamiliar feeling.

"Being with Farron was like living in a fairytale," Fiolla continues, sparing her the interrogation. "He was smart, powerful, wealthy…everything a girl could ask for. Except he would never commit. He used empty words and never meant any of them. So, when he told me he was in love with me, I couldn't force myself to believe him."

"Is that what he told you?"

"Yes, right before he left."

"Words didn't fly a helicopter into a BCS termination center with guns blazing to rescue you from certain death. I'm no subject matter expert, but isn't that the kind of grand gesture every woman wants?"

Michele is wading into uncharted waters. She doesn't know anything about grand gestures. Dating isn't a thing in her world. The closest grand gesture she ever experienced is Rykos warning her and Haven that the PSS was about to raid the urch rave when they first met. She supposes that counts. She'd be dead or captured if it weren't for that. It also feels like a lifetime ago.

"Everything he ever did for me had strings attached. I can't help but feel that wasn't any different."

"Or maybe he truly loves you. All I know is that we're alive because of it."

"What do you mean?"

Fiolla hasn't had time to think about the bigger picture. She believes he used her and wasn't there to stop the BCS from sinking their talons into her when she was most vulnerable. She doesn't see the chain of events that resulted.

"Farron didn't need to save you, Fiolla, but he did. If he had failed, he might not have bothered rescuing us. We would have been handed over to the BCS and killed. Zyree would have been turned back over to Intercorpex and probably killed. Ortan would have disappeared, and the BCS would have succeeded in massacring tens of thousands of quli laborers. None of us would be here to expose Denali's plan for world domination."

Fiolla shrugs and pulls her knees up to her chest as she stares out at the surrounding buildings. "Maybe he felt he owed me."

Farron hurt her. What's worse, Michele knows she was a party to his deceptions. Even if she wasn't, nothing she could say would make a difference.

"I prefer to think of you guys as star-crossed lovers."

She laughs. "I wouldn't have expected an urch to know about Romeo and Juliet."

"You'd be surprised what's available to read in the underground."

"Farron left to stop his father. I think part of it was because of me."

"Would Zyree have anything to do with that?" Her head jerks over at Michele. "You got pretty emotional when he left to fight the BCS. You don't need to explain why. Zyree is a good man and not hard to look at."

"We're in a similar situation, is all," she says, trying to dismiss her feelings. "We're outsiders who are here because the people we swore to serve tried to kill us."

Michele nods. "That's a powerful connection."

"Yeah, I suppose it is."

With duty comes sacrifice. Each of the people in Valhalla has sacrificed separately, and now they are sacrificing together. Michele has already sacrificed so much. It's even more complicated when it comes to Rykos. She is responsible for setting him on his path, so her heartbreak is self-inflicted.

"I haven't had the chance to properly thank you for your help dealing with Zeykala. It was invaluable. I don't think I could have done what you did."

"I appreciate you trusting me with that responsibility. I'm somewhat surprised you didn't ask for my help earlier, given my previous position."

"I didn't think it'd be appropriate."

"Why not?"

It's a legitimate question. Michele wanted to ask but always talked herself out of it. Fiolla didn't owe them anything. Farron rescued her, not them. They may have been giving her a haven, but that doesn't translate into her helping the cause. That's something she needed to volunteer for on her own.

"You've been through a lot and had no reason to trust us. I didn't want you to feel like I was out to exploit you. Thank you for the information about Adiz. I'm not sure what would have happened had he not been uncovered."

"What are you planning on doing to him? You can't keep him chained in the bunk room forever."

"I know. I'm not sure yet. I haven't had much time to think about it."

Fiolla lets out a breathy laugh and shakes her head.

"You know, when I was alone with Zyree, he asked me if I trusted you. I wasn't sure how to answer that at the time. When you're programmed to think a certain way, preconceptions are hard to overcome. That changed after Ortan took control of Archangyl. You could have created chaos in the world with one tap of your finger and didn't. I've never seen anyone be so respectful of the power they hold."

"Reducing the world to ashes won't make it a better place."

"No, it won't, but neither will the executives you're fighting. They're not going to negotiate with you, Michele. When Ortan said that the flaw in your plan was that you could never hack the financial network, he was only half-right. The biggest problem you face is that corporations and patricians won't ever let you change the world in a way that reduces their power."

"I know. I have a plan for that. I'm hoping you'll be willing to help me."

"Of course. Can you answer one question for me, though? Did you mean what you said about me being strong?"

"I did, and you showed that today. Trust me, you'll need that strength again. We may have won this battle, but the fight for the soul of humanity is only just beginning."

CHAPTER NINETY-TWO

THE PATRICIANS

The Eagle's Nest
Chesapeake Geographic Area
Potomac Metro Municipal Corporation

The grounds of the Eagle's Nest manage to be mysterious and beautiful at the same time. The artificial lighting is arranged with such meticulous care that, even in the early evening, the statues and fountains cast perfectly planned shadows. Every hedge, garden, sidewalk, and fixture was designed to have a specific aesthetic purpose. No expense was spared.

The house itself is a monster. Far bigger than his Greenwich estate, the Eagle's Nest has three sprawling floors divided into a main residence and two wings. The home has been in the family since before the collapse, but it's a shame that all this is enjoyed by only one person now.

Denali is escorted through an opulent grand foyer. Everything from the wall moldings to the fixtures is ornate down to the finest detail. He has visited this estate several times for galas and has never ceased to be amazed. Nobody would fail to be awed, which is the point.

"Good evening, Baroness," he says after being shown into the formal living area and announced to his host.

"I hate when you call me that," Talya Bettancourt says. "Fix our guest a drink, and then you are dismissed."

Her servant complies, and a moment later, he's handed a crystal snifter of the most expensive and rare scotch the world has to offer. That alone might make this worth the trip.

"I'm surprised you slithered out of your hole in Greenwich, Denali. What do you want?"

Not too many people can call his estate a "hole" and be taken seriously. She is an exception. If his mansion is akin to a fortress, then hers is a palace. It's a shining symbol of the wealth and power that the Bettancourt family has amassed on the backs of America Incorporated employees.

"You know better than anyone that some business is best handled in person. I'll get right to the point. I need you to release a portion of your gold stores to me."

"I bet you do. Am I unilaterally funding your hostile takeover now?"

"Others have already made their contributions. The math has changed. Rumor has it that Liberteum somehow gained control of the financial network. My Bytecoin transactions are frozen, and I need your gold as a stop-gap measure until it is restored."

"You're not the only one excluded from the currency network, Denali. My accounts are also inaccessible."

He didn't know that she was affected, but it makes sense. Liberteum would have frozen every patrician out of the financial network.

"That is why we maintain gold supplies. It's also why I need some of yours."

Talya shakes her head. "I cannot grant your request. I've already heavily invested in your coup d'état. I don't see the point of pouring in good money on top of bad money."

"We have an arrangement."

"That I have fulfilled. You promised more patrician control over corporations. If anything, we have less."

"And you promised to weaken AME by removing Valen and installing Zeykala, not cripple it by installing a reckless policy you knew could plunge it into civil war."

Talya smirks at the accusation. "Some of her decisions were regrettable."

"Spare me the pointless blame deflection. You had countless conversations with Valen about bringing the qulis under the corporate umbrella. Let's not pretend that the announcement was Zeykala's idea."

"It's a smart business move that would pay dividends if it were handled correctly. Yoking the power of a potent labor force by integrating it into the parent corporation would increase our stock value three-fold."

Her audacity is astounding, even for a patrician. For a woman who considers herself an intellectual, Talya has no concept of how the world works. The only thing more impressive than her title and opulent wealth is her ignorance.

"Valen warned you that qulis would never accept such an arrangement, and he was right."

"Again, it was mishandled."

"By the woman you hand-picked as his successor."

"You're passing judgment on me? That's a bold move, considering the mess you've made. I would think you'd have chosen a more deferential tactic. I'm under no obligation to grant your request."

"It wasn't a request. Your gold is needed, and you will supply it," Denali says, sure to leave no room for negotiation.

Talya gracefully rises from the sofa and strolls around the room, admiring the artwork from Impressionist masters including Renoir and Monet. Her movements convey a sense of power and control meant to cower people into thinking they're at a disadvantage. The problem with using it on the wily patrician is that Denali knows better.

"I chose to participate in your endeavor, thinking it would be best for both our families. I was wrong. The Bettancourts built America Incorporated. I risked decades of their work on a gamble that isn't paying off."

"You will cement their legacy for eternity, Talya. Nothing has changed."

"I almost lost my prima status to Shalius Covington. Was that your idea of cementing my legacy, Denali? You and he were close friends, and he was a member of The Trust. Deny you had anything to do with that."

"Shalius was exercising his own agenda," Denali says as calmly as he can, finishing his drink in the process.

"Spare me. The Covingtons wouldn't have embarked on something so reckless without your knowledge or approval."

Talya walks behind the sofa and out of Denali's vision. She may stab him in the back with an ancient letter opener or break a Ming Dynasty vase over his head. This is a high-stakes version of the old game "chicken," and he refuses to flinch first. He will not give her the satisfaction of craning his neck or shifting to continue facing her.

"The Trust does not control the actions of its membership. Our dealings are evidence of that."

"There was a time I might have believed that. You needed Shalius's support, so you made a deal with your old friend. If he supported your plan, you would deliver America Incorporated to him at my expense. You double-crossed me."

She's speculating. There is no way Talya could know of that arrangement. The only other person who knew was Shalius himself. He's dead and wouldn't have discussed the plan with anyone when he was alive. She connected the dots, and words won't convince her otherwise. Denali knows he won't get what he came here for.

"I cannot offer a defense to an agreement that didn't exist. Isn't that at the root of every conspiracy theory ever imagined?"

"Only this one did. Leave, Denali. As our partnership no longer has a chance of reaching mutual goals, so consider it severed."

Her servant materializes, flanked by a pair of armed guards. Denali wouldn't be surprised if they are the sum of her guard detail. Talya has never been security-minded. She has enough influence over the BCS to compel them to do her dirty work.

"Very well. Goodbye, Baroness."

Without further discussion, he retreats down the path and climbs into his waiting helicopter. The pilot fires up the engine and lifts off when the rotors come up to speed. Denali admires the estate again. It really is beautiful. Too bad it's wasted on a woman like her.

"Commander, are you in position?"

"Yes, sir. We have thermal identification of all occupants. We're just awaiting your 'go' order."

He doesn't waste even a second thinking about it. "You have it. Focus on the bottom floor living area first. That's where Talya is."

"Roger. Executing."

His pilot loops the aircraft around and puts it in a hover over the bay. Without their running lights on, Denali doesn't see his two lethal black escorts until the orange exhaust plumes propel missiles off their pylons and through the inky black sky. He watches with anticipation as they streak toward their targets.

They hit their mark, and the entire first floor of the main mansion erupts in a sheet of fire and smoke. The living embodiment of hubris and conceit was just snuffed out of this world.

"Targets eliminated."

"Move the ship to the dock and have the men disembark. The vault is buried under the north patio. You can access it via a tunnel access in the receiving bays located off the main drive."

The architectural plans of this estate that Denali procured at a steep price are worth their weight in the stacks of gold they will reveal.

"Yes, sir. Anything else?"

He stares long and hard at the mansion. Fire suppression systems have been activated on the first floor. They are of no use to the now-deceased occupant or the art and priceless antiques meticulously scattered throughout the estate. Denali shakes his head one last time. It's such a shame.

"Reduce the mansion to ashes."

The order is relayed, and the gunships fire their remaining missiles. They crash into the mansion, and explosions rip through the wood and stone. The machines circle like birds of prey, sowing destruction on any section left untouched by previous volleys. The birds retreat when their ordnance is expended, leaving the raging fires to obliterate what remains of the gilded estate.

The flames are so bright that light dances around the inside of his helicopter. Today was Talya's final day on this Earth, and the destruction of her home is a fitting end to the elite Bettancourt dynasty. All that's left now is to retrieve the spoils she left behind.

CHAPTER NINETY-THREE

LIBERTEUM

Valhalla
Midtown Geographic Area
New York City Municipal Corporation

Their voices herald their arrival long before anyone in the operations room sees them. Noise carries in that claustrophobia-inducing tube that serves as a spiral staircase. Michele and Fiolla emerge from the dank, dark access into the brightly lit operations center and stop while their eyes adjust to the light.

"I really hate those stairs," Fiolla says, happy to emerge from the confined space.

"I'd say you get used to them, but you never do," Michele says.

They were gone for much longer than Zyree expected. "What have you guys been up to?"

"Koltayne and I paid our final respects to the Emissary, and then Fiolla and I were chatting."

"About what?" Ortan innocently asks.

"Girl talk," Fiolla says, offering Michele a sheepish grin.

Zyree turns to Ortan and shakes his head. "That's code for don't ask any more questions."

"I knew *that.*"

Ortan turns his attention back to his display and then spins his chair to face them. He starts to say something and stops. After he does it a second time, Michele's curiosity is piqued.

"You look troubled. What's up, Ortan?"

"This."

He flicks his hand in the air, and a video message plays on the display behind him. Administrator-General Lyris is sitting at a desk and speaking to the camera. The announcement is to all ICX employees to make all necessary preparations for the resumption of trading. He states they will be reopening the stock market to usher in a new era of blah, blah, blah. Zyree stops listening. Everything that follows is just empty words.

"Where did you get this?" Michele asks. This message wasn't meant for public consumption.

"I pulled it off Intercorpex's internal communications server."

"You hacked in?" Jasper asks, still amazed at what Ortan is capable of.

"There are more backdoors into their systems than front doors."

"This is bad," Zyree says, weighing the outcomes and their probabilities in his mind.

"Why? Wasn't taking down Intercorpex part of the plan?" Fiolla asks. "We control Bytecoin. Why do we care if they try to resume trading?"

"Because the market will crash instantly. These global terrorist attacks have created massive instability, and the stock market hates instability. With the patricians locked out of their accounts thanks to us, they will rush to cash out their holdings for gold."

"Corporations are clinging to power because their stocks still have value," Zyree concludes. "The moment they go to zero, that perception shatters. Services will break down, employees will revolt, and there will be chaos in the streets."

"Then they'll turn to the only power left with the strength and resources able to help stabilize the situation," Michele finishes.

"Denali Keating," Fiolla murmurs. "That's why Farron is so desperate to stop him. He knew about this part of the plan."

An uncomfortable silence grips the room. The buzz of their earlier victory has been killed by a cold, harsh reality. Denali has a playbook and is flipping pages faster than they can counter him. It may already be too late to do anything about it.

"Sorry, I didn't mean to be the bearer of bad news," Ortan says. "Zyree, we have to move faster than we thought we would."

"Farron can deal with his father," he announces to the group. "We can't stop Denali from destabilizing corporations, but we can stop his plan of collapsing the exchange. We're fighting a war on three fronts: Farron has his, you and Ilaria have yours against the BCS, and now I have mine. It's time for me to return to Intercorpex and cut Lyris's strings."

"Don't forget about Chiana," Ortan warns. "You know she's there with him."

"Who's Chiana?" Fiolla asks with an accusatory edge to her voice.

"Zyree's former colleague who tried to kill him what, three times now?"

He stopped counting. Chiana is skilled, but she is too reliant on technology and is overconfident in her abilities. She is formidable, but he knows that she has weaknesses he can exploit.

"I can handle Chiana. I have a score to settle with her anyway."

"Stop! You all need to stop!" Fiolla barks, commanding the attention of everyone in the room. He's never seen her so animated and fired up. "Enough of the kneejerk responses to everyone else's actions. We succeeded today because we had a plan. We may have pieced it together on the fly, but we had one. Now we need another. We're not going to win by counterpunching and hoping one of them lands. It's time to stop playing defense and start playing offense."

"Time is not on our side, Fiolla," Michele warns. "It took me and my father years to plan Archimedes."

"Look at the people in this room. We all bring a different set of skills to the table. We may have come together by accident, but you couldn't build a more capable team if you tried. We're the weakness in Denali's scheme – the one variable he can't account for. It's time we leverage that."

"Do you have something in mind?"

"I think I do. It's going to take all of us to refine it and make it work, though. If we're going to succeed in freeing the world, we need to start by breaking our own chains."

CHAPTER NINETY-FOUR

AMERICA, INC.

The White House
Corporate Governance District
Washington-Arlington Municipal Corporation

The door to the Oval Office swings open and Zeykala's nemesis is led in by a pair of BCS agents. She's glad she acquiesced to Virtari's demand that they be allowed back into the building. Watching Valen led here by armed guards was stimulating and satisfying.

"I see you still haven't had time to change the décor," he says, surveying the room. "I wouldn't think a little thing like insurrection would have stopped you from getting new drapes."

"You're enjoying this, aren't you, Valen?"

"More than you can imagine. Director Virtari, it's fancy meeting you here. I'm surprised you agreed to the board's demand for a transition."

"It's in the best interests of the corporation," the director says, trying to keep this professional. The snide former CEO isn't making it easy.

"Director Virtari informed me that his agents have brought you up to speed with the challenges we're facing."

"Yes, they were quite in-depth. It took a while. What was absent was your plan to restore order in the cities. With the number of qulls emboldened enough to challenge the corporation, I would have thought you'd have one."

"We do."

"Would you care to share it?"

The condescension in his voice makes Zeykala want to reach across this desk and choke him. "Of course. However, the quli uprising is not our most pressing problem."

"You're speaking of Liberteum. How exactly did your people get ambushed at the exchange point, Virtari?" Valen asks, turning to the director, who is leaning on the far wall of the room. "I mean, who even knew where it was? It's inconceivable that the vaunted Bureau of Corporate Security would allow that to happen unless the Pentagon didn't want the exchange to happen in the first place."

"Losing the leader of Liberteum was regrettable," Virtari deadpans.

"Devastating might be a better word for it. Is it true the terrorists have control over Bytecoin?"

"They have control over the currency and transaction systems and seem to have access to corporate communications, transportation, and who knows what else. They could be listening in on this conversation for all we know."

"Oh, I doubt that."

He places a blocker on Zeykala's desk. Designed to disrupt eavesdropping attempts, they are strictly forbidden for anyone outside of security personnel and high-level executives. Even he shouldn't have one once he left his position as CEO.

"I thought we confiscated this from you," Zeykala says, giving him a nasty glance.

"You didn't collect the spares. I like being prepared. What do we know about how Liberteum infiltrated our networks?"

"You would know better than us," Virtari mumbles.

"How exactly would I know?"

The answer was more innocent than the man standing in front of them. "Because you had someone embedded in Liberteum."

"I'm afraid I don't know what you're referring to."

His face shows no emotion or surprise. He wasn't thrown at all by the accusation leveled at him. Zeykala is almost impressed. The man lies so effortlessly. He would have made a great pre-collapse politician.

"Let me jog your memory," Virtari says. "Several years ago, you worked with the BCS to dispatch several highly trained agents into the New York City underground with the sole mission of gathering intelligence on the urches living there. One of them infiltrated Liberteum and began relaying coded information back to you via a forum on the GlobalNet. The mole is still active, and you recently tried relaying instructions to him. Everything that has happened—"

"Okay, enough," Valen says, raising his hand. "How did you discover this information?"

"Does it matter?" Zeykala asks with a fair amount of condescension in her voice.

For once, she feels like she has the upper hand with her predecessor. Valen expertly uses information, and now she knows something he doesn't. It's empowering.

"It does to me."

"Fiolla gave it to us."

"Gave it to you?" Valen asks.

"Less than willingly," Virtari chimes in.

Valen is not a stupid man. He knows what that means. If this doesn't work, they may have signed their own termination orders.

"And where is Fiolla now?"

"She's alive, unfortunately. We were in the middle of terminating her when she was rescued by Farron Keating. Did you know he was also working with Liberteum?" Virtari asks, measuring the former CEO's response from a distance.

"I find that hard to believe. He's a patrician of the gentez-majorez."

"Then you will find it ironic that both he and Fiolla are currently with the terrorist leader Michele in New York. Or did your spy already tell you that?"

"That's not possible. Fiolla is a loyal executive."

"I can show you the playback of the video if you'd like. Did you know she was a terrorist spy, or were you working with her?"

"Why would I knowingly consort with a terrorist?"

"The same reason you concocted a secret plan to slip a BCS agent into their ranks: coordination. Valen, you could have prevented thousands of deaths. The number one threat to the corporation could have been eradicated. Intercorpex would never have halted trading, and our currency system wouldn't be held hostage. Instead, you kept this mole a secret when you were removed from office and never informed Director Virtari of the mission. That's a cover-up."

"I did no such—"

"Are you claiming you didn't have Fiolla message your Liberteum contact via the GlobalNet?"

Valen flashes a knowing grin. "This won't work, Zeykala. Your attempt at spinning an intelligence mission into something nefarious is nothing more than a futile attempt to keep your job. Or, should I say…my job."

"You commit treason, and you think I'm trying to score political points?"

"Zeykala, you've done far worse to make it to this office. Your hands aren't clean, so stop pretending you have the moral high ground."

The retort drips with condescension. Valen thinks he's winning, and now he's determined to get under her skin. There's a reason he was known as a shrewd negotiator when he was CEO. Like all great leaders, he instinctively understands what buttons to push to get what he wants.

"The truth?" Valen continues. "I understood the bigger picture of what threat Liberteum posed and dared to do something about it. You've failed to learn that lesson, and that's how you lost New York City. It's how Virtari ended up at gunpoint by one of his own drones."

Valen is more dangerous than she realized. The details surrounding what happened outside of One Guardian Plaza are classified at the highest levels. He was not briefed on that and shouldn't know the details.

"Let's get back to the matter at hand," Zeykala interjects. "You can justify your activities any way you like, but you betrayed this corporation."

"That shows how little you understand the job the board has asked you to do."

"We'll see."

Zeykala glances over at Virtari. That's the signal. There are cleaner ways to do this, but none are more satisfying.

"Yes, we will. Tomorrow, I resume the duties of a position that never should have been taken from me. My admission of running an operation to infiltrate Liberteum will not change the board's minds."

"I have something else in mind, Valen."

"What are you going to do? March me up to Meade and have me terminated?"

Epic stare-downs require focus. When someone has your undivided attention, it means you aren't paying attention to your surroundings. It's tradecraft for BCS agents – don't miss the forest for the trees. Valen's lack of situational awareness is about to be his downfall.

Zeykala flashes an evil smile. "I don't plan on waiting that long."

Virtari pulls the razor-sharp knife from his belt as he yanks Valen's head backward. In one fluid motion, he slides the blade deep across the man's throat. The former CEO tries to scream as he clutches at the open gash to stem the loss of blood. It will do no good.

With the carotid artery severed and his windpipe cut, his death is imminent. Valen collapses to his knees as he chokes on his own blood. Falling forward and sprawling onto the carpet, he stares up at Virtari with eyes wide in surprise until the expression freezes in death.

Zeykala hovers over him with satisfaction. She can't count how many times she's dreamed of this moment, and she got her wish. By eliminating one threat, she may have invited countless others. Caveat emptor. It's an old Latin expression that means, "Let the buyer beware." Her fate is now intertwined with Virtari's. In the eyes of some, they'll both be traitors to the corporation now.

ACKNOWLEDGMENTS

The plot thickens. This was the last novel that was originally released before the rewrite. I have two left, and I'm eager to finish the series. It's not because I'm tired of it – quite the contrary. I'm looking forward to how the story ends. Will Michele and Rykos find happiness together? What will become of Zyree and Fiolla? Will Zeykala and the corporations maintain power, or will Denali Keating and the elite patricians realize their dream of world domination? Will Farron let that happen? So many questions left to answer....

This saga has taken much longer to finish than I originally planned. I appreciate you for sticking with it and for all my new readers willing to give this a read. I am truly thankful for everyone who has read my novels. Considering the great authors who spend countless hours bringing their stories to life, I'm honored that you've chosen to read mine.

Once again, we are going to play a game of, "Where did Mikael mention his wife in the acknowledgments?" Hint: it's not in this paragraph. I am reserving this space for my beloved mother, Nancy, my sister Kristina, my brother-in-law, Ken, and my nephew Gibson, who is growing up way too fast. Thank you for all your support

It won't be in this paragraph either, honey. Keep scanning. I have great friends who help keep me energized. Thank you to Jenn, Steve, Billy, Amy, Aimee, Stefan, Gabby, Bill and his son Chris, Meg, Chris and Jess, and so many more.

Okay, I've made her wait long enough. To the love of my life, Michele, I couldn't do any of this without you. You are my rock, and your support is the foundation for everything I have accomplished.

I have a confession: I may have caused my cover designer to drink heavily for this one. Book cover creation is challenging under normal circumstances. I usually have an idea about what I want. There are occasions when I'm at a loss, and this was one of them. Still, Dave at JD&J Design came through once again. Thank you for your patience and outstanding work!

Despite having written twenty novels, I still find parts of the English language elusive. I mean, there are rules and then exceptions to them. How non-native English speakers learn the language is almost confounding. So, I will continue to screw up "toward" and "towards" and guess wrong in choosing "further" or "farther." Fortunately, I have Mike Waitz of Sticks and Stones Editing to giggle as he corrects these errors.

ABOUT THE AUTHOR

Mikael Carlson is the award-winning author of the novel *The iCandidate* and the Michael Bennit Series of political dramas. He also has written two other ongoing series: Tierra Campos Thrillers and Watchtower Thrillers. His newest series, America, Inc., is a retelling of the futuristic dystopian Black Swan Saga that serves as a cautionary tale of life in a world following a global economic collapse.

A retired veteran of the Rhode Island Army National Guard and United States Army, he deployed twice in support of military operations during the Global War on Terror. Mikael has served in the field artillery, infantry, and in support of special operations units during his career on active duty at Fort Bragg and in the Army National Guard.

A proud U.S. Army Paratrooper, he conducted over fifty airborne operations following the completion of jump school at Fort Benning in 1998. Since then, he has trained with the militaries of countless foreign nations.

Mikael earned a Master of Arts in American History in 2010 and graduated with a B.S. in International Business from Marist College in 1996.

He was raised in New Milford, Connecticut, and currently lives in nearby Danbury. Connect with him at www.mikaelcarlson.com.

www.ingramcontent.com/pod-product-compliance
Lightning Source LLC
Chambersburg PA
CBHW051440190726
48289CB00001B/283